THE HIGHEST PRAISE FOR

AND ONE TO DIE ON

"This cheerfully brazen homage to *Ten Little Indians* . . . has all the sparkle and complexity her fans have come to expect."   —*Kirkus Reviews*
"Sharp, stylistic prose, unique characters, wicked humor, and a skillfully interwoven plot all contribute to an excellent read."   —*Library Journal*

AND THE OTHER HOLIDAY MYSTERIES BY JANE HADDAM

BLEEDING HEARTS

"A rattling good puzzle, a varied and appealing cast, and a detective whose work carries a rare stamp of authority . . . This one is a treat."
                                              —*Kirkus Reviews* (starred review)
"Charmingly original."   —*Publishers Weekly*
"Absolutely delightful."   —*Romantic Times*
"Once you get to know Gregor and Bennis and Father Kasparian, I guarantee you'll want to come back for more."   —*Indianapolis News*

NOT A CREATURE WAS STIRRING

"Vintage Christie [turned] inside out . . . *Not a Creature Was Stirring* will puzzle, perplex, and please the most discriminating readers."   —*Murder Ad Lib*

PRECIOUS BLOOD

"A fascinating read." —*Romantic Times*

ACT OF DARKNESS

"Juicy gossip abounds, tension builds and all present are suitably suspect as Demarkian expertly wraps up loose ends in this entertaining, satisfying mystery."
—*Publishers Weekly*

A GREAT DAY FOR THE DEADLY

"Haddam . . . plays the mystery game like a master. . . . A novel full of lore, as of suspense, it is bound to satisfy any reader who likes multiple murders mixed with miraculous apparitions and a perfectly damnable puzzle."
—*Chicago Tribune*

A STILLNESS IN BETHLEHEM

"High-quality puzzler." —*Publishers Weekly*
"Classic mysteries are back in vogue, and Jane Haddam's . . . Gregor Demarkian series is one of the finest."
—*Romantic Times*

FEAST OF MURDER

"Haddam offers up a devilishly intricate whodunit for fans of the classic puzzler."
—*Tower Books Mystery Newsletter*

THE GREGOR DEMARKIAN HOLIDAY SERIES
BY JANE HADDAM

Not a Creature Was Stirring
(Christmas)

Precious Blood
(Easter)

Act of Darkness
(Fourth of July)

Quoth the Raven
(Halloween)

A Great Day for the Deadly
(St. Patrick's Day)

Feast of Murder
(Thanksgiving)

A Stillness in Bethlehem
(Christmas)

Murder Superior
(Mother's Day)

Bleeding Hearts
(Valentine's Day)

And One to Die On
(Birthday)

Festival of Deaths
(Hanukkah)

Dear Old Dead
(Father's Day)

Fountain of Death
(New Year's Day)

Baptism In Blood
(Christening)

And coming soon in hardcover:
DEADLY BELOVED
(Wedding)

AND ONE TO DIE ON

JANE HADDAM

BANTAM BOOKS
New York Toronto London Sydney Auckland

This edition contains the complete text
of the original hardcover edition.
NOT ONE WORD HAS BEEN OMITTED.

AND ONE TO DIE ON
A Bantam Book

PUBLISHING HISTORY
Bantam hardcover edition published / April 1996
Bantam trade paperback edition / April 1997

ISBN 0-553-56448-X

Published simultaneously in the United States and Canada

Bantam Books are published by Bantam Books, a division of Bantam Doubleday
Dell Publishing Group, Inc. Its trademark, consisting of the words "Bantam Books"
and the portrayal of a rooster, is Registered in U.S. Patent and Trademark Office
and in other countries. Marca Registrada. Bantam Books, 1540 Broadway, New
York, New York 10036.

PRINTED IN THE UNITED STATES OF AMERICA

OPM   10 9 8 7 6 5 4 3 2 1

This book is dedicated to Gregory James DeAndrea.
Hi.

AND ONE
TO DIE ON

PROLOGUE

THE
ACCIDENTAL
MIRROR

Tasheba Kent - 99 year old actress

Cavender Marsh - Tasheba's Husband

Hannah Kent Graham - Cavenders daughter
and Real Estate Agent

John Graham - Hannah's Husband

Richard Fenster - Devoted fan of Tasheba
computer nerd and collects movie star
memorabilia.

Mathilda Frazier 's Works at Halbard's
Auction House and are assisting with
auction.

Carlton Ji - Researching Death of Lilith
Brayne (Tasheba's Sister)

Lydia Acken - Lawyer - looking over legal
aspects of auction.

Kelly Pratt - Accountant

Geraldine Dart - Employed by Tasheba
Kent and Cavender Marsh.

— 1 —

Sometimes, she would stand in front of the mirror and stare at the lines in her face, the deep ravines spreading across her forehead, the fine webs spinning out from the corners of her eyes, the two deep gashes, like ragged cliffs, on either side of her mouth. Sometimes she would see, superimposed on this, a picture of herself at seventeen, her great dark liquid eyes staring out from under thick lashes, her mouth painted into a bow and parted, the way they all did it, then. That was a poster she was remembering, the first poster for the first movie she ever starred in. It was somewhere in this house, with a few hundred other posters, locked away from sight. She had changed a lot in this house, since she came to live here, permanently, in 1938. She had changed the curtains in the living room and the rugs in the bedroom and all the wall decorations except the ones in the foyer. She had even changed the kind of food there was in the pantry and how it was brought there. She had felt imprisoned here, those first years, but she didn't any longer. It felt perfectly natural to be living here, on a house built into the rock, hanging over the sea. It even felt safe. Lately she had been worried, as she hadn't been in decades, that her defenses had been breached.

Now it was nearly midnight on a cold day in late Oc-

tober, and she was coming down the broad, angled stairs
to the foyer. She was moving very carefully, because at the
age of ninety-nine that was the best she could do. On the
wall of the stairwell posters hung in a graduated rank,
showing the exaggerated makeup and the overexpressive
emotionalism of all American silent movies. TASHEBA
KENT and CONRAD DARCAN in BETRAYED.
TASHEBA KENT and RUDOLPH VALENTINO in DES-
ERT NIGHTS. TASHEBA KENT and HAROLD HOLLIS
in JACARANDA. There were no posters advertising a
movie with Tasheba Kent and Cavender Marsh, because
by the time Cavender began to star in movies, Tasheba
Kent had been retired for a decade.

There was a narrow balcony to the front of the house
through the French windows in the living room, and
Tasheba went there, stepping out into the wind without
worrying about her health. They were always warning
her—Cavender, the doctors, her secretary, Miss Dart—
that she could catch pneumonia at any time, but she
wouldn't live like that, locked up, clutching at every addi-
tional second of breath. She pulled one of the lighter chairs
out onto the balcony and sat down on it. The house was on
an island, separated by only a narrow strip of water from
the coast of central Maine. She could see choppy black
ocean tipped with white and the black rocks of the shore,
looking sharp on the edges and entirely inhospitable.

Years ago, when she and Cav had first come here,
there was no dock on the Maine side. She had bought the
house in 1917 and never lived in it. She and Cav had had
to build the dock and buy the boat the first of the grocery
men used. They had had to make arrangements for the
Los Angeles Times to be flown in and for their favorite
foods, like caviar and pâté, to be shipped up from New
York. They had caused a lot of fuss, then, when they were
supposed to want to hide, and Tash knew that subcon-
sciously they had done it all on purpose.

Tash put her small feet up on the railing and felt the
wind in her face. It was cold and wet out here and she
liked it. She could hear footsteps in the foyer now, coming
through the living room door, on their way to find her, but
she had expected those. Cavender woke up frequently in

the night. He didn't like it when he found the other side of the bed empty. He'd never liked that. That was how they had gotten into this mess to begin with. Tash wondered sometimes how their lives would have turned out, if Cavender hadn't been born into a family so poor that there was only one bed for all six of the boy children.

The approaching footsteps were firm and hard stepped. Cav had been educated in parochial schools. The nuns had taught him to pick his feet up when he walked.

"Tash?" he asked.

"There's no need to whisper," Tash said. "Geraldine Dart's fast asleep next door, and there's nobody else here but us."

Cav came out on the balcony and looked around. The weather was bad, there was no question about it. The wind was sharp and cold. Any minute now, it was going to start to rain. Cav retreated a little.

"You ought to come in," he said. "It's awful out."

"I don't want to come in. I've been thinking."

"That was silly. I would think you were old enough to know better."

"I was thinking about the party. Are you sure all those people are going to come?"

"Oh, yes."

"Are you sure it's going to be all right? We haven't seen anyone for so long. We've always been so careful."

Cav came out on the balcony again. He reminded Tash of one of those Swiss story clocks, where carved wooden characters came out of swinging wooden doors, over and over again, like jacks-in-the-box in perpetual motion.

"It's been fifty years now since it all happened," Cav said seriously. "I don't think anybody cares anymore."

"I'd still feel safer if we didn't have to go through with it. Are you sure we have to go through with it?"

"Well, Tash, there are other ways of making money than selling all your memorabilia at auction, but I never learned how to go about doing them, and I'm too old to start. And so are you."

"I suppose."

"Besides," Cav said, "I'll be glad to get it all out of

here. It spooks me sometimes, running into my past the way I do around here. Doesn't it spook you?"

"No," Tash said thoughtfully. "I think I rather like it. In some ways, in this house, it's as if I never got old."

"You got old," Cav told her. "And so did I. And the roof needs a twenty-five-thousand-dollar repair job. And I've already had one heart attack. We need to hire a full-time nurse and you know it, just in case."

"I don't think I'll wait for 'just in case.' I think that on my hundred and third birthday, I will climb up to the widow's walk on this house, and dive off into the sea."

"Come to bed," Cav said. "We have a lot of people coming very soon. If you're not rested, you won't be able to visit with them."

Cav was right, of course. No matter how good she felt most of the time—how clear in her mind, how strong in her muscles—she was going to be one hundred years old at the end of the week, and she tired easily. She took the arm he held out to her and stood up. She looked back at the sea one more time. It wouldn't be a bad way to go, Tash thought, diving off the widow's walk. People would say it was just like her.

"Tell me something," she said. "Are you sorry we did what we did, way back then? Do you ever wish it could have turned out differently?"

"No."

"Never? Not even once?"

"Not even once. Sometimes I still find myself surprised that it worked out the way it did, that it didn't turn out worse. But I never regret it."

"And you don't think anybody cares anymore. You don't think anybody out there is still angry at us."

"There isn't anyone out there left to be angry, Tash. We've outlasted them all."

Tash let herself be helped across the living room to the foyer, across the foyer to the small cubicle elevator at the back. She came down the stairs on foot, but she never went up anymore. When she tried she just collapsed.

She sat down on the little seat in the corner of the elevator car. Cav's daughter. Her own sister. Aunts and uncles and nieces and nephews. Lawyers and accountants and agents and movie executives. Once everybody in the world had been angry at them. When they had first come out to the island, they'd had to keep the phone off the hook. But Cav was probably right. That was fifty years ago. Almost nobody remembered—and the people who did, like the reporter who was coming for the weekend from *Personality* magazine, thought it was romantic.

Good lord, the kind of trouble you could get yourself into, over nothing more significant than a little light adultery.

The elevator came to a bumping stop.

"Here we are," Cav said. "Let me help you up."

Tash let him help her. Cav was always desperate for proof that he was necessary to her. Tash thought the least she could do was give it to him.

— 2 —

Hannah Kent Graham should have let the maid pack for her. She knew that. She should have written a list of all the clothes she wanted to take, left her suitcases open on her bed, and come out into the living room to do some serious drinking. Hannah Graham almost never did any serious drinking. She almost never did any serious eating, either. What she did do was a lot of very serious surgery. Face-lifts, tummy tucks, liposuction, breast augmentation, rhinoplasty: Hannah had had them all, and some of them more than once. She was sixty years old and only five foot three, but she weighed less than ninety pounds and wore clothes more fashionable than half the starlets she saw window-shopping on Rodeo Drive. Anyplace else in the world except here in Beverly Hills, Hannah would have looked decidedly peculiar—reconstructed, not quite biological, made of cellophane skin stretched across plastic bone—but she didn't live anyplace else in the world. She didn't care what hicks in Austin, Texas, thought of her, either. She was the single most successful real estate agent in Los Angeles, and she looked it.

So far, in forty-five minutes, she had managed to pack two silk day dresses, two evening suits, and a dozen pairs of Christian Dior underwear. She was sucking on her Perrier and ice as if it were an opium teat. In a chair in a corner of the room, her latest husband—number six—was sipping a brandy and soda and trying not to laugh.

If this husband had been like the ones that came before him—beachboys all, picked up in Malibu, notable only for the size of the bulges in their pants—Hannah would have been ready to brain him, but John Graham was actually a serious person. He was almost as old as Hannah herself, at least sixty, and he was a very successful lawyer. He was not, however, a divorce lawyer. Hannah was not that stupid. John handled contract negotiations and long-term development deals for movie stars who really wanted to direct.

Hannah threw a jade green evening dress into the suit bag and backed up to look it over.

"What I don't understand about all this," she said, "is why I'm going out there to attend a one hundredth birthday party for that poisonous old bitch. I mean, why do I want to bother?"

"Personally, I think you want to confront your father. Isn't that what your therapist said?"

"My therapist is a jerk. I don't even know my father. He disappeared into the sunset with that bitch when I was three months old."

"That's my point."

"She murdered my mother," Hannah said. "There isn't any other way to put it."

"Sure there is," John told her. "Especially since she was in Paris or someplace at the exact moment your mother was being killed on the Côte d'Azur. It was your father the police thought killed your mother."

"It comes to the same thing, John. That bitch drove him to it. He went away with her afterward. He left me to be brought up by dear old Aunt Bessie, the world paradigm for the dysfunctional personality."

"There's your father again. That's it exactly. What you really want to do, whether you realize it or not, is brain your old man. I hope you aren't taking a gun along on this weekend."

"I'm thinking of taking cyanide. I also think I'm sick

of therapy-speak. You know what all this is going to mean, don't you? The auction and all the rest of it? It's all going to come out again. The magazines are going to have a field day. *People. Us. Personality.* Isn't *that* going to be fun?"

"You're going to find it very good for business," John said placidly. "People are going to see you as a very romantic figure. It'll do you nothing but good, Hannah. You just watch."

The really disgusting thing, Hannah thought, was that John was probably right. The really important people wouldn't be impressed—they probably wouldn't even notice—but the second-stringers would be all hot to trot. The agency would be inundated with people looking for *anything at all* in Beverly Hills for under a million dollars, who really only wanted to see her close up. If this was the kind of thing I wanted to do with my life, Hannah thought, I would have become an actress.

The jade green evening dress was much too much for a weekend on an island off the coast of Maine. Even if they dressed for dinner there, they wouldn't go in for washed silk and rhinestones. What would they go in for? Hannah put the jade green evening dress back in the closet and took out a plainer one in dark blue. Then she put that one back, too. It made her look like she weighed at least a hundred and five.

"What do you think they have to auction off?" she asked John. "Do you think they have anything of my mother's?"

"I don't know. They might."

"Aunt Bessie always said there wasn't anything of hers left after it was all over, that everything she had was in their house in France and it was never shipped back here for me to have. Maybe he kept it."

"Maybe he did."

"Would you let him, if you were her? Reminders of the murdered wife all around your house?"

"You make a lot of assumptions, Hannah. You assume she's the dominant partner in the relationship. You assume that if he has your mother's things, they must be lying around in his house."

"*Her* house. It was always her house. She bought it before she ever met him."

"Her house. Whatever. Maybe he put those things in an attic somewhere, or a basement. Maybe he keeps them locked up in a hope chest in a closet. They don't have to be where your aunt is tripping over them all the time."

"Don't remind me that she's my aunt, John. It makes me ill."

"I think you better forget about all this packing and go have something to drink. Just leave it all here for the maid to finish with in the morning, and we can sleep in the guest room."

"You only like to sleep in the guest room because there's a mirror on the ceiling."

"Sure. I like to see your bony little ass bopping up and down like a Mexican jumping bean."

Hannah made a face at him and headed out of the bedroom toward the living room. She had to go down a hall carpeted in pale gray and across an entryway of polished fieldstone. Like most houses costing over five million dollars in Beverly Hills, hers looked like the set for a TV miniseries of a Jackie Collins novel. The living room had a conversation pit with its own fireplace. It also had a twenty-two-foot-long wet bar made of teak with a brass footrail. Hannah went around to the back of this and found a bottle of Smirnoff vodka and a glass. Vodka was supposed to be better for your skin than darker liquors.

Hannah poured vodka into her glass straight and drank it down straight. It burned her throat, but it made her feel instantly better.

"You know," she said to John, who had followed her out to get a refill for himself, "maybe this won't be so terrible after all. Maybe I'll be able to create an enormous scene, big enough to cause major headlines, and then maybe I'll threaten to sue."

"Sue?"

"To stop the auction. You're good at lawsuits, John, help me think. Maybe I can claim that everything they have really belongs to my mother. Or maybe I can claim that the whole auction is a way of trading on the name of my mother. Think about it, John. There must be something."

John filled his glass with ice and poured a double shot of brandy in it. This time, he didn't seem any more interested in mixers than Hannah was.

"Hannah," he said. "Give it up. Go to Maine. Scream and yell at your father. Tell your aunt she deserves to rot in hell. Then come home. Trust me. If you try to do anything else, you'll only get yourself in trouble."

Hannah poured herself another glass of vodka and swigged it down again, the way she had the first.

"Crap," she said miserably. "You're probably right."

—— 2 ——

The first time Richard Fenster put a poster of Tasheba Kent on the ceiling of his bedroom, laid down on his bed, and masturbated while looking into those big dark eyes, he was thirteen years old. He was now thirty-six, and if he wanted to abuse himself in homage to the greatest movie star who ever lived, he no longer had to make sure his door was locked and keep himself from crying out in the clutch of passion. His mother and father still lived in the tiny two-bedroom house in Newton where he had grown up, but Richard didn't. He had a nifty one-bedroom apartment just upstairs from this store he operated in Cambridge, where he could be private any time he liked. In fact, he owned the whole building, and nobody lived here he couldn't stand. It was absolutely the best arrangement, and there were days when Richard couldn't believe he'd lucked into it.

Actually, luck had nothing to do with it. Richard wasn't doing what his parents wanted and expected him to do, which was something along the lines of being the next in line for a Nobel Prize in physics. Richard had been declared a math prodigy at seven, sent to MIT at fifteen, and received a doctorate in theoretical mathematics from the California Institute of Technology before he was twenty-four. At that point, he had decided that he'd had enough. He may have been a math prodigy, but he had never been that interested in math. Working with numbers came easily to him, but it also bored him silly. As it turned out, however, it was a highly translatable skill. Richard was in his second year of doctoral work at Cal Tech the first time he bought a block of stock. That first time, he used money from his fellowship, which was supposed to go into his living expenses. He never had to miss a meal. Three months after buying the stock, he sold, at a profit of almost 15 percent, a nice haul even after having to pay capital gains tax. He bought another block and then another, throwing dice on quick turnovers and hunches that came from so deeply inside him, they might not have been hunches at all. His success was astonishing even to him, and he was used to being successful.

What made Richard Fenster a rich man was the Black Monday minicrash of 1987. Just before it hit, he had pulled himself out of the stock market totally, not because of any business intelligence or sober analysis of the state of the deficit, but in a fit of pique. He had spent the Monday before the Monday of the crash bidding on the fan Tasheba Kent had used to seduce Ramon Navarro in *Flame of Desire*. He had lost it to an aggressive little man who reminded him of Peter Lorre and who had much too much money to be beaten. Richard had cashed out of the market because he was angry that he hadn't had the cash when he needed it. The next thing he knew, he was buying back in at rock-bottom prices that wouldn't be seen again for quite a while. Six months later, the market bounced back and he sold out again. It was scary, how much money he made. It was scary to look through the careful financial records he kept on his Macintosh and realize he was worth well over six million dollars.

By then, of course, Richard had been out of Cal Tech for some time and living in New York City. He had a room at the Y for a while and then a fifth floor walk-up studio on West Ninety-fourth Street. He bought his clothes at army-navy stores and thrift shops in Chinatown. He ate from street vendors and take-out places and called "really eating out" sitting down to a Whopper at a Lexington Avenue Burger King. He cared for only two things: his computer and his collection of Tasheba Kent memorabilia.

Anyone who saw him on the street would have tagged him as a hopeless nerd, a rat-faced keyboard jockey, a failure.

He moved back to Massachusetts because he thought it was time to settle down, and because he liked Cambridge, and because the shop made sense. He sold movie memorabilia of every kind, from the ordinary to the very, very rare, from the silents to the present, and books and magazines about the movies, too. Reel To Reel had the best collection of artifacts from 1950s big bug movies west of the Mississippi. It had the best collection of props from 1930s musicals anywhere outside the MGM warehouse. Most of all, Reel To Reel was the acknowledged headquarters for every passionate cinema fan in the United States, and there were more of them than Richard ever imagined.

It was not Richard Fenster's reputation as a fan but his reputation as a dealer that had gotten him invited to Tasheba Kent's one hundredth birthday party, and he knew it. The party was a ruse. Tasheba Kent and Cavender Marsh were obviously in desperate need of money. They were going to sell all their things and use the cash for nursing homes or live-in help or whatever else it was people that ancient needed for their day-to-day lives. Richard supposed it was expensive to be old, although he didn't know it for sure. He hated his parents with the passion of a Greek hating the Turks, and his parents were the only relatively old people he had any contact with. Richard did know that he was willing to spend a great deal of money to get his hands on a significant portion of that collection. He was sure Tasheba Kent and Cavender Marsh and their agents at the auction house knew it, too.

Richard Fenster's idea of packing for a weekend was to stuff all his clean jeans, all his clean shirts, all his clean underwear, and his one extra sweater into a canvas duffel bag and sling the duffel bag over his shoulder. His idea of arranging for transportation up to Maine was to hitch. It was Katha Drosset who had talked him into taking the plane to Augusta and hiring a car from there, and now Katha was sitting on a tall four-legged bar stool shoved up against his five-drawer bureau, smoking a marijuana cigarette and looking bored. The bureau had come from the

Salvation Army. Katha had come from Miss Porter's School and Sarah Lawrence College. Richard had sex with her whenever she was willing to get on top, so that he could lie on his back in bed and stare into the eyes of Tasheba Kent when he came.

"So tell me," Katha said, her voice sounding too high and tight coming through a rush of marijuana smoke, "just what is it you're going to do up there all weekend, aside from meet this woman who's been your idol forever now that she's turned into a walking corpse?"

"Look the merchandise over." Richard's yellow velour shirt had a tomato stain on the collar. It might have been better not to have taken that one even if it had been clean.

"I bet I know what you want to do," Katha said. "I bet you want to ask them all about the death of Lilith Brayne."

"I wouldn't bring it up. I'd probably get thrown out of the house."

"They wouldn't be able to throw you out of the house, unless they meant to drown you. I looked at that stuff they sent. It's the luxury version of Alcatraz you're going to."

"It's nothing of the sort. Is that my western belt under the bed over there?"

"You gave your western belt to that wino in Harvard Square who was trying to keep his pants up with one hand and drink muscatel with the other."

"Oh, yeah."

"It's your rubber rattlesnake you see under the bed. Don't you think it's strange, that nobody's ever written a book about it?"

"About what?"

"About the death of Lilith Brayne. It was a famous case at the time. All those books you have say so. And they all say Cavender Marsh murdered her and got away with it, too."

"They don't say that, Katha. If they did, they'd get sued."

"I still say it sounds like just the thing. People are always digging up old Hollywood murders and writing best-sellers about them. I'm surprised you don't write this one yourself."

"I'm a lousy writer. And I don't want to write a book about the death of Lilith Brayne. It's Tasheba Kent I'm interested in."

"They were sisters."

"I don't think it was a murder," Richard said. "I think the coroner's report was probably accurate. More accident than anything else."

Katha lit another marijuana cigarette, held her breath, and stared dreamily at the ceiling. "I bet what's-his-name doesn't think so," she said as she let the smoke out of her lungs. "You know, the guy that came here from *Personality* magazine last week. I bet he thinks it was a murder. I bet he wants to write about it, too."

"He probably does."

"I think you ought to get in there first," Katha said. "Look at all the time and trouble and money you've put into Tasheba Kent. You've got moral rights in this case. Or squatter's rights. Or something."

"Right," Richard said. "Don't you think you've had enough of that stuff for today?"

"I never have enough of this stuff, Richard. It's better than air."

"Well, it's got more of a kick."

Richard was down to his two sweaters, the red V-necked one with the hole in the shoulder seam and the brown crew-necked one with the hole in the right elbow. Which to wear and which to take? The hole in the elbow was more embarrassing than the hole in the shoulder seam. Richard stuffed the brown sweater into his duffel bag and threw the red one onto the top of his bureau.

"That'll do it," he said. "Maybe I'll get lucky this weekend. Maybe she'll take to me, and sit me down and tell me all about her life."

"Don't be asinine," Katha said scornfully. "She's going to be a hundred years old. It probably takes all the brainpower she has left just to decide what she wants for breakfast."

Aside from clothes, the only important thing Richard had to take to Maine with him was his laptop with its little collection of discs. That folded into a case the size of a briefcase and never really had to be packed at all.

Richard fastened the top of the duffel bag and put it on the floor against the wall. He put his laptop on the floor next to it, so he wouldn't forget it when it was time to leave.

He wished he had good reason for believing that Katha's predictions on the state of Tasheba Kent's mind were wrong, but he didn't. It was just the kind of thing about which Katha tended to be deadly accurate.

Richard went into the bathroom, shut the door, and sat down on the closed cover of the toilet seat. In the beginning, having Katha around felt like a good idea. She was an assistant in the shop and a companion the rest of the time. She was somebody to talk to on a regular basis, which was something Richard had never had before, except when he was living at home. Lately, having her around had begun to make him feel as if he were living at home. She nattered and pried and criticized, just like his mother. Her standards were different, but her methods of attack were precisely the same.

The worst of it was, of course, that he didn't really like having sex with her. Sometimes he positively hated it. She was too thin and too angular. She smelled of marijuana. She cluttered up the bed. What he wanted was to be left alone with the great dark eyes on his ceiling, the parted bowed mouth, the hint of decadence in the rounded flesh of breast and arm.

Sometimes, waking up in the dark with Katha curled into a ball beside him, Richard got a sudden flash of a historical moment: Tasheba Kent and Cavender Marsh making love to each other on the moonlit beach at Cap d'Antibes.

The vision always made him feel as if his intestines were going down the garbage disposal.

—— 4 ——

Mathilda Frazier's office overlooked Madison Avenue, and whenever she got angry—really, impossibly, undeni-

ably angry—she would stand at her windows and drop
sunflower seeds onto the heads of pedestrians walking
along the sidewalk three stories below. Mathilda had no
idea what she would do if she got promoted. That would
mean moving upstairs, literally. By the time she got to the
fifth floor, she could drop all the sunflower seeds she
wanted, nobody would notice. This did not mean that Mathilda Frazier did not want to be promoted. She wanted it
desperately. If she hadn't, she would never have put up
with the kind of abuse she was getting from Martin
Michaelson over the phone.

"Women weren't brought up the way you were back
in whenever-it-was," Martin was saying. "They didn't
have the same assumptions. They were brought up to be
women."

"Right," Mathilda said. She preferred to drop dry
sunflower seeds in their seedpods. The dry-roasted kind
were oily, and tended to get stains all over her suit.

"I don't think you realize how profoundly alienating
women like you can be to women with traditional values. I
don't think you realize what kind of antagonisms you create."

"My mother is a woman with traditional values, Martin. We get along just fine. And you can hardly call
Tasheba Kent a paragon of traditional values. This is a
woman who played the sexual aggressor in twenty movies
starting back before women had the vote."

"The vote isn't the point either, Mathilda. The point
here is that Tasheba Kent was always very male-positive.
She saw men as a good thing. Not like you."

"Wonderful, Martin."

"I'm just trying to warn you. This is an important
account. I don't want you to blow it."

Actually, Mathilda thought, dropping a whole fistful
of sunflower seeds this time, so that they fell like snow on
the head of a young man dressed for the starring role in
Jesus Christ Superstar, what Martin really wanted was to
get her to quit. This *was* an important account, and it was
driving him absolutely crazy that she had gotten it. What
made it worse was that nobody had handed it to her. Martin's usual tactic, when Mathilda got work he wanted for

himself, was to blame it on "affirmative action"—a policy that Halbard's Auction House, being a British company, did not in fact follow. Anybody could tell that much just by looking around at the third floor, where all the auction coordinators worked. It wasn't that there weren't plenty of women, because there were. It wasn't that there weren't plenty of black people and Asians and Indians from New Delhi and other people who might qualify as marginal in the ordinary scheme of things, because Halbard's had a better record at that kind of thing than most American companies. The problem was that 99 percent of these people had British accents, and of the 1 percent left over, a fair number had Scots accents. That was the official and unofficial hiring practices policy at Halbard's: hire British if at all possible, even if you have to bring a load of secretaries in on the boat.

With Tasheba Kent, though, Mathilda could not have been upstaged, or assigned out, or any of the other things Halbard's upper management liked to do to make sure the Americans didn't get their hands on anything important. The Tasheba Kent auction was Mathilda's by right. She was the one who had seen the article—on a back page of the "Metropolitan" section of *The New York Times*, near the bottom—where Tasheba Kent's lawyer had been quoted as saying that Miss Kent and Mr. Marsh were considering an auction of their movie mementos and personal things. She was the one who had called the lawyer to offer the services of Halbard's Auction House. She was the one who had gone over the list of probable sale items with an acerbic young woman named Geraldine Dart. Nobody at Halbard's could deny that the Tasheba Kent auction had been constructed out of almost nothing by Mathilda Frazier herself, and there was absolutely nothing Martin Michaelson could do about it.

"Mathilda?" Martin demanded. "Are you listening to me?"

"Always, Martin," Mathilda said.

"I just want to be sure you're listening to me. I just want to make sure I'm getting through to you. If you aren't careful, this trip of yours could get to be an absolute *disaster*."

"Well, Martin, that's always true, isn't it?"

"What are you going to do if you get there and just put her right off? You don't realize it, but you're *very* abrasive."

"Thanks, Martin."

"You're very aggressive and *unfeminine*. You really are. I know that's not supposed to count anymore, but this is an older woman you're going to be dealing with."

"I know who I'm going to be dealing with, Martin."

"Some women can be very competitive without losing their femininity, but it's like walking a tightrope. Most women just haven't got what it takes."

"Do you have a dictionary of clichés in your office, Martin, where you can look things up whenever you're at a loss for words?"

"What?"

"Never mind. Listen, Martin, I've got to get off the phone now. I've got to go down the hall and see Phyllis."

"Yes. Of course. None of us can afford to keep Phyllis waiting. But you'll think about it, won't you?"

"Think about what?"

"About not going to Maine, of course. Maybe it would be the best thing. Then Tasheba Kent would never have to know that the two of you don't get along."

"Good-bye, Martin."

Mathilda hung up and rubbed her forehead. I'm not going to go check myself out in a mirror, she told herself, I'm just not. Martin Michaelson wouldn't recognize femininity if it walked up and bit him on the ass. In the end, she couldn't help herself. She fished an ancient compact out of the bottom of her purse and surveyed her eyes and eyebrows and eyelashes, her nose and cheekbones, the line of her jaw. Everything seemed to be in place. Nothing seemed to have "masculinized" while she wasn't looking. She hadn't started growing whiskers on her chin or—or *what*, for God's sake?

Mathilda threw the compact back into her purse and the purse over her shoulder and left her office to go down to the other end of the hall. Phyllis Green was an American and the head of the auction coordination department. That way, Halbard's had managed to promote her without moving her upstairs into the pure British precincts of upper management. Phyllis had decided to put up with this for reasons known only to herself. Unlike her staff—which was mainly made up of twentysomethings just graduated from the art history departments of the Ivy League and Seven Sisters—Phyllis was in her fifties and a veteran of the equal pay wars. If she hadn't liked the arrangements at Halbard's, she would either have left or hauled the auction house into court.

"Phyllis?" Mathilda asked, knocking on the open door.

Phyllis looked up from a pile of papers on her desk and waved Mathilda inside. "I thought you'd gone already. Aren't you supposed to be in Maine?"

"I'm leaving first thing tomorrow morning."

"Well, you'll be lucky to get out of here. Do you know what I've spent my time doing all day? Going through the details of the Impressionist auction. Fifty paintings by Pissarro just sitting up there on the sixth floor, lying around like so many pieces of wood, and nobody's cataloged them yet."

"I thought that was Janey Lewis's auction. What happened to Janey?"

"Jumped ship for Christie's."

"Oh."

"Well, you've got to expect it," Phyllis said. "Christie's will actually promote Americans. So. Is there something you need from me, or did you just want to talk?"

Mathilda sighed. "Actually, I just needed an antidote to Martin Michaelson. I just got him off the phone."

"Oh, dear."

"I don't know why I let him get to me, but I do."

"He gets to everybody. He knows all the right buttons to push."

"I guess I just wanted to hear you say I really was the right person to handle this auction, and Tasheba Kent isn't going to loathe me on sight, and I haven't lost my femininity, whatever that means—"

"It means you haven't stopped making yourself look incompetent," Phyllis told her. "Personally, I insist that

the women who work for me lose their femininity as soon
as they accept my offer of a job."

Mathilda laughed. "I know I was being ridiculous. I
just can't help myself. That man just gets me going. I wish
he'd do something awful and get himself fired."

"Bring this auction off successfully and I'll get you
promoted to senior AC," Phyllis said. "Then he can die of
apoplexy."

"He won't, you know. He'll just sit around at lunch
and complain about how this company has been intimi-
dated by the radical feminists."

"Go to Maine," Phyllis said.

Mathilda went back down the hall to her office instead. The phone was ringing, but she didn't pick it up. It
was probably just Martin, wanting to pick up where he
had left off.

Mathilda got her file on the Tasheba Kent auction out
of her file cabinet, spread the contents across her desk, and
began to go over the probable sale lists one more time.

—— 5 ——

For Carlton Ji, journalism was not so much a career as it
was a new kind of computer game, except without the
computer, which suited Carlton just fine. Two of his older
brothers had gone into computer work, and a third—Win-
ston the Medical Doctor, as Carlton's mother always put
it—did a lot of programming on the side. For Carlton,
however, keyboards and memory banks and microchips
were all a lot of fuss and nonsense. If he tried to work one
of the "simple" programs his brothers were always bringing him, he ended up doing something odd to the machine,
so that it shut down and wouldn't work anymore. If he
tried to write his first drafts on the word processor at
work, he found he couldn't get them to print out on the
printer or even to come back onto the screen. They disappeared, that was all, and Carlton had learned to write his
articles out in longhand instead. It was frustrating. Computers made life easier, if you knew how to use them.
Carlton could see that. Besides, there wasn't a human be-

ing of any sex or color in the United States today who really believed there was any such thing as an Asian-American man who was computer illiterate.

Fortunately for Carlton Ji, his computer at *Personality* magazine had a mouse, which just needed to be picked up in the hand and moved around. It was by using the mouse that he had found out what he had found out about the death of Lilith Brayne. He didn't have anything conclusive, of course. If there had been anything definitive lying around, somebody else would have picked it up years ago. What he had was what one of his brothers called "a computer coincidence." The coincidence had been there all along, of course, but it had remained unnoticed until a computer program threw all the elements up on a screen. The trick was that the elements might never have appeared together if there hadn't been a program to force them together, because they weren't the kind of elements a human brain would ordinarily think of combining. Computers were stupid. They did exactly what you told them to do, even if it made no sense.

Carlton Ji wasn't sure what he had done to make the computer do what it did, but one day there he was, staring at a list of seemingly unrelated items on the terminal screen, and it hit him.

"FOUND AT THE SCENE," the screen flashed at him, and then:

GOLD COMPACT
GOLD KEY RING
GOLD CIGARETTE CASE
EBONY AND IVORY CIGARETTE HOLDER
BLACK FEATHER BOA
DIAMOND AND SAPPHIRE DINNER RING

Then the screen wiped itself clean and started, "TASHEBA KENT IN PARIS." This list was even longer than the previous one, because the researcher had keyed in everything she could find, no matter how unimportant. These included:

SILVER GRAY ROLLS-ROYCE WITH SILVER-PLATED TRIM
DIAMOND AND RUBY DINNER RING
BLACK BEADED EVENING DRESS
AMBER AND EBONY HOOKAH
BLACK FEATHER BOA
VIVIENNE CRI SHOES WITH RHINESTONE BUCKLES

If the black feather boa hadn't been in the same position each time—second from the bottom—Carlton might not have noticed it. But he did notice it, and when he went to the paper files to check it out, the point became downright peculiar.

"It was either the same black feather boa or an identical one," Carlton told Jasper Fein, the editor from Duluth House he was hoping to interest in a new book on the death of Lilith Brayne. Like a lot of other reporters from *Personality* magazine, and reporters from *Time* and *Newsweek* and *People,* too, Carlton's dream was to get a really spectacular book into print. The kind of thing that sold a million copies in hardcover. The kind of thing that would get his face on the cover of the Sunday *New York Times Magazine,* or maybe even into *Vanity Fair.* Other reporters had done it, and reporters with a lot less going for them than Carlton Ji.

"You've got to look at the pictures," Carlton told Jasper Fein, "and then you have to read the reports in order. The police in Cap d'Antibes found a black feather boa among Lilith Brayne's things just after she died. That was on Tuesday night—early Wednesday morning, really, around two-thirty or three o'clock. Then later on Wednesday morning, around ten, they interviewed Tasheba Kent in Paris, and *she* was wearing a black feather boa."

Jasper Fein shook his head. "You've lost me, Carlton. So there were two feather boas. So what?"

"So what happened to the first feather boa?"

"What *happened* to it?"

"That's right," Carlton said triumphantly. "Because after the black feather boa was seen around Tasheba Kent's neck at ten o'clock on Wednesday morning, no black feather boa was ever found in Lilith Brayne's things in the south of France again. That feather boa just disappeared without a trace."

Jasper Fein frowned. "Maybe the police just didn't consider it important. Maybe it's not listed because they didn't see any reason to list it."

"They listed a lipstick brush," Carlton objected. "They listed a pair of tweezers."

"Twice?"

"That's right, twice. Once at the scene and once again for the magistrate at the inquest."

"And the only thing that was missing was this black feather boa."

"That's right."

Jasper Fein drummed his fingers against the tablecloth. They were having lunch at the Four Seasons—not the best room in the restaurant, not the room where Jasper would have taken one of his authors who had already been on the best-seller lists, but the Four Seasons nonetheless. Carlton had no idea what lunch was going to cost, because his copy of the menu hadn't had any prices on it.

"Okay," Jasper conceded. "This is beginning to sound interesting."

Carlton Ji beamed. "It certainly sounds interesting to me," he said, "and I'm in a unique position to do something about it. I'm supposed to go up to Maine and spend four days on that godforsaken island where they live now, doing a story for the magazine."

"Love among the geriatric set?"

"I can take any angle I want, actually. My editor just thinks it's a great idea to have Tasheba Kent in the magazine. Hollywood glamour. Silent movies. Love and death. It's a natural."

"Did you say those feather boas were identical?"

"They were as far as I could tell from the photographs, and there are a lot of photographs, and most of them are pretty good. The descriptions in the police reports are identical, too."

"Hmm. It's odd, isn't it? I wonder what it's all about."

"Maybe I'll have a chance to find out when I go to Maine. Maybe I can get someone up there to talk to me."

"Maybe you can," Jasper said, "but don't be worried if you don't. They're old people now. Tasheba Kent must be, my God—"

"One hundred," Carlton said.

"Really?"

"Among the other things that are going on during this weekend I'm supposed to attend is a hundredth birthday party for Tasheba Kent."

"There's the angle for *Personality* magazine. That's the kind of thing you want to play up over there. Not all this stuff about the death of Lilith Brayne."

"To tell you the truth," Carlton said, "I'm going to have to play up the death of Lilith Brayne. My editor's going to insist on it."

Jasper Fein looked ready to ask Carlton how that could, in fact, be the truth, when Carlton had said only a few moments before that his editor would take any angle he wanted to give her. Jasper took a sip of his chablis instead, and Carlton relaxed a little. At least they understood each other. At least Jasper realized that Carlton was going to hang onto his ownership of this idea. Now they could start to talk business for real, and Carlton had a chance of ending up with what he wanted.

Carlton wasn't going to talk money now, though. He wasn't going to talk details. He was going to wait until he got back from Maine. Then he'd have more to bargain with.

——— 6 ———

Lydia Acken sometimes wondered what her life would have been like if she had been born fifteen years later than she was, if she had gone into law school when the law schools were trying to include women instead of keep them out, if she had joined the firm when it was desperate to prove that it did not discriminate in hiring or promotion on the basis of sex. Lydia Acken was sixty years old and a partner at Holborn, Bard & Kirby—but a partner in trusts and estates, which was where the firm put women in the bad old days. Lydia had long ago stopped wondering if she had any interest in trusts and estates. The answer was probably no, but in her time she hadn't felt she had any choice. The most brilliant woman in her Harvard Law School graduating class—the woman who had, as a matter of fact, graduated first in her class—had ended up having to open an office of her own in the small town she had come from in Ohio. Nobody would hire her, because she wanted to be a litigator and she refused to do trusts and estates and she had no interest at all in divorce cases. "Don't be like her," recruiters would tell women also looking for jobs in their firms. "She acts like a man."

Now the firm was full of women, in every department. The younger women didn't think there were enough of them yet, but from Lydia's point of view, the change was astonishing. There were six women litigators in the firm now, two of them partners. There was a woman at the head of corporate liaison, when in the old days the fact that the firm hired any women lawyers at all was kept as secret from corporate clients as sex used to be kept from Victorian children. The new young women were different from the women of Lydia's generation. They weren't soft-spoken or particularly polite. They didn't bow meekly to the idea that a professional woman simply couldn't have a home and a family life. They not only got married—Lydia had been married, for twenty years, to a man who had left her in her fifties to marry his twenty-three-year-old personal assistant—but had children, too, sometimes rushing out in the middle of contract negotiations to deliver, and rushing back two days later before they'd even had a chance to catch their breath. Lydia was in awe of these young women, of their energy, of their intelligence, of their courage, of their wit. She wasn't sure that even if she had been born fifteen years later, she would have been able to compete.

Now it was four o'clock on the afternoon of the day before she was supposed to leave for Maine, and Lydia was sitting at the desk in her office, finding it impossible to concentrate. What she was supposed to be doing was going over the legal ramifications of the auction of the personal effects of Tasheba Kent and Cavender Marsh, what belonged to who, what was already willed to somebody else, what the tax implications were for each sale of each item at each possible price. The situation was complicated by the fact that a fair amount of what Cavender Marsh owned might be said to be more correctly the property of his dead wife. The circumstances surrounding the death of Lilith Brayne were so chaotic and disorganized, Lydia could see immediately that the auction was rife with potential lawsuits. For one thing, the daughter, Hannah Graham, had never had her interests properly represented. If Hannah got herself some decent legal representation now, she could cause real trouble.

This was exactly the kind of complicated mess Lydia had always been so good at straightening out, the kind of legal and emotional minefield she had always been so good at negotiating. Now she seemed to sit over the pages for hour after hour without being able to pay attention to them at all. Hannah Graham wanted to make a fuss to stop her father from selling her mother's things? Well, so what? What did it matter if Cavender Marsh got to sell those things or not? Tasheba Kent wanted to make sure that her black feather boa went to some kind of show business museum, and not to a fan collector, because fan collectors sometimes did really disgusting sexual things with mementos of their favorite stars? Why, in the name of God, should that be Lydia Acken's problem?

What Lydia's mind kept going back to, over and over again, was the sight of a storefront window on a side street in the East Village, a window she had passed by accident the first time, when her cab had been stuck in traffic and made a wrong turn. "LEGAL SERVICES," the sign in the window had said, first in English, then in Spanish, then in some sort of Asian characters, then (Lydia hadn't been sure about this) in the Cyrillic alphabet. Her cabdriver swore heavily in Spanish and speeded up. Turning the corner onto Third Avenue, Lydia was just able to catch the one sign on the one corner that hadn't been torn down and hauled away: East Sixth Street.

She had come back on a Saturday afternoon, walking down the avenue from St. Mark's Place with increasing uneasiness, knowing that her plain denim skirt and white cotton blouse and blue canvas espadrilles were all wrong.

The clothes she wore were all made of natural fibers, for one thing. They were also much too clean. The people around her looked not only worn, but grungy. They had dirt ground into the pores of their skin, so deep it looked as if it might never come out. Their clothes were almost invariably not only polyester and rayon, but the cheapest versions of these, the kinds that crackled like paper and chafed the skin. The children wore pants that were too big for them or too small for them or that just didn't sit right on their hips—but there weren't many children. The ones Lydia saw were either Spanish or Asian. They chattered away in languages she didn't understand.

When she got to the storefront with the sign about legal services in its window, she went in through the plate-glass door and sat down on a worn couch with green plastic cushions. All around her she saw women in sagging dresses and too-tight jeans, tired women and bruised women and women who looked as if they'd rather be dead. There were also a couple of men, but they kept to themselves, in a corner, as if they had stumbled into an old-fashioned hen party. The men looked as if they'd rather be dead, too.

A very young woman with what Lydia now knew was called an "Isro" was sitting at a desk near the back, answering the phone and calling out the names of women who were then allowed to pass through the door behind her desk. The very young woman looked harried and annoyed. At the front of her desk there was a listing stack of brochures, printed in plain black and white, nothing fancy. "EAST VILLAGE LEGAL SERVICES," the brochures announced on their covers. Lydia got up and went to the desk to take one.

"Do you want to sign up to talk to one of the lawyers?" the young woman with the Isro asked her.

"No, no," Lydia said, retreating.

The young woman lost interest in her. Lydia sat back down on the couch and looked through the brochure. Like the sign out front, it was printed in four different languages. Lydia stuck to the English and found out that East Village Legal Services was made up of lawyers who devoted all or part of their time to providing members of the

East Village community with the legal help they needed to "negotiate the system," specializing in welfare law and "disputes with social services professionals" and battering and wife-abuse cases. At the very bottom of the English section, thick black letters spelled out IF YOU ARE A LAWYER. Underneath there was a short paragraph that said simply, "If you are a lawyer and would like to donate your time at EVLS, please contact Sherri at 212-555-2876."

I could devote all my time to something like East Village Legal Services, Lydia found herself thinking, at the oddest times, for days afterward. If I scaled down the way I lived, I wouldn't have to work at all anymore. I wouldn't have to worry about getting paid.

It was a crazy idea, and it didn't help her any with working out the details of the Tasheba Kent auction or getting ready to go to Maine. Lydia was even having a hard time packing. When she put her black wool dinner dress into her suit bag, she asked herself why anybody ever bothered to go to the trouble of dressing for dinner. When she zipped her mid-heeled dress pumps into the shoe pockets of her suitcase, she wondered how she could ever have decided to buy such silly shoes. Everything she did in her life was wrong, everything was silly, and nothing she tried helped her to settle down. Even her tranquilizers didn't work. Her tranquilizers had gotten her through her divorce without so much as a headache.

There's something wrong with me, she thought now, staring at her desk, and it's not natural.

Natural or not, she had to go to Maine. She got her attaché case off the floor and began to stack her papers into it. At the end, she put in the brochure from East Village Legal Services, too. She had been carrying it with her everywhere for days, and she didn't see why she shouldn't bring it to Maine.

Maybe it would operate as an antidote to all these ridiculous people she really didn't want to see.

—— 7 ——

Kelly Pratt had been staring all day at a piece of paper that said "Brayne Estate—Disposition," and all it had gotten him was a backache and a throb in his head the size of the Heart That Ate Cleveland. It didn't help that the first item under the title had been a disclaimer: *"Effects of Lillian Kent, Hereinafter known as Lilith Brayne."* It helped even less that the calculations had been done well before the general use of computers, and that a couple of the figures had been corrected, by hand, in the margins. Kelly was supposed to make something sensible of this piece of paper, to present to the lawyer and to Tasheba Kent and Cavender Marsh, and he just hadn't been able to do it. Now he was practically on his way up to Maine, with his suitcase packed and his best yachting clothes laid out for him on the navy blue satin wing chair back in his bedroom, and all he could think about was what an idiot he was going to look like when the three of them got around to asking him questions.

Kelly Pratt was a tall, broad man in his early fifties, going to paunch but hiding it well, who wished he had changed his last name at the same time he had changed his first. He had changed his first—which had been Hubert, for God's sake, *Hubert* Pratt—right after he had gotten out of the army and right before he had gone into college. Being called "Hubie" for two straight years in Korea would have been enough for anybody. He had chosen "Kelly" because, in spite of the fact that he was working his way to business school and a sensible career in accounting, he had secret fantasies of becoming an actor. There was an actor everybody said he looked like, named John Forsyth, who had a television program in afternoon reruns that year called *Bachelor Father*. The father in question on that program had a niece who lived with him named Kelly. That was where Kelly got his name. It would have bothered him endlessly if anybody had realized that he had taken his name from a girl, but nobody did, so that worked out all right.

Now, thirty years later, Kelly Pratt looked even more like John Forsyth than he had then, and John Forsyth had been in a new television program, and Kelly liked to imagine himself as Blake Carrington. That was the good thing about this trip to Maine. Spending the weekend with a couple of old movie stars was exactly the kind of thing Blake Carrington would do, although he probably wouldn't bring their accounting work along to go over the figures. Normally, Kelly would never have gone on an errand like this himself. The tiny accounting company he had started with his best friend from college, Abraham Kahn, had grown. It wasn't the size of the giants like Arthur Andersen or Deloitte, but it took up three floors of a good building in midtown Manhattan and kept a hundred and fifty people on payroll. When they started out, Kelly had wanted to do as much corporate work as they could get, but Bram had been adamant. "Do personals," he'd said, "big accounts, but personals." And Bram had been right. Kahn and Pratt handled the business affairs of three stars of the Metropolitan Opera, two internationally famous symphony conductors, all six of the principal characters on the most important soap opera still shot in New York, and the entire roster of the most successful team in the history of the National Football League. Kahn and Pratt even appeared on and off in Liz Smith's column. It had become a status symbol of a sort for Kahn and Pratt to agree to handle you. Lately, there had even been a trickle of rock-and-roll stars through the door, including a woman who spent more of her time on stage half-naked than reasonably clothed. Kelly had been all excited about it, but Bram had refused to let him take her on. Rock stars made Bram very, very nervous.

Now Bram was sitting in the visitor's chair in Kelly Pratt's office, smoking a pipe, his long legs stretched out across the carpet. Kelly sometimes thought it was Bram who should have changed his name. Tall and lean, with the chiseled features of a Yankee aristocrat, Abraham Kahn could have passed himself off as a John Endicott or a Martin Cadwalader any time he wanted to. Instead, he belonged to the Harmonie Club and a Conservative synagogue and kept an Israeli flag hanging on a pole next to an American one in a corner of his office.

Bram had his legs crossed with one ankle on the other

knee. His pipe was sending smoke signals up to the ceiling. Every time he looked at the paper Kelly had given him, he sighed heavily.

"It doesn't make any sense," Bram said finally.

Kelly exploded. "I know it doesn't make any sense, Bram. I know that. I was hoping for something a little more constructive."

"How much more constructive could I be? Just look at this sheet, Kelly. Whole chunks of money just seem to go missing. Except for the daughter's trust, of course. That's intact."

"That would have to be intact," Kelly said. "It was administered by the Chase Manhattan Bank. They're too damn high-profile a company to pull any crap."

"Yes, well, the problem is, you couldn't really say that anybody pulled any crap in this case. You couldn't say much of anything. It never occurred to me before, but living without computers must have been heaven for con men and cheats."

"Most people would say that living with computers has been heaven for con men and cheats."

Bram waved this away. "That's because too many of the people who are trying to catch the con men and the cheats don't know how to run the computers. Remember what I've always told you. We get hit by a hacker, we don't prosecute him, we hire him."

"Yes, Bram, I know. You've told me this before."

"If this had been done on a computer, we might be able to trace it." Bram sighed. "But the way it is—do you think they were paying bribes?"

"What? Who?"

"Cavender Marsh and possibly Tasheba Kent. Wasn't there a rumor at the time it all happened that Cavender Marsh had killed his wife?"

"The death was ruled accidental," Kelly said.

"I know what it was ruled," Bram said impatiently. "But look at this. Lilith Brayne died on a Wednesday, and when she did she had almost a million francs in her account in Paris. That's what? About two hundred thousand dollars?"

"Something like that."

"On Friday she had only eight hundred seventy-five thousand francs. That's exactly twenty-five thousand dollars gone."

"I know that. That's the kind of thing that's bothering me."

"On the following Tuesday," Bram went on, "the account went down to seven hundred and fifty thousand francs. Another twenty-five thousand dollars gone."

"Yes," Kelly said in a singsong voice, "and on the following Thursday there was another twenty-five thousand gone, and on the Monday after that there was another twenty-five thousand dollars gone. Five hundred thousand francs, one hundred thousand dollars, disappeared in the course of two weeks. Just gone."

"I wonder how they got it."

"That doesn't worry me," Kelly said. "Cavender Marsh was her husband, after all. He would have had access."

"Maybe. But wasn't there a lot of publicity about this thing?"

"Hell, yes. It wiped the Nazis off the front pages for six days."

"Well, then. He couldn't have just taken it, could he? He couldn't have just walked into the bank and withdrawn money from a dead woman's account without someone remarking on it. Especially this much money."

"They use the Napoleonic Code in France, or they did then. In the Napoleonic Code, everything a wife has belongs to her husband."

"I don't care what some code says. It would still have been an enormous scandal. There aren't any checks?"

"No checks," Kelly said. "No paper at all."

"And since this is the world before computers we're talking about, no withdrawals from the side of the bank, either." Bram shook his head. "Not that any bank would let you withdraw that much on a cash card. Ah, what a mess. Is this going to be significantly important to the work of the weekend?"

"It depends," Kelly said. "There's a daughter. Cavender Marsh's daughter. It depends on what kind of a mood she's in."

"Cavender Marsh and Tasheba Kent had a daughter?"

"No, Cavender Marsh and Lilith Brayne had a daughter, about three months before Lilith Brayne died. She got sent to California to live with an aunt after all the fuss was over."

"You mean they dumped the kid on an aunt and went off together? Cavender Marsh and Tasheba Kent?"

"Yup," Kelly said.

"Good God."

"So you can just see what kind of a mood she's likely to be in. I've talked to that lawyer, Lydia Acken, and she says she's tried to explain what it's going to be like, to Marsh and Kent, but she just can't get through. They think it all happened much too far back. They think everybody is as mellowed with age as they are."

"Oh, this is going to be fun."

"I'd feel a lot better if I could clear up these discrepancies," Kelly said, "but I can't, and I don't think anybody anywhere could, and you know what that means."

"Lawsuits," Bram said solemnly.

"Lawsuits," Kelly agreed.

"If I were you, I think I'd develop a tendency to migraine headaches, so you can repair to your room with a killing headache whenever the going gets rough."

"If I did that, I'd probably spend the whole weekend in my room."

Bram was handing back the paper. Kelly took it and put it on the blotter on his desk. He didn't have to pack it into his briefcase because he had copies. This was a copy, too. The original was in a bank vault somewhere down on Wall Street, in the safekeeping of the Lilith Brayne Trust.

"What do you think it is about really rich people," Kelly asked, "that makes them so damn suicidal?"

— 8 —

When Geraldine Dart took this job she had with Tasheba Kent and Cavender Marsh, she thought of it as a definitive break in the history of her life. Up until the moment when Geraldine had first taken the little motorboat from the landing at Hunter's Pier, across the choppy-glass surface of the Atlantic to the island, she had been just another girl who had graduated from high school but not gone on to college. She could type ninety words a minute and take excellent shorthand, but she didn't have the money to go to one of the big secretarial schools—and even if she had had it, she didn't think it would have helped her much. Geraldine Dart had been the object of jokes since she was a tiny child. Tall, thin, awkward, worse than plain, and born to a pair of clam diggers on top of it—everybody had always assumed that she was stupid as well as both ugly and poor, but it wasn't true. Geraldine actually had a very fine mind, and—what was more important, and more rare—a very clear-sighted, unsentimental way of looking at things. She knew that the women who ended up being private secretaries or personal assistants to the heads of giant corporations, the women who made the truly spectacular salaries in secretarial work, had all at least started out pretty. They were hired for being pretty. Women like Geraldine got jobs in typing pools and word-processing departments and back offices, where they could safely be ignored. Geraldine had decided that it was smarter to save her money and look around for interesting work. Once she had a job she liked, she could settle down a little and decide what she wanted to do next.

Actually, what Geraldine wanted to do next was to buy a house, a three-family place right in the middle of Hunter's Pier, and rent it out. She had been saving her money for four years now, working on the island and getting to live in, and she almost had enough. She went across to the mainland every Thursday afternoon to deposit her salary check in her savings account. Tasheba Kent and Cavender Marsh made fun of her, she knew that. They thought she was a stuck-up little Baptist prude, because she went to church every Sunday and wore her skirts full and long and her blouses high on the neck. Geraldine didn't care. She bought the cheapest clothes she could find. They were large and long not because she was afraid of sex, but because she knew how angular and ugly her body was. She went to church on Sunday not because she was pious and committed to God and religion, but because she needed as much legitimate time away from the island as she could get. The island was a suffocating place, and its inhabitants were odder than Geraldine could have been if she'd taken an overdose of strangeness pills for a year.

Today was only Wednesday, but Geraldine was going over to the mainland anyway. The excuse she had given Cavender Marsh was that there were some last-minute things she needed to pick up, what with all the guests coming for the weekend. This was not true. Geraldine never left anything to the last minute. She was the most ferociously organized person on earth. Because Cavender Marsh left everything until it was too late and couldn't organize his way from the living room to the bathroom, the old man had taken her at her word and told her to have a pleasant day. He hadn't even protested when she'd said she was going to drive the boat over herself, instead of waiting for Tommy the handyman to do it for her.

Geraldine preferred taking the boat over herself because it gave her a chance to think, and because she didn't much like Tommy the handyman. Tommy's people had lived just down the beach from Geraldine's when Geraldine was growing up. It was Tommy's opinion that Geraldine had gotten Above Herself. Geraldine liked the ocean even when it was choppy, and the wind even when it was cold. She liked the little boat because she could handle it easily and because it didn't go too fast. In spite of the fact that Geraldine had lived on the edge of the Atlantic Ocean all her life, she couldn't swim.

She pulled the boat into the tiny dock set off for it at Hunter's Pier and threw the rope around the wet and rotting dock post. Then she anchored her purse firmly onto her right shoulder and climbed up onto the pier. The pier was wet and slippery. The air was wet and much colder than it should have been for this time of year. As always when she brought the boat in by herself, she wished she had the courage to buy herself a pair of jeans. Then she reminded herself of how ridiculous she would look in them, and put the whole thing out of her mind.

Geraldine had reached the end of the pier and the start of the boardwalk when she heard her name called—or a version of her name, which on the pier came to the same thing. She stopped and looked right and left for Jason Rand.

"Gerry," he was calling. "Gerry. Wait up a minute."

Jason Rand was the only person who had ever called Geraldine anything but "Geraldine" in her life, or "Miss Dart," which was worse. He was a tall, bulky man in his late thirties or early forties, with thick black hair that was going to gray and skin that had seen too much wind. He was also the man who owned this pier and rented out the spaces on it. If Hunter's Pier had been a fancier kind of place, Jason might have called what he owned a marina.

Jason was climbing out of the small shack he used as an office, tripping over nets waiting on the boardwalk to be repaired and anchors left to turn to rust by boatmen who didn't take care of them. Jason was always complaining about how many of the men who rented his pier spaces didn't care about the boats they used to make their livings. He said too damn many of them only cared about the booze they drank and the pot they smoked. Geraldine had lived around clammers and boatmen long enough to know that he was right.

Geraldine waited where she was and let him catch up to her. He was wearing a thick down vest over a worn plaid flannel shirt with rolled-up sleeves. His jeans had chalk marks all around the knees.

"I'm glad I caught you," he said. "I wasn't expecting you. It's only Wednesday."

"Big weekend up at the house," Geraldine told him. She didn't elaborate, because he had heard it all already. "You look like you've been knee-deep in muck all morning."

"I've been doing some caulking in the bathroom in the office. You in a hurry? You want to come over and have some coffee?"

Geraldine agreed.

They went down the boardwalk together, Geraldine stepping carefully in her wedge-heeled rubber-soled shoes, Jason swinging along heedlessly, used to the terrain. When they got to the shack, he opened the door for her. Geraldine stepped down into the large main room and took a seat on one of the benches. The room was dirty, as rooms of this kind usually were, but not as dirty as it could have been. Jason was a neat man, and his coffee pot was shined and spotless and his white porcelain coffee mugs were spotless, too. Geraldine didn't know any other man who was orderly like that. She found it attractive.

Jason poured her a mug of coffee and handed it over. Then he handed over the milk and the sugar and a spoon.

"Don't tell me," he said. "Neither of the two old folks can get their act together, and they've got you running around at the last minute like a chicken with its head cut off."

"Not exactly," Geraldine said slowly. She stirred milk and sugar into her coffee and frowned. "You want to know the truth, I've been lying to people all day. I've been saying I had to come into town and do some errands, but I didn't really. That's not it."

"What is it?"

Geraldine had put her purse down beside her on the bench. She picked it up and rummaged around in it until she found a piece of photocopy paper, folded in quarters. She handed it over to Jason Rand.

"Look at that," she said. "That's the guest list for this weekend. Look at the names."

"Is there supposed to be someone on here I recognize?"

"Look at the name on the bottom."

"Bennis Hannaford," Jason read. "Isn't that that guy that writes the books about the knights and the unicorns that they've always got all over the front of the B. Dalton's down in Portland?"

"It's a woman, actually," Geraldine told him. "But that's the same one. Look at the name next to hers. In the parentheses."

"Gregor Demarkian." Jason blinked. "That's familiar, isn't it? I wonder why."

"*Why* is because of all that fuss that happened in Bethlehem, Vermont, a while ago. Don't you remember that? Somebody was running around knocking people off with shotguns and this Gregor Demarkian came in and found out who. That's what he does. He specializes in murder investigations."

"You mean he's some kind of a policeman?"

"I think he's more like a private detective. People call him in when they have a problem they can't solve. Which is what worries me."

"What is?"

"What is he doing here? This Bennis Hannaford is some kind of family connection of Cavender Marsh's. He's her mother's cousin or something, I don't remember. But Demarkian isn't anything to anybody. He isn't even married to Bennis Hannaford. So why is he coming along?"

"Did Kent and Marsh invite him along?" Jason asked.

Geraldine shook her head. "Bennis Hannaford insisted on bringing him. From what I hear, she didn't even give an explanation. She just said that if they wanted her here, they'd have to have him, and that was that."

"Well, Geraldine, an awful lot of people don't get on so well with their relations. Maybe this Bennis Hannaford didn't want to spend a weekend with her mother's cousin without having a little protection along."

"That's what Cavender Marsh thinks. And I would think it too, except that it's Gregor Demarkian we're talking about. I mean, everybody says that Cavender Marsh murdered his wife so that he could marry Tasheba Kent. Some people even say Miss Kent helped him do it."

"Cavender Marsh never did marry Tasheba Kent," Jason pointed out.

"That's true," Geraldine said. "But they did go away together after it all happened. And they've been living together out on the island ever since. They might as well have been married."

"It was all a long time ago. What good would a private detective do anybody now? It didn't even happen in this country."

"I know. But I've been thinking about this, Jason, and I've got an idea that might make sense. It's about Hannah Graham."

"Cavender Marsh's daughter? What about her?"

"Well," Geraldine said, "after her mother died, she got dumped on some aunt or something out in California, while Miss Kent and Mr. Marsh came out here to the island. I don't think she's seen her father since, except in his old movies. I know he doesn't write to her now. Anyway, she's coming for the weekend."

"And?"

"And the lawyer, Lydia Acken, is very upset about the whole thing, because she's convinced that Hannah Graham is out for blood. I heard her talking to Mr. Marsh about it, over the phone. Not that she was getting anywhere with Mr. Marsh. He's one of those people who doesn't hear anything he doesn't want to hear. But you see what could be happening."

Jason shook his head.

"Miss Graham could have hired Mr. Demarkian herself, and this thing with Bennis Hannaford might be a cover they worked up among the three of them. I know you couldn't get Mr. Marsh arrested for murder at this late date. And you couldn't get him arrested in Maine. But there's a lot of money involved here, the auction and all their things going up for sale. If Mr. Demarkian could prove finally that Mr. Marsh had killed his wife, then Miss Graham might be able to work a kind of blackmail. If you see what I mean."

"I thought you told me that these were all rich people."

"Oh, that doesn't matter, Jason. They don't think the way we do. As far as they're concerned, there's no such thing as enough money."

Geraldine had finished her coffee. If she stayed to drink another mug, she wouldn't have time to go to the newspaper and look through their files for what they had on Gregor Demarkian. She wouldn't be able to go to the library either, to see what was in the magazines. She pushed the mug away from her and stood up.

"Well," she said. "I've got to be going. If I stay away too long, I'll never get finished back at the house."

"They work you too hard," Jason said. "You ought to quit that job and find yourself a better one."

"There isn't a better one. They pay me two fifty a week and my room and board, and come Christmas I'm going to have the money for the house."

"Buy that one on Division Street if it's still for sale.

My brother worked the construction on it. He says it's solid as a rock."

"I'll worry about what's for sale when the time comes."

There was nothing else to say. It really was time for her to be going. She looked at her coffee mug again and moved to the door.

"Well," she said again. "I hope you have good luck caulking your bathroom."

"Stop in again before you go on back," Jason told her. "Tell me if you have anything to report."

Geraldine stepped out onto the boardwalk. The air was still cold and wet. The wooden floor under her feet was still slippery. The ocean still looked like choppy black glass. Yet, for some reason, the scene was brighter and gayer than it had been before Geraldine went in for her mug of coffee.

—— 9 ——

Out on the island, Cavender Marsh was shambling along the deck at the back of the house, carrying a prelunch glass of wine in his right hand and looking into the sea. He had stopped for a moment with his back to the French windows that led into the library when he saw it—his face, caught in a suddenly still square of dark water, reflected in an accidental mirror. A moment later, it was gone. The wind came up and the water grew choppy and white-tipped again. More clouds rolled over the sun and turned the day to night.

Old, Cavender Marsh thought. I'm old, old, old. I'm twenty years younger than she is, but I'm still old.

He thought about himself, then, in France and before, about the movies he had made and the feeling he had gotten from seeing his pictures on the posters that hung in front of movie theaters. He had been famous in that decade. She had been nothing, passed over, out of date, and unfamiliar. Gone.

His wineglass was half full and he drank it off. He thought about those two last weeks in France and his face in all the papers, the reporters who had come looking for them only because he was who he had been. He wondered if the Duke of Windsor had ended up feeling like this.

Beneath him, the ocean swirled and roared and slapped against the black rocks that made up the island, slapped and slapped, as if it could drill holes in the granite and pour itself through to the other side.

Cavender Marsh crushed his wineglass into shards and threw the pieces into the sea.

PART 1

A Passion
Like Obsidian

CHAPTER 1

— 1 —

Gregor Demarkian was not used to thinking of Bennis Hannaford as a competent person. He wasn't even used to thinking of Bennis as an adult—and that was in spite of the fact that, if his calculations were correct, she should be turning forty sometime soon. Back on Cavanaugh Street in Philadelphia, where they both lived, Bennis was often treated like a cross between a force of nature and a certified lunatic. "Bennis the Menace," Father Tibor Kasparian called her, and everybody understood what he meant. Bennis came from a rich family out on the Main Line and had made a pile writing sword and sorcery fantasy novels: obviously, she had too much money. Bennis dated rock musicians with rings through their noses and respectable-looking politicians on the rise who turned out later to have connections with Saddam Hussein: obviously, Bennis had too little sense. "Too much," Bennis's best friend on the street, Donna Moradanyan, once said, "is practically Bennis's real name."

It was now seven o'clock in the morning on the Thursday they were supposed to go up to Maine, and Gregor was sitting in the dining room of the Boston Hilton, watching Bennis cross the carpet to join him for breakfast. Forty or not, Bennis looked good. There were streaks of

gray in her great cloud of black hair—Bennis treated Lida
Arkmanian's suggestions that she "do something about
herself," like use lipstick or color her hair, the way a
Hasidic rabbi would treat the suggestion that he ease his
hunger with pork—and her hands looked longer and wir-
ier and more muscular than they had when Gregor had
first met her. Gregor was more impressed with the fact
that she didn't have a line on her face and that she had
managed to stay so thin.

"I haven't had any children, Gregor," Bennis would
point out to him, whenever he brought this up. "What do
you think it is that puts serious weight on most women?"

Gregor had known plenty of women who had put on
serious weight for no good reason he could tell. That came
of having lived significant portions of his life in Armenian
ethnic neighborhoods. He had known other women—
while he was with the FBI in Washington—who were thin
to the point of emaciation but who did nothing else with
their time. If you asked these women how they were, they
obsessed for fifteen minutes on the exact number of calo-
ries there had been in the celery-and-lemon sandwich
they'd had at noon. Bennis didn't do that, either. She was
just this slight figure, five foot four and fine boned without
being fragile, walking along in the costume he thought of
as her uniform: Eddie Bauer blue jeans; L.L. Bean turtleneck; J. Crew long red cotton sweater. If the major catalog
companies ever went out of business, Bennis would have
to go naked.

Halfway across the dining room, Bennis stopped to
talk to a waiter. She smiled. She nodded. Her face lit up as
if the conversation she was having was the most charming
exchange she had ever engaged in in her life. The waiter,
who had started out cool, thawed. Bennis talked to him a
few more moments, nodded vigorously one more time,
and then moved on.

"The fuss you have to go through to get waiters to go
off their menus," she said as she sat down across from
Gregor, "is enough to make me want to take to alcohol at
dawn. Good morning, Gregor. How are you?"

"I'm fine. How are *you*?"

"I'm in a perfectly lousy mood. How did you expect me to be?"

"I wasn't venturing to guess."

Bennis got out her cigarettes and lit one up. "I used to live in Boston," she said, almost dreamily. "I used to own an apartment here and go out with a member of the Boston city government. I did that for years. I don't know how I stood it."

"Now, now."

"I hate Boston, Gregor. I *hate* it."

Gregor shook his head. "If you ask me, it wasn't Boston you had the trouble with. It was Cambridge."

Bennis made a face, and the waiter arrived with a pitcher of orange juice.

—— 2 ——

Actually, Gregor knew exactly what was bothering Bennis, and he knew it had nothing whatever to do with Boston. The trouble had started back on Cavanaugh Street, when Bennis had decided that going up to Maine to accommodate her family was not a good enough reason to put extensive mileage on her tangerine orange two-seater Mercedes convertible. That was when she had decided to accept the invitation of a woman named Darcy Bentley to do a reading of her work and a signing at the Cambridge Full Fantasy Bookstore.

"It was the combination that should have tipped me off," Bennis said later, after it was all over, while she was lying across the bed in her hotel room smoking her first cigarette in three months. "It was that adjective *full*. A *full* fantasy bookstore in a regular small town would have been all right. A regular fantasy bookstore in a college town would have been all right. A *full* fantasy bookstore in a college town is asking for trouble."

What seemed to be trouble, from the beginning, was Darcy Bentley, who reacted to her first sight of Bennis Hannaford as if she had just been granted a face-to-face audience with God. Gregor had seen it happen before, in airports and restaurants, when the real fanatics among

Bennis's six million or so regular readers bumped into their idol on the way to the ladies' room. Darcy Bentley was something beyond a fanatic, however. She was a slight young woman with frowsy brown hair and a frowsy white face, made only marginally interesting by a pair of very large, very dark eyes. As soon as she saw Bennis she held out her hand and gushed, "Oh. You came in disguise. I was so hoping you'd read to us in your Zedalian ceremonial robes."

"The problem with people like Darcy Bentley," Bennis told Gregor later, adding a tall glass of Drambuie on the rocks to her cigarette in an effort to calm herself down, "is that they don't have to take anything else seriously, so they take this seriously instead. Except they take it seriously in the wrong way. I mean, there is no Zedalia. I made it up."

"How do you know Darcy Bentley doesn't have anything else serious to worry about?" Gregor asked her.

Bennis shrugged. "That little flower-print hippie dress of hers came from Jennifer House. I'll bet it cost three hundred dollars."

In the store, Gregor didn't notice Darcy Bentley's clothes, only her face, which seemed to have taken on an odd glow. Bennis Hannaford had arrived, and Darcy Bentley was like a moon, taking its warmth from the sun.

"Oh, we're so excited to have you here," Darcy Bentley kept saying, over and over again. "You have no idea. We've been hoping for something like this for years."

Somewhere in the middle of these effusions, the door to the store swung open and another woman came in. She was shorter and fatter and older than Darcy, but her height and weight and age were beside the point. What struck Gregor was her outfit, which had gone beyond the bizarre and entered the realm of the flagrantly eccentric. On her head the fat woman wore a tall conical cap of embroidered jade green satin. From its point, two dark green satin ribbons fluttered down, as if she were a maypole. Her dress was embroidered jade green satin, too. If you could call it a dress. It fell to her feet and hung like a judge's robes or a graduation gown. It was her footwear that impressed Gregor the most, though. Each of her embroidered jade green slippers had a cluster of jingle bells on the toe. The jingle bells jingled when she walked.

"Oh, Natalia," Darcy crowed, as soon as she saw this woman come in. "I'm glad you're the first one here. This is *Bennis Hannaford*."

"How do you do." Instead of holding her hand out to be shaken, Natalia dropped to one knee and kissed the hem of Bennis's tweed skirt. Bennis nearly jumped out of her skin. Natalia struggled to her feet. "I see you've come in disguise," she said. "That may have been a very wise thing. I seemed to attract some of the most peculiar reactions on the bus coming over here today."

"This is Gregor Demarkian," Bennis said, in a weak voice.

Natalia was perfectly happy to shake Gregor's hand.

After that there was a lengthy silence, during which Darcy and Natalia gazed adoringly at Bennis, and Bennis cast around desperately for something to say. Gregor was just beginning to get desperate himself, when the door opened and three more women came in. Like Natalia, they were in costume, two in peaked hats and robes and one in embroidered satin trousers and an embroidered satin tunic. In Zedalia, Gregor surmised, the women of the nobility must go around exclusively in embroidered satin. Gregor had read one or two of Bennis's books, but he could never remember what was in them. With the knights and the ladies and the unicorns and the magic, they never made any sense to him. Like Natalia, the three new women dropped to the floor and kissed the hem of Bennis's skirt. Bennis leaned over until her lips were touching Gregor's ear and hissed, "I need a *very* large glass of Scotch and a cigarette."

Gregor needed the Scotch himself. He had never smoked. The three women stood up and smiled shyly at Bennis. Darcy Bentley introduced them as Katania, Melinda, and Allamanda. Obviously their names, like their costumes, had been taken from one novel or the other of Zedalian life. From what Gregor remembered, there was a companion world to Zedalia in Bennis's novels, called Zed. Zed was populated entirely by men. He wondered if there were little groups of men somewhere who dressed up in the costumes of Zed and practiced on each other the secret handshakes and underground codes of Zed's nobility. It was depressing to think about it, but there probably were.

"Oh, Miss Hannaford," Katania said. "I'm so glad to meet you. There are so many questions I want to ask you."

"We *all* want to ask you," Melinda said.

"I want you to answer one question right away," Allamanda said. "I just can't wait for the answer."

"Sure," Bennis said recklessly. "Ask away."

"Well," Allamanda said, quite seriously. "Do you write your books yourself, or are they channeled?"

It went downhill from there, way downhill, and rapidly, like a boulder falling off the side of Mount Everest. More women came in, and as they did Gregor began to realize that no one was going to show up at this reading who was not in costume. What was more, both the costumes and the behavior grew increasingly odd. At some point, the crowd reached critical mass, and they began to talk funny. Gregor caught perfectly sensible syllables, but they didn't seem to translate into words.

"*Zia dum gorno rok,*" Darcy Bentley seemed to be saying to Natalia.

"*Gorno tok dem barnia beldap,*" Natalia answered.

"What's going on here?" Gregor asked Bennis. "Do you know what they're talking about?"

"No," Bennis said.

"Do you know what's going on here?"

Bennis sighed. "They're speaking Zedalian," she explained. "There's a chapter in *Zedalia in Winter* that supposedly outlines how to translate Zedalian into English and vice versa."

"Supposedly?"

"Well, you couldn't prove it by me, Gregor. I've never tried to make it work."

Bennis didn't try to make it work now, either. When people spoke to her in Zedalian, she ignored them, and when Darcy asked her if she could read in Zedalian—"We thought it might be a relief for you to hear your work in its original language; and we all understand it here."—Bennis adamantly refused. For a moment, Gregor thought she was going to refuse to do the reading at all, but she was much too much of a professional for that. She got out the manuscript she had been working on back in Philadelphia—at readings, Bennis had explained to Gregor on the drive to Boston, the audience always prefers works in progress—and recited three pages of it with suitable vocal flourish. When people cried out "Great Goddess, hosanna," in the middle of everything, for no reason at all, she acted as if she hadn't heard them. When the reading was over and Natalia leapt to her feet to do a bell dance around a paperback copy of *Zedalia in Love and War* she had thrown to the floor, Bennis simply got up, went over to the desk, and took her pen out in preparation for signing books. Nobody seemed to notice that she was not participating in the festivities. Nobody seemed to notice much of anything. A lot of people had joined Natalia in her bell dance.

"What it is, I think," Bennis told Gregor back at the hotel, while she dragged on a Benson & Hedges menthol as if it were an oxygen mask, "is that people need to identify with something, and they don't want to identify with their families anymore. Families are supposed to be a drag. So instead, they identify with a fictional landscape, like Zedalia."

"If you drink any more of that stuff," Gregor told her, "you're going to be in no shape to drive us to Maine tomorrow morning."

"What worries me, Gregor, is that I might be contributing to the spread of schizophrenia. I might be causing schizophrenia that wouldn't otherwise exist in the world."

Back at the bookstore, all Bennis had been interested in was getting finished and getting out, but it hadn't been easy. The customers had hundreds of books for her to sign, and even after she'd signed them, they hadn't wanted to let her go. No sooner had Bennis pushed away the last copy of any of her books existing anywhere in the Cambridge Full Fantasy Bookstore, than Darcy Bentley and Natalia came running up, carrying something large between them that was covered by a sheet.

"Look," Darcy Bentley squealed, pulling the sheet off

with her left hand. "Look what we got for you. And it was just a miracle that we were able to find it."

What they had found was a gigantic porcelain replica of a Stone Age fertility goddess, four feet high and almost as wide, with great drooping heavy breasts and a belly the size and shape of an NBA regulation basketball. Underneath the belly there were feet, but there didn't seem to be legs. On the head there were long wild tresses of hair that stood up at the ends. Around the neck curled a long snake with flashing green eyes.

The statue had flashing green eyes, too. That's because the eyes on the snake and on the statue's head were tiny green light bulbs, and the whole thing was kept working by four CC batteries and a little nest of plastic-coated wires.

"Isn't it wonderful?" Darcy demanded. "We took one look at it and *knew* that *nothing* else on earth would ever come so close to expressing the spirit of your books."

—— 2 ——

Sitting in the Hilton dining room in front of her pitcher of orange juice and an enormous fruit salad, Bennis looked more depressed than Gregor had ever remembered seeing her. She was only picking at her fresh pineapple, which was her favorite thing on earth after dark chocolate. She hadn't touched her coffee. She had drunk most of the pitcher of orange juice, but Gregor thought that that was mostly because she was hung over. She had to be hung over. After coming back from the bookstore last night, she had put away half of a large bottle of Drambuie, and no dinner.

"Come on." Gregor nudged her foot gently under the table. "Cheer up a little. We've got a long drive."

"I know we do," Bennis said. "But do you know what I was just thinking?"

"No."

"I was just thinking that they aren't alone. Those people at the bookstore last night. They're more colorful about it than most people, but most people are crazy."

"Are they?"

Bennis nodded gloomily. "Take the people we're going up to Maine today to see. Cavender Marsh. Do you remember Cavender Marsh?"

"Movie star from the '30s," Gregor said. "Had an affair with his wife's sister. Wife died, possibly a suicide. He ran off with the sister. We've been through all this before."

"I know we have. I know we have. But bear with me. In the first place, his name isn't really Cavender Marsh. It's John Day. He was—what? My mother's first cousin once removed?"

"He was your mother's second cousin. Your mother's first cousins once removed were the children of her cousins. Your mother's second cousins are the children of your mother's parents' cousins. And there isn't anything crazy about a man changing his name when he becomes an actor. People do it all the time."

"I think you'd have to be from the Main Line to understand how a connection like my mother's second cousin could get me into a mess like this," Bennis said. "I'm from the Main Line and I barely understand it."

"I was just trying to point out that, your pessimism notwithstanding, there doesn't seem to be anything on the lunatic fringe here yet."

Bennis speared a piece of pineapple and bit off the end of it. "I think there's enough on the lunatic fringe in this thing to satisfy a psychiatrist for a decade. Her name isn't really Tasheba Kent, by the way. It's Thelma."

"Kent?"

"That's right. And her sister called herself Lilith Brayne, but her name was really Lillian Kent. Can you imagine anyone wanting to name themselves Lilith, especially in the United States in the '20s, with all that Bible-thumping and anti-Darwin stuff going on?"

"Sure. It was probably worth its weight in publicity."

"Well, if it was, it was the wrong kind of publicity," Bennis said. "Tasheba was the sexy bad-girl one. Lilith was the ever-pure virgin who got tied to the railroad tracks by the villain. They used to have Tasheba Kent–Lilith Brayne film festivals when I was in college."

"I don't think I've ever seen either of them in the movies. I don't even remember the case, although I was alive at the time. I think I was five."

"The case was absolutely huge," Bennis said, "and it was crazy even if nothing else was. I mean, Lilith Brayne was ground up by a hacksaw or something—"

"She fell into an irrigation sluice and was battered by the steel wire grate," Gregor corrected mildly. "Why do you do things like this? You always make the gore more gory than it was."

"It was pretty gory, Gregor. There was an article about it a couple of years ago in *Life*, one of those retrospective things. It said that not much was left of her but her face."

"They were probably exaggerating," Gregor said.

"And then the two of them that were left ran off to that island, and they've never come out and rejoined the world. Don't you think that's lunatic enough? Tasheba Kent was all washed up, but Cavender Marsh still had a pretty important career going. And he just walked right away from it."

"I doubt if there would have been much of it remaining when the scandal died down," Gregor said. "There's only so much you can get away with, even if you're a Hollywood actor. Wasn't there a child involved?"

"They ditched her on a relative. She was three months old, and Cavender Marsh never saw her again. She's supposed to be out at the island this weekend."

Gregor frowned. "That's not a very good idea. This will be the first time she's seen her father since all that happened in 1938?"

"That's right."

"Maybe they've been corresponding," Gregor said, "or talking on the phone."

Bennis shook her head. "There's been nothing like that at all. I asked my brother Christopher about it. He always knows everything about everybody we're connected to. He says Cavender Marsh has never said so much as a single word to his daughter in all this time, never even sent her a birthday card or a Christmas present, and it wasn't his idea for her to come to the birthday party, either. His lawyer insisted. It has something to do with selling their things at auction, just like having me there does. The lawyer insists on having a representative of the heirs on each side of the family there to oversee what goes into the sale. Although why any of us on our side are supposed to care is beyond me. You know how the Main Line feels about Hollywood. After Cavender Marsh became an actor, my grandmother wouldn't have him in the house."

"I wish your brother Christopher could have taken your place on this weekend. Then I wouldn't have had to come up myself. Eat your fruit salad, Bennis. I want us to get started in plenty of time. I don't want us to be late for that boat."

"We won't be late."

"I would like to arrive on time without having had you drive me at your usual pace. And drink coffee. I want to make sure you're awake."

Bennis got out another cigarette and lit up instead. "Really, Gregor," she said. "You're such an old fuddy-duddy about cars."

— 4 —

Gregor didn't know if he was an old fuddy-duddy about cars. He did know that in a sane world, compassionate laws would have prevented a woman like Bennis Hannaford from buying a car that was described as "a true 140." "A true 140," Bennis had explained to him, was a car that ran best at 140 miles an hour. Driving it more slowly was possible, but not very good for the engine. Gregor didn't think Bennis had ever driven him at 140 miles an hour. If she had, he must have passed out cold and forgotten all about it. But she did drive him fast enough to turn his stomach into a mass of knots and make his head feel stuffed full of cotton wool.

"There's no point in driving as fast as you do," Gregor told Bennis, over and over again. "You barely save five minutes of time on any one trip, and you're spending a fortune on speeding tickets."

"Five minutes is a lot of time," Bennis replied solemnly. "Five minutes here and five minutes there. It can really add up."

"What it's going to add up to is your losing your license. And I'm not going to blame the state of Pennsylvania one bit."

Gregor wouldn't have blamed the state of Massachusetts if it had impounded Bennis's car and forced her to go on foot. He had heard his share of jokes about Boston drivers, but he didn't think even Boston had ever been able to handle Bennis Hannaford.

"That was a speed bump we just bounced over," Gregor pointed out, as they came tearing out of the parking garage. "It was supposed to slow you up."

"It didn't."

Bennis went down a one-way street, turned right onto another one-way street, turned right again. It was getting close enough to rush hour so that the streets were filling up. There were a lot of eighteen-wheeler trucks on the road. There were a lot of people on bicycles weaving in and out among the cars. Bennis was driving as if she were on a pristinely clear test track at the Bonneville Salt Flats, and they hadn't really gotten started yet.

"Maybe we should take U.S. One," Gregor suggested. "You know, the scenic route."

"Too slow," Bennis answered. "I want to get on I Ninety-five."

Gregor gave up. He checked his seat belts twice, making sure that both the lap belt and the shoulder strap were tight. Then he closed his eyes. He got along so much better with Bennis driving if he couldn't actually see what it was she was doing.

What was it again that Bennis had said, about Tasheba Kent and Cavender Marsh and all those other people who were supposed to be in Maine for the weekend, that had upset him so much? Oh, yes. Cavender Marsh's daughter. Some lawyer had insisted that Cavender Marsh's daughter be on hand for the birthday party, even though she hadn't seen or heard from her father since she was three months old.

Gregor Demarkian had spent twenty years in the Fed-

eral Bureau of Investigation. He had spent the last ten of
those years either organizing or heading the Department
of Behavioral Sciences, which was the division of the Bureau that coordinated nationwide manhunts for serial killers. He had stood at the edge of a shallow grave and
watched a team of forensic pathologists bring fourteen
bodies up into the light. He had sat in a darkened room
and listened to a boy of seventeen tell him—in a voice that
was eerily reminiscent of an old-fashioned grade-school
teacher's lecturing a class on the proper way to parse a
sentence—that before he slit the throats on the prostitutes
he abducted, he cut off the smallest toe on each of their
right feet for a souvenir. Gregor Demarkian knew crazy
when he saw it, and he didn't throw the word around
carelessly.

In this case, however, he thought he was justified.

Whoever had decided to ask Cavender Marsh's
daughter along on this weekend was crazy—and Cavender
Marsh was just as crazy to have gone along with it.

(HAPTER 2

— 1 —

She was standing on the boardwalk leading to the piers when Bennis and Gregor drove up, a trim, compact woman with pure white hair and small hands and a deep purple suit that somehow wasn't flashy. Gregor Demarkian noticed her right off. In fact, she gave him something of a shock. There he was, bouncing along in his self-inflicted stupor, ignoring Bennis's driving completely—and then he was sitting straight up in his seat, rigid and cold and eager all at the same time. It took him a minute to understand what was wrong. Bennis was guiding the tangerine orange Mercedes into the big open lot with the sign on it that read, "PARKING SHORT AND LONG TERM." The wind was turning the sea into black glass and whitecaps and crawling down his neck. The trim, compact woman with white hair was pacing back and forth on the boardwalk, moving very carefully in her mid-level stacked heels. Bennis backed the car into the space closest to the parking lot attendant's shack, and Gregor finally got it: the trim, compact woman reminded him of Elizabeth.

Elizabeth was the reason Gregor had left the FBI and gone back to the small Armenian-American neighborhood where he had grown up, on Cavanaugh Street in Philadel-

phia. Elizabeth was Gregor's wife of many years, and just
before he had retired she had died of cancer after a last,
long, agonizing year that Gregor still saw over and over
again in his dreams. He had been so exhausted by her
dying, he had decided he never wanted to deal with death
again. He certainly never wanted to deal with death deliv-
ered by lunatics and psychopaths again. He hadn't realized
how wearing living with all that was. Elizabeth had always
protected him from it. Elizabeth had made it possible for
him to be an emotional blank at the Bureau, because she
had always been waiting at home to warm him up when
he was through. Once she was gone he had two choices.
He could either go on working and become an emotional
blank for good, the law enforcement equivalent of the psychopaths he chased. Or he could quit.

The woman did not really look like Elizabeth. Her
body type was very similar, but her face was too tame.
Elizabeth had been an Armenian-American woman with
high cheekbones and large black eyes. This woman was
some derivation of Northern European and rather middle-
of-the-road in terms of looks. Hazel eyes. A short, straight
nose. Small, pretty teeth. It was her attitude that reminded
Gregor of Elizabeth, and the way she carried herself. This,
Gregor thought, was a woman of enormous self-respect
and enormous competence. This woman believed that
manners were important and that true femininity resided
in common sense.

Bennis got the car parked to her satisfaction, pulled
her keys out of the ignition, and sighed.

"I hate leaving it out here in the open like this. I mean,
there must be joyriders even in a place like Hunter's Pier,
Maine."

Gregor looked around. "There doesn't look like
there's much of anybody in Hunter's Pier, Maine."

"Don't be snide, Gregor. People around here probably
just have the sense not to build their houses too close to
the ocean. Can you imagine what it's like in the middle of
a storm?"

"I don't want to imagine it."

Bennis got out of the car. "I'm going to talk to the
attendant and see if I can't make some kind of reasonable

arrangement for the protection of this car. Why don't you go over to the boardwalk and talk to the lady. She has to be one of us."

Gregor thought she was too, but he was curious. "Why would you say that?"

Bennis looked disgusted. "Well, Gregor, I wouldn't expect it's customary for your ordinary inhabitant of Hunter's Pier, Maine, to go running around town in a *real* Chanel suit. Will you get out of the car now and go make sense?"

Gregor got out of the car. He was wearing a suit, as always, although today, in deference to the weather and the venue, he had a sober navy blue sweater on under his jacket instead of a vest. He walked across the asphalt of the parking lot and stepped over the low concrete curb to the boardwalk. The trim, compact woman was watching him.

"Excuse me," she said, in a pleasant, no-nonsense voice, as he began to walk toward her. "Are you Mr. Fenster or Mr. Pratt?"

"Neither," Gregor said, catching up to her. "I'm Gregor Demarkian. I'm here with Bennis Hannaford."

The trim, compact woman looked over Gregor's shoulder, not at Bennis herself, but at Bennis's car. "Oh, yes," she said. "Miss Hannaford. Mr. Marsh's relation."

"Vaguely."

"I'm Lydia Acken," the trim, compact woman said, holding out her hand for him to take. "I'm very glad to meet you. I was—intrigued—when I saw your name on the final guest list."

"There's nothing to be intrigued about," Gregor said firmly. "Miss Hannaford is a friend of mine. She seemed to think this situation was one that might call for moral support."

Lydia Acken laughed. It sounded like water from a spring, clear and soft. "It probably will. I should have thought of that myself. But still, Mr. Demarkian. It *is* intriguing. A famous detective and investigator of murders, coming to a house of someone once accused of murder."

"When Cavender Marsh was accused of murder, I was five years old. Quite frankly, I don't care what he did when I was five years old. I don't care if he butchered an entire village on the Côte d'Azur. It's none of my business."

"I, too, was five years old when Cavender Marsh was accused of murder," Lydia Acken said. "We must have been born in the same year. But I grew up hearing about the case, you see. My mother was a rabid fan of Lilith Brayne's back in the '20s, and she went on and on and on about the death and the people involved in it. She was a very isolated woman. I suppose she didn't have much else to do."

Gregor saw Bennis coming out of the parking attendant's shack. She was hiking along with her shoulder bag balanced against her back and a glum look on her face. Gregor didn't think she'd gotten the answers she wanted out of the parking lot attendant. She stepped over the curb and came walking toward them on the boardwalk. The rubber soles of her shoes made her the only one of the three who looked really steady on her feet on the wet wood.

"Look up the road." Bennis pointed into the air behind Lydia Acken's left shoulder. "Look at what's coming."

Both Gregor and Lydia turned to see what Bennis was pointing at. At first, all Gregor saw was a blur of motion on the road. Then the blur came into focus and he realized what it was: a white-and-gold Cadillac stretch limousine, one of the custom-made extra-long ones, with whitewall tires and shiny wheel spokes plated in chrome.

"Oh, my," Lydia Acken murmured.

At just that moment another car pulled into the parking lot, a small white Toyota Corolla with rental stickers across the back bumper. The Toyota wedged itself into one of the spaces facing the sea and came to a stop. A tall young man, very slight and very flexible, unfolded himself from behind the wheel. The young man was very Asian-and very American-looking at the same time. He also looked very hip. His straight black hair was parted at the side and seemed to sweep around his head when he moved. His tight black jeans and black leather jacket had come right out of a SoHo specialty store. New York,

Gregor thought automatically, and tucked the information away in the back of his brain.

The tall young man gave his keys to the parking lot attendant without much discussion—oh, the joys of driving a car you don't care what happens to—and walked toward them with a rolling gait that had been copied, Gregor was willing to bet, from a 1950s Marlon Brando movie. The tall young man was looking at the white Cadillac limousine just the way the rest of them had been, but unlike them he was not in awe. He had a smirk across his face.

"Hi," he said, as he climbed over the curb. "Are you people all waiting to go out to Tasheba Kent's island? I'm Carlton Ji."

"Oh." Lydia said it repressively. "The reporter."

"Reporter?" Gregor asked.

Carlton Ji came the rest of the way to them. "Hi," he said, sticking his hand out to Gregor. "Who are you? How much do you want to bet it's going to take Her Highness Miss Hannah another five minutes to get down here, just so she can be sure that everybody in town has had a chance to see her?"

"Who's Hannah?" Bennis asked.

"Hannah Graham," Carlton Ji said with relish. "Lilith Brayne's daughter. Everybody's always saying that she's Cavender Marsh's daughter, but it takes two. I think she's much more like her mother."

"She's certainly dramatic," Lydia Acken said.

Carlton Ji suddenly realized that Gregor Demarkian was either not going to shake his hand, or had shaken his hand and then taken his own away without Carlton noticing. Whatever the explanation was, Carlton's hand was hanging in the wind with nothing whatsoever to do. Carlton stuck it into the back pocket of his jeans.

"I work for *Personality* magazine," he said to nobody in particular. "This is going to be a great weekend. I can hardly wait."

The white-and-gold limousine had turned off the main road and begun its winding way through the narrow streets that led to the pier. There were not very many of these streets and none of them was very long, but the car was inching as carefully as if it had been crossing a minefield with a map. Maybe Carlton Ji was right, Gregor thought. Maybe Hannah Graham was making an entrance. If that was her intention, she was doing a very good job. All through the tiny town, people had come out to see the limo pass. There was even a pack of boys sitting on the one flat roof in town, above the pharmacy. The car stopped at every corner, in spite of the fact that there were neither traffic lights nor traffic. Children ran out and touched it and then raced back inside the houses and stores. Hannah Graham probably thought they were impressed, but Gregor doubted it. He thought they were laughing at her, as being another damned fool southerner who didn't have sense enough not to spend her money on stupidities.

The car turned the last of the corners it had to negotiate to get to the pier. It bumped across a couple of potholes and came to a stop at the little ramp that led from the street to the boardwalk. The people who worked on the pier were now out and watching like the rest of town. The parking lot attendant was standing in the open door of his shack. A grizzled, middle-aged man had come out of the larger shack farther down on the pier and started to mend his ropes outside.

"This almost has to be an anticlimax," Bennis told Gregor. "I mean, what would you need to equal that entrance? Muhammad Ali? The Charge of the Light Brigade?"

"I think you'd need the Virgin Mary on a cloud of angel dust at the very least." Lydia Acken had a faint smile on her face.

Actually, Gregor thought that the emergence of Hannah Graham matched the grandeur of her car's arrival— not because she was such a spectacular figure, but because she was so weird. The limo came to a stop. The driver's door opened and a lanky black man emerged wearing a gold-and-white uniform, complete with cap. He walked around the limo and opened the passenger door closest to the curb. He leaned in and gave his arm to the woman inside. Then he helped her onto the ramp with all the care

a jeweler would have taken with one of the tsarina's
Fabergé eggs.

The first thing that came to Gregor's mind was that
this woman was a walking corpse. She was too thin, too
brittle, and much too frequently operated on. She had no
subcutaneous fat on her at all. Her too-tightly stretched
skin covered the bones of her face the way a sheet of Saran
Wrap would have covered a skull. The veins in her hands
looked like a system of tributary rivers suddenly sprung to
life on the dead white surface of a desert.

"My God," Bennis said under her breath. "When I get
old, I'm going to let myself get wrinkled."

The next thing Gregor noticed was the clothes. Hannah Graham was wearing navy blue silk trousers—
ordinary enough, except that there were a series of heart-
shaped holes running up the sides of each leg, exposing
more blue veins and dead white skin. Then there was the
top, a tunic arrangement entirely covered with sequins in
fifteen different colors, making a pattern across her high,
bouncing chest of a male and female symbol intertwined.
Then there were the dark glasses, which had sequins too.
Bizarre.

"Saline implants," Lydia Acken told Bennis in a
whisper. She was staring at Hannah Graham's chest.

"Nose job," Bennis whispered back.

The driver had gone around to the back of the limousine and begun to unload Hannah Graham's luggage.
There was a lot of it—at least three large suitcases and two
suit bags, a cosmetics case, a jewelry case, a portable shoe
tree with a dozen pairs of shoes in it, an overnight case,
and a pair of hatboxes. Hannah watched it being unloaded, then walked away from it. Gregor noticed that
even the hatboxes were leather and part of a matched set.
Every piece had the initials *HK* on it in flowing script, like
the signet of a monarch.

"The *HK* is for 'Hannah Kent,' " Carlton Ji whispered
to Gregor. "She won't use Marsh because she despises her
father."

Hannah Graham walked up the ramp to the boardwalk, put her sunglasses on top of her head, and squinted
at the assembled company. She's blind as a bat and those

sunglasses are prescription, Gregor thought. Hannah Graham settled her attention on Lydia Acken.

"Are you all waiting to go out to Tasheba Kent's island?" she asked. Her voice, like her body, was brittle.

Lydia Acken was the soul of politeness. She couldn't help herself. "Yes, yes," she said. "Of course we are. And you must be Hannah Graham. I'm Lydia Acken. I'm your father's lawyer. And Miss Kent's, too, of course."

Hannah Graham looked out to sea. "When is the next boat expected to arrive?" she asked.

For a moment, they were all nonplussed. It was such a silly question, and she had asked it with such calm certainty.

"I'm afraid it isn't like that, Miss Graham," Lydia said apologetically. "There isn't any regular boat service from Hunter's Pier to the island. Miss Kent and Mr. Marsh keep a boat, and they'll be sending it over to ferry us across very soon, with their handyman driving or maybe Miss Dart. I called as soon as I got here and that was half an hour ago. I'm sure it won't be long now."

Hannah walked back and forth on the boardwalk, still looking out to sea, a thoughtful expression on her face. She was wearing wedge-heeled, cork-soled sandals, but she was perfectly steady on her feet.

"Do you mean that there's no way to get out to that island unless my father and that woman send a boat for you?" she asked.

"Well, I'm sure you could hire a boat at this end," Lydia Acken told her, "but why would you want to? If you've been invited, you can get over absolutely free."

"You might want to surprise them, though," Hannah said. Her gaze was still on the water. "This is that woman's hundredth birthday, isn't it? Maybe some secret admirer somewhere wants to send her a cake."

"You can't get out there at all when the weather's bad," a voice said.

They all turned to look at the man who had come out of the larger shack on the pier to mend his ropes. He had let them fall to the boardwalk at his feet and now he tilted his chair back to rest against the shack.

"You can't get from there to here when the weather's

bad, either," he went on. "Too many rocks. Too hard to dock."

Hannah Graham walked over to him. She looked him up and down. "Do they ever come out, Tasheba Kent and Cavender Marsh? Do they ever come into town and just walk around?"

"Not anymore they don't," the man at the shack said. "They did when I was a kid, but that was forty years ago."

Hannah Graham put her glasses back on her nose. "Somebody I knew once said that island was just like Alcatraz."

"A lot of people say that," the man at the shack replied. "I don't think Alcatraz had fifteen marble bathrooms."

Now, faintly, Gregor could hear the sound of an outboard motor. It was not a very powerful outboard motor—he hoped they had something bigger out there; with a hundred-year-old woman in the house, they needed it—and its hum was almost drowned out by the sound of the sea slapping against the pilings of the piers. The man at the shack was the only one to have caught it besides Gregor. He stood up and shaded his eyes with his hand.

"There she is. That's Gerry coming in."

"Who's Gerry?" Carlton Ji asked.

"Geraldine Dart. Miss Kent's and Mr. Marsh's secretary," Lydia Acken answered.

"I didn't know secretaries knew how to drive boats," Carlton Ji said.

The boat was now close enough so that all of them could hear it, and see it too. It was a small launch with a sharply edged prow and a squared-off rear. Gregor tried to remember what the rear end of a boat was called. The boat looked to him like the right size for a small example of what people called a cabin cruiser, except that it didn't seem to have a cabin.

As they watched, the boat slowed down and began to almost drift toward one of the empty docking places. When it got close enough to the wood to actually hit it, its motor cut off almost completely. The man at the shack moved down the boardwalk and out along the dock toward the boat. A plain young woman was standing in the bow and preparing to throw a rope at a post. She threw the rope to the man from the shack instead.

"Hello, Gerry," the man from the shack said. "These here are your passengers."

"Hello, Jason."

Gerry grabbed the hand Jason was holding out to her and let herself be helped onto the pier. Then she stood straight and looked over at the assembled company. She's something worse than plain, Gregor thought, but even so he liked her face. There was vitality in it, and humor, and intelligence. She had checked them out and looked them over and decided she wasn't impressed with them at all.

"Oh, Miss Dart," Lydia Acken said, coming forward. "It's very good to see you again. I don't know if you remember me. I'm Lydia Acken."

"I remember you, Miss Acken." Miss Dart looked past the group to the enormous pile of luggage Hannah Graham's driver had unloaded from the limousine. "I'm only taking people in this trip," Miss Dart announced. "Somebody will come back for the luggage later."

Hannah Graham thrust herself forward. "I can't possibly allow you to leave my luggage here. I have valuable things in it."

"Someone will be back for the luggage later," Miss Dart repeated.

"I don't think you realize who I am," Hannah Graham said.

Geraldine Dart gave Hannah Graham such a withering look of contempt, it would have turned any normal human being to stone.

"I don't have to know who you are," she said. "All I have to know is that if I put all these people and all that luggage into this one little boat, it'll sink."

With that, Geraldine Dart turned on her heel and marched back down the pier to the boat.

"Any of you who want to go out to the island," she called back, "come on ahead. I'm leaving now."

—— 2 ——

"Hold onto the sides and hold onto them tight," Geraldine Dart ordered a few minutes later, when they were all loaded onto the boat and it was breaking away from the dock and into the open water. "The weather is getting a little bit raw."

It was true. There had been so much going on back there, with Hannah Graham and Carlton Ji and Jason at the shack, Gregor hadn't noticed it. Now he saw that the wind was high and stiff and the ocean had a hostile rhythm. Above their heads, the late afternoon sky was thick with storm clouds.

"Do you suppose he was telling the truth, that man back there?" Bennis asked. "Do you suppose there really isn't any way to get on or off the island if the weather is bad?"

"Oh, that's true enough," Geraldine Dart said from the wheel, not bothering to turn around to see who had spoken. "The weather doesn't have to be all that bad, either. You don't need a hurricane or a nor'easter. It's the rocks, you see."

"It does look very rocky," Lydia Acken said worriedly.

"I think they're making it all up," Hannah Graham said. "I think the both of them are just trying to scare us."

Everybody ignored her.

"I wouldn't think this would be the optimum situation," Gregor said slowly. "Miss Kent is very old. And Mr. Marsh, even if he isn't as old as Miss Kent, he must be nearly eighty."

"Just about," Geraldine Dart agreed.

"I always forget that there's such a great difference in their ages," Lydia Acken said. "They're both so old, I think of them as elderly and let it go at that."

The boat hit an air pocket and bounced first upward, then down hard onto the surface of the sea. Gregor felt his stomach roll dangerously.

"We tried to talk them into moving into town a couple of years ago," Geraldine Dart said. "They wouldn't hear of it. I guess they like it out there."

"I'd hate it out there," Bennis said. "Just look at that place. Does Vincent Price live in the attic?"

That place was just visible now to the front of them, a tall Victorian pile with cast-iron railings around the large square of its main roof and smaller squares of the roofs on the turrets. It was at least three stories high, not counting the attic. The house rose up off the rock like the physical embodiment of the wrath of God. Gregor had never understood why the Victorians had painted so many of their buildings brown and black in that way, but this was an extravagant example of the style. The windows were tall blank sheets of glass divided into four parts and curved at the top. Bennis was right. Vincent Price ought to be living in the attic.

"Did Tasheba Kent build this house herself?" Carlton Ji asked. "It doesn't look like her style at all."

"Tasheba Kent bought the house," Lydia Acken said. "It was built by a man named Josiah Horne back in 1837. First he made a lot of money selling rum and slaves. Then he got religion and went running around the country preaching repentance and revival. Then he got an attack of the guilts or a case of clinical depression and built this place out here. He moved in and nobody saw him for twenty years."

"They found him dead in there in 1857," Geraldine Dart said cheerfully. "Been dead for a couple of years, too, and his body rotted and eaten away to almost nothing, sitting bolt upright in his best chair in front of the fireplace in the library. The place was filthy. He'd never let a cleaning lady in to do for him. He never let anybody in. He would never have been found at all, but some people from his church wanted to hold a revival and they didn't have the money for it, so they came out here to see if he'd give them what they needed."

"That must have been before born-again religion became a profit-making enterprise," Carlton Ji said.

Hannah Graham was glaring at Geraldine Dart. "She's just trying to frighten us again," she hissed. "We shouldn't let her get away with it. The next thing you know, she'll be telling us the place is haunted."

"It *is* haunted," Geraldine Dart said calmly. "And I'm

not making it up. You can read all about it in a book called *Ghosts and Legends in Rural New England*. We've got it in the library."

"She's making it *up*," Hannah Graham snapped.

The boat was pulling closer and closer to the island. Gregor could see the dock jutting out from the rocks, and then a long steep flight of wooden stairs. *Long* and *steep* were the operative adjectives. The stairs were more like a ladder than like ordinary stairs. He wondered if that was the only way up to and down from the house. It seemed to be.

"I can't believe Miss Kent and Mr. Marsh can handle those stairs," Gregor commented. "I'm not sure I'm going to be able to manage them."

Geraldine Dart was pulling the little boat up next to its dock. She had gone forward to throw her mooring rope around the post. She secured it there, then came back to the rest of them.

"Mr. Marsh handles the stairs all right," she told Gregor, "but the next time Miss Kent gets off this island, it's going to be in a helicopter or a coffin."

(HAPTER 3

— 1 —

It was two o'clock in the afternoon, and Richard Fenster was sitting in a blue molded plastic chair in Logan Airport, fuming. All he could think of was how, if he had hitchhiked the way he had intended to, he would be in Maine by now. If he wasn't, he would at least be moving. Instead, he was sitting here in this chair, and there was no relief in sight. The first of the bomb threats had hit at eleven fifteen, less than ten minutes before his plane was due to board. The all-clear had been sounded twenty-two minutes later, but it hadn't done him any good. There had been another bomb threat, and another one after that, and another one after that. Every one of them had to be checked out. That meant closing this entire end of the airport and holding up all traffic until teams of guards could search through closets and bathrooms and utility spaces and even passengers' luggage. That meant no planes taking off while the searching was going on. That meant more and more time wasted and more and more reporters arriving to look into it all. By now, the situation was reaching legendary proportions. It was going to be one of those things, like Woodstock, that everybody wanted to have been a part of. If Richard hadn't been in such a hurry, he would have been enjoying himself.

The only other person in this small waiting room was a young woman in a very formal suit—navy blue raw silk with a short jacket; high-necked white silk blouse peeking up over the jacket's plain round neckline—who kept pacing back and forth and staring at the clock on the wall above the check-in desk. She had a handful of sunflower seeds she seemed more interested in playing with than eating. She would move them from one hand to the other over and over again, then bump her elbow on a concrete post or one of the chairs. The sunflower seeds would scatter everywhere, and she would have to go back to her handbag to get another handful to play around with. Richard had tried a couple of times to talk to her, but she hadn't been having any. Obviously, young women in raw silk suits didn't fraternize with men in ragged jeans and cotton sweaters.

There was the sound of footsteps in the hall and they both looked up. This was the very last waiting room at this end. Nobody came down here unless they wanted to take a MaineAir flight to Portland or Augusta. Richard couldn't remember where he was supposed to land to get to Hunter's Pier. He watched the hallway carefully, and a few seconds later a man came striding down it, a beefy overblown man with too much color in his face who looked a little like John Forsyth. He was followed by a MaineAir reservations clerk who had to run to keep up with him.

"The problem is, Mr. Pratt, this end of the airport has been closed all day," the clerk was saying, out of breath from running. "We haven't been able to take off since six fifteen this morning."

"I'm not supposed to take off until quarter to three," Mr. Pratt told her, still striding along. He was carrying one large suitcase. He came into the waiting area and set it down. He nodded first to the young woman and then to Richard. Then he sat down.

The reservations clerk looked around, too. "These are the passengers from the eleven twenty-four flight," she said. "They haven't left yet."

The young woman in the raw silk suit came closer.

"Are we going to leave soon? It's getting to be ridiculously late."

The reservations clerk looked distressed. "Oh, we know, Miss Frazier, we know. It's absolutely terrible. But there's nothing we can do about it. Airport security simply won't let us leave."

"They're going to have to let us leave sometime," Miss Frazier said.

"They must realize by now that these bomb threats are hoaxes," Richard said. "There have been at least four of them. There hasn't been a bomb yet."

The reservations clerk whipped around, looking more flustered by the second. "Oh, Mr. Fenster, yes, of course that's occurred to everybody. But you really can't blame airport security. Maybe all the bomb threats have been hoaxes up until now because somebody is trying to wear us down. Maybe somebody is trying to get us to stop paying attention. Then, as soon as our guard is down—"

"Oh, Jesus," Miss Frazier moaned.

"That's a load of crap," Richard said.

"No," the newly arrived Mr. Pratt said, "I don't think it is. Better safe than sorry. I don't want to get blown out of the air."

"The only thing they have to do to make sure we don't get blown out of the air," Richard told him, "is to check out the plane."

The reservations clerk was sliding from flustered into angry. In Richard's experience, clerks were like nurses. They could be pleasant to the people they were supposed to be serving just as long as those people were accommodating and polite. One whiff of independence and rebellion, and they were ready for war.

"Well," the reservations clerk sniffed now, "I know it's been a frustrating day, but it's been a frustrating day for *all* of us. MaineAir will be in the air as soon as it's safe to fly."

"Will MaineAir post a general boarding announcement?" Mr. Pratt inquired.

"Of course," the reservations clerk sniffed. "MaineAir is always careful to follow mandated airport procedures."

She turned her back on them and walked off into the

corridor, bouncing along in her uniform suit, huffy and mad.

"I just thought if I had to wait forever anyway, I might as well get myself a drink," Mr. Pratt said. "Either of the two of you want to come along?"

"Sure," Richard said, getting out of his seat and stretching. He held out a hand. "I'm Richard Fenster."

"I'm Kelly Pratt," Mr. Pratt said, shaking his hand.

Miss Frazier was looking from one to the other of them, always pausing a little bit longer on Richard. She looked nonplussed.

"Excuse me," she said finally. "Did you say your name was Richard Fenster? *Richard* Fenster?"

"That's right," Richard said.

"The Richard Fenster who's going up to Hunter's Pier, Maine, for the weekend?"

"That's right again," Richard said.

"Hey," Kelly Pratt said. "*I'm* going up to Hunter's Pier, Maine, for the weekend."

"I take it you're going there, too," Richard said to Miss Frazier.

Miss Frazier was now looking more than nonplussed. She was looking downright annoyed. She kept giving Richard the once-over, up and down, back and forth, checking out every hole in his sweater and every frayed thread in his jeans. Richard was beginning to think she had them both mentally cataloged.

"I'm Mathilda Frazier. I'm with Halbard's Auction House. I'm the one who's coordinating the auction of the personal effects of . . . well, you see what I mean."

"I see what you mean," Kelly Pratt said. "This is wonderful. I'm Kelly Pratt of Kahn and Pratt. We're the accountants."

Mathilda Frazier ignored him. "You don't look at all the way I expected you to look," she told Richard. "You are the same Richard Fenster I'm thinking of? The one who bought the gold evening sandals Tasheba Kent wore in *Dark Passions*? At Christie's in London?"

"For one hundred fifty-two thousand dollars." Richard nodded. "That's me."

"You mean you paid a hundred fifty thousand dollars

for a pair of evening slippers? Used?" Kelly Pratt was astounded. "I think you need to get yourself some decent financial advice. Obviously, you're a young guy who's made himself a lot of money he doesn't know what to do with."

"Mr. Fenster is a collector," Mathilda Frazier said.

"Mr. Fenster is in need of a tall glass of Budweiser," Richard announced. "Is there actually a bar around here somewhere? I'd kill for something cold."

"You have to go down to the core and out of the boarding area and around to the right," Kelly Pratt said. "I know the way. It won't take long. When you get that beer into you, though, you've got to tell me about those evening slippers. Do you do that kind of thing often?"

"I do it once or twice a year."

"That must be a very expensive hobby, Mr. Fenster. That must be worse than keeping racehorses."

Kelly Pratt was out in the corridor, trying to get them started on their way to the bar. Richard Fenster was holding back, to see what Mathilda Frazier would do.

"You coming along?" Richard asked her finally.

Mathilda Frazier seemed to start, and then sigh, expressions of emotions that seemed to have nothing to do with him at all. Then she got her handbag from the seat she had left it on and nodded.

"All right," she said. "After a day like this, I suppose I could use a glass of wine."

—— 2 ——

If Mathilda Frazier had been asked to name the fairy tale she liked least as a child, that fairy tale would have been *The Ugly Duckling*. Mathilda Frazier didn't like reversal-of-fortune stories of any kind. In her mind, the world was supposed to be an orderly place, where the people who started out being the best went on being the best forever. It bothered her no end that of the women she had graduated from high school with, only one of them was already a really enormous success—and she had been the plainest, nerdiest, most unhip girl in the class, the girl who had never gotten invited to anything, the girl who was considered an absolute square and a bore. The fact that this girl had turned out to be a success in rock music—all tarted up and dressed in miniskirts and bustiers—made the situation even worse.

There were plenty of reversal-of-fortune stories out there, Mathilda knew, and every one of them made her angry. She couldn't hear the name of Bill Gates without wanting to spit. If there was an up-from-nowhere story about a movie star or a novelist in one of the magazines, complete with before-and-after ugly-duckling-to-swan photographs to illustrate the transformation, Mathilda paged right past it. Obviously, Richard Fenster was an ugly duckling who had turned into a swan. In spite of the fact that he was still ugly—and so badly dressed he might have been taken for a street bum, except that he was so clean—he was impressively rich. All the auction houses had had his finances checked out, discreetly, and those checks always said the same thing. Richard Fenster had money to burn, and he liked to burn it—but all he was willing to burn it on were things that had belonged to Tasheba Kent.

On the walk from the waiting area to the bar, Mathilda Frazier developed a violent dislike of Richard Fenster. She disliked the clothes he wore, the way he walked, the manner in which he tilted his head to the left when he spoke. She disliked his accent, which was a thick south Boston twang. She disliked the thick stainless-steel Timex watch he wore on his right wrist. Most of all, she disliked his arrogance. She was sure it was evident in everything he did. The man breathed arrogance, she told herself. The man sweated arrogance every time he overexerted himself. He was impossible.

The airport bar was a plastic-looking place where even the real looked fake. The ferns in the great clay pots at the entrance were real, but at first sight they seemed to be molded out of polyethylene. The wood of the bar and the tables was real, but it looked simulated.

The bar was mostly empty, so they took a table next to the low brick wall that divided the bar from the corridor. The table was right under a loudspeaker, so they would be sure to hear about it if their flight ever decided to take off. Kelly Pratt didn't want to wait for the waitress. He found out what they were all having and rushed off to the bar.

"Maybe it's alcoholism," Richard Fenster said.

Mathilda Frazier couldn't ignore him—rule one in the trade was that you never offended high bidders—so she said something noncommittal about their all being nervous. What it was they were all supposed to be nervous about, she couldn't have said.

Fortunately, Kelly Pratt did not take long. He came back carrying three dissimilar glasses—a tall one for the beer, a stemmed one for the wine, a squat one for his whiskey and soda—and spread them out on the table. Mathilda looked at hers and decided that the wine looked like urine. She took a sip and decided that it tasted like urine, too. Normally, Mathilda did not drink house wines. She ordered from the wine list and made sure she got the proper year.

Kelly Pratt took a long swig of his whiskey and then looked around the table happily.

"You don't know how pleased I am to run into you two," he began. "I hate flying on these small planes. They make my stomach ache. And going up to Maine." He shrugged. "Either of you ever been up to this Hunter's Pier place before?"

Mathilda and Richard shook their heads.

"I should have gone up when we were first in negotiations for the auction," Mathilda said. "It's almost unheard-of for us to schedule a major auction of this kind without some representative of the company physically checking out the material. But we tried and tried and—they're extremely secretive."

"Oh, yes," Kelly Pratt agreed. "You never see them. I've never been out to the island, and they've never been in to my offices in New York. When I have something I need them to sign, I have to send it Federal Express. Or by messenger."

"I don't think secretive is really what they are," Richard Fenster said. "I think it's more like gun-shy. You forget what it must have been like for them, when the scandal broke. And the death, too. It would have been bad enough if Marsh had just left his wife for Tasheba Kent. But with Lilith Brayne dying or committing suicide or whatever it was in that awful way . . . ." Richard shrugged.

"I think their behavior was peculiar in spite of all that," Mathilda said. "Back at the office we have these pictures of them, taken at the time, that one of the researchers found and put up all around our section. You know, newspaper pictures, black-and-white things, taken during the investigation. And there she is, Tasheba Kent I mean, with this big black thing wrapped around her neck—"

"A black feather boa."

"A black feather boa," Mathilda ignored Richard's interruption, "and these dark glasses, huge ones, covering up the entire top half of her face, and if you ask me, that's no way to be inconspicuous. I look at those pictures and all I can think of is that she was doing it on purpose. Dramatizing herself. Getting her picture in the paper as much as possible."

"Oh, I don't think that can be right." Kelly Pratt shook his head. "We do the accounting for them now, you know. I've seen all the records. Even the old ones. I can tell you right off that these are very private people. Have been, from the beginning. If you ask me, they spend more time hiding their affairs than they really need to."

"Maybe they do now," Mathilda said crisply, "but I think then was a different story. Was your firm doing the accounting for them then?"

"Well, now," Kelly Pratt admitted. "Our firm wasn't even in existence then. I wasn't even born then."

"I think they were trying to pull it off," Mathilda said. "I think they thought that if they made it enough of a big glamorous deal, a kind of love story for the ages, they might be able to come out on the other side of it without Cavender Marsh's career being permanently ruined. Do you know what else we've got in our office, besides all those pictures?"

"Haven't a clue." Richard Fenster hadn't touched his beer.

"We've got a copy of an interview Tasheba Kent gave

to *Photoplay* magazine about two weeks after Lilith Brayne died. It was a telephone interview, by the way. According to the text, Miss Kent was in seclusion, prostrated with grief over the tragedy. Well, she may have been prostrated with grief, but it hadn't affected her voice. She certainly did talk a lot."

"What did she say?" Kelly Pratt asked curiously.

Mathilda tried another sip of her wine. It was just as bad as it had been the first time.

"Well, the thing that struck me the most was this long monologue she gave about the course of love. About how she and her sister were never really two separate people, but two halves of a single person. And now that one half was gone, the half that was left was not just devastated, but emotionally on the brink of death herself."

Kelly Pratt looked confused. "Do you mean they were identical twins?"

"No," Richard Fenster said. "Tasheba Kent was a year older than Lilith Brayne."

Mathilda frowned. "They didn't even look that much alike, if you ask me. Lilith had a sweeter and more regular face. And she'd just had the baby, of course, so she'd put on a little weight. She was round and sort of maternal-looking in a glamorous kind of way. Like Demi Moore now. Tasheba Kent was always the bone-thin, hawk-faced, predatory type. She looked like a vulture."

"She was beautiful," Richard Fenster countered. There was a slight edge to his voice. "And I think you're putting far too much emphasis on one movie-magazine interview. In the first place, those magazines were notorious for misquoting stars and misrepresenting facts. In the second place, even if she did say exactly those specific things, I think it was perfectly understandable. Her sister had just died. The cause of death was in at least some ways connected to the affair she was having with her sister's husband. A little rogue guilt seems to be right in order here."

"I don't think she was feeling guilty at all," Mathilda told him. "I think she was having a grand old time. The *tone* of the whole piece is just wrong. You should have read it. Lilith is gone and now she has Cavender Marsh all to herself, but that isn't enough, because she wants your sympathy too. Lilith may be dead, but it's Tasheba who is suffering."

Richard Fenster looked thoughtful. "You should get a copy of that *Photoplay* for the auction. I'd be interested to own it."

"If Tasheba Kent is your idol, I'd think you'd want to *destroy* every copy of the thing in existence," Mathilda said. "It certainly doesn't put that woman in a very good light."

"Attention," the loudspeaker over their head blared, through a rain of static that almost made the word sound like an expletive in a Balkan language. "Attention all passengers of MaineAir flights one seventy-seven and two twenty-nine. That's MaineAir one seventy-seven and two twenty-nine. Flights will be boarding at gate number—" more static "—in fifteen minutes. That's—"

The static drowned the rest of the message out.

"I don't think they've changed the gate, do you?" Kelly Pratt asked.

"Only way to find out is to walk that way and ask the first MaineAir person we find." Richard Fenster stood. "Are you coming, Miss Frazier?"

Mathilda considered asking him to call her "Ms." but decided against it. It was unnecessarily antagonistic, and it really wouldn't make sense for her to turn Fenster into an enemy. He had collected so much stuff already. He might want to have an auction of his own one day.

Mathilda grabbed her bag and stood up.

"I'm coming," she told him, in as pleasant a voice as possible. It wasn't very pleasant.

In the course of having a single drink that none of them had finished, Mathilda Frazier had gone from disliking Richard Fenster to absolutely loathing him.

—— 3 ——

Back on the island, Tasheba Kent was lying on top of the bedspread in her four-poster, king-size, curtained-and-canopied bed. The window curtains were drawn, and had been since noon. The tray with Tasheba's lunch on it was sitting on the vanity table, untouched. Around about eleven thirty, she had heard the sound of voices down in the foyer, as some of the guests arrived. Since then, things had been very quiet. Tasheba stared up at the underside of the canopy and wondered what was going on down there, who had come, what they were doing, what they were saying about her. The items for the auction were laid out on three long tables in the library, watched over by a man they had hired from the village. Each of the three of them had their own table, with the things that had belonged to more than one of them parceled out at random. She wondered if they were looking through those things now, pawing over them, trying to make them come right. God only knew she had pawed through them often enough herself in the last sixty years. By now she ought to know that no matter how many times she replayed the story, she could never make it come out right.

Sixty years.

She reached over to her night table and picked up the Tiffany's brass carriage clock that she'd had at least since the year it all happened. She and Cavender didn't get into Tiffany's anymore. It was a good thing the clock was well made and hadn't needed repair. Tasheba didn't have her glasses on and the room was dark. She tilted the clock back and forth in the thin wash of grayness that seeped through a crack in the window curtains. Four fifteen, the clock seemed to say. That was a good time, four fifteen. It was Cavender's time to be alone.

Tasheba moved very slowly, first onto her side, then almost over onto her stomach. She had to be careful. She had grown very frail. Simple things had become very difficult or even impossible. She braced herself against the night table and levered herself up into a sitting position, with her legs hanging off the side of the bed. Her big platinum and diamond dinner ring cut into the flesh of her fingers as she pushed against the night table's edge, making her want to cry out.

Once she was sitting up, it was easier. She got down to the floor without any trouble at all. She moved across the room at first by holding on to furniture, like a child learning to walk. After a while, it got better. The joints in her legs became operative. The muscles in her calves and thighs gained strength and determination. It was as if her body forgot how to move while she was asleep and had to learn all over again each time she woke up.

There were French doors leading to a balcony over-looking the pool terrace hiding behind long curtains on one wall. Tasheba got the curtains pulled back and the French doors open and went outside. The pool terrace seemed to be deserted, but she couldn't see all of it. Cavender usually had a drink there every day at this time, getting a jump on the cocktail hour. Maybe he had stayed inside today to entertain their guests.

"Cavender?" Tasheba called out, hearing the high whining querulous tone in her voice and hating it. "Cavender, are you down there?"

There was the sound of metal scraping against the fieldstone of the terrace and then a cough. Cavender came into view underneath her.

"You aren't wearing a robe," he said, looking up. "You aren't wearing slippers, either. Go back inside and put something on."

"I just want to ask you a question," Tasheba said. "It won't take very long."

"You don't have to ask me any questions. Everything's fine. Everything's wonderful. Go back to resting up before dinner."

"People came," Tasheba said. "I heard them."

"Some people came. Bennis Hannaford and that friend of hers. Lydia Acken. The reporter from *Personality*. Oh. And Hannah Kent Graham. It turns out that that's what she calls herself. Hannah *Kent* Graham. After her mother instead of after me."

"I think that's very sweet," Tasheba said quietly. "I think it's rather—amazing that she didn't call herself after her aunt Bessie."

"Maybe she didn't like her aunt. I never understood how anyone could. I didn't talk to her, by the way. I didn't even let her see me. I couldn't face it. She's grotesque."

"She's your daughter."

"That's not something that ever mattered a damn to

either one of us. Go back to bed now. You've got a long night ahead of you. You've got an even longer weekend."

"Are the rest of them coming?"

"They got held up in Boston with some problems with their plane, but they're coming. Yes. They'll be here as soon as they can."

"I wish it was over and done with," Tasheba said. "I wish I didn't have to be so worried all the time."

"You don't have to be worried. Go back to bed."

There was a nice breeze coming in off the ocean, cold but pleasant. Tasheba felt as if she could have stood on the balcony all night. But it was silly. It was ridiculous not to care now whether she lived or died, just because she was old.

I never expected to get this old, she thought, as she went back into the bedroom and shut the French doors tight behind her. I never expected to live much past the age of forty.

She stretched herself out on her bed again and stared up at the underside of the canopy.

In a way, she had died just around the time that she was forty.

She just hadn't stopped breathing.

CHAPTER 4

— 1 —

Gregor Demarkian had devised a quick-and-easy way to determine whether a large house, owned by rich people, was run by the husband or the wife: if house guests were required to come down to dinner in black tie, the house was run by the wife. If house guests were not required to come down to dinner in black tie, the house was not necessarily run by the husband. Gregor had known his share of informal women. It was just that husbands never wanted to dress up for dinner on their own territory, unless they were having a party for five or six hundred people and inviting the president of the United States.

The instructions on the little card Gregor had found on the table beside his bed—along with an ice bucket, a glass, and a bottle of mineral water—had said, "Cocktails at seven, Dinner at seven thirty, Black Tie." The card had been written out by hand and had nothing else on it, so Gregor hadn't been able to pretend to investigate it. He had simply explored his bedroom for a while, decided that there wasn't very much to see, and stretched out on the bed to read. The bedroom was a small but very high-ceilinged square containing almost all the sins of Victorian interior decoration. The furniture was made of wood too heavy and too dark to have looked graceful in anything smaller than a football field. The curtains on the windows were made of heavy dark damask. Every available surface was clogged with painted figurines in porcelain and plaster, all in varying stages of terminal sentimentality. On Gregor's bedside table there was a porcelain group, consisting of a very large mother figure with three tiny children clutching at her knees, titled "Angel of the Home." Gregor had to put it away on one of the bookshelves before he felt comfortable moving the ice bucket and the mineral water off the tray.

What there wasn't, in this room, was any sign of the life Tasheba Kent and Cavender Marsh had lived before coming to Maine. In fact, as far as Gregor could see, there was very little of that part of their lives anywhere in the house. Maybe their private rooms were full of the memorabilia of Hollywood and the movies. Downstairs and in the guest wing, there was only a long line of movie posters climbing the wall of the main staircase. There weren't even any books about the movies lying around. Gregor had gone into the library after lunch; all he had found were books on gardening and the complete works of Agatha Christie.

Of course, there were three long tables full of memorabilia, meant for sale at this auction. Those things might once have been scattered around the house and then been collected up to be sent to New York. Gregor didn't think so, because he never seemed to run into any feeling of absence anywhere. There were no blank shelves anywhere that he could see. There were no empty, unfilled places on coffee tables or sideboards. These little figurines were very old, even if they were maudlin and not very valuable. They hadn't been bought last week to be shoved into the gaps left by cigarette lighters and rhinestone-encrusted minaudières.

Gregor tried to check the set of his tie in a mirror that was more elaborately carved frame than glass. Fat cupids chased even fatter maidens around the edges of a silver lake. He could see one side of his tie or the other, but not both at once.

Gregor went to the door of his bedroom and looked out into the guest room hall. All the other doors on this corridor were closed, as they had been all afternoon. He heard no noise. Either his fellow guests had gone down to cocktails early, or they were being very quiet about getting dressed. Gregor knocked on Bennis's door and got no answer. He tried the doorknob, found that it turned easily, and poked his head inside. It was impossible to get Bennis to take security seriously. She left doors open and suitcases unlocked and checkbooks and credit cards lying around on tables. The only precautions she would take had to do with her car, and that was more because she was overprotective of the car than that she believed she could be the victim of a carjacking. Bennis was not in her room. There was a mess of papers on the bed—she had been working— and a pile of cigarette butts in the ashtray on the bedside table, but Bennis herself was gone.

Gregor retreated into the hallway, nonplussed. Maybe he had read the card wrong. Maybe there was a code to messages like that one to which he wasn't privy. Gregor was not an unsophisticated man. In spite of the fact that he had grown up poor in the days when Cavanaugh Street had been not only an Armenian immigrant conclave but something of a slum, his career since had brought him into contact with more rich people than any sane man would want to know. He had been to dinner at the White House (twice, under two different presidents) and on a long weekend in the Virginia hills where the Duke and Duchess of Windsor were spending a vacation. Granted, during that weekend he had been part of the security force, not one of the guests, but that hardly mattered. Gregor Demarkian knew how to operate in the world. It was only around people related to Bennis Day Hannaford that he began to suspect conspiracies and to believe that whatever social occasion he was involved in was really a trap, meant to make him look like an idiot.

He was still standing in the hallway, staring at Bennis Hannaford's bedroom door, when a door down the corridor opened and a woman came out. Gregor looked up and saw Lydia Acken locking up very carefully behind herself. The lawyer wore a long pearl white dress in plain, unadorned taffeta. There was a string of pearls around her neck. She had her white hair brushed back into a neat chignon designed to let little curling tendrils escape around her face. She had pearl stud earrings in her ears and a small white taffeta handbag in her hands. She looked, Gregor thought, almost unbelievably attractive.

Lydia finished locking up and came down the hall to him. He was, after all, standing at the head of the stairs.

"Are you waiting for your friend?" she asked him pleasantly. "I noticed her especially on the pier. She's really quite beautiful."

"Bennis?" It was true, of course, that Bennis Hannaford was beautiful. It was just that Gregor never noticed it. "I don't know," he said now, "I suppose I've known her so long, it just doesn't register anymore."

"Maybe that's why she's holding you up." Lydia nodded at Bennis's closed door. "Maybe she feels she's being taken for granted, and she's making you wait so you'll appreciate her more."

"*Bennis?*" Gregor said. "Oh. Oh, no. I mean, it's not —we don't—it isn't like that, you see—we're—"

"Oh." Lydia Acken blushed scarlet. "Oh, I *am* sorry. I just assumed—and of course I shouldn't have—that's what comes of trying to be modern when you don't have the faintest idea what it is that's going on—"

"No, no," Gregor said quickly. "I can see how you thought what you thought. Lots of people think it. It's just that it doesn't happen to be the way—"

"My mother always told me I didn't have sense enough to mind my own business," Lydia said miserably.

"Bennis isn't home," Gregor threw in, feeling desperate. "I came across the hall to see if she'd fix my tie, but she's already gone."

Lydia Acken stopped in the middle of the muttered recriminations she was still directing at herself and looked up into Gregor's eyes. Then a smile began to spread across her face, and she bit her lower lip to stop its spreading.

"Oh, dear," she said. "Have I made a fool of myself, or what?"

"You made no bigger a fool of yourself than I made of myself. By the way, is my tie crooked?"

"Yes. Yes, it is, as a matter of fact. Here, give me a minute and I'll fix it."

Gregor stood very still. Lydia rose up on tiptoe and fussed around at his throat. The tickle against his Adam's apple was comforting and familiar. Elizabeth had always fixed his ties for him and straightened out his collars. These are the kinds of things, Gregor thought, that any man can do for himself, but that most men don't really want to.

"There," Lydia Acken said. "You look fine now. Are you going to wait for Miss Hannaford to come back, or are you going downstairs for cocktails?"

"I suppose I'm going downstairs for cocktails. I don't know when Bennis is going to be back, or even if. Can I come downstairs with you?"

"Yes," Lydia said. "Of course you may. I'd like that. Maybe on the way down I'll pump you for the information everybody in the house is just dying to find out about you."

"Really? What information is that?"

"Information on what you're doing here, of course," Lydia said. "I ran into Geraldine Dart this afternoon after lunch, in a back hallway while I was looking for the loo, and she's absolutely convinced that Hannah Graham hired you to find out what really happened to Lilith Brayne."

"I can't imagine what would induce me to work for Hannah Graham. A personal visit from God Almighty, maybe."

"Well, Hannah Graham also thinks you've been hired to find out what happened to her mother, or maybe to cover it up, but she thinks I hired you. Has somebody hired you? Are you here to find out what happened to Lilith Brayne?"

"In the first place," Gregor said, as they started side by side down the stairs, "nobody can hire me. I don't have a private detective's license, and I don't need money. Sometimes I look into things that interest me. I no longer investigate anything for money."

"You're a very intelligent man."

"In the second place," Gregor continued, "as far as I know, everybody already knows what happened to Lilith Brayne. A tragedy. An accident. A mess. But none of my business."

"I wish it were none of my business." Lydia sighed. "You know, Mr. Demarkian, when I went off to law school, back in the early fifties, when girls just didn't get accepted, I had this vision of starting out on a great adventure, a modern crusade full of knights and dragons and damsels in distress. And what did I get? Tasheba Kent and Cavender Marsh, two very old people who still think sex is the only point of life and who are just as silly and narcissistic in everything else they do."

"Call me Gregor," Gregor said.

"My name is Lydia. Lydia Ann. I've never liked it."

"We'll have to think of a suitable nickname, then. Look. I think we're the first ones down. I wonder where everybody's gone."

Lydia Acken's eyes flashed. "Hannah Graham has probably gone off for a spot of surgery before drinks," she said tartly.

Then she marched off ahead of Gregor into the living room.

―――― 2 ――――

Tasheba Kent's official birthday, and official birthday party, weren't until Saturday, but while Gregor had been upstairs reading his book somebody had begun decorating the living room anyway. Most of the decorations were the standard sort of thing that could be found in any Hallmark card shop. There was a string of shiny-surfaced multicolored cardboard letters held together with tin swivel fasteners tacked up just above eye level on one wall, spelling out "HAPPY BIRTHDAY." There were blue-and-white crepe-paper streamers wound barber-pole fashion around the two decorative posts that separated the living room from the study beyond it. There were quilted crepe-paper-and-cardboard stand-up happy faces in blue and yellow and green, scattered across the coffee tables and end tables and shelves, each proclaiming "HAPPY BIRTHDAY" in a riot of exclamation points. It would have looked like the setup for a children's party, except that here and there there were indications that the woman

for whom all this fuss was being made was not young.
There was a metal walker tucked discreetly into a corner.
There was an arm brace lying on the floor next to one of
the larger couches. There were magnifying glasses everywhere, as if the person who needed them could never remember where she had put them down.

Lydia Acken walked over to the letters on the wall,
touched the shiny surface of the *T*, and shook her head.

"Somehow, I wouldn't have thought this was
Tasheba's style. Of course, it may not be out here for her.
It may be out here for us. One more prop to make the
auction a success."

"Maybe Tasheba Kent has gone a little senile," Gregor
said. "At a hundred years old, she'd be entitled."

"She might be entitled, but I know it hasn't happened," Lydia said. "I speak to her on the phone quite
often. She's in remarkably good shape for somebody her
age. I had an aunt who died at seventy-five who wasn't
anywhere near as alert."

"I think she's practicing voodoo," somebody said
from the living room doorway.

Gregor and Lydia turned around to see Hannah Graham, wearing what might have been the single oddest
piece of clothing Gregor had ever encountered. It seemed
to be made of round plastic discs, bone white but painted
over with designs in metallic blue and red and green, held
together with white metal staples. It was very short, riding
high on Hannah's thighs, showing off skeletal legs with
bright blue veins laced through them. It was both backless
and strapless, exposing arms as thin as pipe cleaners and a
back whose skin was so dry it looked like sandpaper. The
whole extraordinary ensemble was set off by a pair of
spike-heeled sandals at least four inches high, that Hannah
Graham seemed to have trouble walking on.

Hannah Graham came into the room and picked up
one of the quilted crepe-paper-and-cardboard happy faces.
She put it down again and went over to look at the blue-
and-white streamers.

"My God," she said. "What a hokey lot of nonsense. I
wonder how she thinks she's going to get away with it."

"I don't think *she's* trying to get away with anything,"

Lydia said stiffly. "I don't think any of these things here were her idea. They were probably put out by Miss Dart or Mr. Marsh."

Hannah shot Lydia a cynical look. "I'll bet Miss Dart doesn't do a thing around here without permission. I'll bet my father doesn't either. He's not talking to me, by the way."

"Don't be ridiculous," Lydia said. "We've barely got here. He hasn't had a chance."

"I've given him several chances," Hannah countered. "He runs away every time he sees me coming. He locks himself in bathrooms. But he won't be able to avoid me all weekend. I'm faster than he is."

Oh, wonderful, Gregor thought. This is going to be just as bad as I feared. Then he looked toward the living room door again and saw a very young woman come in, someone he had not met, a girlish-looking woman with red-gold hair in a conservative long dress. Behind her were two men, the older in a tuxedo like Gregor's own, the younger in a plain blue suit.

"Oh," the young woman said. "This must be the right place for us to go."

Hannah Graham was giving the young woman a hard look, one of the hardest Gregor had ever seen. It was a river of pure hate, made stronger by the fact that Hannah was not going to get a chance to do anything about it. Hannah had dieted and exercised and gone under the knife enough so that she looked nothing at all like an ordinary woman in her late fifties, but she looked nothing at all like a woman in her twenties, and that was what she was trying to look like. This was a woman in her twenties, and it showed.

Lydia Acken came forward with her hand outstretched. "How do you do," she said. "I don't believe we've met. My name is Lydia Acken."

"We haven't met but we've talked," the young woman said. "I'm Mathilda Frazier, from the Halbard Auction House."

"Oh, yes," Lydia said.

Mathilda turned to the two men behind her. "The tall one is Kelly Pratt—"

"Kelly and I have met many times," Lydia said.

"—and the other one is Richard Fenster. He's a very important collector and dealer of movie memorabilia."

"I know Richard Fenster." Bennis came in with Carlton Ji in tow. She was wearing a strapless red sheath that seemed molded to her, and Carlton Ji looked stoned. "Richard deals in memorabilia from science fiction and fantasy movies," Bennis went on. "We've been in touch."

Gregor looked around and realized that they were all there, all the people who had been on the guest list, everybody who was expected for this party except for the people who actually lived in the house. The clock on the wall above the Happy Birthday letters said five minutes after seven. Gregor wondered where Geraldine Dart was.

He didn't have to wonder for long. She came through the living room door carrying a long silver tray of identical cocktails, exactly eight of them, one for each person in the room, not including herself. Gregor had no idea what the drinks were. They looked like they had grenadine in them. Obviously, guests in this house were supposed to take what they were served and make the best of it.

"Here we go," Geraldine said, giving Hannah Graham a swift look of wariness and delight that passed so quickly it might not have occurred at all. "Everybody take one of these, and then we'll be ready for the arrival of the king and queen."

The arrival of the king and queen turned out to be a production with a lot in common with the way Bennis Hannaford's more ardent fans liked to conduct their introductions. First, a gong sounded in the hall—not a chime or bell or the bass note of an old clock telling the hour, but a real gong, the kind of sound that could only be made by a felt-tipped hammer smashing against a large brass disc. Then Geraldine Dart shooed a few stragglers away from the living room doorway, and the procession began.

Cavender Marsh came in first. He was a very old man dressed in a tuxedo, but he still looked spry and alert and admirably, almost miraculously, trim.

The Tasheba Kent who followed him was something of a shock. The actress was an ancient woman, bearing all the usual marks of great age. Her skin was as soft as tissue paper and looked as thin. There was a lot of it, with wrinkle after wrinkle falling down the side of her face and along the bones of her arms. She did not have a dowager's hump, but she was hunched over. Her head and neck hung low between her shoulders. She was not really able to stand up straight. She was not fat, but her body had lost whatever shape it ever had. Her breasts did not curve upward and outward. Her stomach was a round mound jutting out from beneath her rib cage.

None of this would have been particularly disturbing, if Tasheba Kent had been dressed like an old woman, or even in simple conservative clothes. Instead, she was dressed like the silent movie vamp she had once been. Her dress was a tight black tube of beaded satin, hugging every wayward contour. Wrapped around her shoulders was a black feather boa and a beaded satin shawl. Around her forehead was a beaded satin headband; the hair it held back was jet black and as thick as a full-cream chocolate mousse. It was a wig and it looked like a wig, but it was less grotesque than Tasheba Kent's makeup. That was so highly colored and so thickly applied, it belonged more properly on a clown. Tasheba Kent's eyes were laden down with at least three sets of false eyelashes and rimmed with kohl. Her lips were painted into a bright red cupid's bow. Her cheeks were rouged into two shiny bright apples.

"Good God," Lydia Acken whispered into Gregor's ear. "Like niece, like aunt. Here we go again."

But Gregor didn't think that was really true. It was most definitely not the same, what Tasheba Kent was doing and what Hannah Graham was doing. Hannah actually expected to fool people. At least when the serious competition—meaning women like Mathilda Frazier and Bennis Hannaford—was out of sight, Hannah thought she would be able to wipe away time. Gregor didn't think Tasheba Kent had any illusions about the way she looked. She knew she was grotesque. She wanted to be grotesque. She was reveling in it.

Now why, Gregor asked himself, would a woman want to do something like that?

——— 3 ———

After the entrance, dinner was inevitably an anticlimax. They sat around the long table in the dining room, eating impossibly bland food off Royal Doulton plates by the light of three eight-stick sterling-silver candelabra. They made polite conversation with each other of the kind common to people who do not know each other well and never expect to. The dining room table was strewn with happy birthday reminders, including a set of little plastic balloons with "100" written across each one. People kept picking those up and commenting on them, as if they were significant in some way.

Gregor had managed to get himself seated on Lydia Acken's right, so when the conversation turned to ghosts just before dessert, he was not desperately bored and searching for something new to occupy his mind. Neither was Lydia, as far as he could tell. They had been talking for the last twenty minutes about his early years with the Federal Bureau of Investigation, about how he had felt about J. Edgar Hoover ("a bigot and a psychopath"), about why he had stuck it out ("the idea of the Bureau is a good one, if you see what I mean"). They had just gotten started on the way the confidential files had been disposed of in the three long days after Hoover's death—"the blackmail files," they used to be called; the dirt Hoover had on senators and congressmen and presidents—when Cavender Marsh said what he did about the concubine.

"That's who I think it is wandering around this house in the night," Cavender Marsh said, his deep bass voice booming down the table from his place in the host's chair. "I think the old man couldn't bear the idea of shutting himself up in this place alone, so he got himself a hired companion, and then one day she wanted to leave and he decided to cut her throat and stuff her body in the well. And her soul has been here ever since, trying to take revenge."

"Oh, don't be silly," Tasheba Kent said, in a wavery voice, from her own end of the table. "Now, don't any of you people worry about a thing. Cavender doesn't even know if old Josiah Horne ever had a companion living out here with him at all, never mind a lady companion that he used for a mistress and then murdered. And we've had all the wells checked out at least three times since we moved here, and nobody's ever found a body or a skeleton in one."

"If the place is haunted, I'd think it would be haunted by Josiah Horne himself," Carlton Ji said. "From what Miss Dart told us on the boat, he sounds strange enough to haunt a place all on his own."

"This is just some game they're all playing," Hannah Graham announced scornfully, "to keep us off balance. There aren't any ghosts, here or anywhere else. I'm not going to let them scare *me*."

Geraldine Dart was sitting at the end of the table on Tasheba Kent's left, close enough to cut the old woman's food and help her with her utensils if she needed help. She was wearing a plain black dress and a long necklace of black glass beads and a terrible pair of glasses that went up into points at the outside corners, like the kind of thing divorcées wore forty years ago. Now she took the glasses off and put them down on the table next to her wineglass.

"You know," she said in a slow careful voice, "I really was telling the truth on the boat this morning. There really is a ghost, and I really have seen her. Three times, as a matter of fact. In the main family wing, upstairs near the bedrooms."

"Miss Dart is always telling us all about it," Cavender Marsh boomed cheerfully.

"It can't be Josiah Horne because it's most definitely the ghost of a woman," Geraldine Dart continued. "And she can't be a recent arrival because she's dressed in an old-fashioned dress. Long to the floor with a high collar. That sort of thing."

"Does she talk?" Richard Fenster asked curiously.

"She's never talked to me," Geraldine Dart said. "She just stands at the window at the end of the hall up there, looking out. Then when she hears me, she turns to see who I am. Then she just fades away."

"I think I'm disappointed," Carlton Ji said. "I think I'd prefer to have chains rattling and blood dripping from the ceiling, like in that Shirley Jackson novel."

"I think I'd rather have a love story," Mathilda Frazier said. "You know, she sets herself down in front of the portrait of her lost lover and pines away for him."

"She couldn't be pining away for him," Kelly Pratt said reasonably. "She's already dead."

"Well, I don't know what she's doing," Geraldine Dart told them, "but she seems to be harmless enough. One minute to twelve midnight exactly, when she comes. Some of you ought to go up there tonight and see if you can catch sight of her."

"Maybe we will," Bennis Hannaford said.

Down at the middle of the left side of the table, Hannah Graham shot out of her seat, wadded her blue linen napkin into a ball, and sent the ball flying at the nearest candelabra. She almost hit it. If she had, she would have set something on fire.

"You little bitch," Hannah snarled at Geraldine Dart. "Don't think I don't know what kind of shit you're pulling. Don't think I'm going to let you get away with it, either."

Then Hannah Graham kicked her chair over backward, so that it hit the floor with a crash, and went marching out of the dining room.

CHAPTER 5

— 1 —

For Carlton Ji, the great questions of late-twentieth-century existence—if the races would ever be able to learn to live with each other; whether a cure would be found for cancer or AIDS; how the world was going to be supplied with the technological comforts it wanted without poisoning itself in the process—could be boiled down to a single proposition, the quintessential interview question for *Personality* magazine: How does it make you *feel* when you think about these things? There were people even at *Personality* who knew that this question was idiotic. How an immunologist *felt* about AIDS was far less important than what he *knew* about it. No matter how miserable the contemplation of race hatred made you, it would not tell you how to solve the problems of Bosnia-Herzegovina. Feelings, though, were what *Personality* dealt in, especially the mushily maudlin feelings of well-heeled people about their miserable childhoods. It was amazing how many highly successful television actresses and bankable movie stars—none of whom had ever been known to shut up for fifteen seconds on any other subject—had suffered in silence for decades on the subject of their mothers' shopping addictions or their fathers' love affairs with emotional coldness and the National Football League. *Personality* used to

publish revelations far more powerful and far more in-
flammatory than either of those, but they had had to give
it up, because they kept getting sued. It turned out that
you could not print accusations about an ordinary, non-
public person if you could not prove them to be true. It
also turned out that "somebody said so," even if the somebody was the hottest romantic comedy lead since Carole
Lombard, did not constitute proof.

For Carlton Ji, the insidious part of all this was how
much it made him want to be like these people, and how
hard he tried to rewrite his life to fit the paradigm their
lives all seemed to fit. He had actually grown up in fairly
pleasant surroundings, in one of the nicer suburbs on
Long Island, with a father who worked full-time as a
banker and a mother who worked part-time as a research
biologist at a small chemical company. He had three
brothers and a sister, plenty of pocket money without having to work for it, and the kind of high school career that
leaves more happy memories than the other sort. Second
cousins coming in from miserable apartments in the city
and endless hours of after-school work in the family restaurant looked on his life with awe. For some of them, the
mere fact that he had his own room that he had to share
with nobody else, that he could just go into and shut the
door, meant that he was being brought up like an imperial
prince. Carlton never paid any attention to these second
cousins, because they made him uncomfortable, and because he could never get over the feeling that their lives
were somehow their fault. Other people had come over
from Asia, and from worse places, too. Other people had
had to start small. Why did it seem to be only his second
cousins and their parents who never got anywhere with it?

For Carlton Ji, everybody was responsible for his own
fate, unless he was being sabotaged by his dysfunctional
family. In Carlton's own case, his family got him every
time. That was why, no matter how brilliant he had tried
to be at the dinner table tonight, Bennis Hannaford hadn't
paid the slightest bit of attention to him.

Everybody else went into the living room for liqueurs
after dinner—except for Tasheba Kent, who was looking
extremely tired and extremely frail—but Carlton drifted

off on his own, feeling disenfranchised and disgruntled. The best thing to do with a mood like this was to express it. The problem with expressing it was that that was likely to get him into trouble. Business etiquette had not been invented with the emotional health of the whole human being in mind. Carlton wandered down to the library and looked in on the exhibits. The man from town who was supposed to be guarding the room looked him over once or twice, as if he were a sea slug, but did nothing to stop him from going in. Carlton looked over the loot on the three tables and decided it bored him. Tasheba Kent's table had a lot of jet-black fans and beaded dresses. The dresses on Lilith Brayne's table ran more to pastels. Cavender Marsh's table held not much of anything. By the 1930s, when Cavender Marsh had been famous, movie stars were no longer living their lives in a sea of props. Or maybe they were, but the props were subtle ones, that didn't become famous in and of themselves. Carlton thought about the sale, at auction, of "the last cigar Charlie Chaplin ever chewed on in a movie," and decided that people were just plain crazy.

He left the library by the far door and found himself in a narrow service hall. The hall was lined on both sides by plain wood doors. Carlton opened one and found a laundry room. He opened another and found a pantry. He opened a third and found a lot of old trunks, some with broken sides and shattered clasps, piled up inside and on top of each other with no concern for order or logic. Voices floated down to him from the living room, deep and courteous, high-pitched and discontented.

"I think it's a tort, behavior like that," Hannah Graham's voice was saying. "I think you ought to be able to sue somebody over that."

Carlton ought to have been surprised that Hannah Graham was back in the fold, after that grand exit with the thrown napkin, but he wasn't. Hannah Graham was the kind of woman who would always make her way back to the fold, because she was the kind of woman who couldn't stand thinking that something interesting might be going on without her.

Carlton went to the end of the hall and opened the

door there. He found a small square landing with stairs leading up to the left and another door, directly opposite to the one he was coming through. He went to that door and opened it. He groped around on the wall and turned the light switch on. This room was a kind of walk-in medicine cabinet. Three of the four walls were lined floor to ceiling with shelves, and these shelves were crammed with bottles. A lot of bottles contained vitamins, bought in bulk quantities from a mail-order house. "AS ADVERTISED IN *PREVENTION* MAGAZINE!" the labels on these bottles said. Carlton found enough vitamin E to drown in and enough vitamin A to poison a rabbit farm. He found so many combinations of B vitamins, he began to wonder if the B's had some nonnutritional usefulness, like being good for polishing silverware. One of the other shelves was full of aspirin and acetaminophen in as many different brands as possible. Another shelf had painkillers like Advil and Motrin. Another shelf was full of antibiotics, in spite of the fact that they were supposed to be available only by prescription. Carlton got down on his knees and looked at the shelves closest to the floor. Two of them had nothing on them at all. The third contained prescription blood pressure medication made out to Cavender Marsh. Carlton Ji picked up one of the bottles and found out that it was both full and well past its expiration date. Obviously, somebody in this house, Geraldine Dart if not Tasheba Kent and Cavender Marsh themselves, had found a way to get around the laws and stockpile their prescriptions.

Carlton went out on the landing, turned off the light in the little room, and closed the door behind himself. That had been interesting but unproductive. There had been no clue to the things he wanted to know up there. He looked up the dark staircase. This was a servant's staircase, of course, and maybe nobody used it anymore, at least at night. He had checked all four walls and been unable to find a switch. He had looked up into the blackness and been unable to see a lightbulb or a light fixture or a lamp. What did the servants do in this place when there were servants, if there were ever servants? Did they carry candles?

Carlton thought about going back to the others. He

decided against it. He would just wander around mooning about Bennis Hannaford, and she would just go on ignoring him. He could try to confront her, but he didn't think that would be a good idea. Carlton had a very good eye for the kind of people who would treat his claims to wounded vulnerability with contempt. He climbed a few steps and looked up into the darkness. Things would get better as he went higher, he realized, because there was a window on the landing above him. The problems would come between landings. The half flights were long and steep and narrow. They boxed off whatever light was coming through the windows and made the climber wait for it.

Carlton went up to the first landing. The window there was tall and thin. He looked out and saw black rocks and a black ocean and the tiny lights of a buoy at sea. He was at the back of the house in more ways than one. He wasn't looking across to Hunter's Pier from here.

Carlton went up another half landing and found another window. He went up another half landing yet and found another window yet. There were, apparently, going to be windows on every landing but doors only on every other one. He went up another half landing and opened the door there. He had lost track of where he was. He was looking out on a meanly proportioned hall, lined with plain wood doors again. He opened one of the doors and found a miserable little bedroom. It was equipped with a metal bedframe and a thin mattress and a single small wood table. He went back to the landing. Servants' quarters, definitely. How glad he was that he hadn't had to be a servant in a nineteenth-century house.

He went up the next half flight of stairs, stopped to look out at the night again—same scene, lots of black, illuminated buoys—and then went up the half flight after that. This was the end. The landing had a door on it, but no further stairs. Carlton opened the door. He was surprised to find that the vast room beyond seemed to be brightly lit. It wasn't, of course. This was the attic, an undifferentiated space whose low walls were lined with periodic windows. The windows on the far side of the space looked out on the front of the house and let in the light from the powerful security arcs out there. Carlton closed the attic door behind him and took a deep breath of musty air.

Attics, Carlton thought, can be interesting places. There might be anything at all stuffed into them. He walked across the middle of the room to the front windows, looking around as he went. This attic was not neglected. There was no carpet of dust and grit under his feet. Somebody had been sweeping the floor up here.

He got to the front windows and looked out. The sea looked angrier than it had when he had come over on the boat. The water seemed to be rising higher against the dock than he remembered it doing. The wind was rising, too. It was pressing against the side of the house the way Sisyphus had pressed against his boulder. Out there in Hunter's Pier, everything was quiet. Lights glowed on the docks and in the windows of houses and bars. The flagpole where the flags of the United States and the state of Maine had flown when they came in this morning was bending in the wind.

Carlton had turned around to contemplate the contents of the attic, to decide where he was going to start searching for something he could use, when he heard them for the first time—except that he didn't think of them as "them" yet, only as "it," and what he thought he heard was the squeaking of a metal hinge in need of some 3-In-One oil. He looked back at the door he had come in through, wary. It was still shut. He looked around for another door and found it, to his right, but it was shut, too.

The squeaking, he realized, was coming from above his head. He looked up and saw nothing. It was too dark up there, beyond the reach of the light from the windows. The darkness seemed to be breathing, but Carlton was certain that was his imagination. His imagination was working so hard right now, he could have conjured up the Loch Ness monster with wings and convinced himself that it was perfectly real.

There was a big black steamer trunk in the very middle of the room, plastered over with theatrical stickers. Carlton was sure it had to belong to either Cavender

Marsh or Tasheba Kent, because he was sure that no one else who had ever been connected to this house had ever had a theatrical background. He knelt down by the trunk. It was the kind that had to be padlocked, but the padlock that had once been threaded through the hasp was nowhere to be found. Carlton lifted the top of the trunk. The hinges squeaked, but they didn't sound anything at all the way the squeaking had sounded just a few moments before. He put the top of the trunk gently on the attic floor and looked into it. On the top there was a wooden tray, lined with felt and divided into sections. In the sections were such uninteresting objects as paper clips, safety pins, and loose glass beads from long-broken necklaces. Carlton took the divider out and put that on the attic floor, too.

Underneath the divider there was the big empty space of the trunk proper. At the bottom of it were a pair of black lace handkerchiefs and a single black sock. There were also three manila envelopes, so old they had almost turned white. Carlton picked up the top one and looked inside. It was full of small black-and-white photographs, some only two inches square, of the kind taken by cheap snapshot cameras in the late thirties and early forties. Carlton pulled some out. The first one showed an easily recognizable Cavender Marsh standing in front of a car parked in front of a beach. Next to Cavender Marsh was Lilith Brayne, looking almost normal in white gloves and a big straw hat. Carlton turned the picture over and read the script on the back: *CM and LM in Nice, 1937.* That must have been the last good summer.

Carlton put this photograph carefully on the floor—it might come in handy, for his article or his book; technically he didn't own it, but as long as nobody could prove where he had gotten it, he would be able to use it—and went on to the next one. This was a larger one, of Lilith Brayne herself, in a swimsuit. The strap of the suit went around the back of her neck and the sides came a third of the way down her thighs. He put this on the floor, too, in another stack, because he didn't want to use it.

The third picture was the largest one yet, almost the size of the snapshots people took today, and it was a kind of family portrait. Cavender Marsh was there, and Lilith

Brayne was there, and Tasheba Kent was there, too. Lilith Brayne and Tasheba Kent sat side by side on a large white-looking sofa, holding hands. Cavender Marsh stood between them and behind them, smiling determinedly at the camera. Carlton turned the photograph over. *Just the three of us in 1936.* Then he turned it back and contemplated the faces of the three people in it.

He was just beginning to wonder what it was about this photograph—something off, something wrong, the emotional tone not what it ought to be—when the first of them hit him, screeching through the air like a World War II kamikaze pilot, smacking him in the side of the head with all the force of a mugger's cosh and a set of claws besides. Carlton put his hand up to his head; he felt the ooze of blood. Another one came at him from behind. He felt it claw the skin at the back of his skull.

"Shit," Carlton said. "Shit, shit, shit."

They were all moving now, restless and angry, hundreds of them up in the rafters.

Bats.

He had to get out of there.

He got up to make a run for the door, and five of them hit him at once.

—— 2 ——

Kelly Pratt was not the sort of person who worried about what he thought of as serious things. He let himself fret about his name and his hair and his waistline, but he thought it was bad for his health, mental and physical, to get too worked up at major crises that were not his own. The missing one hundred thousand dollars that had once belonged to Lilith Brayne was a crisis that was not his own. If he followed the advice he usually gave to himself, what he would do about it was to investigate it as thoroughly as he could, come to whatever conclusions were professionally warranted, and otherwise leave the mess alone. It was not his responsibility to do now what the French police should have done then.

What made him uneasy about holding to this course

of action now was the presence of Gregor Demarkian among this group of guests. Kelly knew that Gregor Demarkian was going to be here for the weekend. His name, like all their names, had been on the guest list included with the formal invitations they had all received from Tasheba Kent and Cavender Marsh through Geraldine Dart. For some reason, Gregor Demarkian's name simply hadn't struck Kelly at that time. Of course, he realized now that it should have. Those invitations were not only formal but formalities. Everybody had been invited by telephone first, and their acceptances secured, before the invitations had gone out. That left the question of why Gregor Demarkian had been invited in the first place. The cover story was that Gregor Demarkian was only here as the companion of Bennis Hannaford, but Kelly Pratt didn't believe that. For one thing, Miss Dart had made it perfectly clear to him—and, he supposed, to everyone else—that "companions" of any kind were not welcome on this weekend. Tasheba Kent was an old woman, and too many people tired her out. For another thing, it was obvious to anybody with eyes that Gregor Demarkian and Bennis Hannaford were not "companions" in the sense that word was usually meant. Bennis Hannaford was not sexually attracted to Gregor Demarkian, and Gregor Demarkian was principally interested in the old lady lawyer. Kelly Pratt didn't understand that. Gregor Demarkian was a successful man. He was even a famous one. Kelly himself was neither so successful nor so famous, but since his divorce fifteen years ago he'd had relationships with a number of women, and they had all been under thirty-two. Why anybody who didn't have to would want to put up with a middle-aged nonentity like Lydia Acken was beyond Kelly's comprehension.

Kelly might still not have approached Gregor Demarkian, on the principle that he would only be borrowing trouble, except that it turned out to be so easy. Nobody had really had the heart for drinking liqueurs after Hannah Graham's little fit at dinner, especially after Hannah returned and insisted on talking the whole thing out over and over again. Everybody had been minimally polite for the least amount of time they could be. Then they had all drifted off to their rooms or to other parts of the house. Only Hannah Graham had remained in the living room, drinking mineral water on ice and getting sourer and more hostile by the minute.

That's a woman who would be much happier if she'd let herself drink something serious, Kelly Pratt told himself, watching Gregor Demarkian go into the library and begin to look over the things spread out on the tables. Lydia Acken had gone to bed and Bennis Hannaford had disappeared, so Demarkian was on his own for the first time in the evening. Kelly Pratt went to the library door. Demarkian stopped for a long time in front of the table with Lilith Brayne's things on it. He picked up shoes and fans and necklaces and put them down again. He picked up a vase and read what was written on the bottom of it.

Kelly Pratt couldn't help himself. "Is there something wrong?" he blurted out. "Is there something there that should be there?"

Gregor Demarkian looked around in astonishment. "I don't know. I was just wasting time."

Kelly Pratt blushed. "I thought you might be detecting something. You looked so intent. You almost looked angry."

Demarkian turned back to the table. "I was just trying to figure out why it is people buy things like these. They had so much stuff. Beads. Fans. Shoes. Handbags. It goes on and on and on. And what for?"

"I don't know," Kelly said.

"It's interesting to look at the differences in their taste, too," Demarkian said. "They were sisters. From what I understand, before the royal mess over Cavender Marsh, they were even fairly close. But they didn't begin to like the same things."

"They liked Cavender Marsh," Kelly pointed out.

Demarkian laughed. "That's true enough. And they both liked him too much, if you ask me. I don't understand the things people do for what they call love."

"I don't either," Kelly Pratt said. He was feeling much better now. There was something about the way Gregor Demarkian had laughed that had taken the sting out of him. In fact, Kelly couldn't remember now why he had thought that Gregor Demarkian was such a formidable and dangerous man. He really didn't look like much, once you got close to him. Tall. Broad. Running to fat. The face was a horror story. Big-nosed and almost painfully ethnic, it was the kind of face that any man with real ambition would have worked on these days. If Kelly Pratt had had that face, he would have signed himself into a clinic in Switzerland as soon as he was able to afford it.

Kelly walked over to the table of Lilith Brayne's things. Lilith Brayne seemed to have favored lilac and old rose in her personal life. The things on Tasheba Kent's table were much more of a piece: all black, all vampy and fussed up with beads and jet.

"So," Kelly Pratt said. "Tell me. Do you have any idea what really happened to Lilith Brayne?"

Gregor Demarkian sighed. "Don't tell me. You think I'm out here to investigate that, too."

"Well, you must be out here to investigate something. That's what you do."

"I also take vacations sometimes. I also take time off and read books. Sometimes I even write articles for law enforcement journals."

"You wouldn't want to take a vacation here. And you could read books anywhere. This place has terrible light."

"As far as I know, there isn't even any reason to question how Lilith Brayne died," Gregor Demarkian said. "We're talking about an investigation by a perfectly qualified police force that took place in 1938. It's not as if new evidence had leapt into public view that we now have to take account of. It's not as if we could go back and look at the evidence they had then, either. It's all finished and done with. There's no point in going on with it."

Kelly Pratt went over to the table with Cavender Marsh's things on it and looked at that for a minute.

"Tell me something," he said. "If somebody did have new evidence, or if they knew something nobody had noticed at the time, what would you tell them to do?"

"It would depend," Gregor Demarkian said.

"On what?"

"On what he wanted to use the new evidence for. You have to understand, right away, what you couldn't do with such evidence. Even if you were able to prove now, conclusively and without loopholes, what the police tried and failed to prove then—meaning that Cavender Marsh murdered his wife—you still wouldn't be able to do anything about Cavender Marsh. The man is almost eighty years old. Even if you could convince the French government to retry him, you couldn't convince the United States government to extradite him. And my guess is that it would be a billion-to-one against getting the French government to retry him, especially since the French government that tried him in the first place was the one that existed before the Nazi invasion, which is related only in theory to the one that exists now."

"You mean you think it would be a waste of time," Kelly Pratt said.

"Not necessarily," Gregor Demarkian said cautiously. "Sometimes, in old cases like these, there is someone—a son or daughter, a surviving spouse or a particularly close friend—who feels that advertising the truth of the case will clear the name of someone who was falsely accused or maliciously misrepresented. Sometimes corrections of that kind are absolutely necessary for the sake of justice."

"And in this case?"

Gregor Demarkian shrugged. "The death of Lilith Brayne was pronounced an accident, not a suicide. As far as I can tell, it was also Lilith Brayne whose reputation came out best after all the publicity. If you leave things just the way they are, Lilith Brayne looks good—and if you have something against Cavender Marsh, you don't have to go on with it either, because half the people who do read the story will be perfectly willing to believe that he killed his wife and got away with it without your producing any new evidence at all. The only reason I could see why anybody would want to fiddle with new evidence in this case—except for some disinterested third party who's decided to write a book about it and could use the publicity—well, the only reason to go on with it would be to try to clear Cavender Marsh once and for all, wouldn't it? And I can't think of a person on earth who would want to do that."

"No," Kelly said. "I couldn't either. That Hannah Graham wouldn't want to."

"Hardly."

Kelly Pratt fidgeted. "Well," he said, "what about just curiosity? Or being uncomfortable. What about knowing something that just makes you nervous?"

"Do you know something like that?" Gregor Demarkian asked.

Kelly Pratt nodded, reluctantly. "Yeah. Yeah, I do."

"And you want to tell it to me."

Gregor Demarkian was not feeling too keen about this. Kelly Pratt could tell. Everything about the man's body language said the intellectual and emotional fortifications were going up. Maybe Kelly had been wrong. Maybe Demarkian hadn't come up here to investigate the murder of Lilith Brayne after all.

Actually, it didn't really matter. Kelly Pratt had been bursting ever since he came across this information, and telling Bram Kahn about it had done nothing to relieve his distress. Gregor Demarkian was a professional. Gregor Demarkian might actually know what it was all this was supposed to mean.

"Look," Kelly Pratt burst out. "Back in 1938, one hundred thousand dollars was a hell of a lot of money."

CHAPTER 6

— 1 —

There were no telephones in the bedrooms at Tasheba Kent's house. There were no telephones anywhere in Tasheba Kent's house that Gregor could see, although he knew that there had to be at least one somewhere or, even better, a shortwave radio. You didn't run a house like this, way out in the middle of the ocean on a rock, with two very old people in it, without having some way of communicating with the standard emergency services. The only emergency service Gregor wanted to contact was his best friend, Father Tibor Kasparian, back on Cavanaugh Street in Philadelphia. Tibor was where Gregor went when the world got to be too much for him. Gregor had a feeling that Tasheba Kent's house was too much for him. The house and its inhabitants were a deliberate assault on reason. Even its guests were only half-sane. There was Lydia Acken, but there was also Kelly Pratt.

When Gregor finished listening to Kelly Pratt's chaotic and convoluted story, he went back into the living room and found it empty. Even Hannah Graham had disappeared, although she had left a wineglass full of ice and mineral water on the bare wood of the coffee table, where it was leaving a stain. Gregor put the glass back on the bar and went out into the foyer. It was empty, too. For the moment, the whole house seemed to be empty, and quiet and not quite dark. He looked up the great main staircase to the landing that led to the guest rooms on the left and the family rooms on the right. There was nobody up there, either, but the electrified chandelier was lit. It sent a cascade of light and shadow bouncing down the steps, looking atmospheric and not quite real.

It's this house, Gregor told himself in disgust. It looks like a movie set. And it's Geraldine Dart, too, and all that nonsense she was talking at dinner. I've started to spook myself. The next thing I know, I'll be seeing that idiotic ghost.

Gregor climbed the staircase with determination. At the landing, he stopped and looked into both of the bedroom wings. The hallways were empty and lit only by the dim wall fixtures placed between the third and fourth doors on each side of each corridor. No lights came from beneath the doors, but Gregor knew that didn't mean anything. This was an old house built by a rich man. The doors might fit so closely against their jambs, no light could escape.

Gregor went to Bennis Hannaford's bedroom door and knocked. There was the sound of a muffled "just a minute" and then a cascade of fluttering paper. Gregor heard Bennis say, "Oh, shit."

Bare feet padded across the room; the door opened. Bennis stuck her head out, saw Gregor, and looked relieved.

"Come on in," she said, stepping back. "I thought you were that idiotic Carlton."

Gregor came into the room. Bennis was in a pair of pajamas and one of his old terry cloth bathrobes. The galleys for her latest book had fallen off the bed and scattered across the floor. She sat down cross-legged in front of them and began to put them in order.

"Listen to that," she said. "Every time I hear the rumble of thunder in the distance, I think of Geraldine Dart, blithering away about how there's no way off this island if the weather is even a little out of sorts."

Bennis was right. There was thunder in the distance. Gregor hadn't noticed it before, but now that his attention

had been called to it, it was perfectly clear. He went to
Bennis's window and looked out. Her room faced the back
of the house, so there wasn't much he could see, but he did
catch a jagged bolt of lightning far in the distance.

Gregor sat down in the chair in front of Bennis's vanity table. Bennis was pitching her papers onto the bed. She
looked tousled and agitated and restless and tired.

"So," she said, throwing herself on the bed as well,
"what have you been up to? I've been trying to convince
the proofreader of this book that there's no such thing as a
'chaise lounge.'"

"You do that every book."

"I know, but I never win. I saw you captured by Kelly
Pratt. I'm sorry I didn't rescue you."

"I don't know if I'm sorry or not. He was telling me a
very interesting story, a kind of minor real-life logic problem. It was all about the death of Lilith Brayne, of course.

"Because that's all anybody around here ever talks
about," Gregor continued. "At least, that's all they ever
talk about to me. The more they talk, the more I remember about the case, or about things around the case, but
I'm still no expert. You should have warned me this was
going to happen. I would have boned up before we got
here. It would have been more entertaining for everybody
concerned. Including me."

"I didn't know what it was going to be like." Bennis
reached to her night table for her cigarettes, got one out
and lit it with a hot red plastic Bic lighter. Then she took a
deep drag and blew a cloud of smoke into the air. "If you
want to know what it's been like for me, it's been Carlton
Ji. That's not quite fair. He left me alone after dinner. But
still. And if it hasn't been Carlton Ji, it's been Hannah
Graham. She really is the most poisonous woman."

"I agree," Gregor said.

"Well, you should have heard her after dinner. I don't
know where she went after she stormed out, but she didn't
stay away much longer than it took us to retire to the
living room for liqueurs, and then all she could talk about
was her lawyer. Scaring somebody with false stories of the
supernatural was a tort, whatever that means—"

"It means something defined as wrong in law," Gregor said.

"Whatever. Anyway, what Geraldine Dart did to her was a tort and she could sue, and if Cavender Marsh had any sense at all—if you ask me, Gregor, this entire scene was played for the benefit of Cavender Marsh—where was I? Oh, yes. If Cavender Marsh had any sense, he'd make Geraldine Dart apologize. It was really awful and it was weird, too, like one of those conversations that are really taking place in code except you don't know how to decipher them. If you know what I mean."

"Not exactly," Gregor said drily.

Bennis sighed. "I don't know what I mean either, I guess, but you can imagine what it was like. Everybody went upstairs as quickly as they could, but I kept getting caught. I wish I could be like your friend the lawyer. She cut Hannah Graham off right in the middle of a sentence and said, 'Excuse me, I have to go to bed now.' And then she just left."

"I was in the library looking over the collection of things that are supposed to be auctioned. I don't know anything about the auction of this sort of thing, but I wouldn't think Halbard House would be interested in being part of it if it wasn't going to be profitable. It isn't what I expected, though. There are a lot of shoes."

"What did you think there would be?"

Gregor shrugged. "Jewelry. Expensive knickknacks of the kind people used to have all over their houses when I was younger, clocks in the bellies of Indian elephants and ashtrays made out of sharks' teeth welded together with gold. There's something good you can say about the '60s. It put a stop to all that."

"No, it didn't." Bennis shook her head. "You just stopped knowing people who indulged in it. If there were valuable things like that to sell—intrinsically valuable things, you know, because they had gold in them or precious gems—this would be a different kind of auction. It might not even be an auction."

"Maybe not. I still don't see why anybody is going to want to bid on a pair of 1920's curved-heeled high-heeled shoes with straps with big rhinestone butterflies on them going across the instep. I'm describing this badly. They were on Lilith Brayne's table. I kept trying to figure out how she managed to walk in them without the butterflies ripping the tops of her feet to shreds."

"I used to wear clogs when I was in college," Bennis said. "I tried some on a couple of months ago and I nearly broke my foot. I don't know how anybody ever walked in them, but I used to, and I don't remember it being much of a problem."

"I've always thought women had very peculiar feet," Gregor said.

Bennis had finished her cigarette. She stubbed the butt out in her glass ashtray and reached for her pack again. After months of going without, Gregor realized, she was now smoking exactly as she had before she had ever quit at all.

Bennis took a deep drag, blew a new stream of smoke into the air, and said, "I think when we get back to Philadelphia, I'm going to start a collection of pictures of all the weird and uncomfortable things men have worn for the sake of fashion over the years, and every time somebody like you tries to tell me how strange women are about clothes, I'm going to— What was that?"

That was a crack, sharp and harsh, like the sound of a two-by-four being broken in half. Gregor stood up, instinctively on the alert, and as he did the lights went out.

"Oh, damn," Bennis said irritably. "A power failure."

"I don't think so," Gregor told her.

The next thing they heard was another crack, this time stronger and closer, and then a high giggling cackle that seemed to rain down upon them from somewhere above their heads. Then there was a bright flash of lightning very close, followed by a clap of thunder loud enough to burst eardrums.

"Damn, damn, damn," Bennis said, more anxious now than irritable. "I hate electrical storms."

"Where are your candles?" Gregor asked her.

Bennis didn't answer. Gregor got up and looked around for them himself, on the vanity table, on the bookshelves near the door. He finally found a candelabra with three candlesticks in it on top of Bennis's bureau. He picked it up and walked it over to her, guided by the glowing tip of her cigarette.

"Here," he said. "Light these."

"Good idea." Bennis took the candelabra from him and used her Bic to get the candles lit. The light that resulted wasn't much to talk about, but it was something. Bennis handed the candelabra back to him. "Don't go away now, Gregor. Wait until the lights come back on. I really do hate electrical storms."

"We're both going to leave," Gregor said firmly. "Get up and follow me now."

"Why?"

The cackling came again, high-pitched and hysterical, piercing wood and glass until it seemed to fill up their ears.

"What the hell is that?" Bennis demanded.

"The *House on Haunted Hill*," Gregor said sarcastically. "Get up and get moving."

—— 2 ——

The rest were all out in the hall already, in various states of dress and undress. Some were holding candles. Some hadn't realized they had candles to hold. Gregor tried to sort them out and make sure they were all there, but in the darkness it was too confusing. He saw Lydia Acken in a nightgown and sedate blue kimono, and Kelly Pratt in a pair of designer jeans Gregor suspected he'd pulled on hastily over nothing at all. After that, the faces and bodies seemed to shift and meld and dissolve.

Above their heads, the cackling came again, much louder and clearer out here. Lydia Acken jumped and shivered.

"What is that?" she asked plaintively. "It sounds like the sound track from a horror movie."

"That's about it," Gregor said.

"You mean somebody is watching a horror movie around here somewhere?"

That was Richard Fenster, Gregor thought. Instead of answering him, Gregor went out onto the landing and across to the start of the family wing. The doors on this corridor were all closed, but as Gregor watched one of them opened. Geraldine Dart came out of it, holding a candelabra with six lit sticks and pulling the belt of her robe more tightly around her. She saw Gregor and nodded. Then she shut her bedroom door and came down the hall to the landing.

"I thought your ghost never said a word," Gregor told her.

"This isn't my ghost," Geraldine Dart replied. "This is nothing like my ghost."

Gregor decided to let it pass. The cackling giggle was shrieking through the house again, sounding ever louder but ever more banal. Gregor went back to the guest wing with Geraldine Dart in tow and said, "I think we'd better all go downstairs. It's not going to stop until we do what we're supposed to do."

"How do you know we're supposed to go downstairs?" Bennis demanded.

"Because downstairs is the only place we can go," Gregor said. "I suppose there's an upstairs—"

"Two more floors and an attic," Geraldine Dart said.

"Can we get up there?" Gregor asked her.

Geraldine Dart thought about it. "The doors to the wings up there on this staircase are all locked," she said, "and there's no access to the attic from here. There are a back family staircase and a servants' staircase. They both have access to the attic. I don't know what's locked on them and what isn't. We never use those staircases anymore."

"I wouldn't want to go upstairs anyway," Mathilda Frazier said. Her voice was shaky. "That—that noise is coming from up there."

The noise came again, almost hiccuping now. Gregor saw Lydia Acken shiver again.

"The point," he told them, "is that we're *supposed* to investigate. It's not going to stop until we have investigated. We really can't go up, it's much too complicated, so we'll have to go down."

"But what will we find when we investigate?" Kelly Pratt asked.

"Nothing in particular," Gregor said. "It's a game

more than anything else. I wonder if that security guard went home or if he's sleeping in the house."

"He's sleeping in the chauffeur's apartment over the garage," Geraldine Dart said. "He got off at eleven o'clock, but we couldn't get him back to the mainland. The storm had already started by then."

"You mean there's a storm?" Mathilda Frazier sounded truly frightened. "You mean we can't get out of here?"

"It's just temporary," Geraldine Dart said irritably. "This isn't Alcatraz."

Lightning flashed past the window at the end of the hall, illuminating them all for just a second. Then the thunder hit in a rolling sharp slap. Kelly Pratt jumped a little and squealed. Mathilda Frazier rubbed the palms of her hands against the sides of her arms. Bennis lit another cigarette.

Gregor thought it was too bad that the security man wasn't in the house. He could have used the help of someone who had not been subjected to Geraldine Dart's ghost stories. Or maybe he had. Maybe Geraldine Dart told these ghost stories in Hunter's Pier and everywhere else she went. Maybe they were her preferred form of entertainment.

The cackle came again. It did a crescendo that sounded calculated and false. In the middle it suddenly switched out of soprano and into bass.

"Oh, wonderful," Richard Fenster muttered. "Something new."

"Two ghosts." Mathilda Frazier giggled, almost hysterical. "Isn't that just what we need? *Two* ghosts."

Gregor touched Geraldine Dart on the arm. "You don't happen to have a flashlight anywhere around, do you?"

"Downstairs in the kitchen," Geraldine said.

"You don't keep one in your own room?"

"No," Geraldine said. "No, I don't."

"Funny," Gregor said. "I would have thought power failures were a fairly frequent occurrence in a place like this."

Geraldine Dart started to explain herself. Then the

cackle rang out again, and she stopped. Gregor Demarkian ignored both Geraldine and the cackle.

"Come on," he told the whole group of them. "Let's go downstairs and get this over with."

—— 2 ——

They went in a body with Gregor at the head, like a group of kindergarten children being herded around a museum by a teacher. They went down the stairs into the foyer and looked around. There was nothing there, of course. If there had been, they could have seen it from the top of the stairs. They went into the living room and looked around there, too, but as Gregor had suspected, there was nothing there to find. Their candles cast odd shadows on the walls, and all the birthday decorations looked sinister, but that was only to be expected. The way things were right now, Gregor thought, an episode of *Leave It to Beaver* would have looked sinister.

Gregor picked up one of the smiley faces and turned it over in his hands, but it was just what it had been before, quilted crepe paper and cardboard. Nobody had slashed it up with a knife or painted it with blood or sprayed it with poison. He put it down again and picked up a silver table lighter. It wasn't a piece he had noticed before, but he couldn't see anything special about it, so he put that down, too. The cackle started up again, but it seemed muffled and remote down here. Nobody looked as nervous as they had before.

"What are we supposed to be doing down here?" Richard Fenster asked. "Is this some kind of treasure hunt? Are we supposed to be discovering something?"

"We're supposed to be making idiots of ourselves in a very public manner," Gregor told him. Then he turned to Geraldine Dart. "Why don't you go get us those flashlights now? We're going to need them if we ever intend to get the power back on."

"You mean you want to go down to the basement to fuss with the fuse box right now?" Geraldine asked.

"No, not right now," Gregor said. "Right now I'm

going to go looking around in the library, which is the next logical place to look."

"Oh," Geraldine said. "I don't know if I could let you do that."

"Don't be stupid," Kelly Pratt said. "You said that guard went off duty at eleven. It's got to be nearly one now. Any one of us could have come down here in the last two hours and stolen every single piece on those tables."

"Well," Geraldine Dart said.

"It's too bad you don't keep a flashlight in your bedside table," Gregor said blandly.

Geraldine Dart blushed. "All right," she told him. "I'm going. I'll be right back. But for God's sake, don't touch anything."

Geraldine half ran out of the room, heading toward the foyer, and Gregor found himself shaking his head. Then the cackle started up again, and he sighed.

"The *House on Haunted Hill,*" Gregor said again.

"That's the name of a movie," Bennis told him.

"I know," he said. "You've watched it at least three times in my presence, with Donna Moradanyan and Tibor. You ought to pay more attention."

"You mean that laugh we hear is from a movie?"

"From a tape made from the movie, I think. Somebody just got a tape recorder and recorded all those laughs at the beginning and the end over and over. Can't you hear that thing repeating itself?"

The cackle came again. Everybody was still. Finally, Richard Fenster said, "He's right. It is repeating itself."

"But who would do something like that?" Lydia Acken demanded. "It's terrible. And those two old people upstairs. They could be frightened into strokes."

"I don't think so," Gregor said. "In fact, I think they're probably in on it. That's why they haven't come downstairs yet."

"If this is some kind of setup and they really are in on it," Mathilda said, "there's going to be some serious trouble."

"But why would they do something like that?" Lydia asked. "Why? What's the point of all this?"

Gregor had a few ideas as to the why and wherefore

of all of this, but they were complicated. Instead of answering Lydia's question, he went into the library. It was as unchanged as the living room had been, which was what he had expected. He left it and came back to the rest of them.

"All right," he said. "I think we can be confident that we've done everything that we could be expected to do. The lights ought to come back on any minute now."

"This is incredible," Kelly Pratt said.

Gregor thought this was more than incredible. He thought it was execrable. As soon as they all calmed down, he was going to get Geraldine Dart in a corner and take her apart at the seams. He would do the same to Tasheba Kent and Cavender Marsh, but he was afraid that the sound of his voice at full volume would frighten them to death. They deserved to be frightened to death, he thought. This was the worst kind of practical joke. And it wasn't funny.

Above their heads and on the side tables, the lights flickered. Gregor had forgotten that he had left them all on when he had come to bed. He checked his watch and saw that it was one fifteen. There was nothing more in the way of hysterical, sinister cackles.

"There," he said, when the lights stopped flickering and came fully on. "That's the end of that. I think we can probably all go to bed now."

"You go. I'm going to have a drink." Mathilda Frazier sounded irritated.

Then Geraldine Dart came running into the room, carrying a handful of flashlights and completely out of breath.

"I did it," she exclaimed triumphantly. "I went all the way down to the basement by myself and changed the fuses, all by myself. What do you think of that?"

Gregor was about to say that it was the least he would have expected of her, but at that moment a woman's voice came at them from out in the foyer, and it stopped him dead.

"Ger-ald-ine?" the voice called out in a singsong. "Ger——al——dine?"

"Isn't that Miss Kent?" Bennis asked uncertainly.

Geraldine Dart looked suddenly scared to death. "Yes,

that is Miss Kent," she said in a panicky voice. "But I don't understand—"

"Ger——al——dine," Tasheba Kent sang out again.

Geraldine Dart rushed out of the room, dropping the flashlights as she went. Gregor followed her. He was followed in turn by the rest of them, led by Bennis. Gregor stopped in the foyer and looked up the stairs. Tasheba Kent had come about a third of the way down from the second floor, and she was still coming. She was dressed in a royal purple negligee with ruffles down the front and royal purple slippers. Her black wig had been pulled haphazardly over her white hair so that it looked like some kind of a lunatic hat. Geraldine Dart seemed frozen at the foot of the stairs. Gregor Demarkian didn't think he had ever seen anyone look that green.

"Ger——al——diiiiiiiine," Tasheba Kent sang out in a long wailing hum.

Then she blinked, and seemed to shrivel. Then she fell. At first she just collapsed against the steps and stayed put. Then she started to roll.

"Oh, my God," Geraldine Dart said. "Oh, my God. She's going to break her neck."

Gregor Demarkian was running for the stairs before he knew it. So was Kelly Pratt. They pushed Geraldine Dart out of the way and bounded up toward Tasheba Kent. They reached out to stop the old woman rolling. She slipped past their hands and went slamming into their legs. Kelly Pratt lost his balance and staggered backward. Gregor had to twist himself into knots to keep his place. He reached out to stop the top half of Tasheba Kent's body from rolling any farther down the stairs. The bottom half of her was braced against his legs. He got her by the head and felt her wig come off in his hands. Then he reached out and grabbed her again, and this time he got what was left of her skull.

What was *left* of her skull.

Gregor dropped Tasheba Kent's head and stepped back a little. Geraldine Dart started to scream.

"Oh, my God, oh, my God, oh, my God," Geraldine Dart said.

Gregor leaned down and turned Tasheba Kent's head

over, so that he could get a better look at what had happened to her.

As far as he could tell, someone had taken a large round heavy object and caved in the entire left side of her head.

PART 2

THE
DEMONOLOGY
OF ICE CREAM

CHAPTER 1

— 1 —

Gregor knew he had been wrong, terribly wrong, about everything that was going on in this house. It had all seemed so simple, and now this woman was lying against his legs, bloody and dead, and nothing made any sense at all. Outside, he could hear the wind. It was whistling through the roof gutters and making windows rattle. Inside, Mathilda Frazier had started crying in a low, steady, unrelentless way. Bennis Hannaford was patting her ineffectually on the back and looking helpless.

Gregor stepped away from the body. It had come to rest. It wasn't going to roll anymore.

"The first thing we need to do," he said in a calm, measured voice, "is to find a phone."

"Right," Kelly Pratt burst in. "That's what we need. We need the police."

"But we're not going to be able to get the police over here tonight," Geraldine Dart objected. "The storm will make it impossible."

"Don't be ridiculous," Kelly Pratt snapped. "It's not much of a storm at all."

Mathilda Frazier began to cry harder. "It's just like she said before. It doesn't have to be much of a storm. All you need is a little rain and wind, and then you're *trapped.*"

"Could we at least have some more light in here?" Gregor asked.

This, it turned out, was easy. The chandelier at the top of the stairs was on a dimmer and could be turned up. There were bracket lights on the wall next to the rising staircase. When these were turned on, Gregor knelt down next to the body. He was not a pathologist. There could be a hundred things here he was bound to miss because he didn't know what to look for. He knew he had to look now, as closely as he could, because if he didn't he might not be allowed to look once the police arrived on the scene. Even without being a pathologist, the situation looked relatively simple. The crater on the side of Tasheba Kent's head was at least three inches in diameter and irregularly shaped. Gregor guessed it had been made by a golf club or something like it, with a long handle for leverage and a round thick metal or wooden piece at the end.

A check of Tasheba Kent's body and face revealed little. The one really disturbing thing was the wig. The old woman had taken her makeup off before she went to bed. There were no bright red and black blotches anywhere on her wrinkled face. Even the blood in the crater was going dirty brown. Underneath the wig, Tasheba Kent's hair was thick but very white, with that tinge of hard dark yellow the hair of old people sometimes gets. The wig, though. Gregor tapped his fingers against the stair rail, bothered. The wig just did not make sense.

"She put it on after she was hit," Gregor said suddenly.

"What?" Bennis asked him.

"The wig," Gregor explained. "She put it on after she was hit. That's the only way it makes sense. She was very careful about her appearance. She overdid her makeup and she wore clothes that were much too young for her, but she was careful. She would never have put a wig on that way, half on and half off, without looking at it in the mirror and checking the fit, and rearranging it if she had to."

"Maybe she did check the fit," Richard Fenster said

doubtfully. "She was a hundred years old. Maybe she looked in the mirror and her eyes weren't any good, and she thought it did fit."

"If that's what she did, she would have had to have lost her sense of touch as well as her sight. There's a good three-inch gap between where the wig ends and where her hair ends on the side without the gash, and the wig hasn't been pulled into the gash on the side with it. Did she sleep in a bedroom by herself?" he asked Geraldine Dart. "Or did she share a bedroom with Cavender Marsh?"

Geraldine Dart looked totally confused. "She shares a bedroom with Cavender. What difference does that make?"

Gregor stood up. Tasheba Kent started to roll again. He leaned over and caught her. He wished they could move her into the living room or the dining room or any-place else where she might stay still, but he knew they couldn't do that. The police would want everything in place when they arrived.

Gregor stepped carefully over the body—it made him wince, but there was nothing else he could do—and started up the stairs again.

"Miss Dart," he called back over his shoulder. "Come up here with me. I need you to show me which of those bedrooms belongs to Tasheba Kent and Cavender Marsh."

At first, Geraldine Dart protested. "You don't want to wake him up out of a sound sleep for something like this," she protested, running up the stairs at Gregor's back. "You'll give him a stroke. We need to find a way to break this to him gently."

"Don't worry," Gregor told her. "I don't think we're going to have to break it to him at all tonight."

Gregor reached the landing. Geraldine Dart rushed by him and went to a door in the middle of the left-hand wall. When she opened this, Gregor thanked her, passed inside the room, and looked around. The room was dark. The curtains that covered the windows on one wall were faintly backlit, as if there was a security light outside but not too close. The big dark bed had a canopy and a set of curtains but was otherwise a series of black lumps in the dark. Gregor reached around on the wall until he found the light switch and flicked it on. A chandelier almost the size of the one that hung over the foyer burst into light, lighting the room as cruelly as a movie set.

"Mr. Demarkian," Geraldine Dart protested.

"Gregor? Gregor, what's going on?" That was Bennis, coming in from the hallway. The rest of them were out there, too, moving around in a clump, because they were afraid to be alone. Gregor ignored them all.

He went over to the side of the bed closest to the door and looked down on the sleeping Cavender Marsh. The old man was tucked neatly under a top sheet and a pale blue blanket, both pristinely folded back and as unwrinkled as if they had been covering a doll. There was no doubt, however, that Cavender Marsh was breathing. His chest rose and fell rhythmically. His nose emitted a high-pitched, highly polite little snore.

"Why hasn't he woken up?" Geraldine Dart asked anxiously. "Is he in a coma?"

"Of course he isn't in a coma," Gregor said. "He's just asleep. He probably took a sleeping pill."

"Mr. Marsh doesn't take sleeping pills," Geraldine Dart said.

"Then somebody gave him one, or more likely two or three." Gregor went around to the other side of the bed.

At first, Gregor didn't see anything unusual. The bed-clothes were more rumpled there than they had been on Cavender Marsh's side, but any bedclothes anywhere would have been. Gregor Demarkian had never seen anyone sleep with such perfect lack of movement as Cavender Marsh was displaying tonight. On Tasheba Kent's side, the blanket was twisted and the top sheet was pushed down under it. Gregor pulled up the top sheet and untwisted the blanket and examined them both. They were clean. The pillow was wadded into a ball. Gregor unwadded it and found that it was perfectly clean, too. He almost thought he had been wrong in his conjectures, but then, as he was drawing his head out from between the bed-curtains, he caught sight of the ruffled border around the canopy over his head. Just at the start of the first curve, the border was soaked in blood.

"Oh, God," Geraldine Dart said. "Oh, God, it's still wet. How did it get like that?"

"She probably brushed against it as she was getting out of bed," Gregor said.

"Do you mean she was already bleeding when she got out of bed? How could she have been?"

"Very easily," Gregor said. "People do a great deal after they've had a head trauma, even if they're the next best thing to technically dead. She was sitting up when she was hit, though. If she'd been lying down, there would be blood all over the pillowcase and the sheets."

"Sitting up," Geraldine Dart repeated. "I don't believe that. You didn't know Tasheba Kent, Mr. Demarkian. A hundred years old or no hundred years old, she wouldn't have sat there and let somebody come at her with a poker—"

"Not a poker."

"—or whatever it was. She just wouldn't have."

"All right, she wouldn't have," Gregor said, "so that isn't what she did. She sat up in bed and listened to this person talk, and when she wasn't expecting it this person whipped out a weapon and coshed her on the head. Then she started acting very strangely."

"You mean she put on the wig," Bennis said, edging closer.

Gregor checked the wall behind the place where Tasheba Kent's pillow had been. There was a faint stain there that might have been fresh blood. He wasn't going to know for sure until he got some lab technicians to check it out. He walked away from the bed and looked at the carpet next to it. There were no stains there, but a little farther along, near the bed's foot, there was an unmistakable red splotch. They would have to check the nightgown under Tasheba Kent's negligee. There had certainly been no splotch of blood on the negligee. That meant that Tasheba Kent not only hadn't been wearing it in bed—interesting enough, Gregor thought, if she had been talking to a visitor—but hadn't been wearing it when she went to her vanity table, either. Gregor was sure that Tasheba Kent had been going to her vanity table. There was an empty wig stand there.

Gregor traced Tasheba Kent's possible path around the bed to the vanity table, but didn't find any bloodstains. He sat down at the vanity table and looked over the jars and implements without really knowing what most of them were. There weren't any bloodstains there, either. The wig stand was different. There was a big red-brown smear on the back of it, at the place on a person that would have been the start of the nape of the neck. Gregor got a Kleenex out of his pocket to protect the stand from his fingerprints and picked it up. Then he put the stand down again and sighed. Everything he saw confirmed the conjectures he had made downstairs about what had happened up here tonight, but it was impossible to get any really important information out of physical evidence without the help of the lab technicians.

"Tell me," he said, turning to Geraldine Dart, "what time did she come up here tonight?"

"Time? I don't know if I could pinpoint a time. It was right after dinner. Maybe nine thirty or ten o'clock."

"It was ten minutes to ten when we all went into the living room," Bennis said. "I checked my watch."

Gregor nodded. "Now, Miss Dart. Tasheba Kent didn't come up to her room alone."

"No, no, of course not," Geraldine Dart said. "I brought her up here myself. I used the elevator at the back of the foyer."

"And you settled her down to sleep."

"I helped her to get ready for bed and then I gave her her glasses and the book she's been reading. Miss Kent always read a little before she went to bed. Of course, she didn't read very well anymore. She could barely see words on a page. But she'd read a paragraph or two every night."

"Glasses," Gregor repeated.

He left the vanity table and went back to Tasheba Kent's side of the bed, but there was no mystery about the glasses. They were on the bedside table next to the lamp, neatly folded up and unstained by blood or anything else. Gregor went back to the vanity table.

"After you got her ready for bed, what did you do?" he asked Geraldine Dart.

"I came downstairs to see that everything was going all right in the living room."

"And was it?"

Geraldine shrugged. "Hannah Graham was back. I don't know where she'd gone to when she walked out on dinner, but she was back. She had Cavender cornered and she was railing at him, so I had to pry the two of them apart."

"Did Cavender Marsh go to bed then?" Gregor asked.

Geraldine shook her head. "He went and talked to Richard Fenster for a while. Cavender doesn't like to go to bed early. He says it makes him feel like a hick."

"Did he seem all right to you at that point?"

"Yes, he did, Mr. Demarkian, but I didn't stay long after that. Cavender doesn't need to be helped to bed in the same way Tasheba does—did. And I was tired. I made sure everybody had something to drink and knew where to get more, and then I went up to bed."

"What about you?" Gregor asked Bennis.

"I finished my liqueur and went up to bed," she said. "That was later than you'd think. Almost quarter to eleven. I was talking to Mathilda about buying books at auction. If it hadn't been for Hannah Graham, I think we both would have stayed longer. We were having a very interesting conversation."

"What did Hannah Graham do?"

Bennis made a face. "She behaved like Hannah Graham," she said. "She's impossible, Gregor, really. She's the *most* abusive woman."

"Practically the only way you could get away from her last night was to go into the library," Geraldine said. "I told her at one point that she might want to look over her mother's things, that Cavender wouldn't be averse to her having some of them, and she acted as if I'd just threatened to poison her. She didn't follow you when you went in there, either. And I know she wanted to talk to you."

The idea that Hannah Graham had wanted to talk to him—and might still want to talk to him—was not a comforting thought, but Gregor put it firmly out of his mind for the moment.

"Do either of you remember Cavender Marsh going to bed?" he asked the two women.

Both Geraldine Dart and Bennis Hannaford shook their heads.

"Do either of you remember him acting at all strangely? Suddenly and overwhelmingly tired? Or as if it seemed he'd had too much to drink when you knew he hadn't."

Both women shook their heads again.

Gregor got up and went to the door of the bedroom to look out on the hall. They were there, standing in a little knot under the dim glow of the bracket lights, looking sullen and afraid. Richard Fenster was drinking out of a hip flask and leaning against the wall. Lydia Acken was standing very erect, with her arms wrapped around her waist. Her skin looked powdered gray.

"All right," he said. "I know that this is a little unusual, but we're going to be stuck out here alone for a little while, and I'd like to get a few things straight before the police arrive. Does anybody here mind answering a couple of questions?"

"I mind," Hannah Graham said belligerently.

Mathilda Frazier let out a sharp bark of anger. "Oh, for God's sake. Why do you always have to cause trouble for everybody in your vicinity? Why can you never cooperate about anything?"

"I'm not causing trouble," Hannah said. "I'm just sticking up for myself. He doesn't have any right to ask us questions."

"I'd rather have him ask me questions than have a cop ask me questions," Richard Fenster said. "I'd rather have him investigating this murder, too. He doesn't have any kind of ax to grind."

"It doesn't matter if the police ask you questions, because you don't have to answer them," Hannah Graham shot back. "Any decent lawyer could tell you that. You don't have to tell the police a thing."

"No, you don't," Kelly Pratt said, "but they can punish you for that. They can make it very hard for you to leave the state. They can let things leak to the media—and oh, God, how this one is going to attract the media. Like blood attracts sharks."

"Don't be ridiculous." Hannah Graham looked momentarily uneasy. "The media aren't going to care one way or the other about this. She was just a has-been old movie star. She hasn't been in the public eye in years."

"She wasn't just a has-been old movie star," Richard Fenster said. "She was once the most famous woman in America. And she was involved in one of the most famous murder investigations of the century. And now she's been murdered herself."

"My mother died by accident," Hannah Graham said. "That's what all the papers said at the time. That's what the police decided."

"It was still a murder investigation, even if it wasn't a murder," Richard Fenster said. "There is going to be a mess when this gets out. People go out of their way to get this man to handle their messes, and here he is right in the middle of this one and willing to do it for free. Why shouldn't we take advantage of his being here?"

Hannah Graham had been standing at the very far edge of the group, a little behind where Mathilda Frazier was seated on the floor. Now she moved forward until she was standing right in front of Richard Fenster and flicked a finger at his hip flask.

"I don't have to talk to anyone I don't want to talk to," she said. "And I'm not going to, no matter what you say. And besides, I don't think he's such a great detective. If he were, he wouldn't be questioning us. He'd be out looking for Carlton Ji."

"What?" Gregor said.

Hannah whirled around, triumphant. "Carlton Ji," she said again. "You remember. The odious little Chinaman. Well, he isn't here. And he hasn't been here. He didn't come downstairs with us when the screaming started. He didn't come down later, either. And he was gone before that. He wasn't with the rest of us in the living room after dinner."

"Maybe he was in the library," Gregor said.

"He wasn't while I was there," Richard Fenster said

thoughtfully. "And I was there for a good half an hour. The only other person who came in was Lydia Acken."

"He wasn't there while I was there," Lydia said. "And he wasn't in the living room just after dinner, either, Mrs. Graham is right about that."

"I didn't see him, either," Kelly Pratt said.

"I saw him *right* after dinner," Geraldine Dart said. "He *was* in the library for at least a minute or two. Then I don't know what happened to him."

"Don't ask me," Bennis told Gregor. "I never saw him at all."

Hannah Graham's triumph had grown into something bigger and worse. She was afire with self-righteousness and self-justification.

"There!" she exclaimed. "There! Didn't I tell you. He disappeared right after dinner, and the Great Detective didn't even notice. I don't think this man is anything but a lot of hype in *People* magazine, and I'm not going to answer his questions no matter what any of the rest of you say. And I'm not afraid of the local police either. Tasheba Kent is dead and Carlton Ji is missing, and I say all anybody has to do to solve this case is find out where the little bastard has gone. I'll bet he's halfway to San Francisco by now."

—— 2 ——

Carlton Ji couldn't be halfway to San Francisco by now. Gregor Demarkian knew that. The timing wasn't right. At least, Carlton Ji couldn't have gotten off the island if he was in fact what Hannah Graham believed he was, the murderer of Tasheba Kent. A woman with a head wound that severe might be able to walk around for as long as five or six full minutes before collapsing, but after that it would have been impossible. Tasheba Kent had to have been struck in the head just about the moment that eerie cackling laughter had started. She might have been struck by Geraldine Dart or by Carlton Ji or by one of the people who had gathered in the hall and on the landing while the racket was going on, but whoever had struck her had not then gotten off this island. The storm was going full blast. There would have been no way for the murderer to have gotten off.

Still, Carlton Ji was missing. There was no doubt about that. They went to his room and found it empty. His bed hadn't been slept in and his suitcase, although rummaged through, hadn't been unpacked. Gregor didn't think the rummaging had been a search job. It looked more like the kind of thing someone would do when he was looking for a clean pair of socks. They checked all the other bedrooms, too, just in case Carlton Ji had wandered off and fallen asleep and not been woken by all the subsequent noise. They checked the bedroom closets, too, and any containers—a steamer trunk in Geraldine Dart's room; an oversize wardrobe in a guest room in the family wing—big enough to hide a body. Then they checked the rooms downstairs. They looked behind the living room couch. They looked under the tables in the library where the things for the auction were kept. They even opened the sideboard in the dining room.

"There are those other floors," Bennis told Gregor, after they'd failed to find either Carlton Ji or any trace of Carlton Ji anywhere else in the house. "Maybe we'd better try those."

"I think we're going to have to," Gregor agreed, "but I don't see how we're going to do it tonight. We're all exhausted. Christ, I wish we could get hold of the police."

"I wish we could, too. Do you think Carlton Ji killed Tasheba Kent?"

"I don't know."

"Do you think he's dead?"

"I don't know that either."

The storm thundered overhead. "I don't like this," Bennis said. "I've never heard you be so uncertain. Usually when I ask you questions like this, you tell me it's perfectly obvious what happened and if I just used my head, I could figure it all out for myself."

Gregor let Bennis go back to looking around the dining room and went out into the foyer. From there he could see Lydia Acken making her way down the utility hallway to the kitchen, hesitantly opening door after door and peering inside. Every time she opened a door, she seemed to shudder. Every time she closed one she looked relieved. Gregor went up to her and tapped her on the shoulder.

"Oh," she said, jumping. "Oh, I'm sorry. I didn't mean to squeak. I've just been looking in these closets, and every time I open a door I'm just sure I'm going to find—well, and then there's another one, you know, another hallway like this, on the other side of the house. I don't think I'm going to be able to stand it."

"You don't have to search the other hallway as well as this one," Gregor told her. "You can let somebody else do that. Are these all closets?"

Lydia laughed thinly. "They're all specialty closets. You wouldn't believe it. There's one with nothing but baseball equipment in it. There's another one with nothing but rubber rain boots. This is an incredible place."

Gregor opened the next door down and found a closet full of sets of flatware. They were stacked in boxes on the floor and the shelves. He opened the next door after that and found what appeared to be chauffeurs' uniforms, all separated neatly into sizes. Lydia Acken laughed again.

"Oh, dear," she said, somewhat shrilly. "Oh, dear. Do you think the two of them were insane? Or do you think these things were left over from a previous tenant? What would anybody want with so many chauffeurs' uniforms?"

"I think I want to give up on these closets for a minute and go look into the kitchen," Gregor said. "Do you want to come with me? We can get back to this hall later."

"I want to come with you," Lydia Acken said quickly.

Gregor motioned her along the hallway and they went, Lydia staying just a little behind, as if she were sure a lion was going to jump out at them, and she didn't want to be in the way of an attack. In spite of the fact that Gregor had said what he'd said about the closets, he looked in a couple more of them as they went along. One was full of old books that had not been cared for and smelled of mildew. One was full of plastic cat feeder dishes. They came to a heavy swinging door and Gregor pushed it open. Beyond it was a brightly lit room that was obviously a kitchen, but so large and well-equipped it could have served a small hotel.

"Here we are," Gregor said—and then he saw it, stuck to the wall next to the refrigerator, a perfectly ordinary everyday plastic phone. Gregor couldn't remember another time in his life when he had been this relieved. He couldn't remember another time in his life when he had been this desperate to get in contact with the local police.

"Just a minute," he told Lydia Acken.

He strode across the room to the phone and picked up the receiver. He dialed 0 for Operator and stood back to wait. A few seconds later he hit the disconnect bar and started all over again.

The reason it took so long for Gregor to realize what was going on was due to his own disbelief. It was such a cliché, he was sure that it couldn't have happened. It was such an obvious next step in the drama, he was positive that no self-respecting twentieth-century murderer would have indulged in it. It was the kind of thing that happened in books but never in real life to real people with real things to worry about—except, of course, that it had.

The phone was dead.

CHAPTER 2

— 1 —

The phone cord had been cut at the side of the house just outside the kitchen window. Somebody had climbed up onto the sink and leaned out the window there to get at it, using a smooth-edged slicing blade from the knife rack and leaving it—the blade covered with bits of black rubber—on the drainboard when the job was through. This was not the worst of what was going on. It was just the thing that upset Geraldine Dart the most. For some reason, unlike the bloody death of Tasheba Kent, unlike the sight of Cavender Marsh in his peaceful uninterruptable sleep, the slashed phone cord made it clear to Geraldine that everything had now gone permanently and irretrievably wrong.

It was almost dawn by the time they were all able to go upstairs, and even then Geraldine had to herd them there. She would have left them alone if Gregor Demarkian had asked her to. She was glad he didn't, because the thought of the bunch of them loose in the downstairs rooms of this house made her skin crawl. One of them had smashed something round and heavy into the side of Tasheba Kent's head—or Carlton Ji had, and to Geraldine that amounted to the same thing. One of them had given Cavender Marsh a lot of sleeping pills and cut the cord on the phone, too. Then there was the record, which had been played much too loud and much too long. Somebody must have gotten into the pantry and changed the settings.

If there was one thing Geraldine wanted to do, it was to go into the pantry and get a good look at the CD machine. She had already been in the pantry once since Tasheba Kent died—ostensibly to check for Carlton Ji or Carlton Ji's corpse—but with the way things had been then, she had barely had a chance to notice that the machine was, in fact, still there, never mind whether its volume control was up or if it had been set to replay. It was just about that time that the Demarkian man had discovered that the phone was out. Then everybody had gone running into the kitchen, hysterical and angry, and she had had to follow them. She hadn't wanted to appear conspicuous. She hadn't been hysterical then, because she hadn't expected the lines to be cut. She had only thought that the phone lines were down between the island and the mainland. That happened without the need of outside interference at least once a month.

The Demarkian man seemed to have forgotten all about the ghostly laughter of the beginning of this evening. For that, Geraldine was more than grateful. She knew she would have to explain it to somebody sometime. If she didn't talk to Gregor Demarkian, she would have to talk to Dick Morrow, who served as sheriff for Hunter's Pier, or to the state police. She didn't want to talk tonight, while she was tired and upset and hadn't had a chance to think.

Outside, the storm was really turning into something special. That hadn't been in the forecast. Geraldine had been checking the forecasts all week. The worst she had heard was that they were supposed to get "a little rain" on Thursday night. This was more like the start of a wet-weather nor'easter, complete with howling winds and rain that turned unexpectedly to hail, pelting the windows and the side of the house with round hard balls. This house was so solidly built, it was possible not to notice that the weather out there was awful. You had to really listen to hear the hail. Geraldine was the only one who was really listening. The rest of them, she could see, thought things were going to get better when the sun came up.

Which it would, of course. It was just that the sun might not come up until Saturday afternoon.

Geraldine had gotten them all to the second floor. Now she shooed them in the direction of the guest wing.

"I'm not going to set up breakfast until nine o'clock," she told them. "Nobody is going to want to eat before then. You should all go to bed and get some rest."

"Rest," Mathilda Frazier said. "Oh, God."

"I'm not just going to lock my door, I'm going to bolt it, and I'm going to put a chair in front of it, too," Hannah Graham declared. "I'm sure I'm not going to be able to get any sleep. How can I know that this house isn't full of secret passageways?"

"Of course it isn't full of secret passageways," Geraldine said wearily. "It's just a house."

"It's going to be a house with a lien on it to pay the fees from a lawsuit when I'm through," Hannah Graham said.

"I don't think you're ever going to be through," Bennis Hannaford told her. "I'm going to go to bed."

"I'm going to bed, too," Mathilda Frazier said.

"We aren't going to make any sense until we get a little sleep," Kelly Pratt said.

Hannah glared at the rest of them in contempt. Then she stalked away, down the hall to the door at the end, which belonged to her bedroom. Maybe we should have put her in the family wing, Geraldine thought. She rejected the idea. Hannah Graham might be related by blood to Cavender Marsh and Tasheba Kent both, but in every spiritual sense the woman belonged to another species.

"I'm going to go to bed myself," Geraldine said. "I'll set my alarm and get up at quarter to nine. I'll have breakfast on the sideboard for anybody who wants it. Don't feel you have to get up."

Mathilda Frazier looked down the stairs. "I wish we could move her. I know all about . . . not tampering with the evidence and all that, but . . . I wish we could move her."

"I do, too," Geraldine said gently. "But Mr. Demarkian says not, and Mr. Demarkian is the only one of us who knows what he's doing around here. Go to bed now?"

Mathilda Frazier nodded, and the rest of them took their cue from her. Even Gregor Demarkian began drifting obediently off. Geraldine watched until all of them were safely in their rooms. Then she turned away and went into the family wing.

The first thing she did was to stop in and look at Cavender. He was lying exactly as they had left him, perfectly still and on his back. His chest was rising and falling in even, rhythmic sweeps. He seemed to have a smile on his face. Gregor Demarkian had said there was nothing to worry about. Cavender wasn't exhibiting the symptoms of true coma or showing signs of going into respiratory failure. If anything, according to Demarkian, he was exhibiting admirable fitness of lung and heart, especially considering the fact that he'd been smoking cigars since he was nineteen years old. Geraldine trusted Demarkian, but she wanted to check anyway. Demarkian was a detective, not a doctor. There were probably a lot of things about the human body he didn't know.

Cavender was fine. Even standing right next to him, Geraldine couldn't find anything, no matter how small, to worry about. There was no hitch in his breath. When she laid her ear on the covers above his chest, she heard no murmur or stumble in his heart. Stop being ridiculous, she told herself. You're just trying to postpone the inevitable.

It was true, too. The last thing Geraldine Dart wanted to do right now was to walk back down those stairs past Tasheba Kent's body, but it had to be done. She left Cavender Marsh's room and went out into the hall, but she didn't turn toward her own bedroom door. She went out to the landing and looked into the guest wing. Everything seemed to be quiet over there, perfectly silent, dead. All the doors were closed and no lights were showing under them, even in the two cases where Geraldine knew the doors were out of true.

Geraldine went down the stairs, quickly at first, then slowing down as she got near the bottom. Tasheba's body was lying on a diagonal, so it wouldn't roll anymore, but it still took up most of the steps it touched. Geraldine scooted around Tasheba Kent's feet so quickly, she almost lost her balance and fell. By the time she got to the foyer, she was running. She turned to look back, but there was nothing to see but a sheet. Gregor Demarkian had said that leaving her where she was didn't mean they couldn't cover her up. Geraldine thought he had been stretching things a little.

Whatever he had been doing, she was past it now. She didn't have to go upstairs again if she didn't want to. There were couches all over the first floor that she could sleep on. Earlier tonight, she had gone around to the pantry by the back hall. Now she didn't want to waste the time, or spook herself going through all those dark hallways, so she went straight from the foyer to the kitchen. The utility hall that connected these two was short and very well lit. Getting to the kitchen, Geraldine turned on all the lights she could and tried not to look at the knives in the knife rack next to the stove. To get to the pantry, she had to go all the way across to the door that led to the way out at the back. Then she had to cross an almost unheated little mud room, climb four steps, and let herself through another door into the back utility hall. This hall was not well lit. The principle that seemed to have been operating when this house was wired for electricity was that servants were able to see in the dark.

Geraldine left the door between the mud room and the back hall open, as she had left the door between the kitchen and the mud room open, so that some of the kitchen light would filter through and help her do what she was doing. The pantry door was two doors in from the mud room door, just past the beginning of the back stairs. Geraldine didn't look up there any more than she had looked at the knives in the kitchen. She hated those back stairs. They were like something out of a novel by Alexandre Dumas. They should have belonged to a dungeon or a torture chamber. The two or three times Geraldine had been forced to climb those stairs, she had taken a flashlight and been careful to wear the plain gold cross she had been given in Bible class at the Hunter's Pier First Full Gospel Baptist Church.

Now she hurried into the pantry, leaving the door open behind her. At the last minute, just to be cautious, she took a can of peas and a can of kidney beans and propped them against the open door. Then she went back in among the cans of vegetables and the sacks of flour and the big jars of honey and maple syrup and looked around. The CD player was just where she had put it in the first place, back around midnight. Its speakers were still aimed at the square mesh microphone that was connected to the intercom system. The microphone had been turned off, but there was no mystery about that. Geraldine had done it herself, that last time she had come in here, looking for Carlton Ji or his body. If she hadn't, her breathing or her footsteps would have gone bouncing around the house just the way the cackling laughter had, although they would have been quieter.

Geraldine looked over the facing of the player, checking out the settings. As she had suspected, the volume had been turned way up, into the reddest part of the red zone. The program had been fiddled with, too. Instead of being set for one play-through of the disc on the turntable, it was set for seven. If it had been set for ten or eleven, Geraldine might have thought she had made the mistake herself. She had been nervous and jumpy. Her hand might have shaken as she was punching the instructions into the machine. She could guarantee that she hadn't been calm enough to be paying full attention. She did know that she hadn't pushed "seven" though. She could remember putting her finger down on "one."

Geraldine checked the timer, but that hadn't been tampered with. She had set the machine to go on at one. Whoever had fiddled with it had left it to go on at one. The disc had not been changed, but Geraldine would have been shocked if it had been. She had brought no other discs to the pantry. The rest of the collection was up in Cavender Marsh's bedroom, tucked away on the top shelf in Tasheba Kent's closet. Obviously, somebody had either followed her to the pantry when she had come to set the machine, or they had stumbled into the pantry while they were snooping around and decided to take advantage of what they found. Was that last scenario actually possible?

Geraldine supposed it was. With the exception of Gregor Demarkian, Geraldine wouldn't trust any of the people in this house as far as she could throw them.

The thing to do now was to get this silly machine out of here, before anybody else had a chance to use it. Since she'd put it here herself, she couldn't see why it would be "tampering with evidence" for her to remove it. She wasn't trying to hide anything. She had every intention of telling Demarkian and Dick Morrow and even the state police just what it was she had done and why.

Geraldine opened the door to the turntable and took out the disc. The plastic case the disc belonged in was lying across three cans of Campbell's pork and beans on the shelf above the player. Geraldine got it down and put the disc inside. She closed the turntable door, unplugged the machine, wrapped the cord around her hand four times to make sure it wouldn't dangle, and put the player under her right arm the way a running back would carry a football. Then she turned around and started to leave.

It was a moment that made her believe, forever afterward, that she had no instinct of self-preservation. She was standing in the doorway to the pantry, not five feet from where she had been just a moment before, and she had not felt his presence. She had not heard him walk up. She had not heard him breathing. He was a complete surprise, and as soon as she saw him, Geraldine felt the breath knocked out of her. Never mind the fact that he was grinning in a furious and nasty way that made him look deranged.

"Well, well, well," Richard Fenster said, shifting his weight a little to the right. Now he was blocking the entire doorway. There was no way Geraldine could get out without pushing against him. "What is it we're doing here?"

Geraldine nearly dropped the CD player to the floor. "Oh, for God's sake. What is it you think you're doing?"

"I think that what we're going to discuss here is what it is you're doing," Richard Fenster said. "Don't you agree?"

Geraldine Dart agreed. She had to agree. She wasn't getting out of this pantry until Richard Fenster let her out.

—— 2 ——

Hannah Graham did not believe in taking pills if you didn't have to, but she did think there were a lot of circumstances under which you had to, and one of those was if she couldn't get to sleep at night. Sleep was very important, because lack of it could make you wrinkled. Lack of it could also make you crazy, because the only way anybody could hold onto her sanity was through dreams. This was all a little fuzzy, but Hannah knew what she meant, and what she was afraid of. Right now, she was scared to death that she would lie on her bed for hours and not be able to relax at all. Unfortunately, although she had brought a small suitcase full of nothing but medication, none of the medication she had brought was sleeping pills. She had twenty-two different kinds of vitamins, including liquid vitamin E to rub on her hands and face to keep them from aging. She had six different kinds of tranquilizers to meet every need from mild upset to major emotional breakdown. She had enough different kinds of painkillers, both over the counter and bootleg prescription, to open her own Mobile Army Surgical Hospital. But she did not have a single pill to put her to sleep. Not one.

The bed in Hannah's room had a canopy that arched up into the darkness at the top of the room like a gently rolling hill. On the wall next to the window was a steel engraving of a Victorian lady sitting at her boudoir, frowning into a mirror that was not telling her what she wanted to hear. On the vanity table there was a tortoiseshell brush and comb and hand mirror set, with the handles carved into swirling ribbons and fat little bows. Hannah thought about taking a tranquilizer, but a tranquilizer wasn't what she wanted. A tranquilizer would calm her down enough so that she could go to sleep, but it would block out all her dreams. She would wake up fuzzy and nauseated and not alert, which she couldn't afford. Hannah knew this from experience.

Hannah got out of bed and checked herself in the vanity table mirror. She looked all right in a dim light, and there were nothing but dim lights in the hall and the bedrooms of this wing. Even in the gloom, though, she could see the start of a sag at the corner of her jaw. It was time to go in and get herself seen to again. This was what came of putting yourself through too much stress, and drinking wine and eating ice cream to calm yourself down. For Hannah, ice cream was the root of all evil. It jumped out of refrigerators at you. It ambushed you in stores. Its entire reason for existence was to make the upper-middle-class women of America look fat.

Her hair was impossible. She could try to do something about it, or put on a wig, but all that seemed like too much trouble at this hour of the morning. She fished a blue silk scarf out of the suitcase she had left open at the foot of her bed and tied it around her head. It didn't exactly go with either her dressing gown or her nightgown, but it would have to do.

Hannah let herself out into the hall. It was empty and dark and quiet, but she was sure that most of the people in the bedrooms would still be awake. This was not the kind of night that sent you to your pillow and an uncomplicated trip to dreamland. She went down to the door halfway down the hall and on the opposite side from her own and knocked. She heard moving in there that she was sure had to be pacing.

"Just a minute," Mathilda Frazier's voice called out. Then, closer to the door, "Who is it?"

"It's Hannah Graham," Hannah said.

On the other side of the door, the bolt was pulled back and the knob was turned. Mathilda Frazier opened up a crack and scowled out.

"What is it you want?" she asked Hannah Graham.

This was ungracious enough, but Hannah wasn't really surprised. This was one of those new young women who tried to compensate for their lack of breeding and ordinary good looks by trying to be more aggressive than any man. If Mathilda Frazier had been a resident of Beverly Hills, Hannah Graham would not have had her in the house.

"I've come to ask you if I can borrow a couple of sleeping pills," Hannah said.

Mathilda made a face. "What makes you think I've got sleeping pills?"

"I heard you telling Kelly Pratt you were going to take one."

"I never told Kelly any such thing."

"Yes, you did. It was right before dinner. I don't remember who was doing what to annoy you, but somebody was doing something."

Mathilda Frazier hesitated. Then she seemed to make up her mind.

"Come on in," she said grudgingly. "I don't have very many, but I suppose you can have two. I don't think we're going to be on this island for another night anyway."

"Don't you?" Hannah asked.

Mathilda's room was almost identical to her own, but mirror image. Mathilda had a bed with a canopy and a vanity with a curved-top mirror and a steel engraving, but her steel engraving was of a little boy carrying a balloon. Hannah sat down on the vanity stool. Mathilda had done a lot more unpacking than she had, if you could call it unpacking. Three suitcases were lying open on the bedroom floor, spilling slips and bras and blouses and pantyhose everywhere.

Mathilda got a plastic prescription bottle out of her cosmetics case and opened the cap. She shook two pills out onto her hand and walked them across the room to Hannah.

"Here," she said, handing the pills to Hannah. "These are a fairly strong prescription. They ought to knock you right out."

"Thanks." Hannah knew what kind of prescription they were. She had some of her own back in California. She would classify them as middle of the road. The pills were blessedly small, though, and she was able to swallow them dry.

"Can I ask you something?" Mathilda Frazier said. "What was it you meant before? Do you think the police are going to make us spend another night in this house?"

"I think the police are going to want to get us out of here as soon as they can," Hannah said. "I just don't think we're going to get off this island. At least, not tomorrow."

"But why not?"

"Listen to the wind," Hannah told her. "And it's not just the wind, either. Go look at the weather."

Mathilda hesitated again, as if she thought Hannah was out to trick her in every way she could. Then she walked over to the window and pulled back the curtains. "It's still so dark out there. It's hard to see anything at all. You're right about the wind, though. The wind is just plain awful."

"Do you hear those pinging sounds?"

"Like hard rain hitting a metal roof."

"That's hail hitting the side of the house," Hannah said. "It's going to get worse all day Friday, too. I heard it on the radio."

Mathilda let the curtain drop and came around to sit on the edge of her bed. "God, I hate this. This is just the most creepy thing. And the idea of that man wandering around here—where do you think he's gone to? Do you think he's hiding in the attic or the basement or someplace else we haven't looked?"

"I think he's long gone," Hannah said. "I think he killed Tasheba Kent and took off out of here. I don't care what Gregor Demarkian says."

"But why would he kill Tasheba Kent? That's what I don't understand. I mean, I think it's obvious that he must have done it. There isn't any other reason for him to be missing, unless he's—" Mathilda blanched. "Oh, dear."

"I don't see why he would be dead," Hannah said, completing Mathilda's thought. "Unless he killed himself trying to escape in the storm. I couldn't see any reason for any of us to have killed him. None of us had ever met him before."

"I can't see why anybody would want to murder Tasheba Kent," Mathilda said. "I mean, the woman was practically a century old and she spent all her time out here in the middle of nowhere. She wasn't a danger to anybody. And she couldn't have lasted very long anyway. Why would anybody want to go to the trouble of murdering a woman who was almost a century old?"

"I don't think of her as a woman who was almost a hundred years old," Hannah said. "I think of her as the woman who was responsible for the death of Lilith

Brayne. And it seems to me that there must be dozens of
people who would want to see her dead."

"Well, from your point of view I suppose that's perfectly natural." Mathilda didn't sound as if she meant it.
"I'm sorry," she went on, "but I took two of those pills
nearly twenty minutes ago, and I'm getting a little sleepy."

"Of course." Hannah stood up.

"I hope you're wrong about the storm," Mathilda told
her. "I don't want to spend another night in this house. I
don't want to spend another minute in it."

"Well, maybe it will let up," Hannah said.

Going back to her room, though, Hannah knew that
the storm was not going to let up, not on Friday, and
maybe not on Saturday, either. The man on the radio had
been very explicit. This was the first of the great winter
storms arriving early. They were likely to be socked in
hard for the rest of the weekend.

— 2 —

Down at the end of the hall nearest the landing and the
stairs, Bennis Hannaford was sitting cross-legged, writing
notes in the margins of her galleys that she knew she was
going to have to black out later. They had a lot of four-
letter words in them, and even more sarcasm. They were
the kinds of things that made copyeditors and proof-
readers quit in tears, or threaten to sue. Bennis couldn't
help herself. She was exhausted. She was agitated. She
wasn't going to be able to get to sleep for hours. She had
to do *something*.

When the knock came on the door, Bennis had just
finished her fourth cigarette in a chain of cigarettes, a
chain that she had every intention of going on with until
she could go downstairs for breakfast. She took a deep
drag of it and went to her door.

"Who is it?"

"Gregor," Gregor said.

Bennis opened up and ushered him inside. "Come on
in," she told him. "I'm just sitting on my bed quietly going
mad."

Gregor sat down on the stool to Bennis's vanity table and stretched out his legs.

"Stop going mad for a moment and try to concentrate," he said. "This is important. I want you to tell me everything you know about the death of Lilith Brayne."

CHAPTER 3

If Gregor Demarkian had had to rely on the report of Bennis Hannaford for information about the death of Lilith Brayne, he would have been up a tree without a ladder. Bennis knew the things everybody knew, and not much more. Cavender Marsh had been married to Lilith Brayne while having a very passionate, and very public, affair with Tasheba Kent. Cavender Marsh and Lilith Brayne went away together to the south of France, alone, to see if they could put their marriage back together. Lilith Brayne showed up dead and cut to pieces in a sluice, apparently after accidentally falling to her death from the stone balcony of their rented villa. The French police investigated Cavender Marsh for murder but finally decided he couldn't have committed it. The movie magazines of two continents convicted Tasheba Kent of murder without worrying much about what evidence there was in any direction. The verdict of *Silver Screen* and *Photoplay* and their sisters was that Tasheba Kent had driven her beautiful, betrayed sister to suicide by first driving her beautiful, betrayed sister to despair.

It was the kind of information most people would have been satisfied with, but it was not the kind of information Gregor Demarkian needed. He wasn't craving after exact times to the second or elaborate suspect location charts at this late date. He just needed some details. Kelly Pratt's story about the missing one hundred thousand dollars was interesting, because Gregor could come up with an explanation for it—but if his explanation was true, things were much more odd here than he had expected. Before he jumped to conclusions like that, he ought to know more about what he was doing. After a while, he made Bennis get up and come downstairs with him. She didn't want to walk past Tasheba Kent's body, but Gregor didn't think anybody did, and it had to be done. They searched all the bookshelves in the library and the living room and came up with nothing. Then they went upstairs again and Gregor started searching through the bedrooms in the family wing.

"Let's just hope they don't keep it in Geraldine Dart's room," Gregor told Bennis. "Then I'll have to wait until morning, and I can't sleep."

"Keep what in Geraldine Dart's room?" Bennis asked.

When Gregor found what he was looking for—in Cavender Marsh's room, on a bookshelf that seemed to have been built just to hold them—he showed her.

"Scrapbooks," he explained, pulling one of the big leather-bound volumes off the top shelf. "I knew they wouldn't be able to resist keeping scrapbooks."

There were dozens of album-size scrapbooks on the bookshelf, six rows of them, some in black and some in light brown and some in leather that looked almost white. At the bottom there were three in black leather with gold lettering on them. Bennis pulled one of these out and opened it up.

"You're right," she said. "They did keep a scrapbook with articles about the murder investigation in it. How odd."

"It would have been odder if they hadn't," Gregor told her. "They kept scrapbooks of everything else."

They both looked over at the still-sleeping form of Cavender Marsh, still perfectly still, still perfectly happy.

"I wish I knew what kind of medication he was on," Bennis said. "I'd get some for myself."

Gregor took down all three of the books with the gold

lettering, and then one each at random of the other kinds—black leather, white leather, light brown leather—and put them aside. The glow-in-the-dark digital clock on Cavender Marsh's bedside table said six twenty-two, but the sky outside his bedroom windows was still black. Gregor put the scrapbooks in a stack and lifted them up. They were each at least five inches thick and a foot and a half wide. They made him stagger a little.

"What do you want the other ones for?" Bennis said, pointing to the three without gold lettering. "They can't all be about the death of Lilith Brayne."

"Even the ones with the gold lettering aren't all about the death of Lilith Brayne," Gregor told her. "They're just about Cavender Marsh and Tasheba Kent together. I need the background."

"Background," Bennis repeated.

"You ought to go back to bed and get some sleep. Just because I'm going to be up doesn't mean you have to be."

"Are you sure you ought to be taking these things out of Cavender Marsh's room without permission?" Bennis asked him.

Gregor took her back to her room and then went back to his own. He spread the scrapbooks out on his bed and opened each one. The all-black ones were full of stories about Cavender Marsh, movie magazine stories with headlines that promised to reveal "his startling confession" and "his secret shame." The articles seemed to date from an era well before the arrival of Tasheba Kent and Lilith Brayne in his life. Gregor knew that when Cavender Marsh had decided to marry Lilith Brayne—a woman who was not only twenty years older than he was but who looked it—the story had caused a sensation. It had spilled off the fan magazines and into the regular press, even into *The New York Times*. A congressman from Kentucky had made a speech about it from the floor of the House of Representatives. The cardinal archbishop of Boston had given a radio speech explaining why the Catholic Church found such backward-lopsided matings unnatural. There was no hint of any of that in the scrapbook Gregor had chosen at random. There was no hint that Cavender Marsh had ever even met Lilith Brayne.

The white leather scrapbooks belonged to Lilith Brayne. The one Gregor had concentrated on movie stills and newspaper stories from the early part of her career. Lilith always seemed to be posed from the side and back, looking over her shoulder. It made her neck look long and swanlike. Every once in a while she was photographed from the side, but that didn't work as well. Her nose was very long and very pointed. Caught at the wrong angle, it looked like a sewing needle stuck on the front of her face. Several of the pictures were full-length shots, usually of Lilith looking not quite flapperish but very stylish in 1920s café society clothes. In those pictures, she was wearing the black shoes with the rhinestone buckles Gregor had seen downstairs, or copies of them.

The light brown leather scrapbooks belonged to Tasheba Kent, and the one Gregor had laid hands on was the most dramatic of any he had seen yet. Lilith Brayne had done a fair amount of work to appear "normal" even while she was a movie star. Tasheba Kent had gone over the top and stayed there. The scrapbook Gregor had was from the height of her career. All the clippings of movie advertisements from newspapers and magazines showed her name above the title, usually in bigger letters than the title. The pictures of Tasheba Kent herself were melodramatic. Her dresses were so tight, it was difficult to understand how she could have moved in them. Her cigarette holders were so long it was difficult to understand how she could have smoked in her car without setting her driver's hair on fire. Her eyes were rimmed with so much kohl, they looked like they had been blackened in a fight. Tasheba Kent had a long, thin nose very much like her sister's, but she did nothing to hide it. She exaggerated it, the way she exaggerated everything about herself. Exaggeration, not individuality, was what you noticed when you looked at her. It was as if there were nobody at all named Tasheba Kent, just a series of constantly shifting surfaces, sparkling and flashing and much too bright.

After that scrapbook full of Tasheba Kent, the one about the death and trial was almost boring, and the other two—which mostly had to do with Tasheba and Cavender going away together, and retrospective articles on the level of Where Are They Now—were worse. In the 1938 photo-graphs, all three of the principals looked oddly subdued; 1930s styles didn't suit either of the sisters as well as 1920s styles had. Then, too, they were older, in that way women got older before the advent of aerobics tapes and small-weight lifting and macrobiotic diets. What struck Gregor was how depressed and tense they all looked, even before the death of Lilith Brayne. There was a picture of Cavender and Lilith standing on the deck of an ocean liner, surrounded by confetti and balloons. Both were smiling determinedly at the camera, but underneath it all they looked grim. There was a picture of Tasheba Kent sitting at a small round table at an outside café in Paris. She had adapted the 1930s styles as much as she could to her own personal taste. Since the style didn't adapt very well, she had simply made herself look patently bizarre. Her cigarette holder was much shorter, though, and her dark glasses covered the wrinkles around her eyes. She looked like a vampire bat that had just turned itself into a self-important middle-aged woman.

In the pictures from the period of the investigation, Tasheba Kent seemed to get stranger and stranger by the second. In *The New York Times* photograph of her arriving at the jail in southern France where Cavender Marsh was being detained, she had added a black mink coat to the glasses and the cigarette holder. In the *San Francisco Chronicle* picture of her at her sister's inquest, her throat was wrapped up in a black feather boa. What was even more distinctive was the way her makeup seemed to thicken, the closer she got to the point where she would have to answer questions herself. In the *London Times* photograph of her on the stand at the inquest, she had discarded the mink coat and the dark glasses and the feather boa, but her face was a mask of foundation and paint, so thick Gregor could almost see the texture of it through the cheap newsprint black-and-white grain.

Gregor went back to the articles about the death of Lilith Brayne and read them through. Then he went back to the articles about the inquest and read those through, too. When he was finished, he had some sympathy with the people, like Hannah Graham, who thought the French police had taken a dive in this case. In the very beginning, there were indications that the police were asking the right questions, but those indications did not last long. In no time at all, Gregor was scowling furiously at what seemed to him to be blatant evidence of raw incompetence. Of course, that went along with some of the theories he had formed earlier, before he had looked at this material, but he wasn't sure that he wanted it to. The other possibility was that the newspapers were simply doing a very bad job of reporting. The French police might have been perfectly competent, but their competence might not have seemed like news to international editors in San Francisco and London and New York. But Gregor doubted it.

Gregor went through the light brown scrapbook one more time and concentrated on articles and magazine pieces and news reports from Los Angeles, to see if the perspective was any different. In theory, newspaper editors in Los Angeles ought to have a better idea than newspaper editors in other places what a bunch of movie stars was up to. Reading through the material, this was not a theory that seemed to be borne out by the physical evidence. The *Los Angeles Times* said all the same inane things the papers in other cities said. It just placed the story higher on its front page and gave it bigger headlines.

Gregor put the scrapbooks in a heap on the floor next to his bed and stretched out with his head on the pillow. Then he got the little traveling alarm clock he brought with him everywhere and set it for quarter to ten. His mind was racing, but it was racing on a kind of automatic pilot. The speed of his thoughts was not interfering with the need of his body for sleep. Gregor closed his eyes and let himself slide away, into a world where Tasheba Kent and Lilith Brayne and Cavender Marsh were all alive and much younger than they could have been today, where they wore curved-heeled shoes with rhinestone buckles and black feather boas and evening suits with velvet on the lapels.

Never get taken in by appearances, Gregor told himself just as he began to fall into a dark and dreamless sleep.

They always trip you up.

—— 2 ——

The alarm clock on Gregor's bedside table emitted little high-pitched squeaks, like a mouse in danger of immediate execution, that never failed to wake him up. When Gregor opened his eyes, he found himself lying almost sideways across the bed, as if he had been wrestling with something in his sleep. He sat up and got himself turned around. The first thing he noticed was that the weather hadn't gotten any better. It was lighter now than it had been when he had gone to sleep, but that wasn't saying much. A thin stream of gray was forcing itself through the heavy curtains across his bedroom windows. A stiff wind was forcing itself against the windows themselves, making them rattle and creak. Gregor got out of bed and went to look out. The fog was so thick, he couldn't see a dozen yards out to sea. Close to the island, the ocean was angry and strong, smashing against the rocks in great heavy swells that exploded into foam as soon as they connected to the land.

If Gregor hadn't been so hungry, he would have taken a shower before he went down for breakfast. As it was, his stomach felt not only empty but full of sandpaper. He was queasy and weak. He was sure he wouldn't feel any better until he had eaten at least four eggs. He dressed in what he thought of as casual clothes, and what Bennis called his "Ozzie Nelson outfit." It consisted of good gray slacks, a white button-down shirt, wool sweater with a V-neck, and a tie. Then he went downstairs in search of the dining room and breakfast, hoping against hope that it hadn't already been removed.

Gregor had no need to worry. Once he was out of the guest wing and onto the second-floor landing, he could smell food and coffee. Once he was halfway down the stairs, he could hear people talking in the kind of tense, exasperated voices he supposed were only natural under the circumstances. Getting ready upstairs, Gregor had half hoped to find the dining room empty except for Lydia Acken, whom he very much wanted to talk to. Now he knew that even if Lydia Acken were eating her breakfast right this minute, he would never have a chance to get her alone. He could hear at least four different voices, snapping at each other.

Gregor made his way around the shrouded body of Tasheba Kent, through the foyer, and into the great double doors of the dining room. He was surprised to see that they were all there, with the exception of Cavender Marsh, although some of them looked far more awake and alert than others. Hannah Graham and Mathilda Frazier looked particularly awful, as if they were forcing themselves upright and inhaling too much coffee to keep themselves that way. Kelly Pratt, on the other hand, looked well-pressed and refreshed, as if he'd had a perfectly adequate night's sleep. Lydia Acken was somewhere in the middle. She looked awake enough, but as if she would rather not be.

Gregor came the rest of the way into the dining room, said "Good morning," and headed for the sideboard where silver serving trays were set out in a row. He got himself a plate, a cup, and a saucer. He filled the cup with black coffee and the plate with breakfast sausages and scrambled eggs. Then he turned around and put the plate, the cup, and the saucer down at one of the empty places on this side of the table. That was when he noticed they were staring at him. They had all stopped talking. They had all stopped eating. They were just sitting very still, watching him move.

Gregor sat down in front of his food. He cleared his throat. "Well," he said. "Good morning."

Gregor was sure that he had already said this once. He wasn't sure that any of them had heard. None of them answered him now. Gregor picked up the fork at his place and speared a piece of breakfast sausage. Even Bennis looked shocked.

"Excuse me," Gregor said carefully. "Have I missed something here? Is there anything wrong?"

Bennis lit a cigarette and blew a stream of smoke into the air. "It's amazing. He's really going to eat that thing."

"Of course I'm going to eat it," Gregor said. "I've been up all night. I'm starving."

"Most of us have had a little trouble this morning working up an appetite," Richard Fenster said tartly.

"Except for Kelly," Mathilda Frazier said in a listless voice. "He's just as bad as you are."

Kelly Pratt was in the middle of finishing off an enormous piece of toast piled high with butter and jam. He swallowed the last big chunk of it and grinned.

"I don't see what you're letting it put you off your food for," he said. "It's just a body and you can't even see it. It's covered with a sheet. I say just ignore it and get on with your life."

"I can't just get on with my life if I'm stuck on this damn island," Hannah Graham snapped, "and I can't just ignore the body of someone I'm related to, sprawled out dead and stiff in the middle of the staircase I have to use every time I want to go upstairs. Of course it's put me off my food. It's grotesque."

Down at the far end of the table, Geraldine Dart stirred. "You know, Mr. Demarkian, it really is awful to have her there. And it's not like we're going to be able to do something about it any time soon. The weather reports—"

"The weather reports are lousy," Richard Fenster finished for her. "It's supposed to be more or less like this all day. Then it's supposed to calm down tonight, but what they mean by calming down isn't going to help us much."

"It could be as late as Sunday before we are able to get off of here and get some help," Geraldine Dart said, "and the idea of leaving her there like that, in the middle of the stairs, where we all have to keep stepping over her—" Geraldine shook her head and shuddered.

Lydia Acken took a very small bite of her toast, thought better of it, and put the toast down on her plate again. "You know, we also have Cavender Marsh to consider. He's going to come out of that sleeping pill–induced sleep of his sometime. When he finds out what's happened, he's going to have a shock. Having to step over the body of the woman he's been living with for over fifty years is going to be entirely too much for his constitution."

Gregor took a bite out of his sausage and then another. Then he put his fork down on his plate and thought it over. He didn't really believe that the sight of Tasheba Kent's body would be too much for the constitution of

Cavender Marsh. He didn't think much of anything would. If there was one solid impression Gregor had come away with from his perusal of the scrapbooks, it was that all three of the principals in the death of Lilith Brayne had been narcissistic to the point of pathology. Gregor thought Cavender Marsh might be surprised to find his long-time companion dead—although he might not—and that he might even be curious about how it had all come about. Gregor did not think that Cavender Marsh would be shaken to his foundations, or in peril of having a stroke.

On the other hand, the people at this table had a point. If it was really going to be that long before they could contact the mainland and get the police out here, there was no sense at all to leaving Tasheba Kent's body on the stairs. Preserving a crime scene was one thing. Preserving everybody's sanity was something else.

Gregor put salt and pepper on his scrambled eggs and continued to eat. "Are you sure about that weather forecast?" he asked Geraldine Dart. "Can you trust the station you're getting it from?"

"I can trust the source the radio station is getting it from," Geraldine said. "I'm tuned to the same station all the fishermen use. This is supposed to be one of the worst storms we've seen in twenty years. There's snow coming down a little ways north of us, and that's bad for October even for Maine."

"How calm does it have to be out there before we can get off the island? Or would it be easier to get somebody from the mainland out here?"

"It would be easiest to get us off the island if we had the right kind of boat," Geraldine answered, "but we don't. If we had something fairly big and somebody who knew how to drive it, we could probably go as soon as it actually stopped hailing. But all the boats we have here are small."

"Would anybody here know how to drive a bigger boat if we had one?" Gregor asked.

"I don't think so," Geraldine said dejectedly.

"What about people coming out from the mainland to here?"

"Well, the problem with that is our dock, you see. It's

not a very good one and it's not very well positioned. I mean, it's as well positioned as it could be, but this is all rock out here. The area right next to the shore is very dangerous. I go back and forth all the time, and I've smashed up a couple of small boats over the years myself, and on perfectly clear days, too. You have to pay attention, and if the sea is at all rough, you can't."

Gregor took a long sip of coffee. "I see what you mean. I also accept the fact that Sunday is just too far away. We can't leave her lying on the steps that long."

"Oh, thank God," Mathilda Frazier said.

"Do you have someplace we could put the body?" Gregor asked Geraldine. "Is there a study or someplace like that, someplace out of the way? It would be absolutely best if we could lock it up."

"There's a television room on this floor," Geraldine said. "It's around the back of the staircase off the foyer. Miss Kent hated television and didn't even want to see a set around, but Mr. Marsh loves it, so we kept it back there. It's out of sight but it's easily accessible."

"That sounds perfect." Gregor finished off his coffee, wiped his face with his cloth napkin, and threw his napkin on the tablecloth next to his unused butter knife. "I'm going to have to have some help moving the body. Mr. Fenster? Mr. Pratt?"

"I'm on my way," Kelly Pratt said, standing up.

"Count me out," Richard Fenster said. "I have no intention of touching a corpse no matter what it died from. I most particularly have no intention of touching that corpse."

"Oh, my, what a big man it is," Hannah Graham said nastily.

Bennis Hannaford crushed her cigarette out in the ashtray next to her coffee cup and pushed back her chair. "I'll go," she said. "I'm at least as strong as he is and I'm probably more emotionally stable. And I'd do anything not to have to step over that body again."

Gregor was about to argue—in the world in which he had grown up, women were not forced to move corpses or do other heavy things if there were men around to do it for them—but he knew what kind of a fight he would cause if he raised his voice in protest, and he just wasn't up for it. Instead, he nodded at the two of them. They followed him to the foyer and stood at the foot of the stairs, solemnly staring at the body of Tasheba Kent under its white linen sheet. Geraldine Dart came, too. She was the only one who knew the way to the television room.

"All right," Gregor said. "We have to be very careful here, because the corpse is going to be very stiff. And bodies in rigor are very brittle. If you hit them too hard against a corner or a piece of furniture, it's not impossible that pieces of them might break off."

"Yuck," Bennis said.

"I'll take the shoulders," Kelly Pratt told her. "They'll be heavier and harder to move. You take the feet."

To find out where the shoulders were and where the feet were, Kelly Pratt had to take the sheet off Tasheba Kent's body. Gregor was watching Bennis's face, but she didn't flinch. She just waited until Kelly Pratt got a grip under Tasheba Kent's arms and then picked up at her end.

"Which way?" Bennis asked Gregor and Geraldine.

Geraldine scurried around and pointed them in the right direction. Gregor followed behind them as they went, past the elevator doors, off into a corner. Geraldine got the door open and the lights on. Kelly and Bennis maneuvered the body into the room and waited for further instructions.

"Lay it out on the couch," Gregor told them. "It might as well be there as anywhere else."

"It really is stiff," Bennis said. "Does it stay like this forever?"

"No, it doesn't," Gregor said. "It doesn't stay like that very long at all, and it's a nuisance while it's going on. Once you get her down, we'd better cover her up again. She's going to begin to look fairly awful by the time Sunday comes around."

Bennis and Kelly put the body down on the couch—much more carefully, Gregor noticed, than they needed to. The linen sheet had dropped off in the foyer. Bennis went back out to get it. She returned with it folded over her arm. For some reason, she couldn't get it so that it hung perfectly, without showing any part of the corpse. She took it off again and went to reposition the body on the couch.

"What's this?" Bennis said suddenly. She dropped the sheet to the floor and leaned closer to the ruffles of the negligee that rose high on Tasheba Kent's neck. "Gregor, come quick, take a look at this."

Gregor was feeling guilty about leaving Bennis on her own to do all these unpleasant things. After his initial impulse to act like the stereotypical sexist male, he had simply mentally relaxed and allowed her to take all the responsibility she wanted to for something that really should have been his own job. Now that she was calling for him, however, he was galvanized into action. He rushed forward much more quickly than he had any reason to, as if she had just announced an emergency.

What Bennis had, however, was not an emergency. It was a cufflink, made of heavy gold with a flat top in the shape of an old-fashioned movie camera, that she had found stuck in the neck ruffle of Tasheba Kent's negligee.

"Look at that," she said, handing the piece over to Gregor. "What do you think that is?"

"I know what that is," Geraldine Dart said. "It's one of Cavender's favorite cufflinks. He was wearing them when he came down to dinner last night."

CHAPTER 4

— 1 —

Eventually, you had to spend a little time sleeping. Richard Fenster had tried to find a way around it, but there it was. The human body was not made to go forever without sleep. Especially when it got older—and Richard was getting older; he hated to admit it, but it was true—it needed to expend significant amounts of time horizontal, blacked out, in another place. The problem was that it couldn't be in that place and this one at the same time. And that was dangerous.

Richard Fenster had taken the discovery of Cavender Marsh's cufflink with a grain of salt. When Geraldine Dart had run into the dining room babbling about it, he had gotten up for another piece of toast, and let the rest of them oooh and aaah about it. Gregor Demarkian hadn't been very impressed, either, but nobody was paying any attention to Demarkian but Richard. Geraldine had gushed out her report. Kelly Pratt had asked the questions that established the fact that they couldn't actually see the cufflink, because Gregor Demarkian had put it away in an envelope for the police. Mathilda Frazier had advanced the first of the amateur detective theories by announcing, "I don't believe this has anything to do with anything at all. Husbands hug wives all the time. That doesn't mean they've just bashed their heads in."

Richard had a whole list of objections to this line of reasoning, starting with the fact that Tasheba Kent and Cavender Marsh had never been married, but Mathilda Frazier was already convinced that he was after her ass. He didn't want to give the woman any more cause for conceit than she already thought she had. Instead, he got up from his chair again.

"If I don't get some sleep, I'm going to collapse," he told them.

They looked at him as if he had just pitched a fit in the middle of the table.

"I don't even read murder mysteries," he said querulously. "You people may be fascinated by all this stuff, but I'm not."

"So go to sleep," Mathilda Frazier said.

They had resumed their conversation as soon as he left the dining room. Richard could tell by the excited tones in their voices, and the way a giggle seemed to run just under the surface, without ever breaking into light. He looked at the stairs where Tasheba Kent's body had lain. He found a couple of flecks of blood on the runner carpet. Nothing much.

Richard went around to the back of the staircase and past the elevators. He stuck his head into a back hall before finding the television room. The television room wasn't much, just a small square place that might have started life as a walk-in closet, with a couch and two chairs and a Magnavox twenty-seven inch in it. There was a VCR and a couple of tapes, too, but the tapes were nothing shocking. *Blade Runner*. *The Hunt for Red October*. Like every other man on earth, Cavender Marsh liked action-adventure and good guys versus bad guys.

Richard shut the door to the television room. He pulled back the white sheet and looked into Tasheba Kent's face. What he really looked into was Tasheba Kent's makeup. In spite of what they had all thought last night, she was wearing quite a bit of it—just not as much of it as she had been wearing at dinner. Richard put his finger on the cold wet skin of the bridge of her nose and traced the line of the nosebone to the cartilage tip. He moved his finger to the left eyebrow and traced the line of it there. It was hopeless. Her eyebrows had been plucked. Her eyes, although free of false eyelashes now, were puffy with age and the abuse of too much paint. Her lips looked stung.

Richard got his handkerchief out of his pocket and tried to wipe some of the paint off, but it wouldn't come. He went over to the one small window and undid the latch. With his luck, this window would be painted shut, or it would be one of those windows that was never meant to be opened. To his surprise, it opened easily. Richard stuck his handkerchief into the rain and waited until it was soaked. Then he wrung it out a little and brought it back inside.

This time, getting the makeup off was much easier. It smeared under the rainwater, but it came. Richard rubbed at the eyes until they were clear of everything but a thin black line of mascara on each eyelid. Then he went back to the window, washed the handkerchief out, and came back to do the sides of her face. The lips were hardest. Lipstick streaked and stuck and got stubborn. Richard had to go back to the window three times before he was finished with that. He got it all, though, and then he sat back to look at what he had left.

The problem, Richard thought a few minutes later, was that it was so hard to know what age could or couldn't do to a human face. This was not the Tasheba Kent he dreamed about, the one whose great dark eyes stared down at him from his bedroom ceiling—but that Tasheba Kent was twenty-two years old. This one would have been one hundred if she had lived. Time and gravity had taken their toll. So had six decades of Cavender Marsh. Having met Cavender, Richard thought he would take a toll on anyone, even Gandhi or Jesus. Tasheba's eyes looked smaller, but the size of them in the picture he had might have been a trick of the camera. The hands looked bigger, but Richard had never really paid attention to her hands. He had been lying when he had told Gregor Demarkian that he would never touch a corpse, and especially this one. Precisely what he wanted to do now was to touch this corpse. He wanted to put his hands on her face and feel the smoothness of her skin. He wanted to put his hands on her arms and feel them tighten into life against him. Sometimes he thought his touch was magic. If he could only lay hands on her in exactly the right way, she would not only rise from the dead but reconstitute herself. The evil witch's enchantment would be broken. Tasheba Kent would be young again.

I am losing my mind, Richard thought in a sudden panic, backing away from the corpse. Now he hurried over to close the window, unhappy to see that a thick patch of damp had formed on the carpet. He went back to the couch and stared at the ancient face again, the wrinkles and folds and ugly slackness. Everybody always said that age brought individuality, but it wasn't true. Tasheba Kent at twenty-two had had individuality. This woman was simply Old, made up of the bits and pieces of generic age, no different from dozens of other old people from one end of the country to the other. There was nothing here to prove that she had once been the most desirable woman alive.

Richard pulled the linen sheet off the corpse. The body that appeared to him stuffed into the ruffled negligee was a lumpy mess. It had no shape at all. Richard ignored it and went right to the feet. The feet had slippers on them, dyed to match the negligee, with a little heel, the kind of thing Richard associated most with movies in which Jean Harlow received visitors in her boudoir. Richard took the slippers off and examined them. Then he dropped them to the floor and looked over the naked feet.

The feet were like the rest of the body in a lot of ways. They were old and puffy, not the slim small elegant things of *Storms of Love*. The toenails were dry and yellow and cracked. In *Island Melody*, they had been shaped and painted—bright red, according to the magazines. Richard picked up the slippers and put them back on Tasheba Kent's feet. He was thinking furiously.

Feet feet feet, he kept telling himself, as he picked the linen sheet off the floor and draped it back over the body. There's only so much that can be done about feet.

Now that he knew what he wanted to do next, he felt much better, not really sleepy at all.

Down in the library on the tables with all the things to be auctioned there were shoes, dozens of shoes.

What he had to do now was to get his hands on some of them.

— 2 —

Mathilda Frazier knew that Gregor Demarkian wanted to talk to her. She had known, since last night, that he would want to talk to everyone. She didn't even object to talking to him, in principle. Lately, Mathilda had been congratulating herself on not being a woman like Hannah Graham. She didn't go looking for excuses to go on the offensive. She didn't throw monkey wrenches into other people's plans just because she felt like being contrary. She understood why Geraldine Dart and Kelly Pratt and the rest of them wanted to let Demarkian do some investigating before the police arrived. She was no more interested in facing a full-scale murder inquiry than anyone else was. It was just that Gregor Demarkian made her so damned *nervous*.

He came up to her just as everybody was filing out of the dining room after the discovery of the cufflink—an event that Kelly Pratt, at least, was treating like some episode in a Sherlock Holmes story—and it couldn't have been a worse time. The sleeping pills she had taken hadn't really worn off. Under ordinary circumstances, she would have been knocked out for hours yet. Apparently, watching an old woman die in front of you made a difference. Instead of conking right out, Mathilda had lain on the top of her bed and tossed and turned. Every once in a while, she'd had very disturbing dreams with dead bodies in them and old women floating on a sea of chiffon. Every once in a while, she had come awake, too, which never happened with these particular pills. That's why she kept getting the prescription refilled. Eventually, she had just given it up and come downstairs. She hadn't wanted breakfast and she hadn't wanted company, but she hadn't been able to

stand the idea of staying alone in her room one moment
longer.

Obviously, the same sort of thing had happened to
Hannah Graham. Hannah always looked awful, but now
she looked awful and ready to disperse into molecules. She
wasn't as quick with the nastiness, either. This morning
she seemed to be a beat behind the beat.

Why couldn't Gregor Demarkian want to talk to Hannah? Mathilda asked herself grumpily, but Demarkian was
paying no attention to Hannah, and Hannah had already
said that she would refuse to talk to him anyway. Gregor
Demarkian was waiting patiently at the dining room door
and smiling in her direction.

"I don't suppose it would work if I said I absolutely
had to fall asleep right this minute," Mathilda said. "I
don't suppose you'd believe me if I said I was about ready
to pass out."

"You look ready to pass out," Gregor Demarkian told
her. "But I only want you for a minute."

"You don't believe in that cufflink, do you?" Mathilda
asked him. "You don't think it's a very important clue."

"On the contrary." Demarkian shook his big head. "I
think it's extremely important. I just don't think it's important in the way everybody else seems to think it's important. If you understand what I'm saying."

"No."

"I just want you to come in here for a second. There
are a couple of things I want to ask you about the auction."

The "here" that Gregor Demarkian wanted her to
come into was the library, dark and gloomy even though
all its lights were lit, its three tables loaded with junk looking like they had no earthly reason for being.

"I wonder where the guard is this morning."

"He's still in the room over the garage," Demarkian
told her. "He isn't due in until eleven thirty. I think the
idea was to make the insurance company nominally
happy, while not spending any more money than absolutely necessary."

"Have you given any thought to the possibility that he
might be the one who killed Tasheba?" Mathilda asked.

"We don't know anything about him. Even Geraldine only seems to know that he's somebody from town."

"I've thought about it," Demarkian said impassively, "but I've also checked it out. It's not feasible."

"Why not?"

"Because all the doors on this house have automatic locks. You leave the house and pull the door shut behind you, and you're locked out. And three different people saw the man leave by the front door."

"Maybe he had a key."

"Geraldine Dart says not."

"I'm sure all the doors in the house don't lock like that," Mathilda said. "The French doors at the back couldn't."

"That's true," Gregor agreed, "but because of the terrain around here, those doors can only be approached through the house. You'd have to be an expert rock climber to get around to them on land even in the best of weather. Last night, the project would have been virtually impossible."

"Oh," Mathilda murmured, sitting down dejectedly in the nearest chair. "I suppose that leaves us with Carlton again. I wish we knew where he was. I wish we knew how he was. I keep thinking about Hannah's scenario, you know, about him killing Tasheba Kent and then trying to escape and then getting drowned. It's a terrible idea."

"Mmm," Gregor said.

He was standing next to the table with Tasheba Kent's things on it, looking down at a set of black bangle bracelets with a pair of earrings to match. They weren't among the more interesting items in the collection. Mathilda didn't expect them to fetch much in the sale.

"There are much better things on that table than those," she told Gregor Demarkian. "The cigarette holders are really valuable, especially the extra-long ones. The one with the silver inlays was the one she used in *Vamp*. She had it made for herself when the movie went into production and then she kept it. We think it's going to bring in more than twenty thousand dollars."

"For a cigarette holder?"

"Oh, yes. It may bring in even more now, after all of this. Auction buyers like mysteries and legends."

Gregor Demarkian picked up the black cigarette holder with the silver inlays, looked it over, and put it down again. "Tell me. How was it decided, which items to put up for auction?"

"It hasn't really been decided yet," Mathilda Frazier said. "We're still in negotiations. All these things on the tables are at least up for discussion."

"Who will decide what will go and what will stay?"

"Well, I decide some of it. There are some things an auction house like Halbard's just can't sell. But I like most of these things. The more complete a collection like this is, even down to pieces you don't expect are going to find a buyer, the better the auction tends to go. And sometimes you get lucky, and somebody like Richard Fenster comes in with a lot of money and a world-class obsession, and buys everything you have."

"Do you think Richard Fenster would be interested in buying all these things?"

"I think he'd be interested in buying everything that belonged to Tasheba Kent, yes. He's the world's most famous collector of her memorabilia. He'd probably also be quite interested in anything belonging to Cavender Marsh or Lilith Brayne that had connections to Tasheba Kent."

Gregor nodded. "Tell me something else now. Upstairs, in the room Cavender Marsh shared with Tasheba Kent, there are dozens of bound scrapbooks, covering every possible era in the public lives of the three of them—"

"Oh, I know," Mathilda said. "I've seen them. Aren't they wonderful? They'd bring hundreds of thousands of dollars at auction. I told both Cavender Marsh and Tasheba Kent that, and then I told Lydia Acken, because I thought she could drum some sense into their heads, but nothing worked. They just don't want to sell those scrapbooks."

"All right. So Cavender Marsh and Tasheba Kent weren't quite as willing to sell their things as I thought they were at first."

"Oh, yes they were," Mathilda said, "or are or whatever you want to call it. Those scrapbooks were practically the only things they held out. It's Hannah Graham that everybody is worried about."

"Hannah Graham?"

Mathilda shrugged. "You'd have to talk to Lydia Acken to get it all straight, because I don't really understand it, but what it comes down to is that there are bases on which Hannah Graham can sue to keep at least Lilith Brayne's things out of the auction. I mean, Lilith Brayne was her mother. And just because her father dumped her off on a relative or something, doesn't mean she and her mother would have been estranged if her mother had lived. That's why we invited her here, you see. We thought if we could get Hannah to come out here and pick a few of Lilith Brayne's things to keep, then she would be less likely to try to stop us from selling the rest."

"And would that matter? If she did stop you from selling any of Lilith Brayne's things at auction."

"It would matter a great deal, Mr. Demarkian. It's like I told you. Auction buyers like mysteries and legends. This is one of the great Hollywood mysteries of all time, a scandal. Two beautiful older sisters after the same younger man. Passion and intrigue and law courts and newspaper headlines and a romantic ending in Hitchcockian seclusion. We'd do pretty well auctioning off just the things that belonged to Tasheba Kent and Cavender Marsh, but throw in the things belonging to Lilith Brayne and we'll do spectacularly."

Gregor Demarkian walked over to the table with Lilith Brayne's things on it and looked down at it. Then he walked back to the table with Tasheba Kent's things on it and looked down on that. There was a frown on his face and two deep lines of concentration across his forehead. Mathilda was fascinated. Was this the way a great detective worked? What was he thinking about? Had there been women great detectives, too? Mathilda made a note to herself to check it out.

Gregor pushed some things around on the table with Tasheba Kent's things on it and then slapped the palm of his hand against the wood.

"A black feather boa," he said. "There was a black

feather boa in all the pictures of Tasheba Kent during the inquest."

"We're selling the black feather boa," Mathilda said quickly. "It's one of my favorite items."

"It's not here."

Mathilda went over to the table with Tasheba Kent's things on it and looked it over. Gregor Demarkian was right. The black feather boa wasn't there.

"I'm going to have Richard Fenster's head in a handbasket," Mathilda said furiously. "He's not going to get off this island until I've had every inch of his room, his luggage, and his person searched."

"Why are you so sure it was Fenster who took it?"

"Because he's the only one here who would have wanted it." Mathilda was pawing through all the things on the table. She didn't see anything else missing, but that didn't mean very much. She hadn't memorized every item. "I'm going to have to get my articles list and go over every piece. Do you notice anything else gone?"

"No," Gregor Demarkian said, "but I never had a very good idea of what was here. The shoes with the rhinestone buckles have been moved around on Lilith Brayne's table, if that means anything."

"It doesn't matter if things have been moved around," Mathilda said distractedly. "People are allowed to look."

Mathilda Frazier's mind was on one thing and one thing only: on Richard Fenster and what he had done to her, taking that feather boa and hiding it away.

Gregor Demarkian had gone back to the table with Lilith Brayne's things on it and picked up the shoes with the rhinestone buckles on them. He was staring at them with a very curious expression on his face.

But Mathilda Frazier was already, mentally, someplace else.

—— 2 ——

Upstairs in the family wing, Cavender Marsh was awake and had been awake for nearly an hour. He was, however, pretending to be still asleep. Earlier, satisfied that they

were all downstairs and likely to stay there for a while, he
had sneaked out to the bathroom to have a good washing
up. Then he had climbed back into bed, smoothed out his
sheets and his blankets, and made himself lie still. He had
noticed the gaps in the bookshelf full of scrapbooks and
deducted that Mr. Gregor Demarkian had been here. He
wondered if Mr. Gregor Demarkian had come in on his
own or if he had gotten the permission of Geraldine Dart.
Cavender Marsh didn't think it mattered. The only thing
that did matter was that nobody should know that
Tasheba Kent was already dead.

Already dead, Cavender thought, and nearly burst out
laughing.

Geraldine Dart was on the other side of the room
now, tidying things up, moving things around. She was
taking away all the bits and pieces of Tasheba Kent's birthday, as if the sight of a Hallmark card in a red envelope or
a two-inch-square jeweler's box wrapped in red foil paper
would give him a stroke. She was even taking the spools of
unused gift ribbon off the top of the desk and putting them
away in the long center drawer.

"What if he wakes up?" she kept saying to herself, in
a guttural mumble that would have been enough to wake
him if he had been asleep. "What if he wakes up?"

When Cavender Marsh woke up—officially this
time—he had every intention of having the next best thing
to a stroke, complete with screaming and crying and pass-
ing out. He had every intention of creating the biggest
scene on record in the history of just about any. He was an
excellent actor, one of the most talented and best trained
of his generation. He knew how to give a convincing performance. He'd been giving one to his dear companion
now for at least sixty years. She had never caught on for a
moment.

"Oh, God," Geraldine Dart was saying, holding a
package of pink-and-white-striped birthday candles in the
air. "Look at these. Just look at these."

Cavender did look at them, for a minute, but then he
shut his eyes again. Geraldine was getting very close to the
bureau mirror. He didn't want her to catch him when he

wasn't ready for her. He heard her pitch the package of candles into the drawer and then pick up something else.

"Oh, God, oh, God," she said again. "This is incredible."

Cavender Marsh had always thought that Geraldine Dart was incredible. He thought she was incredible now, fussing over birthday things that didn't matter anymore. Nobody was going to be having a birthday in this house any time soon. He listened to her going back and forth, back and forth, back and forth. He listened to her moving things and opening and closing drawers. Finally, he listened to her walk past his bed to the door.

"This is absolutely unbelievable," she said, very loudly, to no one at all.

Then she opened the door, went out, and closed the door behind her.

Cavender Marsh waited a little while, testing the atmosphere. There was no one in his room. If there had been, he could have felt them. There were no sounds in the hallway outside except for Geraldine Dart's footsteps, and they were moving away.

Cavender Marsh opened his eyes. Geraldine had done a very thorough job. All signs of Tasheba's impending birthday were gone. Even the little porcelain birthday cake music box had been whisked out of sight, and that had nothing to do with this birthday at all. It had been sent to Cavender himself by a fan from Tacoma five years ago. There had been a pair of red balloons near the window that were gone now. Cavender wondered if Geraldine had taken them with her or shoved them out into the weather to be battered into shreds.

The weather was really and truly awful. Cavender could hear it even if he couldn't see it through the closed curtains. He had lived on this island off the coast of Maine long enough to know what it was all this wind and hail and thunder meant. It was going to be at least another day before they could get off this island, or get somebody onto it to help them out, and that was going to cause a major problem.

Cavender considered the possibility of going on with the pretense of being asleep for another twenty-four hours, but he knew it wasn't feasible. Since he wasn't actually asleep, he was very hungry. He also needed to use the bathroom and stretch his legs and do all the other things people did when they were alert and alive and expecting to stay that way.

A scene, Cavender Marsh decided, was his only way out.

Because he didn't really care if that damned old bitch was dead.

But he did care if he stayed alive himself.

CHAPTER 5

— 1 —

The problem in cases like these, Gregor Demarkian told himself, was not in finding the solution. The solutions were easy, in spite of the confusion that surrounded them. From where he was sitting, he thought it would be only a matter of time. He knew (more or less) what had really happened in the death of Lilith Brayne. He knew what had happened in the death of Tasheba Kent, too. His suspect list was down to three people, and one of those remained under suspicion for purely aesthetic reasons. It never did to assume innocence where guilt was usually found.

The problem in cases like this was in knowing what they were really about, and understanding what was going to happen next. Criminals were not difficult to catch, only difficult to convict. Motives weren't hard to fathom, even in the most pathological serial killer. It was details that tripped you up, every time. Gregor was fairly sure that they were safe now, that everything that was going to happen had already happened, but he wished he could be sure.

The next thing to do was to find Carlton Ji. Gregor knew that. Waking from a fitful nap to a vision of black storm clouds and smashing seas—he had left his window open when he'd fallen asleep this time; the weather was so black, there was no reason not to—he knew immediately that he should have insisted on looking harder when they first looked. Everybody else seemed to have forgotten about Carlton Ji, either accidentally or deliberately. Gregor didn't blame them. The easiest thing to do, right now, with the whole bunch of them stuck together like this with no way to escape each other, was to demonize Carlton Ji as much as possible. Carlton Ji wasn't around to protest. His disappearance was mysterious. They could blame him for everything and go on eating together, drinking together, and arguing with each other, without having to worry if someone was about to stick a tranquilizer in their drink or hit them over the head with a baseball bat.

The second thing Gregor knew he ought to do was to look for the murder weapon, or at least for an instrument of the same kind as the murder weapon. Gregor would make himself look for the murder weapon itself eventually, because murderers were funny. If Gregor himself had committed a murder of this kind under circumstances of this kind, he would have dropped his weapon out a window and into the sea straight off, or gone out on one of the terraces and hurled it as far as it would go. There was no reason at all, on an island like this, to be caught with the equivalent of a smoking gun in your hand. Murderers got attached to their weapons, though. They began to feel about them the way short-breathed family men with too many obligations felt about their life insurance policies. Gregor sometimes thought that killing, outside of war, must be a very difficult thing, even for serial killers like Dahmer and Bundy. Murderers always seemed to want to use the same weapon over and over and over again, as if it were a magic wand given to them in trust by their fairy godmothers. There had been a time in his life when Gregor Demarkian wanted desperately to know why people killed each other. He could remember standing at the side of a shallow trench next to a rural road in southwestern Massachusetts, looking down at the bodies and skeletons of fourteen girls between the ages of eighteen and twenty-two, and wondering what it was, what started it, what made it continue, what brought it to an end. Murderers who killed like that were supposed to be different from other murderers. In Gregor's experience, some of them ac-

tually were. Surely Ted Bundy had been a unique case.
Most of the serial murderers Gregor had dealt with in his
time at the FBI had been surprisingly similar to the nonse-
rial, garden-variety murderers he had dealt with in his odd
little retirement noncareer of sideline investigations. Serial
murderers broke down into two main categories: crazies
who belonged permanently in mental institutions and people (usually men) with practical motives that just weren't
the kind of practical motives most other people could
identify with. The kind of murderer Gregor now dealt
with also broke down into two categories: people who
exploded in blind passion or heedless rage, usually helped
along by alcohol or drugs, and people with practical motives that just about everybody could understand. Members of the general public insisted on believing that there
was a fundamental difference between someone who killed
his wife to get the insurance and someone who caused five
babies in an emergency ward to go into convulsions—and
one to eventually die—because she wanted to show what a
good nurse she could be in an emergency. Gregor could
see how the cases seemed different, but he was certain they
weren't fundamentally. Fundamentally, all murderers were
alike, and their motives could be reduced to a single simple
sentence: *I can get away with it.*

Gregor thought he would start looking for Carlton
Ji—on his own; he never liked asking Bennis's help in a
situation like this, and he didn't trust any of the rest of
them, not even the ones he knew perfectly well hadn't
committed this murder—by finding the back stairs Geraldine Dart had been talking about. But at the last minute he
decided to make a detour. It was now two o'clock in the
afternoon. Most of the guests in this house were undoubt-
edly either taking naps, as Gregor had been, or trying to.
Gregor thought he would try the person he wanted anyway. If he woke her up, he could always apologize and go
back to his original plan. He walked down the hall to
Lydia Acken's door and tapped gently—too gently, he
thought, to wake her out of a sound sleep. He had nothing
to worry about. As soon as he tapped, he heard movement
behind the door. Then the door opened and Lydia's head

popped out, an anxious look spread across her face like makeup.

"Oh," she said, "Mr. Demarkian. Oh, come right in. I tried to take a nap, but I couldn't fall asleep, so then I was trying to get some work done, but I wasn't managing that, either. I've never been involved in a murder case before. Is it always this—worrying—to the participants?"

"It is to some of them," Gregor said, coming inside. Lydia's room was just like all the other bedrooms in this wing, with the same furniture and the same curtains and the same rugs. It was as if somebody had gone through with the interior decoration equivalent of a tract house plan, doling out accoutrements like parts from an assembly line. Gregor sat down on the stool that went with the vanity table and picked up an amateurishly printed brochure emblazoned with the words *EAST VILLAGE LEGAL SERVICES*. "What's this?" he asked her.

"That," Lydia said, taking the brochure out of his hand, "is my present escapist fantasy. East Village Legal Services is a group down around St. Mark's Place that does free legal work with indigent people who need help negotiating the city bureaucracy or that kind of thing."

"It sounds interesting."

"I know it does. It sounds a great deal more interesting than trusts and estates and the annual partners' dinner and one more bonus for my pension plan."

"Is it something you do now, in your free time?"

Lydia Acken laughed. "Mr. Demarkian, in a law firm like mine, there is no such thing as free time. Oh, they'd give me a little space to do *pro bono* work if I asked for it. It's good public relations. But someplace like EVLS needs more than that."

"Like what?"

"Like lawyers who have other means of support and who can work full time. Like lawyers who can really concentrate on the cases, because the cases are very complicated. It's not like Legal Aid. It's not criminal things usually. It's more—oh, you know. Child Protective Services took away some woman's child because it was only four months old and she was feeding it taro root and good social work practice says that no child is supposed to have solid food until it's at least nine months old, but back in the Virgin Islands or wherever this woman is from all children get solid food almost immediately because not to do it is supposed to be bad for the child. So then you have a big mess, and the woman wants her child back, and the social worker is some twenty-one-year-old graduate of City College who thinks she knows abuse and neglect when she sees it, and—" Lydia Acken shrugged.

"You sound excited when you talk about it."

"I am excited when I talk about it," Lydia said. "I'm excited when I think about it. I've even worked out how I could quit the firm and live more simply and all the rest of it. I suppose what it comes down to is that I just don't have the courage. White-shoe Wall Street law firms are very womblike, cocoon sorts of places."

Gregor smiled. "I think your courage is fine. I think if you want to do it you will. Maybe you just need to get yourself used to the idea."

"Sometimes I think all I want is to spend the rest of my life dealing with real things that really matter. Not whether putting all the bonds into some multimillionaire's second wife's name will raise estate tax estimates if the estate tax is due and payable the year after next. You have no idea what old rich men are like. They can natter away about this nonsense for months on end."

Actually, Gregor knew very well what old rich men were like. He had met quite a few of them in his time, in person or over the phone, including Bennis Hannaford's father, who had been one of the oldest, one of the richest, and one of the most eccentric. Bennis refused to dignify her father's personality by calling it "eccentric," however. She just came right out and called the old man "the nastiest piece of business I've ever met."

Gregor stretched out his legs. "Believe it or not, I came down here with a purpose. I was wondering if you might know something that could help me out."

Lydia frowned. "I don't know what I could know. I'm afraid I couldn't discuss any confidential business—"

"No, no," Gregor assured her. "This shouldn't come under the definition of confidential business. It's about the death of Lilith Brayne."

"Oh?"

"I've been looking at some scrapbooks that belong to Cavender Marsh and Tasheba Kent, and there are quite a few newspaper stories about the death and the investigation and the inquest, but they aren't big on forensic details, if you understand what I mean. And I've been thinking that there must be copies of the inquest transcripts around somewhere. And the most logical person to have them would be Cavender Marsh's lawyer."

"Oh, dear," Lydia said. "We don't have anything like that in the files at the firm. Of course, we do have some information about the case—"

"Yes?"

"Well, you see," Lydia explained, "we were attorneys of record for Mr. Marsh even at the time, but we're not a firm that handles criminal cases. We certainly don't handle this kind of criminal case. From time to time, we've been involved in SEC investigations and tax evasion actions. We don't handle the actual criminal litigation in those cases, but we cooperate with the contact firms that do. But a murder investigation . . . ." Lydia shook her head.

"I see," Gregor said slowly. "And of course, this case took place in France. I didn't really expect that someone from your firm had gone across the Atlantic Ocean to represent Cavender Marsh at the inquest. I was just hoping there might be some material on the case floating around, and that you might have seen it."

"Oh, no, there's nothing like that," Lydia said. Then she cocked her head in curiosity. "Exactly what is it that you're looking for? What kind of information?"

Gregor yawned. "Oh, well," he said, "the condition of the body mostly, when it was found. The articles I've read all say that Lilith Brayne's body was a terrible mess when they fished it out of the water, but they never tell you what *kind* of mess. I suppose the details were too gruesome to be reported in the popular press, but that doesn't help me any."

Lydia Acken looked amused. "The details weren't too gruesome to be reported in the popular press," she said. "It's just that those two old farts have been censoring their clippings."

"What do you mean?"

"I'll bet you the clippings you saw all made them look pretty good. I'm not saying they looked like saints, mind you—they hardly could have, under the circumstances—but I'll bet those pieces all had that fawning flattered gush of '30s celebrity journalism."

"Not all of them did," Gregor Demarkian said. "Some of them were from sources like the *London Times.*"

Lydia Acken waved this away. "The problem with the respectable press is that they're too interested in being respectable to act like the press. Do you remember my telling you, when we first met, that my mother was a big fan of the case—that she made it a kind of hobby?"

"I remember something of the kind."

"Well, those were the days before television and all the mothers thought children—especially girl children—shouldn't be allowed to go to scary movies, so all I had for excitement were my mother's clippings. And some of them were very, very exciting. *I* know what kind of mess Lilith Brayne's body was in when it was found. It was described in detail years later in *Confidential.* And the things they had to say about Tasheba Kent and Cavender Marsh—if it were me, I wouldn't put that kind of thing in my scrapbooks, either."

"So what did it say?"

"Well," Lydia Acken replied, "in the first place, Lilith Brayne fell over a balcony railing on a terrace high up on the side of a cliff. The terrace was part of a villa she and Cavender Marsh were renting at the time."

"That's in everything."

"I know it is, but give me time. All right. When Lilith Brayne fell, her body apparently bounced off the side of the cliff as it went down, and instead of falling into the little river delta there, or farther out into the sea, it fell into a sluice that processed sewage for the town. You had to read the real sensationalist press to find out that it was sewage that was involved. Everybody else said water, as if she'd fallen into an irrigation ditch. Anyway, aside from the sluice itself, this thing had these big sharp-edged metal blades that turned whenever the water passed over them, that were supposed to chop up the solid sewage into manageable pieces—"

"Oh, my God," Gregor said.

Lydia nodded. "She was cut to ribbons. Of course, she wasn't rendered into small pieces the way sewage would have been. The blades weren't that strong. They couldn't cut through bone. But still. If it hadn't been for this fluke where her head got cut off and pitched outside the sluice by an action of the water, they wouldn't have been able to identify her at all. I don't think there was anything much left of her body."

"Dear Christ," Gregor said. "And this was in *Confidential*, was it?"

"I don't remember. *Confidential* or one of the magazines like it. And they weren't very friendly to Cavender Marsh or Tasheba Kent. There was a reason why Cavender Marsh never worked again after all that happened, in spite of the fact that he was one of the most popular and successful movie actors of his time before it. The hostility to him was enormous. When he and Tasheba got off the boat in New York Harbor, after Cavender had been cleared and they were allowed to come back to the States, there was a positive mob waiting for them, with eggs and old vegetables and all sorts of other things besides. One woman had a whole bottle full of urine she poured right onto Tasheba Kent's head. The police had to be called out in force."

"I think I'm beginning to be sorry that I never developed a taste for the gutter press," Gregor said.

"Oh, I read that sort of thing all the time. It's much more informative than the Op-Ed page of the *Times,* if you just skip all the nonsense about being kidnapped by UFOs and go straight to the murders."

"Right," Gregor said.

"Was any of that any kind of help to you? I know it wasn't the same thing as a coroner's report, but it was probably as well as you'd do even if you had a coroner's report. From 1938, I mean. It wasn't as if they had DNA tracing and all that back then."

"It was a great deal of help to me," Gregor said. "It was one of those details that had to be cleared up, because

I didn't dare get it wrong, and now it is cleared up. So the next thing I have to do is—What the hell is that?"

"That" was a racket in the hallway, consisting of swearing and yelling and banging and stamping, and getting louder and less coherent by the second. Lydia raised her head to listen to it, and sighed.

"That," she told Gregor Demarkian, "is Hannah Graham, having another first-class fit."

—— 2 ——

Hannah Graham was indeed having another first-class fit. Hannah was having it in the middle of the guest wing hall, and Gregor understood as soon as he looked at her that she was having it to collect an audience. He and Lydia were the first to emerge from any of the rooms to see what was going on. They weren't left alone in their contemplation for long. Hannah was jumping and yelling and kicking her door. Then she marched down the hall and kicked every other door she came to that was still shut. When she passed by Lydia and Gregor, Gregor thought she was going to kick them. Instead, she glared at them and started to kick the walls. First Kelly Pratt, then Mathilda Frazier, then Richard Fenster emerged from their rooms. When Bennis Hannaford came out, she gave Gregor and Lydia, still standing together in Lydia's doorway, an amused smile, then lit up a cigarette and worked on looking bored. In no time at all, Geraldine Dart came hurrying in from the family wing, blowing smoke and breathing fire.

"What do you think you're doing?" Geraldine demanded, grabbing Hannah's arm and jerking her to a stop. "You're going to wake up your father. You're going to give him a heart attack."

"The start of World War Three couldn't give that old goat a heart attack," Hannah Graham snarled, jerking her arm out of Geraldine's grasp. "And don't you touch me. Don't you dare. I have every intention of suing the pants off everybody in this house as soon as I get off this damn island, and I'm going to start with you."

"I don't care who you sue," Geraldine Dart snapped.

"I won't have you behaving like this when there's a frail old man in the house."

Bennis Hannaford blew a stream of smoke into the air. "Haven't we had this argument before?" she asked.

But it was Mathilda Frazier, more than any of them, who had finally had enough. Gregor could see it in her face, and in the way she pushed herself forward until she was standing between Hannah and Geraldine.

"Look," Mathilda said to Hannah, "is there a *point* to this commotion this time? I mean, do you have something in particular you want to share with us this time or is this just another one of your periodic bids for attention?"

"Maybe she's the one who took the black feather boa," Richard Fenster said.

Mathilda ignored him. "Because if this is one of your periodic bids for attention," she told Hannah, "I swear to God, this time I'm going to slap your face."

Hannah Graham gave Mathilda Frazier a tight little smile. "I was taking a nap," she said. "I had all my doors locked just like the rest of you probably did, to make sure I was safe. Why don't you all come into my room and see what happened while I was all locked up tight and fast asleep."

A ripple of unease went up and down the hall. Hannah Graham was a world-class bitch, but she wouldn't pull something like this unless she had something to show. They had all been lying down in their rooms with their doors locked. Gregor could practically hear them thinking: *Now what?*

Gregor came forward—it was obvious that nobody else was going to; they were all waiting for him—and presented himself to Hannah Graham.

"So," he said. "What is it?"

"Go in and look," Hannah Graham told him.

Gregor went down the hall to Hannah's room and stepped inside. He was expecting to find a mess—drawers pulled out, luggage turned upside down, clothes scattered across the floor. But the drawers were still neatly in their bureaus and the luggage was still intact and exactly where it belonged. That did not, however, mean that the room had not been tampered with. It had been tampered with in a distinct and elaborate way. It had been decorated for a birthday party.

Helium-filled balloons in six different colors bounced against the high ceiling. Crepe-paper rosettes the size of basketballs were tied to the backs of chairs and the foot of the bed. Crepe-paper streamers were wound around the window frame and left to dangle from the tops of the closet doors. A pile of popper party favors had been left on top of the chest of drawers. A tall layer cake with white icing topped by three fat candles (a one and two zeros, making 100) was on the glass top of the vanity table in front of the mirror. The candles were lit, and the wax was dripping down.

Hannah Graham came in and put her hands on her hips. "So what do you think?" she demanded. "Is this enough for me to start screaming about?"

The rest of them had followed her inside—or almost inside. They made a tight little knot now in the doorway.

"Oh, my God," Mathilda Frazier was saying. "Oh, my God. Just look at all this."

"This couldn't have been done while you were just asleep," Richard Fenster said. "You'd have woken up."

"Maybe somebody slipped me whatever they slipped Cavender Marsh last night," Hannah retorted.

Gregor Demarkian was looking over the crepe-paper rosettes and the crepe-paper streamers and the cake on the vanity table.

"Geraldine?" he asked.

"I'm right here," Geraldine Dart answered in a shaky voice.

"Do you know where all this stuff came from?"

Geraldine Dart nodded vigorously. "Oh, yes," she said. "I made that cake myself. It's been in the big refrigerator in the kitchen since the day before yesterday. And the other things have been in the pantry. Except that the balloons weren't blown up, of course. There were just little plastic packages of them and a big tank full of helium to fill them with."

"Mmm," Gregor said.

He looked around the room a couple of times. Then he got down on the floor and looked under the bed.

"Uh-huh," he said. "Just as I thought. Mr. Fenster?"

"What is it?"

"It's not a body I'm asking you to touch this time, just a large metal tank. I'm a little too old to go hauling that sort of thing around by myself. Would you mind getting it out where we could all see it?"

Richard Fenster got down on the floor, reached under the bed, and began to tug something toward them. A moment later, the top of a large metal cylinder emerged into view. Richard Fenster tugged again; the rest of the tank came out from under the bed. Then he got to his feet and set the thing upright.

"There," he said. "And there's paint on the side that says 'helium,' too."

"Is this the tank you were talking about?" Gregor asked Geraldine Dart.

"Well, it must be," Geraldine said. "I mean, there couldn't be two of them, could there? You have to get them over from the mainland by boat, and it isn't easy. I know from experience. This isn't the kind of thing one of you people could have sneaked over in your luggage."

"No," Gregor agreed, "it's not that."

"I don't think all this happened while Hannah was taking a nap," Kelly Pratt said. "I don't think it's possible. I think she must have been prowling around in the house somewhere and she doesn't want us to know what she was doing."

"It's like I said before," Richard Fenster said. "She took the black feather boa."

Bennis Hannaford pushed her way to the front of the crowd and presented herself to Gregor. "What's going on?" she asked him. "Do you have the faintest idea what this is all about?"

"It's about misdirection," Gregor said.

"Wonderful," Bennis told him. "Would you like to be more explicit?"

"No. I'd like to find out where it is, first, and then I'd like to go on from there."

"Where what is?"

By now, Gregor had considered every corner and piece

of furniture in the room, and come to the conclusion that there was only one possible place.

"It's got to be in the closet," he said, moving forward and opening the closet doors.

Since there was nothing else in the closet—not even Hannah's dresses, which she had left in her suit bag and not bothered to hang up—it came out as soon as Gregor opened the closet door. First it slid forward. Then it slid sideways. Then it came to rest in a heap.

It was the body of Carlton Ji, and it was in very bad shape. The head was full of scratches and gouges. The side of its face had been smashed in by a blunt instrument.

And there was a black feather boa wrapped around its neck.

PART 3

THE
ORCHESTRA
OF GLASS

CHAPTER 1

— 1 —

What Gregor really wanted to know, right this second, was when the music was going to start. Surely there ought to be something, preferably played on an organ, to highlight the impossible drama of this moment. At the very least there ought to be thunder and lightning—but the weather wasn't cooperating. It was still bad, but it wasn't angry-bad. The wind was raging and screaming. Gregor had no doubt that if he looked out the windows, he would find that the ocean was a mess. Thunder and lightning, however, were absent. What was taking their place at the moment was Geraldine Dart's keening, high-pitched and hysterical, as automatic and robotic as the screeching of a car burglar alarm on a residential street at midnight.

I am losing my temper, Gregor told himself. I am losing my temper and that is not a good or smart or safe thing to do.

The whole group had now pushed its way into Hannah Graham's room. They were ignoring Geraldine Dart's noise completely, but they were fascinated with the body of Carlton Ji. Gregor half expected one of them to step forward and try to take Carlton Ji's pulse. Mathilda Frazier seemed to be on the verge of tears. Bennis Hannaford looked as if she wanted to go somewhere and chain-smoke. Gregor knew that she wouldn't do it here. If there was one thing he had taught her in all their time together, it was that it was absolutely forbidden to smoke at a crime scene.

Not that this was a crime scene, Gregor thought. At least, it wasn't the right crime scene. He wondered where Carlton Ji had died.

"If you think I'm going to let this corpse lie here like a lump for the next two days," Hannah Graham said, "you're out of your mind. I want you to get him out of here right this second."

"I'm not going to do anything of the kind right this second," Gregor said. He stepped over the body and looked into the closet. It was not a closet as closets in more modern houses would be understood. When this house was built, closets and cupboards were not ordinarily included in the design of rooms. Those functions were taken over by large pieces of furniture like wardrobes and armoires. This was a wardrobe that had been grafted onto the wall at some more or less recent date. The floor of it was a good four inches above the floor of the room itself. Gregor looked around in the dust in there and found absolutely nothing. He looked on the overhead shelf and found a couple of plastic dry cleaning bags, folded. He swore under his breath. In Armenian.

"I hope you know what you're doing," Hannah Graham told him. "As far as I can see, you're just tampering with evidence."

"Evidence of what?" Kelly Pratt asked her. "The only evidence that's going to be found in here is the evidence that proves you killed him."

Hannah bristled. "Oh, you won't find any evidence like that in here."

"Oh, shut up, all of you," Mathilda Frazier said. "I'm tired of this."

Geraldine Dart had stopped screaming. It would have been a relief, but Gregor didn't notice. He had stopped listening to her a while ago. He bent over Carlton Ji's body and looked into the wound on the side of his face. As far as Gregor could tell, it was the same as the wound on the side of Tasheba Kent's face. They had to have been made with the same weapon. Gregor turned the body on its back and went at the black feather boa. It was wound around and around Carlton Ji's neck, like the woolen mufflers his mother used to wind around his own on cold days when he was a boy in Philadelphia. Gregor got the boa unwound and put it aside, noting to himself how old and delicate it was. A couple of small feathers came off in his hands. Others seemed to be hanging by a thread. He tilted Carlton Ji's neck back and forth, to get a good look at the neck, but there was nothing to see.

"All right," he said out loud. "That was just for effect."

"Effect?" Lydia Acken sounded indignant.

"A lot gets done for effect around here, haven't you noticed that?" he asked her. "Screaming ghosts in the night. Corpses rolling downstairs. Although that was probably accidental."

"I'm glad you said that," Richard Fenster said. "How could anybody possibly have set that up?"

"Oh, I don't know," Gregor said. "Last summer, I took the niece and nephew of a friend of mine to a movie about dinosaurs where the dinosaurs looked absolutely real. People seem to be able to do a lot of things these days."

"Gregor," Bennis said. "I think you're losing it."

Gregor was examining the scratches on Carlton Ji's head. Actually, they were worse than scratches in some places. They were tears. Carlton Ji had been cut and he had bled badly.

"Before he died," Gregor told them, not unhappy to see how mystified they were. He turned to Geraldine Dart and asked, "Where are the bats?"

"Bats?"

"Bats," Gregor said firmly. "Before this man died, he had a major argument with some bats. There are bat droppings in his hair. And there are scratches and gouges on his scalp, which bled heavily, which means they were made while his heart was still beating healthily. There have to be bats somewhere in this house."

"In the attic," Geraldine said hastily. "We've had them in the attic once or twice."

"That figures." Gregor straightened.

"So what are you going to do now?" Bennis asked him. "Do you want to go search the attic?"

"No." The last thing Gregor wanted to do was to go wandering around in a dark attic full of bats that might be just as unhappy to see him as they had been to see Carlton Ji. Bats in the United States were often rabid. As far as Gregor was concerned, the police could take care of them.

"What I want to do is go down to Carlton Ji's room and really look around," Gregor told them. "I want to find his notes."

"You searched his room last night," Kelly Pratt said. "You didn't find anything."

"I didn't search his room," Gregor told him. "I just looked around to see if anybody was there or if there was any sign that Mr. Ji had packed up and taken off. Although it was fairly obvious even then that he had to be dead."

"Was it?" Mathilda Frazier looked utterly bewildered. "It wasn't obvious to me."

"It was obvious to *him* because *he's* the great detective." Hannah Graham sounded triumphant.

"I want to go down there and look through all his pieces of paper," Gregor continued, as if they hadn't spoken. "I want to get into his computer, if he brought one. Bennis? Can you do that?"

"If it's something normal like an Apple or an IBM," Bennis said. "And if he wasn't too much of a hacker."

Gregor rubbed fragments of bat droppings from his fingers. "Somehow, Carlton Ji didn't seem to me to be the type to be much of a hacker," he said.

"Why not?" Kelly Pratt demanded. "He was an Oriental."

Gregor ignored this. "What we need to find out is if Carlton Ji was killed because of something he knew or because he was simply in the wrong place at the wrong time. I tend to the latter theory, but I can't just let it go without checking. So what I want to do next is to go down the hall and make a systematic—"

"My God," Cavender Marsh said. "That young man is dead."

—— 2 ——

They should have been expecting it, of course. They should have known that Cavender Marsh wouldn't sleep forever. They should have been ready to take care of him. They weren't. Even Gregor wasn't. Cavender Marsh came tripping into the room with his spry old man's jaunty gait, leaned down over Carlton Ji's body, and paled.

"He isn't just dead," Cavender Marsh said. "He's been hit. Somebody's killed him."

"Now, Mr. Marsh." Geraldine Dart rushed forward and began to tug the old man away from the body. "It's really quite all right. Mr. Demarkian is a detective, and he's taking care of everything."

"I know Mr. Demarkian is a detective." Cavender Marsh spoke scornfully. "I read *People* magazine just like you do. Why has this young man been killed in my house? Does Tash know about it yet?"

"Oh," Geraldine said. "Well—"

"Miss Kent is in the television room," Mathilda Frazier rushed in with anxious brightness. "We haven't had a chance to tell her about any of this as of yet."

Cavender was incredulous. "Tash is in the television room? The *television* room?"

"The cat was on the roof," Gregor said to the ceiling.

Geraldine Dart had finally managed to get her employer away from Carlton Ji's body and over near the bed, but she hadn't been able to stop him from staring at it.

"Incredible," the old man kept saying. "Incredible. And what was he doing with the feather boa?"

"He was wearing it," Hannah Graham said.

"This is Ms. Graham's room," Kelly Pratt said.

Cavender Marsh looked from one to the other of them, frowning. "I think I'm going to go downstairs and see Tash," he said finally, shaking free of Geraldine's grasp. "I don't like what's going on around here. I don't think she'll like it either."

"But you can't go down and see Miss Kent." Geraldine grabbed for him again. "You just can't. She's resting."

"For God's sake, Geraldine," Cavender Marsh said

with contempt. "Tash wouldn't rest in the television room. She'd rest in her own bed. That's why we put in the elevator."

"I think you should let him go," Gregor told them all quietly. "I think it's an excellent idea for Mr. Marsh to go down and see his wife."

Cavender Marsh took advantage of Geraldine Dart's stunned paralysis in the next moment to slip through her grasp and head out into the hall. He was humming under his breath as he went, or maybe muttering, it was hard to tell. Geraldine Dart emerged from her deep freeze into an explosion. She advanced on Gregor Demarkian with both fists raised and damn near hit him.

"Just *what* do you think you're doing?" she demanded. "Are you out of your mind? To all intents and purposes, you've just murdered that man."

"Oh, I don't think so," Gregor said mildly. "Why don't we follow him downstairs and see?"

"Why don't we follow him downstairs and get ready to administer CPR," Geraldine spat. "My God, how stupid could you be?"

"I'll tell you how stupid I'm not," Gregor said. "I'm not so stupid that I don't realize that anybody who had taken a quantity of sleeping pills sufficient to keep himself asleep as long as Cavender Marsh has been pretending to be asleep—would now be dead."

Geraldine Dart hesitated. Her eyes widened, her lips formed another angry retort. Then she turned and ran out of the room, saying nothing at all. No one stopped her. While she and Gregor had been talking, most of the others had started to follow Cavender Marsh downstairs. They were like the residents of Utah and Nevada who had sat on their porches to watch nuclear test explosions in the desert. Only Bennis was left, and she wasn't going to go until Gregor did.

"Are you saying that Cavender Marsh already knows that Tasheba is dead?" she asked him now. "Or are you saying that he killed her?"

"Let's just say I'm saying that Cavender Marsh knows that there is a corpse in the television room. No, that's not right. He knows that there is another corpse in the house that isn't Carlton Ji."

"You are saying he killed her," Bennis said, narrowing her eyes at him.

Gregor shook his head. "It's more complicated than that. Let's go downstairs now, Bennis. I want to see what happens next."

"You make it sound like a soap opera."

"It's not a soap opera, Bennis. It's a silent movie. Everything that goes on in this house is a silent movie. Never forget that for a moment. If you do, it will make you crazy."

"I'm already crazy. And I haven't noticed anybody being silent up to now."

Gregor began to nudge Bennis down the stairs. She moved along without needing much prodding. Below them, they could see the tag end of the little group of guests, crowding around the television room door—but not too closely around. An explosion was coming and they didn't want to be too near it.

"Come on, hurry up," Gregor told Bennis.

Then he hurried up on his own, without looking back to see if she was keeping pace. He got to the bottom of the stairs and swung around to the back. Mathilda Frazier was standing farthest away. She had her arms wrapped around her upper body like a substitute for a bulletproof vest. Richard Fenster was the closest, practically hanging through the television room door. He had a nasty, sardonic grin on his face.

That young man knows too much and isn't careful about it, Gregor thought. He reached the television room door and pulled Richard Fenster away from it, so that he could get inside. Cavender Marsh was already inside, alone in the small room and looking distinctly confused. The body of Tasheba Kent was still lying where they had left it on the couch, covered completely by a white linen sheet. Cavender Marsh kept walking from the window to the couch and back to the window again. He had a baffled, anguished look on his face, like someone who had just gone into shock.

"I don't understand it," he said, as Gregor came into

the room. "I just don't understand it. Tash is under this sheet?"

"Would you like me to take the sheet away and show you?" Gregor asked politely.

Cavender Marsh walked over to the couch and took a deep and audible breath. He seemed to be trembling, but determined.

"No," he told Gregor. "No, I'll do it myself. You are telling me that she's dead, aren't you?"

"Yes, she's dead."

"Well, all right. She was ninety-nine years old. It's not as if she hasn't lived a full life. It's not as if dying at ninety-nine should come as such a shock."

Gregor said nothing. Cavender Marsh put his hand resolutely on the linen sheet and drew it back. He moved more slowly than Gregor had ever seen him move, drawing out the effect. Tasheba Kent was lying a little on her side, so that all that could be seen of her head at first was the part that wasn't damaged. Her eyes were closed and her lips were slack, but they would both have been just like that if she had been nothing worse than asleep.

Cavender Marsh relaxed a little and squared his shoulders. "All right," he said. "That's not too bad. She looks very peaceful."

"Yes, she does."

"I don't like the way she's lying, though. She never sleeps on her side. She finds it uncomfortable. She says it makes her arm go to sleep."

"I don't think it matters to her now, which way she's lying," Gregor said.

"Of course it doesn't," Cavender Marsh agreed. "It's silly to think it does. But I can't help myself, you know, after all this time. I'll always think of her as still alive."

"That's probably very natural."

"So I'll just move her around a little so that she looks comfortable," Cavender Marsh said.

He put his hands on the shoulders of Tasheba Kent's corpse, and Gregor did not try to stop him. He moved the body around until it was lying on its back and then stepped back to admire his handiwork. The rigor was wearing off. Tasheba Kent's body was much more flexible than it had been, but not yet as flexible as it would get. Her head lolled gently back and forth on the stalk of her neck.

"There," Cavender Marsh started to say, and then he stopped, and frowned. "Wait a minute . . . what's this?"

Cavender Marsh leaned forward, grabbed her face by the jaw and twisted it until he could see the side of her head that had been hidden from him.

"She's been hit," he exclaimed in stupefaction. "She's been hit. Somebody murdered her."

"It does look like that," Gregor told him.

Cavender Marsh jumped away from the body. "This is terrible. This is terrible. There must be some kind of maniac in the house."

"Do you think so?" Gregor asked. "I dealt with maniacs for ten years, and this just doesn't have that kind of feel to me."

"You must be joking." Cavender Marsh was a tower of fury. "This is a hundred-year-old woman we're talking about here. There can't be any reason to murder a hundred-dred-year-old woman. It's insane."

"I thought so myself in the beginning," Gregor said judiciously, "but I've changed my mind. I can think of a couple of perfectly good reasons for murdering this woman."

"Name one," Cavender Marsh demanded.

Gregor could have named two, but he didn't get the chance. The house was suddenly torn apart by a giggle and a laugh, and then a scream rent the air, powerful and piercing.

"Oh, my God," Mathilda Frazier said from outside in the foyer. "It's back again."

"What is that?" Cavender Marsh had gone white.

"That's your ghost," Gregor told him. "Last night it was doing the sound track from *The House on Haunted Hill*. Tonight I think we're doing *The Conqueror Worm*. It might be *The Tingler*."

Bennis stuck her head into the television room. "Gregor?"

"I'm coming," Gregor said.

—— 2 ——

The first thing Gregor Demarkian noticed when he got out
to the foyer was Geraldine Dart. She looked like a character in a *Twilight Zone* episode or a child playing statues.
Her eyes were wide and wild. Her mouth was open. Her
hands were out in the air in front of her, stiff and useless.
Gregor went past her and out toward the front door. The
sound was louder there and the light was better. It didn't
take him very long to find what he was looking for. Up at
the top corners of the front door, imbedded discreetly in
the walls, were two tiny speakers for an intercom system.

"All right," he said. "Miss Dart?"

Geraldine Dart unfroze. "Oh, dear," she whimpered.
"Oh, dear. I don't know what's happening. I really don't."

"Don't worry about what's happening for the moment," Gregor told her. "Answer a few questions for me,
please. Is there a microphone for this intercom system in
the foyer?"

"What? Oh. Oh, no. There aren't many microphones.
We didn't need them. We just had them in the bedrooms
and the bathrooms upstairs. And there's one in the pantry."

"In the pantry?"

"It was a mistake. We got some local man from
Hunter's Pier to put the system in and he made a mistake.
And it wasn't worthwhile to correct it. Oh, my God. The
pantry."

"What is she talking about?" Richard Fenster demanded.

"I've got to go," Geraldine Dart cried.

She turned away from them and rushed down the hall
to the kitchen. One or two of the others started to follow,
but when they saw that Gregor wasn't going to, they
stopped. Gregor stayed where he was and waited. Screams
crashed down around them, soprano-high and hysterical.
Gregor was more and more sure that what he was hearing
was from *The Tingler*. In no time at all, Geraldine Dart
came rushing back, even more frightened and frantic than
she had been before.

"It's not there," she burst out. "It's not there. I don't understand it."

"Did you leave it there?" Gregor asked her. "It was—what? A CD player? A tape machine?"

"A CD player," Geraldine replied miserably. "And of course I didn't leave it there. I wasn't that stupid. I took it upstairs and put it in my room."

"Is there a microphone in your room?"

"Yes, there is. There are microphones in all the rooms on the family wing."

"It's probably still there, then," Gregor said. "I think we'd all appreciate it if you went upstairs and turned it off."

"Wait a minute," Kelly Pratt said brusquely. "Do you mean she did it on purpose? She put some kind of record on a stereo and made us all jump out of our skins?"

"If you'd been listening to me, you'd have known that all along," Hannah Graham said. "I told you they were setting us all up. I told you."

"Go," Gregor told Geraldine Dart. "The noise is getting on my nerves."

"It's getting on everybody's nerves," Mathilda Frazier said.

"But I didn't do this." Geraldine Dart was nearly in tears herself now. "I didn't do this. I have no idea how it happened."

"It doesn't matter who did it," Gregor told her. "It only matters that you make it stop."

Cavender Marsh pushed forward. "It matters to me who did it."

"She was the one who did it last night," Richard Fenster said. "I caught her at it when she was trying to take the stuff away."

Geraldine Dart backed away from them. "I'm going," she said. "I'm going right away. And if it's not in my bedroom, I'll check all the others."

She ran to the staircase and then up, up and up, pounding on the stairs as she went.

Gregor turned his attention back to the rest of them. Gregor had filed away quite a bit of information for future use, but he didn't want to go into any of it now. Richard

Fenster had caught Geraldine Dart removing the CD
player from the pantry after the incident last night. That
was interesting. In spite of all the melodramatic overreact-
ing, Cavender Marsh's blood pressure didn't seem to have
been raised a bit by any of this nonsense, including sudden
bloodcurdling screams loud enough to shake the rafters of
his home. That was interesting, too. Most interesting of all
was what hadn't happened, last night, while all that insane
laughter was going on and Tasheba Kent's body was rolling down the stairs. It was what hadn't happened that
made Gregor so sure that he was right.

Unfortunately, being right wasn't enough. Gregor
Demarkian was going to have to play this farce through
right to the end, whether he liked it or not, and all the rest
of these people were going to have to play it right through
with him. They definitely weren't going to like it, but there
was nothing Gregor could do about that, either.

There was a sudden bounce and skip and giggle above
their heads—Geraldine taking the disc off the CD upstairs
and doing it badly—and then there was silence in the
house again, broken only by the wind.

"I'm going to sue somebody," Hannah Graham declared. "I'm going to sue everybody in sight."

Gregor sighed. "All right," he said, "let's make a
guess. The dining room or the living room?"

"The dining room or the living room for what?" Lydia
Acken asked.

"For the next act in this circus," Gregor said. "I
plump for the dining room myself. It's easy to close off,
which means it would be easy to hide whatever you
wanted to do in there, especially if you had to take a little
time."

"Where's that security guard?" Bennis asked suddenly. "I haven't seen him all day. Isn't that odd?"

"It's very odd," Gregor agreed, "but it's not what
we're going to investigate right now. Now we're going to
go into the dining room and see what we can find there."

It was obvious from the looks on their faces that there
were now quite a few of them who thought, as Hannah
Graham had always thought, that he was crazy. They followed him anyway, and they were rewarded.

Like Hannah Graham's bedroom, the dining room had been decorated for a birthday party, but much more elaborately. There were so many helium-filled balloons it was impossible to see any of the upper third of the chandelier. The chairs were literally upholstered in crepe paper, wound around and around the backs and seats and legs in different colors. A banner spelling out "HAPPY BIRTHDAY" had been attached to one wall. Another banner spelling out the number 100 had been attached to the opposite wall. Every place at the table had been set with special happy birthday paper napkins and special happy birthday paper plates and special happy birthday paper cups. In the middle of the table there was a big quilted crepe-paper-and-cardboard sculpture spelling out "HAPPY BIRTHDAY" in fat, bloated red, white, and blue letters. It was like a children's party with a thyroid condition.

"Oh, my God," Mathilda Frazier said, for what felt to Gregor like the two thousandth time since she had arrived on this island.

Gregor wasn't having any.

"Excuse me," he told the assembled company. "I'm going upstairs to search Carlton Ji's room. If any of you should decide that you have something to tell me, I'd be glad of the company."

"That's it?" Richard Fenster demanded hotly. His face was red. "That's all you've got to say about—about all this?"

"That's it."

"The great detective," Hannah Graham said.

"The great detective has work to do," Gregor told her impassively. "Oh. There is one more thing. Mr. Pratt?"

"What is it?" Kelly Pratt asked.

"Mr. Pratt, when Geraldine Dart comes back downstairs, I would very much appreciate it if you would ask her for the keys to the chauffeur's apartment. Then go over there and release the security guard. He'll probably appreciate it, too. It's my guess that you'll find him tied up on the floor of the bedroom or the bathroom, or possibly on the bed itself. I'm sure he won't have been hidden too well. There wouldn't have been any point to it, and it would have been too difficult. All right?"

"But Gregor, wait," Bennis said. "Won't this solve everything? Won't he be able to tell us who tied him up?"

"I don't think so," Gregor said. "I think he was probably sent over there last night carrying a nicely doctored bottle of something ninety proof and expensive. Now, if you will excuse me, ladies and gentlemen, I'm going to go."

And go Gregor Demarkian did, steadily and relentlessly, out of the dining room and through the foyer and up the stairs.

He'd had as much as he wanted to take of the whole lot of them.

CHAPTER 2

— 1 —

As soon as Geraldine Dart heard that Gregor Demarkian wanted to talk to people—"to anyone who has something to tell him," was the way Richard Fenster explained it to her—she knew she ought to be the first one upstairs. But the thought of it made her weak and teary, and the idea of spending half an hour or so trying to unravel what all this had started out to be—it was just impossible, that was all. She had gone upstairs and found the CD player sitting on top of her bureau, playing the music from *The Tingler* into the intercom microphone embedded in her bedroom wall. The night before she had left the CD player on the shelf in her closet with the little stack of plastic disc casings beside it: *Howls and Whispers, The House on Haunted Hill, Screams in the Night, The Tingler, Song of the Werewolf.* It hadn't been hidden. Anybody could have come in and found it, if they had known she had it. Richard Fenster might have told his story to anyone at all. Geraldine snatched the disc off the machine, then turned the intercom microphone off. She'd had to suppress an urge to shout imprecations into it or to tell them all to get out of the house. They couldn't get out of the damn house if they wanted to, and most of them probably desperately wanted to. Then Geraldine had gone downstairs and found them all in the dining room, and the mess there, and she had just wanted to sit in a chair and cry. It was going to take hours to get all this nonsense cleaned up. It might take days to chase down all the balloons, which had already started to drift into the foyer and other rooms. Then there was Donnie Hacket to take care of. Donnie Hacket was the man they had hired to act as a security guard. Donnie wasn't much security and he wasn't much of a guard. He drank when he could afford to, and he slept too much even when he couldn't. Gregor Demarkian had sent Kelly Pratt over to fetch him, and Kelly had found him tied up with bed linen and laundry rope on the bathroom floor of the chauffeur's apartment, and suddenly Donnie was threatening lawsuits as frequently and fervently as Hannah Graham.

Eventually, Geraldine decided to go back upstairs to see Gregor Demarkian because it was the only way she could think of to get any peace and quiet. Mathilda Frazier and Lydia Acken were busy stripping crepe paper from chairs and folding up the quilted crepe-paper-and-cardboard sculpture. The men were sitting around complaining. Hannah Graham was with them. The sniping was awful. It had been bad all weekend, but now it was ultrafast and supernasty. It was as if they had all decided that they had nothing to lose. They might as well be thoroughly, outrageously, unrepentantly hateful. It was more fun than staring out the windows and trying too hard to be very, very nice.

"Tasheba always hated fans," Cavender Marsh told Richard Fenster. "She said they were vampires of the spirit."

"I don't know who you think you're fooling with the surgery," Mathilda Frazier told Hannah Graham spitefully. "You look older than your father does."

"Do you always have to act as if you were right in the middle of a Rotary Club meeting?" Richard Fenster asked Kelly Pratt. "We have two people dead here, and you're bouncing around like you're cheerleading for the Chamber of Commerce."

The only people who weren't behaving like absolute scum were Lydia Acken and Bennis Hannaford. Geraldine knew from experience that Lydia was always polite to the point of the ridiculous. She could only decide that Bennis Hannaford had decided mentally and emotionally to distance herself from the rest of them. After a little hesitation, Bennis had gone to work helping Mathilda and Lydia clean up. Prodded by comments from Cavender Marsh and Hannah Graham—"Oh, look," Hannah had said at one point. "The great American writer knows just what to do with Scotch tape."—Bennis behaved as if she were blind, deaf, and dumb. Geraldine wasn't used to thinking of Hannah Graham as Cavender Marsh's daughter except in a very formal, abstract way. Now she saw that there was nothing at all abstract about the relationship. Hannah Graham might have been brought up by an aunt. Cavender Marsh might not have seen his daughter in nearly sixty years. But it didn't matter. They were a lot alike.

"What I don't understand is why people with noses like yours wear their hair forward the way you do," Hannah told Geraldine at one point. "I mean, it only makes the protuberance much more *prominent*, doesn't it?"

Geraldine knew she had a large nose. She had heard enough about it in her life. She had stopped really minding years ago. For some reason, however, Hannah's comment really got to her. She was piling paper party plates in a stack and nesting paper party cups together. She stopped where she was and swung around to look at Hannah Graham.

"At least it's my own nose," Geraldine told her.

Hannah Graham sniffed. "Not being able to afford the necessary medical attention," she said, "is hardly something to be proud of."

Keeping her temper would be something to be proud of. Geraldine knew that. If she stayed in this room much longer, she was going to blow up. She was going to hit somebody on their cosmetically improved nose. Carefully, she put the stack of paper plates and the nested cups at the end of the dining room table. She wiped her palms across the top of her skirt and patted her hair. She looked at Bennis Hannaford tying a dozen balloons together with a piece of string.

"Don't look in the mirror," Hannah Graham said.

"Every time you crack a mirror like that, it's seven years' bad luck."

Geraldine went out of the dining room and into the foyer. She went up the stairs and down the guest room wing. Carlton Ji's door was open and light was spilling out. Geraldine stopped in the doorway. Gregor Demarkian sat on the bed, taking stapled sheafs of paper out of a red cardboard folder. The bed was full of other papers and other cardboard folders. One of the cardboard folders, the bright orange one, was labeled "LILITH BRAYNE" in tall black letters. Geraldine raised her hand to the door and knocked.

"Mr. Demarkian?"

"Come in," Gregor said, barely looking up. "Grab the stool and sit down."

Geraldine did grab the stool and sit down. It gave her something to do for a moment. Gregor was still looking over the papers from the red folder. Every once in a while he would nod and mutter to himself. Finally, he pushed the folder away from himself and looked up at Geraldine, for real, for the first time.

"He was writing a book," he told Geraldine. "He'd collected some very interesting stuff."

"About Tasheba Kent?"

"About the death of Lilith Brayne. And about that black feather boa."

Geraldine grimaced. "God, I'm beginning to hate that thing. Not that I ever liked it. It's been sitting around the house for years, collecting dust. But *now*. Why do you think it was wrapped around his neck? Was something done to his neck that it was covering up?"

"Not that I could see. He may have had it with him when he died."

"But why?"

Gregor Demarkian tapped the red folder. "He has quite a bit of documentation here about a rather odd glitch in the evidence records that exist from 1938."

"What kind of glitch?"

"Well," Gregor said, "on the night Lilith Brayne died, one of the things listed as being at the scene—at the general scene, you understand, in the villa, not in the water with her—was a black feather boa. That's the only time a black feather boa is mentioned among her things. When the possessions list was made for the inquest, no black feather boa was on it. No black feather boa was ever mentioned in connection with Lilith Brayne again. But a black feather boa was worn almost every day during the investigation by Tasheba Kent, and worn very publicly, too. You can see it in every photograph of her from the time."

"That's odd," Geraldine said.

"That's very odd," Gregor agreed. His finger absently tapped the red folder again.

"Maybe the explanation is something very simple," Geraldine suggested. "Maybe it was just a mistake. Or maybe it belonged to Tasheba all along, and she'd left it at the villa, and Cavender sneaked it back to her after Lilith died."

"That's not bad. We'd have to find out if Tasheba Kent was ever in that villa before her sister died. The women I know wouldn't have had her in the same town, under the circumstances, but movie stars seem to be unusual people."

"Even ex-movie stars are that," Geraldine said. She stared at her hands. "Well. Here I am. Somebody told me that if any of us had anything to tell you, we should come right up, so—"

"So you've come to tell me about the laughs in the night," Gregor said.

Geraldine nodded. "But I don't know what happened this afternoon. I didn't have anything to do with that."

"I didn't think you did."

"And to tell you the truth, the stuff last night wasn't my idea, either. Well, I suppose you could have guessed that. It isn't the kind of thing an employee does to an employer's weekend party unless she's looking to get fired, and I'm definitely not looking to get fired."

"You like working here?"

"No, I don't," Geraldine said frankly. She sighed. "The old lady was a consummate bitch and Cavender isn't much better. But it's a very lucrative job. The salary is decent and there's room and board besides. I've been putting quite a bit away."

"In an attempt to retire early, I hope."

"Very early." Geraldine laughed. "Anyway, the idea for the ghost business was Cavender's, and I didn't like it much, but it seemed perfectly harmless."

"It was just Cavender Marsh's idea? Not Tasheba Kent's, too?"

Geraldine shook her head. "Cavender was really worked up, you see, about what he kept calling 'the potential for invasion of privacy.' What he meant was that he was afraid the guests would get up here and want to talk about nothing but what had happened in 1938, and he just wasn't going to have it. They didn't talk about it, you know."

"Really? Never?"

"Never while I was around. They might have talked about it when they were alone. The thing about this weekend, though, Mr. Demarkian, was that there were going to be so many people here they couldn't control. Lydia Acken and Mathilda Frazier and Kelly Pratt don't really count. They were all employees, in a way. They weren't going to bring up anything Cavender didn't want to bring up. At least, not for long."

"No, I can see that. Especially in the case of Mathilda Frazier. She wouldn't want to see the auction collapse."

"The problems," Geraldine said, "came with all the other people. Your friend Bennis Hannaford made Cavender very nervous because she insisted on bringing you. He was half sure that his uptight rich relatives had commissioned you to reopen the case and reinvestigate it and come to some final conclusions they could believe in. Cavender's relatives never did accept the accident verdict. The ones who are still alive who were alive then just think that he's a murderer."

"If they do," Gregor told her, "they haven't said anything about it to me. And they haven't said anything about it to Bennis, either. She would have told me."

"Well, you and Bennis Hannaford weren't the only problems. There was Richard Fenster, who was a wild card. There's no telling what a fan like that will do, even a well-heeled one who can spend tons of money at auctions. And Carlton Ji was a reporter. Granted he was a reporter for *Personality,* which isn't exactly like being a reporter for *The New York Times,* but a reporter is a reporter. The big worry, though, was Hannah. I mean, you can just imagine. Carlton was absolutely wild. At one point, he said he was going to sleep with a gun next to his bed."

"Does he own a gun?"

"No," Geraldine said. "But you get the idea of what things were like around here. So you see, when he decided that we ought to create a distraction to keep the guests' minds off past history and onto the present, I went right along with it. It sounded a lot safer than guns." She sighed again.

"It surely was," Gregor told her. "Were these plans discussed with Tasheba Kent?"

"Oh, yes," Geraldine said. "I think she thought it was all very silly and unnecessary, but she went along with it. I don't think she minded all that as much as he did. I don't mean her sister dying. I have no idea how she felt about that. I mean all the scandal and disgrace that came afterward. Her career was already over then. His was just getting into high gear. Tasheba was already a Hollywood legend. Cavender never really had a chance to become one."

"I think he's legend enough because of the scandal. Everybody knows who he is and what's gone on in his life."

"I know, but it isn't the same thing. People don't remember the movies he was in or even if he could act. Anyway, it bothered him more than it bothered her, but she went along with it, and I went into Boston one day last month and bought the CD player and the sound tracks."

"Good selection," Gregor said drily.

"I should have bought more of the generic ones," Geraldine told him. "You know, *1001 Sounds of Terror. Werewolves of the Movies.* You wouldn't believe the kinds of things you can buy. I brought the stuff back here and I got it all set up in the pantry. I was going to set it up in my room, just so I wouldn't have to go running all over the house in the dark just in case something went wrong, but Cavender Marsh said that that was too dangerous. We didn't want anybody to find the machine where it was too obvious that I was the one who was using it."

"So it was all set up in the pantry before any of us ever arrived on the island."

"Days before," Geraldine confirmed. "Then, after dinner, when all the rest of you were having liqueurs and fighting with Hannah Graham, I went into the pantry and set the timer for one o'clock in the morning."

"And then what?"

"And then nothing," Geraldine said. "And then I went up to bed. I didn't go to sleep. I knew I wasn't going to get much. I stayed up and read until all the commotion started."

"And then you came out to us."

"That's right."

"Is your bedroom next to the one that Tasheba Kent shared with Cavender Marsh?"

"Not exactly." Geraldine sounded regretful. "They have an *en suite* bathroom. I'm on the other side of that. I couldn't have heard anything, Mr. Demarkian, no matter what it was."

"That's too bad." Gregor sighed. "What about Tasheba Kent and Cavender Marsh? Were they supposed to come out when the commotion started?"

"Oh, no," Geraldine said. "That was part of the plan. They were supposed to stay right where they were. And then the next morning they were supposed to come down to breakfast and say they hadn't heard a thing. We thought that would be spookier."

"So the first surprise you got was when Tasheba Kent started to come down the stairs?"

"That wasn't a surprise, Mr. Demarkian. That was a *shock*."

"Okay," Gregor said. "Move forward a little. After we had done all the searching, after the rest of us went to bed, you came downstairs again."

"That's right," Geraldine said. "I'd already disconnected the machine, you see. When we searched, I made a point of being the one who went into the pantry, and I unplugged the CD and turned off the microphone. Then I went back after everybody was asleep to remove the machine and to check it, because I knew it had been tampered with. I just knew it. I was right, too. The volume had been pushed up way too high. And there's this push-button doohickey that you can use to tell the machine how many times you want to play something, and it had been hiked way up, into the double digits, so that the laughs just played over and over again forever."

"You sure you couldn't have done those things yourself, accidentally?"

"Positive."

"Who do you think could have done them?"

Geraldine threw up her hands. "I don't *know,*" she cried. "I just don't know. The machine wasn't right out in the open. It was at the very back of the pantry. It wasn't as if somebody could have just stuck their head in there and seen it. Somebody would really have had to be snooping. And why would they be snooping in the pantry?"

"I don't know," Gregor said.

"Cavender and Tasheba and I were the only ones who knew about it," Geraldine said. "And Cavender wouldn't have fiddled with the controls himself. He would have sent me to do it. And before you ask, Tasheba wouldn't have done it either. I'm not saying she couldn't have. She was in incredibly good shape for a woman her age. But if she was going to do anything to that CD player, she was going to shut it off."

"It doesn't seem to make sense, does it?" Gregor asked gently. "I take it you got caught in the act of removing the CD player by Richard Fenster."

"Yes, I did. But I wouldn't make too much of that if I were you, Mr. Demarkian. He said he followed me and I believed him. I don't think he knew where the CD player was beforehand, or even that there was a CD player. And besides—"

"Yes?"

Geraldine got up off the vanity table stool and began to pace around. "I told him most of what I've told you, at least about why we played the disc," she said, "but in spite of the fact that he'd asked for the explanation, he didn't seem to be interested. He had this little smile on his face and he kept staring past my left shoulder. It was like—"

"What?"

Geraldine slapped her hands together. "It was like he knew something the rest of us didn't, and he thought we were all damned fools because we hadn't figured it out. It was as if he had the ultimate piece of insider information. It was just as creepy as some of the other things that have gone on around here this weekend. Creepier. I think he likes to keep secrets, Richard Fenster does. I think it's a kind of sickness."

"I think you don't like Richard Fenster much," Gregor Demarkian said.

Geraldine blushed and looked away. "I'm sorry, Mr. Demarkian. I'm acting like an hysterical little idiot, I know that. And you're right. Richard Fenster makes my skin crawl."

"Maybe he'll do the right thing and come up here to talk to me," Gregor Demarkian said. His eyes were on the red folder.

Geraldine shook her head violently. "He's never going to do that. You don't understand what he's like. He's never going to tell anybody at all. Mr. Demarkian, if you want to know what Richard Fenster has on his mind, you're going to have to go downstairs and drag it out of him. And you're going to have to threaten him with something serious before you even start to get anywhere."

---- 2 ----

Down in the dining room, Richard Fenster—who loved secrets just as much as Geraldine Dart thought he did, or maybe more—was thinking of giving this one up. He did not care for the turn events had taken in this place. Ghostly laughter on a CD hadn't bothered him very much—and the death of that ancient woman rolling down the stairs hadn't disturbed him enough to interrupt his progress to sleep—but since then things had been getting out of hand. The death of Carlton Ji changed things. So did the steady escalation of all the lunatic elements in all their various venues. Sometimes it felt that the lunatic events, and not the murder of Cavender Marsh's paramour, had become the point of this entire weekend. That was not a good sign. Richard Fenster thought he understood murder. He was positive that he understood that particular murder, just the way he understood all the ins and outs of what had happened to those three people. He understood determination and decision and plan. What he didn't like was emotion and eccentricity. There were a fair number of people who would have said that Richard Fenster was very eccentric himself. Richard knew it was a different kind of eccentricity. He would never have played these kinds of giggling, childish, senseless practical jokes.

Lydia Acken was trying to arrange a pile of crepe-paper streamers into something like a manageable ball. Richard took the pile out of her hands and compacted it expertly, a skill acquired after years of having to deal with the shredded newspaper used for cushioning items sent through the mail. He handed the newly formed ball back to her and stood up, ignoring the nasty little exchange then going on between Cavender Marsh and Kelly Pratt. Cavender seemed to be suggesting that Kelly was personally responsible for the abysmal performance of Cavender's money market fund. Lydia put the ball on the dining room table and smiled.

"Thank you," she said. "It's nice to see somebody being helpful to somebody else around here."

"I'm going to take a walk," Richard told her. "It's beginning to get impossibly close in this room."

"It's impossibly close in this whole house," Hannah Graham snapped. "When I get off this island, I'm going to go straight to my lawyers, and they're going to get an earful."

As far as Richard Fenster was concerned, anybody who spent any time at all for any reason around Hannah Graham was going to get an earful, even if they never did anything more provocative than breathe. He left the dining room. He went to the foyer windows and looked out across the choppy ocean to the docks at Hunter's Pier. He could just about see them, in spite of the dark sky and the fog and the mist sent up by the waves slapping against the massive rocks of the island. He could see the dock lights, glowing red and white and green.

"None of you people has any backbone," Hannah Graham was saying, her California caw knifing through the air like static on the radio. "You let these people get away with everything. And what for? What for? Just because you think they're some kind of *celebrities.*"

Richard left the foyer and went into the living room. He was relieved to see that nothing had happened to it since the last time he had seen it. Nobody had overdecorated this room with crepe paper and balloons. Nobody had overturned all the furniture or knocked the pictures and the mirrors out of true. He looked around behind the couches and found them a little dusty, but otherwise uninhabited. He didn't know what it was he half expected to find, but he knew that whatever it was couldn't be good.

When he was sure there was nothing to see in the living room, Richard left it and went into the library. The guard should have been at the door there, keeping an eye on things, but he wasn't. Donnie was sitting in the dining room, drinking a beer he had found in the kitchen and complaining of the hangover he had acquired last night. Richard thought it was probably not a hangover, in the usual sense, but a reaction to whatever pills he had been given. Gregor Demarkian was surely right about that. Richard didn't care, as long as it left him free to look over the library tables on his own.

The trick, he told himself, was not to make a mistake. The trick was not to think you knew something that you only suspected. That way lay trouble.

Richard looked over a few of the things on the long tables—it was really too bad that this auction was never going to come off; he would have bought so much; maybe he could make some kind of deal with the estate and get hold of it anyway—and then took one of the black shoes with the rhinestone buckles and put it under the loose roll of sweater that hung over his waist. Then he took a shoe from a pair on the other table and put that under there, too. The second shoe was not important, not famous, not a trademark, not a prop. It was an ordinary blue leather pump in a style that had been popular around 1935. Its heel dug into his belly when he walked, stabbing him right through the cotton of his shirt and undershirt, so that he had to hold onto it when he walked. If anyone had seen him, he would have looked ludicrous. Fortunately, he thought, no one had seen him.

Richard crossed the foyer again and went around to the back. He opened the door to the television room and looked inside. Nothing had been disturbed in here either. Richard went in and closed the door behind him.

The linen sheet was back on the corpse. Richard wondered who had put it there. He took both the shoes out from under his sweater and put them on the floor.

Know, he told himself. Don't guess. Always double-check.

He took the linen sheet off the corpse again and threw it down without noticing where it landed. Then he picked up the shoe with the rhinestone buckle on it and went for the feet.

He was so intent on what he was doing, he didn't hear the door to the television room open.

His concentration was so perfect, that when the ball of cast iron hit him on the side of the head, he was completely unaware that he was not alone in the room anymore at all.

CHAPTER 3

— 1 —

Gregor Demarkian knew that the paper he wanted to see was sitting in Kelly Pratt's briefcase, which was lying on the vanity table in Kelly Pratt's bedroom. Gregor knew that because he'd seen the paper before—Kelly had brought it to him, as a kind of visual aid, during the conversation they had had about the mysterious 1938 disappearance of one hundred thousand dollars from Lilith Brayne's French bank account—and because Kelly had felt it necessary to explain to him at the time where he kept his briefcase and why he kept it there. It seemed that Kelly Pratt never did anything because it was convenient. He had to have not only reasons but philosophies. He had to believe that whatever he was doing was tied into the Great Chain of Being and the search for the Holy Grail. Gregor didn't remember why Kelly Pratt had thought it was so important to keep his briefcase on his vanity table instead of on his bureau. Gregor liked Kelly Pratt in a number of ways, but the man was intellectually exhausting.

Gregor packed up the papers he had spread across Carlton Ji's bed, putting each back in its proper colored folder. The collection was pathetic, really. Carlton Ji hadn't had half as much as he'd thought he had. He hadn't had a third as much as he'd promised the publisher he was trying to interest in a book about the death of Lilith Brayne. He had, however, had something. And that had been the end of him.

Gregor really did need one more look at Kelly Pratt's piece of paper. He put Carlton Ji's folders on the top of the bureau and left the bedroom. This far down the hallway, he couldn't hear anything coming up from the first floor. He went into Kelly Pratt's bedroom. The briefcase was on the vanity table, just where Kelly Pratt had said it would be. Gregor sat down on the vanity table stool and opened the briefcase with a single flick of the spring lock. Kelly obviously didn't believe in keeping his private papers safely shut away.

The piece of paper Gregor was looking for—the single sheet with the numerical exposition of when and how, after the death of Lilith Brayne, the French equivalent of one hundred thousand dollars had been siphoned from Lilith Brayne's account—was sitting in solitary splendor in the pocket on the briefcase's left-hand side. The deep well on the right-hand side was filled with folders and thick sheafs of paper marked "Real Property" and "Bond Investments" and "Limited Partnerships." Gregor looked at these without much interest. ("Oil Lease Holdings—Cavender Marsh (John Day).") Then he turned his attention to the piece of paper he really wanted to see. "Account of Lilith Brayne (Lillian Kent)," it was headed at the top. Underneath that was a thick paragraph in French that ended with the words *Mme Jean Day.* Gregor looked down the page at the columns of figures, the dates and times of the withdrawals, always made at the busy hours of the day and always in central branches in Paris or (in one case) at what was probably the single branch in the busy market area of a small town. Kelly had made a big thing of the fact that no withdrawal checks had ever been found, but Gregor didn't think that was important. This was 1938 they were talking about. It had probably been 1939 before all the paperwork had been gathered together in one place and sent on to Lilith Brayne's lawyers in New York. There were no computers, and the Nazis were swallowing Czechoslovakia and about to invade Poland. It would be more surprising if a few things *hadn't* got lost.

Satisfied that he had seen what he wanted to see, Gregor closed up Kelly Pratt's briefcase. He went down the hall to Hannah Graham's room and looked in on the body of Carlton Ji, which was exactly where he had left it. Then he went out to the landing. Voices drifted up to him, probably from the library. One of them, inevitably, belonged to Hannah Graham.

"That phony ghost attack last night gave me a bad case of hives," Hannah Graham was saying. "They're still all up and down my back. They're very painful. And the consequences could very well be *permanent.*"

"Oh, for God's sake," Bennis Hannaford said.

Gregor went downstairs. The dining room doors were propped open. Every once in a while a helium balloon tried to pop out. Strings were yanked and the balloon was dragged back in. Gregor crossed the foyer to the back.

As far as he could tell, they were all in the dining room together. If he wanted to stage a confrontation scene, he could do it in a minute or two, after he'd checked to make sure that everything was all right. The doors to the television room were closed. Gregor opened them, stepped inside, and turned on the light.

He didn't see the body of Richard Fenster immediately. He was too busy looking at the television room couch, which was empty of a corpse and a linen sheet and everything else. The body they had laid out here just a few hours ago was gone. It hadn't fallen to the floor or been shoved behind one of the small pieces of furniture. There was no closet in the television room to hide it in. Gregor knew it couldn't have gone far. It would have to have been moved by one person—at the very most, two. There were all those other people in the dining room. Certainly what Gregor most feared could not have happened. The body could not have been taken out and thrown into the sea. Not just yet.

Gregor was turning to leave the television room to search the closets in the utility hall outside when he saw Richard Fenster's body. Richard's legs were sticking out from under a round occasional table that was covered with a pale blue embroidered cotton tablecloth. Gregor had been so sure that the furniture in this room was too small to hide a body, he hadn't even checked. Now he did check. He looked behind sofas and chairs. He looked under the other occasional table. He looked into the one dark corner. There was nothing, just this single pair of legs and feet, emerging from a field of blue.

Gregor knew the feet belonged to Richard Fenster, because no one but Richard Fenster wore clothes like this in this house. He had been sure as soon as he saw the legs that Richard Fenster was already dead. That was why he hadn't rushed to check on him. Checking on him now, Gregor was careful anyway. He moved the table, not the body. He got down on one knee and felt for Richard Fenster's pulse.

Gregor didn't think he had ever been as shocked in his life as when he felt that vein begin to beat against his fingertip. It was a very faint beat, but it was unmistakably there. Gregor dropped Richard Fenster's arm and moved quickly to his head. The wound there was just like the other two he had seen, except that it was lower and a little off-center. The killer had been standing above Tasheba Kent when whatever it was had been smashed into the side of Tasheba Kent's head. The killer had been standing above Carlton Ji, too. In the case of Richard Fenster, the killer had had to swing upward, and it hadn't worked so well. Almost all of the right side of Richard Fenster's face had been caved in. Unlike Tasheba Kent's and Carlton Ji's, very little of Richard Fenster's skull had been destroyed. If they could get him out of here and to a hospital right away, he might get off without even a hair of brain damage.

Gregor went to the door of the dining room and looked inside. The decorations had mostly been taken down. The paper plates and cups had been put in stacks and stowed away on the sideboard. Lydia Acken was setting out the silver candlesticks that had been on the table the night before. Gregor folded his arms across his chest and coughed to get their attention.

"Oh, look," Hannah Graham said in her nasty voice. "If it isn't the great detective."

"That's right," Gregor told her. "It's the great detective. And the great detective now requests the pleasure of your company in the television room. Immediately."

"I'm not going anywhere with you," Hannah Graham said dismissively. "You ought to know that by now."

"I know that if you don't walk across that foyer under your own steam like a civilized human being, I'm going to drag you there by your hair," Gregor said. "I no longer have any interest in putting up with your act. Ladies and gentlemen. If you would, please."

"Where's Richard Fenster?" Mathilda Frazier asked.

Gregor didn't answer her. She would find out where Richard Fenster was soon enough. He turned away from the lot of them and went back across the foyer to the television room. They followed him in a big round herd, like cartoon sheep. Gregor stepped back far enough for the rest of them to get into the doorway and see inside. When most of them didn't seem inclined to do this, Bennis Hannaford came forward and walked into the television room on her own.

"Oh, my God," she said. "There's another one. There's another one dead."

"Who's dead?" Mathilda Frazier asked, hurrying forward. When she saw Richard Fenster on the floor, she went green and backed up, smacking into Kelly Pratt.

They were all crowding close now.

"Jesus Christ," Kelly said. "What's going on around here?"

"I know what's going on around here," Hannah said. "It's a plot. Cavender and Geraldine planned it all months ago. They just waited for us to get here so that they could pull it off."

"Planned what?" Lydia asked. "What could they possibly have wanted to plan?"

Cavender Marsh didn't come anywhere near the television room door. Gregor noticed it, but didn't remark on it.

"Right now," he told them, "there's only one thing we really have to worry about. And that's the fact that Richard Fenster is not dead."

"Not dead?" Hannah demanded. "What do you mean

he's not dead? His face has been smashed in just like all the others."

"Not quite like all the others," Gregor said. "The murderer's stroke was off. More of Richard Fenster's cheek and jaw were crushed than his skull. So now he's alive, and we have to get him off of this island. We have to do it now. We don't have much time."

"But there isn't any way to get him off this island," Mathilda Frazier wailed. "The weather is still terrible. Just look at it."

"I can think of a way we might be able to tell the people on the mainland that we needed help," Geraldine Dart said suddenly. "It might not work, but it might. It couldn't hurt us to try. But we need somebody who knows Morse code."

"I know Morse code," Bennis Hannaford said. "Eight straight years at Camp Winnipesaukee. What do you want me to do?"

—— 2 ——

What Geraldine Dart wanted Bennis Hannaford to do was simple enough. It was so simple, Gregor was embarrassed not to have thought of it himself, hours ago.

"Out in the garage we've got these spotlights," Geraldine explained to the rest of them. "Battery-powered spotlights. We bought them a couple of years ago to serve as backups in case of a power failure. So that people could get in and out of the dock and up and down the stairs in the dark if there was an emergency. I don't know if any of them still work."

"What about the batteries?" Bennis asked. "If the batteries have been lying around for two years, they must have expired."

"No, no." Geraldine shook her head. "Don't worry about the batteries. I'm very careful to keep up-to-date on all the different kinds of batteries we use in this house. It's the lights themselves we have to worry about. It's very damp out in the garage."

"But what will you do with the lights when you get

them?" Mathilda demanded. "What does Morse code have to do with it?"

"Don't you see?" Kelly had a tiny smile on his lips. "They're going to send out a signal. Save Our Ship."

"There's a balcony that looks out toward the front of the house from the living room," Geraldine said. "We can set up there. Maybe there won't be anyone on the mainland looking out at us, but maybe there might be. Maybe Jason might be. And if somebody sees our signal, they'll know we're in desperate need of help."

"But what difference would that make?" Mathilda asked. "Nobody can get out here in this weather. Everybody's been saying that right from the beginning."

"I think it's a very good plan," Lydia said firmly. Her face was very pale. "Maybe somebody on the mainland could think of something really special to do once they knew our situation was really dire. Maybe they could send in a helicopter."

"A helicopter couldn't land here," Hannah Graham objected. "It's much too windy."

"Whatever it's going to be, we'd better get started," Bennis said. "Shall Geraldine and I go out to the garage together, Gregor?"

"That's an excellent idea," Gregor said.

"So what are the rest of us supposed to do?" Hannah demanded. "Stand around staring at the silly jerk's body and twiddling our thumbs?"

"No," Gregor said. "You're supposed to help me search the closets one more time. In case none of you had noticed, and I'm sure at least one of you didn't have to notice, because you knew all about it in advance, Richard Fenster is lying on the floor in there, but Tasheba Kent's body is not lying on the couch. It has disappeared. I suggest you help me find it."

"Oh, dear," Mathilda Frazier wailed. "I hadn't thought of that. Even if Carlton did kill Tasheba, he couldn't have killed himself. That means somebody else killed him. One of us."

"Carlton didn't kill Tasheba," Gregor said.

"We're going," Bennis said, ignoring Mathilda's vapors. "We'll be back as soon as we can. Keep your fingers crossed and wish us luck."

Bennis and Geraldine Dart left the room. A moment later, Gregor heard them leave the house through the front door. Then he turned and faced the rest of the group.

"All right," he said. "Let's get going."

— 3 —

They were good. Even Hannah Graham was good. Cavender Marsh did not help out, but Gregor did not expect him to. He was old, and he was furious, a prisoner of alien forces in his own home. He got even more furious when Gregor refused to allow him to stand guard at the television room door, and assigned Lydia Acken to that job instead.

"You can't possibly be implying that you suspect me of bashing that young man's head in," Cavender fumed. "I couldn't lift whatever it was that hit him."

"I'm sure that's perfectly true," Gregor said calmly, "but I want Lydia at that door."

Cavender stormed off. He went to sit by himself in the living room, muttering imprecations against Gregor Demarkian and all his works and offspring in four languages. Lydia Acken took up her place in front of the television room door.

"This makes me very nervous," she told Gregor. "What is it I'm supposed to do here?"

"Make sure nobody else gets in."

"I don't see how I'm going to bring that off. I couldn't physically restrain someone like Kelly Pratt. I couldn't even physically restrain someone like Mathilda Frazier."

"If someone gives you a hard time, shout. I'll do the physical restraining myself."

Lydia looked dubious, but she let it go. Gregor knew that he was flabby and out of shape, but he let it go, too. It had taken him a lot of work to get flabby and out of shape. He had spent years on the project. That didn't mean he couldn't do what he had to do in an emergency.

Since Gregor knew that this body could not have gone

far, he did not send the group fanning out all over the house the way he had when they were looking for Carlton Ji last night. He sent Kelly and Hannah to search the three closets at the west end of the utility hall. He sent Mathilda and the security guard to search the three closets at the east end. The security guard was sullen and more than a little tipsy. Gregor didn't know where he was getting his liquor, but he was certainly getting it somewhere. Maybe the poor man figured he was owed, after being knocked out and tied up the way he had been.

Gregor took the closets in the middle of the hall himself. They were both the most likely and the least likely ones. They were the most likely because they were the closest and the easiest to get to. Someone in a hurry could have taken Tasheba Kent's body and shoved it into one of these in no time at all. They were the least likely for exactly the same reasons. Someone hoping to hide the body until it could be disposed of would be right to fear that in one of these three closets, it would be much too quickly and too easily found.

In the first closet Gregor looked in, he found nothing at all of interest. In the second, he found three black feather boas wound around hangers and hanging from a rod. He wondered if the one that had been on the table with the auction things had been the original, or at least the one from 1938, or if it had been just another copy, like these so obviously were. Gregor went to the third closet. It was empty of everything except dust.

"Oh, look," Mathilda Frazier exclaimed, backing out of the closet she had been looking through. "One of those shoes."

She held up what must once have been a black high-heeled shoe with a rhinestone buckle. Its sole had been cut to shreds; part of its top was missing.

"Where did you find this?" Gregor asked.

Mathilda pointed into the closet. Gregor got down on his hands and knees to look.

"You only found the one shoe?" he asked her.

"That's right," Mathilda said.

"Mr. Pratt," Gregor called out, "go down to the library and see if you can find the mate to that shoe. It should be on the table with Lilith Brayne's things."

Kelly Pratt hurried away obediently. Gregor went on searching in the closet. This one was stuffed full of all kinds of things, mostly packed away in opaque green plastic bags. Gregor pulled out a moth-eaten old quilt and a Persian lamb coat yellow with age. Kelly Pratt returned.

"It's not there," he announced breathlessly. "There's nothing at all like it on any of the tables."

"That's not surprising." Gregor went left to the next closet. "Have you tried this one?"

Mathilda Frazier shook her head.

"What about the one on the other side?"

"I looked through that one, yes," Mathilda said. "There was nothing at all in it."

Gregor nodded and opened the third door. He was suddenly reminded of Monty Hall's *Let's Make a Deal,* a show he had only watched once or twice in his life, but that had this kind of feel. The difference was that Gregor already knew what was behind door number three.

The corpse from the television room was propped up in a back corner of the closet. It was partially hidden by a hanging dry cleaning bag with a Brooks Brothers gray wool suit inside it. When Gregor pushed the bag aside, the body slumped forward and slid to the floor.

"Oh, my God," Mathilda Frazier squealed.

Just then the front door slammed open and Geraldine Dart and Bennis Hannaford came running in.

"Gregor," Bennis was shouting. "We've got them. They're going to work."

Bennis ran across the foyer and into the utility hall, closely followed by Geraldine Dart. Cavender Marsh emerged from his sulk in the living room and came after them. When Bennis saw the crowd clustered around the open closet door, she strode toward it.

"Didn't you hear me?" she demanded. "We got the lights. We dumped them next to the door as we came in. We're going to take them right out and set them up."

"Your timing is wonderful," Hannah Graham said.

Bennis ignored her and poked her head through the open closet door. "What the—oh, for God's sake."

"We've been having a very interesting time while you were gone," Gregor told her.

Geraldine looked into the closet, too. She blanched.

"I can't believe it. I really can't believe it. Doesn't anybody ever make any sense around here at all anymore?"

"Oh, this makes perfect sense," Gregor said.

"I'm glad you think so." Bennis was getting out her cigarettes, crime scene or no crime scene. Who knew what was a crime scene around here anymore? "Personally, I think somebody put funny little pills in the water around here and we've all become positively certifiable."

"Why would anybody want to move Tasheba Kent's body from the television room into that closet?" Mathilda Frazier said. "Whatever for?"

"Well," Gregor said, "for one thing, because it isn't Tasheba Kent's body."

"But, Mr. Demarkian," Lydia said with mild indignation. "It has to be Tasheba Kent's body. Who else's body could it be?"

"Lilith Brayne's," Gregor said.

"Lilith Brayne's?" Kelly Pratt repeated. "But, Mr. Demarkian, that couldn't be. The kind of a switch you're talking about—somebody would have noticed."

"No, they wouldn't have," Gregor said. "Not after what happened to that body in that sluice."

"But they didn't even look all that much alike," Mathilda Frazier objected. "Everybody always says they were very different."

"They were very different," Gregor told her. "With the makeup off. But they almost never had their makeup off. And with their makeup on, all either one of them ever looked like was what their makeup made them look like."

"They were just about the same height," Bennis Hannaford said thoughtfully.

"I think this is in terrible taste," Cavender Marsh burst out. His body was trembling with rage. "Terrible taste. What makes you think you can come in here and make these ridiculous accusations, for which you have no proof whatsoever, as if you were God Almighty and better than the combined police forces of two countries, which is what it was, by the way, that investigation, two countries—"

"But I do have proof," Gregor interrupted gently. Cavender Marsh fell silent, his eyes blazing. "I have the same proof Richard Fenster had. I have the shoes."

"What do the shoes have to do with it?" Lydia Acken asked.

"They've been torn up," Hannah Graham put in. "You can't tell anything at all from them."

"Not from this particular pair of shoes, no," Gregor agreed. "These were the best ones, but they weren't the only ones. There are dozens of pairs of shoes out there in the library. It doesn't matter which pair you try. It will always come out the same."

"Why were those the best shoes?" Bennis asked.

"The black shoes with the rhinestone buckles were one of Lilith Brayne's trademarks," Gregor replied. "She wore them in her movies, but she also wore them later, after she retired, in much the same way and for much the same reasons her sister went on wearing black feather boas. If you look through some of the scrapbooks Cavender Marsh has kept all these years, you can see them. Tasheba's wearing them in one of the most widely circulated of the photographs ever taken of her and Cavender Marsh together, the one with the two of them standing on the terrace of the villa where Lilith Brayne was assumed later to have died."

"I'm sure this all seems very clever to you," Cavender Marsh spat, "but it doesn't seem all that clever to me. What difference do the shoes make?"

"They make all the difference in the world," Gregor said. "Go out to the library and look at the two sets of shoes. Lilith had very small feet. Tasheba had very large ones. Tasheba's shoes might have fit Lilith, if she stuffed them full of tissue paper. Lilith's shoes could never have fit Tasheba. What Richard Fenster probably found out was that that pair of shoes with the rhinestone buckles fit the feet of the woman who was calling herself Tasheba Kent perfectly—even after all these years."

CHAPTER 4

— 1 —

It was all starting to go wrong. Cavender Marsh could see that. Even if the rest of them couldn't, he could. There she was, lying on the floor dead at last. She had been as hard to kill as the creature in a Boris Karloff movie. He could still see her coming out of the shadows on that terrace in the south of France, floating across the checkerboard marble with a big smile on her face. He could still see Tash out cold at his feet after he had hit her, so close to the edge and so easy to roll over. But that wasn't fair. He had killed Tash himself. He had struck her across the windpipe with the side of his hand. He had stepped on the back of her neck and broken it after she was down. He had done all the things Lilith had said the papers would say he had done. It was just that he had wished at the time that he was doing them to Lilith.

The Demarkian man was waiting. He was being very patient. Considering the fact that there was a man sprawled half-dead on the floor of the television room, the detective was being very patient indeed. Cavender didn't think this would last long. Geraldine Dart and Bennis Hannaford had their signal lamps. They wanted to go out on the balcony to test them. They would have been gone already if they hadn't been so fascinated in what was going to be said around here next.

Cavender said the only thing he could say, under the circumstances. "You don't really believe," he drawled in great deliberation, "that I killed two people and maimed a third in this house this weekend. I'm eighty years old."

Gregor Demarkian sighed. "That's true. You didn't kill any of them yourself. Not this time. You just planned the way they were going to die."

"Really? All of them?" Cavender was carefully contemptuous.

"Richard Fenster may have been your accomplice's idea."

"It was more than Richard Fenster," Cavender Marsh said.

There were stirrings in the crowd. The sympathy was definitely directed away from him this time. The hero of this hour was Gregor Demarkian. Cavender didn't think he had ever seen such a large and solid man.

"Start from the beginning," Bennis Hannaford said suddenly. "I don't understand any of this."

Gregor Demarkian regarded Bennis very seriously and said, "I'll explain it all to you later. I want you to go out and put those lights to use. Do it now."

"All right," Bennis Hannaford said, although she didn't sound happy. "Geraldine and I—"

"No," Gregor Demarkian said. "Just you. I need Miss Dart here."

"Oh, dear," Geraldine Dart said. She wrung her hands, just like a character in a Lilith Brayne movie.

"You can't really believe that I threw my lot in with this plain and unstylish little blob of lower-middle-class sensibilities," Cavender Marsh insisted. "Even your audience doesn't believe it, and they're far more naive about this sort of thing than you and I are."

"He didn't say that you were sleeping with her," Kelly Pratt said.

Bennis Hannaford gave them all one last look and hurried out of the room. Mathilda Frazier began to rock back and forth, from the balls of her feet to her heels.

"The beginning," Gregor Demarkian said, nodding

his massive head, "was a marriage. The marriage of Cavender Marsh and Lilith Brayne. A marriage that could only have been made among actors. He was in his early twenties. She was in her early forties, or maybe even older. It was unheard-of, but they got away with it, in a way. The attitude of the fan magazines, from what I've been able to glean from looking through some scrapbooks, was that Cavender was a fine young innocent who had been corralled and brainwashed by a consummate witch."

Cavender Marsh burst out laughing. "Oh, she was that," he said. "She was surely that."

"Yes," Gregor Demarkian agreed. "I think she was. Anyway, the two of them married. When Lilith got pregnant, the fan magazines didn't thaw to her much, but then Cavender did something to destroy his own reputation. He had an affair. Now that, in and of itself, was not necessarily a bad thing. The press had been waiting for him to get tired of the old woman he had married. There had probably been fill-in-the-blanks instant news stories on file for months about how the brave young beauty saved Cavender Marsh from the clutches of the evil temptress. But the brave young beauty turned out to be not so young. In fact, she was a year older than the evil temptress, and the evil temptress's own sister. At that point, Lilith Brayne began to get a little sympathy from the press."

"I'm beginning to think this is very ageist," Mathilda Frazier interrupted disapprovingly. "What difference does it make how old they both were?"

"In 1938, it made a great deal of difference," Gregor Demarkian said. "It made so much difference, that it began to look to a lot of people that Cavender might have something psychologically wrong with him. This was, after all, an era when women were considered to be aging at thirty."

"Oh, yes," Lydia Acken put in, "that was really true. I remember. My mother told people she was twenty-eight for nearly fifteen years."

"Everything Cavender Marsh did was public," Gregor went on. "His wife's pregnancy was public. His affair with Tasheba Kent was public. He was photographed everywhere, and he always seemed to be in the wrong place at the wrong time. But that wasn't the worst of it. He was involved with two sisters. They were very different in many ways, but they were also very much alike. For one thing, they were both highly competitive. For another, they were both very demanding."

"*Demanding*," Cavender said. "What a word for it. They were both emotional vampires."

"Was Tasheba Kent being—demanding—the night Cavender Marsh killed her?" Lydia Acken asked.

"I don't know," Gregor said. "Mr. Marsh knows, and he may tell us or not, as he cares to. What I do know is that on the night she was killed, Tasheba Kent showed up at the villa in the south of France that Cavender Marsh was sharing with his wife and his three-month-old baby daughter. Tasheba was not supposed to be there."

"She'd been threatened with mayhem if she so much as showed up in town," Cavender Marsh said. His voice was very firm. He did not sound worried. "But not by me, Mr. Demarkian. By Lilith."

"That may be true," Gregor said, "but you killed Tasheba Kent. If it had been your wife who had committed the murder, she would have been arrested and tried for it, because you would never have helped her escape from the law. The only possible reason for your doing what you did, in fact do over the next few months and years, is that you knew damn well that if you did not do it, you would end up in jail yourself."

"But what did he do?" Kelly Pratt asked plaintively. "And what does all this have to do with the money?"

"What money?" Mathilda Frazier asked.

"I'll get to the money in a minute," Gregor said. "The first thing Cavender and Lilith did was to heave the body of Tasheba off the terrace and into the sluice, where it was sure to get severely mangled. The reason for this was not necessarily what you might think. They weren't worried about Tasheba Kent's appearance tipping the police off to her identity, because Tasheba Kent's appearance was what her makeup made it be. By that time, that was true of both the sisters. They weren't so very much alike if you knew them well without their makeup, but if you didn't—and almost nobody did—"

"Including me," Cavender Marsh said.

"—if you didn't, what you thought of when someone said 'Lilith Brayne' or 'Tasheba Kent' was a paint job, and paint jobs are easily manipulated. No, the reason they had to mangle the body was because the one thing that could destroy their whole plan was a full body autopsy."

"But what was their plan?" Lydia Acken asked.

"They were going to pass the death off as the death of Lilith Brayne, an accident that was probably a suicide," Gregor said. "This was a brilliant scenario, especially in the France of the time, which was addicted to tragedies of that sort. It was also psychologically coherent. There was no way to pass the death of Tasheba Kent off as suicide. Nobody would have believed it. And accident wouldn't have gone over too well, either. There had been too many very good reasons, trumpeted in the press month after month, why Cavender Marsh or Lilith Brayne would have wanted to kill Tasheba Kent. If it ever became clear that it was Tasheba Kent who was dead, there was going to be a major investigation."

"I still don't understand what a full body autopsy had to do with it," Mathilda Frazier said. "Do you mean they were worried about fingerprints and things like that?"

"I don't think so," Gregor told her. "I doubt if any of their fingerprints were on file anywhere. What a full body autopsy would have revealed was the obvious. It would have shown clearly that the woman whose body this was had never had a child."

"Oh," Lydia Acken said.

"So," Gregor Demarkian continued, "they rolled the body into the sluice. Then Lilith Brayne took off all her makeup, got Tasheba Kent's handbag, and headed back to Paris looking like nothing so much as another frumpy middle-aged woman. When she got to Paris, she let herself into her sister's apartment, made herself up very heavily, and proceeded to play the part of Tasheba Kent. I don't know what she did about personal maids and that sort of person, but she must have done something, because it worked."

"Lilith was a much better actress than anyone ever gave her credit for." Cavender Marsh said it proudly.

"Cavender gave Lilith a few hours to get away," Gregor went on, "and then called the police. At this point, the two of them began to make a series of mistakes that should have gotten them caught, but didn't. The first of these concerned Tasheba Kent's trademark black feather boa. She'd worn it when she came down to the villa from Paris, and left it lying across the bed in Cavender Marsh's bedroom. Lilith had completely forgotten about it when she'd gone back to town to take up her masquerade. That's why the black feather boa appeared on the first list the police made of the things belonging to Lilith Brayne that were found in the villa."

"Only on the first list?" Kelly Pratt asked.

"That's right," Gregor told him. "That was what got Carlton so excited. He got hold of those lists. After that first one, the black feather boa disappeared. It did appear on the neck of the woman calling herself Tasheba Kent, though. That woman wore a black feather boa prominently for weeks afterward. I can only assume that Cavender Marsh found some way of getting it away from the villa and to his play-acting wife."

"I told the police the boa had belonged to Tash," Cavender Marsh said. "I told them Lilith had stolen it one day when we visited Tash in Paris, because Lilith was obsessed with my relationship with her sister. They said they understood."

"I'm sure they did," Gregor said drily. "Especially after you spread around the French franc equivalent of twenty-five thousand dollars to increase their capacity for empathy. That was your second mistake, by the way. Not that you bribed the French police. That was not only necessary, but customary at the time in cases of the sort this was supposed to be. The mistake was in where you got the money, in four twenty-five-thousand-dollar chunks."

Cavender said nothing. His eyes were on Gregor Demarkian, as if he were a snake charmer.

"Where did they get it?" Lydia Acken asked.

"They got it from Lilith Brayne's bank account," Kelly Pratt put in excitedly. "That's where they got it. But how did they get it?"

"Mr. Pratt found the discrepancy in the bank account," Gregor Demarkian explained to them. "Four very large withdrawals to the tune of the French franc equivalent of one hundred thousand dollars, all made after the supposed death of Lilith Brayne."

"But how could they do that?" Mathilda Frazier asked. "She couldn't just show up at the bank looking like Lilith Brayne, could she? The story must have been in all the papers. She would have caused a sensation."

"You're absolutely right," Gregor told her. "If Lilith Brayne had shown up at a French bank looking like Lilith Brayne and trying to withdraw twenty-five thousand dollars—even once, never mind four times—she would most certainly have caused a sensation. But the explanation is very simple. The money was not in fact withdrawn from *Lilith Brayne's* bank account. It was withdrawn from *Lillian Kent Day's* bank account."

"Who's Lillian Kent Day?" Lydia Acken asked.

"Lillian Kent was the name with which Lilith Brayne was born," Gregor explained. "Lillian Kent Day was the name by which she was legally known in France in 1938, because she was the wife of one John Day, otherwise known as Cavender Marsh. Like a lot of famous people, Lilith Brayne preferred not to be famous every minute of every day. My guess is that the people at the bank didn't even know she was Lilith Brayne. She was just a respectable bourgeois woman called Madame Day."

"I found the discrepancies in the money," Kelly Pratt said proudly. "While I was looking over the background to come up for the weekend. We all wanted to make sure the auction would go off without any lawsuits. So I was working it all up, you see."

Cavender Marsh couldn't tell if they saw or not. None of them was paying attention to Kelly Pratt. They were all looking at Gregor Demarkian, stunned. Cavender Marsh smiled a little to himself.

"You know," he said, "all of this is very interesting, and of course it's also true, but it doesn't explain very much, does it? About what's been happening here this weekend. That's what they all really want to know about. That's what the police are going to want to know about, too."

"I think it explains a great deal," Gregor Demarkian said. "In fact, I think it's the only way we can explain anything of what happened here. You came to this island to live with Lilith Brayne because you had to, not because you wanted to, and you've been wishing her dead for all the sixty years since."

"That still doesn't explain how I killed her," Cavender Marsh said. "It doesn't explain how I could have swung around what must have been a very heavy object, at my age. My condition is good, but nobody's condition is that good at eighty."

"That's true," Gregor Demarkian agreed. "This time you had help. This time you didn't actually kill anybody."

"I didn't actually go hauling bodies all over the house, either," Cavender said. "I couldn't have lifted them."

"That's true, too."

"So you see," Cavender said, "it's not so simple after all."

"Oh, but it is," Gregor told him. "Your wife was killed by the one person on earth who had every reason to want her dead in a nasty and deliberate way, no matter how old or how close to death she was. Her own daughter and yours. Hannah Kent Graham."

"That's ridiculous." Hannah Graham's voice was high and hysterical. "That's totally ridiculous. How can you possibly say something like that?"

"I can say it very easily," Gregor told her. "It all comes down to that most famous line from the Sherlock Holmes stories, the dog that did nothing in the nighttime. You were the only one who could have fixed that CD player, the only one who could have cut the lights, the only one who could have cut the phone lines, the only one who could have done all the things that needed to be done in a very short time on the night your mother died, because you were the only one who was not in the group with the rest of us when all that was going on."

"Of course I was there! Of course I was there! It was just dark and you didn't see me."

"I didn't see you either," Mathilda Frazier said.

"Who did and didn't see her is not the point," Gregor Demarkian interjected, before it became a screaming match. "The point is that I didn't hear her. Ms. Graham, in all the time that we have been in this house, I have only twice heard you shut up for longer than thirty seconds on the subject of just who you were going to sue for what when you got out of here. One of those times was just now, when you were much too interested in what I had to say to interrupt me. The other was the night your mother died—a night, by the way, full of exactly the sort of incidents tailor-made to start you off on one of your litigious monologues. There was no litigious monologue, Ms. Graham, because you were not there to give it. You were running around behind the scenes doing your level best to distract me from noticing anything that might actually be important."

Hannah Graham's sticklike body was backing away down the hall, toward the foyer. She's going to do exactly the wrong thing, Cavender Marsh thought. She's more my child than she is her mother's. She's going to panic.

At just that moment, there was the sound of running footsteps in the foyer. Bennis came charging into the utility hall, waving her arms.

"Gregor!" she shouted. "Gregor, I did it! I got in touch with the mainland!"

Bennis Hannaford was running fast and not watching where she was going. She ran into Hannah and was caught up short, gasping for breath.

"Excuse me," she said, puffing to regain her wind. Then she turned her attention to Gregor again. "It was perfect," she said. "Absolutely perfect. I was blinking away, sure I was no good at all, and then somebody on the shore started to answer me. It was wonderful. He's sending help right away. I told him we had a man here with a severe concussion and we needed an ambulance and everything, and he said to sit tight and he'd get somebody to come out here some way or another right away."

"Was it Jason?" Geraldine Dart asked.

"I don't know. He didn't give me his name. I'm going to go back and wait for more messages."

"Did he say there were going to be more messages?" Mathilda Frazier asked.

"Just in case," Bennis Hannaford said.

Hannah was panicking. Cavender Marsh could see it. She was backing farther and farther away down the hall, and where did she think she could go? Even if Jason or somebody else did manage to get help out here in the middle of this storm—and Cavender was by no means sure they could; that might have been Maine coast macho posturing talking—what could Hannah do then? Did she intend to jump into the sea and swim?

Cavender started forward, some vague thought in his mind of stopping his daughter before she did anything that was both stupid and irrevocable. If there was anything he had learned from the first, and real, death of Tasheba Kent, it was that you must never do anything that you couldn't later flatly deny.

The rest of them were in a knot, talking excitedly. Bennis Hannaford had run out of the room to go back to her signal lights and Morse code. Hannah was almost to that point in her backing up where it would be feasible for her to turn and run.

And then the lights went out.

—— 2 ——

This time, when the lights went out, Hannah Graham knew that it was not a joke. It was not a prank. It was not a fuse. The storm had finally gotten to the power lines on the mainland and the ones that came out here. They were going to be without light for a while.

Hannah Graham's father thought she was panicking. Hannah knew that. She had seen it in Cavender Marsh's eyes as he watched her back away. Not that either of them had ever thought of her as anything but a nuisance. That was why her own mother had dumped her on an aunt to come out to this island and indulge the sexual obsession she had with Cavender Marsh. That was why her own father had gone along with it all. They were a pair of prizes, those two, and ever since the moment when Cavender Marsh had contacted her in California and told her what had really happened in 1938, Hannah Graham had been making plans.

Hannah now knew a number of things the rest of them didn't know. She even knew things that Cavender didn't know. He had expected to be in control of it all, and of her, but he had made the very worst kind of mistake.

The weapon was a thing called a warming iron, a great round blob of cast iron at the end of a very long cast-iron rod. In the days before central heating, you put the blob end into the fire until it was very hot and then put the hot end between the sheets and the blankets at the bottom of your bed to keep your feet warm on chilly winter nights. Hannah had never seen a warming iron before she came to the island, but she had read about them in books on antiques. This one had been lying on the floor of the attic when she had gone in to see what Carlton Ji was up to. And Carlton Ji had been up to no good, of course. Those people were never up to any good. Hannah Graham hated Orientals.

The weapon was in the tall narrow broom closet at the very start of the hall leading back from the foyer to the television room. The closet was too small to hold a body, so it had never been searched thoroughly even once all this weekend. It was also full of vacuum cleaner equipment and easy to hide something made of metal in. Hannah got it out and felt the weight of it in her hands. She had never been so glad of the time she had spent working out with weights.

They were all getting used to the darkness now. They were all beginning to be able to see at least a little in the gloom. Hannah still had the advantage and she knew it. She had walked around this house in the dark many times before. The rest of them had not.

"Hannah?" Cavender Marsh asked tentatively.

Hannah smiled. He was just where she wanted him to be, really. She moved closer to the stairs.

"I'm right here," she called out. "I'm over near the stairs."

"Hannah, listen to me," Cavender Marsh said. "Try to be reasonable for a moment now."

"I am being reasonable," Hannah told him.

"I'd be careful if I were you," Gregor Demarkian warned.

Hannah was worried for a moment, but then she wasn't anymore. Cavender Marsh wasn't paying any attention to Gregor Demarkian. And Gregor Demarkian was nowhere close to either Cavender or the stairs. He was way in back, near the living room door.

"What's going on around here?" Mathilda Frazier asked.

She was way, way in the back, invisible. She didn't want to come out and see what was happening. Kelly Pratt and Geraldine Dart were invisible, too. They were all hiding in the dark. They were all hoping this would just go away. Only Cavender Marsh was advancing across the foyer, walking with his hands in his pockets, as if he thought he could make himself look like Cary Grant.

"Now, Hannah," he began.

He sounded just like Hannah's therapist. Hannah hated her therapist.

"I'm right here," Hannah said again. "I'm really not going anyplace."

"Be *careful*," Gregor Demarkian warned for the second time.

Bennis Hannaford rushed in again. "They are sending a helicopter," she said in a rush of enthusiasm. "It's coming right from some army base to the south of us. We're all supposed to go up onto the roof and wait for it."

"A helicopter can't land on this roof," Geraldine Dart said. "It's not flat."

"We can't get Richard Fenster up to the roof right now either," Mathilda Frazier said. "We probably shouldn't move him."

"Right," Bennis Hannaford said. "I'll go back and explain everything."

Bennis Hannaford rushed out again in the direction of the living room. Hannah stayed in her place at the side of the stairs, her back against the wall, waiting.

"Now, Hannah," Cavender said for the third time, or maybe the fourth or fifth.

"Come over and talk to me," Hannah said. "I don't want to have to shout."

Cavender Marsh came. He came much too slowly and too deliberately, but he came. Even now, it seemed, he had to be a movie star. Even now he had to make entrances and exits and melodramas and foreshadowings. Hannah waited until he was almost right in front of her. Then she swung around him, to his back, raised the warming iron above her head and smashed it down on the foyer's parquet floor.

Cavender Marsh jumped onto the first of the steps and Hannah smashed the warming iron down again, on the step next to him, cracking the step even though she hit it through the thickness of the runner carpet.

"What the hell do you think you're doing?" Gregor Demarkian demanded.

This was not a question Hannah Graham thought she had to answer. Cavender Marsh was running as best he could up the stairs.

Hannah Graham was following him, swinging the warming iron above her head and smashing it down over and over again, like a polo player in pursuit of the ball.

CHAPTER 5

—— 1 ——

She wasn't trying to catch him. Gregor saw that right away. She could run much faster than he could, even carrying that heavy iron instrument. She could have hit him at any time. The shaft of whatever it was was at least four feet long. When Kelly Pratt started to run up behind her to drive her off, she swung it around at him and nearly hit him in the gut. If she had connected, she would have broken his rib cage or his pelvis or caused the kind of internal damages that usually resulted from car wrecks. Kelly Pratt backed up and stopped. Cavender Marsh went higher on the stairs. Hannah Graham followed him, swinging the rod ahead of her, smashing the hard round end of it over and over again into the walls.

"What's she doing?" Bennis asked in a whisper.

Gregor didn't know when she'd come back from her latest run of Morse code signals, but here she was.

"She's driving him," Gregor told her. "Upstairs. I don't know where."

"Don't you think it's dangerous?"

This was a question about on a par with, Is the Pope Catholic? Gregor didn't answer it. Cavender was almost to the second-floor landing now. Hannah was right behind him.

Gregor began to climb the darkened stairs, as quickly as he could without attracting the attention of Hannah Graham, or Cavender Marsh. He needn't have been so cautious. They were paying no attention to him. Cavender Marsh was much too frightened. Hannah Graham was having much too good a time. When they were both on the landing, Cavender Marsh started to dart toward the family wing. Hannah Graham got around behind him and blocked his path. Cavender Marsh tried to make it to the guest wing. Hannah Graham stopped him there, too. She was very fast, when she wanted to be.

"What's she trying to do?" Bennis demanded, coming up behind Gregor on the stairs.

Bennis was very fast when she wanted to be, too. "She's forcing him up the stairs," Gregor told her. "Watch."

Cavender Marsh had to go on up the stairs, to the third floor or maybe beyond, because there was nowhere else to go. The problem was that the stairs were not a straight shot, rising from the second-floor landing in the same well. The stairs were at the back of the landing, tucked in next to the windows. Hannah Graham got there first and smashed the windows into pieces. Shards of glass sprayed into the shadows. Cavender started to back up and found his daughter behind him again. He bolted upward.

"He's going to have a heart attack," Bennis said.

"Maybe that's what she's after," Kelly Pratt told her.

Gregor turned and saw that they were all there, Bennis and Kelly and Mathilda and Lydia and Geraldine, following him resolutely in spite of the fact that they didn't know how they could possibly be of use. Gregor fixed his attention on Geraldine Dart.

"Where do those stairs go?" he asked her.

"To the second and third floors and to the attic. But the doors to the second and third floors are locked."

"But not the one to the attic?"

"I don't know," Geraldine said.

They could all hear the banging of that metal thing on wood, and the sounds of cracking and splintering that always followed it. Cavender Marsh and Hannah Graham were proceeding upward.

"All right," Gregor said. "You told us last night, early this morning, whenever it was. There's another way up to the attic?"

"Yes, there is. There's a staircase off a utility hall behind the library."

"All right," Gregor said again. "I want you to go there and go on up. Take Kelly Pratt with you."

"I'm ready," Kelly Pratt said.

"Just the two of them?" Bennis asked. "What about the rest of us?"

"Ms. Frazier and Ms. Acken are going to stay right here on the landing in case there's another way back that Ms. Dart doesn't know about. You and I are going up that staircase."

"What are we going to do if there is another way back to this landing?" Mathilda Frazier asked. "What could we do? She could kill us with that thing."

"We'll be all right, dear," Lydia Acken said stoutly. "We don't have to put ourselves in danger. We just have to observe."

Actually, they did not have to do anything. Gregor did not believe there was another way back to this landing. He did believe that these two were the weakest ones in the group, and that they needed to be kept out of trouble. He turned to Bennis.

"Are you ready?"

"Of course."

"Then let's go on up."

They left Lydia Acken and Mathilda Frazier huddled together on the small balcony overlooking the foyer, and started up the stairs at the back in the direction of Hannah Graham and Cavender Marsh.

— 2 —

It had been dark in the main body of the house, but nothing like it was in this back staircase. There were windows in the walls, Gregor could see them, but they didn't do much good. The weather outside was still awful. It was only the middle of the afternoon, but it was almost as black as night. Gregor could still hear the sounds of footsteps and crashing iron, but they were far above him now.

"What do you think she's doing?" Bennis asked. "Is she trying to kill him?"

"At least," Gregor said.

"Is she crazy?"

In spite of all the cigarettes she smoked, Bennis was hurrying up the stairs without a problem, never having to stop for rest, never having to gasp for air. It was Gregor, who had never smoked a cigarette in his life, who was having trouble sucking wind.

"I think," he said, "that what she really is is royally angry. You'd be angry too if you had two perfectly good parents who had dumped you on a relative and never bothered to see you again just so they could run away to an island together and—um—"

"Screw," Bennis said helpfully.

They reached the landing for the third floor and Gregor stopped, ostensibly to check the door to the third floor proper but really to catch his breath.

"It was all Lilith Brayne's idea, of course," he said. "Cavender Marsh hated the woman by then, but there was nothing he could have done to get away from her once he'd murdered Tasheba Kent. He'd have gone to the guillotine for it if the case had ever been properly solved."

"Marvelous. Didn't Lilith worry that he'd do to her what he did to her sister?"

"Why should she? That case certainly wouldn't have gone uninvestigated. It would have brought every cop in the state of Maine out here. It would have been asking to be arrested."

"Even after sixty years? Why didn't he just shove her in the sea?"

"I don't know, Bennis. Maybe Cavender Marsh is not one of those people who can kill in cold blood. Maybe he needs to be pushed into a crisis before he can actually do away with anybody. I'm not St. Peter at the gate. I can't see into a man's soul. I just know what Cavender Marsh did do."

"I don't suppose you can call what she's doing killing in cold blood either," Bennis said. "Can you hear anything anymore, Gregor? I can't hear anything."

They were on the landing for the fourth floor now, and Bennis was right. The sounds of footsteps were gone. The sounds of smashing glass and cracking wood were gone, too. Bennis stopped.

"Maybe they went into the attic," she said.

"We have to go up and see."

Bennis ran up the next flight of stairs on her own. When she got to the top, she opened a door and poked her head through it. She withdrew almost immediately.

"Bats," she told Gregor.

"What do you mean, bats?"

"Bats," Bennis repeated. "The attic is full of them. Do you remember Carlton Ji?"

Gregor remembered Carlton Ji. He got to the attic landing and opened the door to the attic himself. On the other side of the attic, another door opened and someone coughed.

"Who's there?" Kelly Pratt asked.

"It's me," Gregor said.

"The trapdoor is open," Geraldine Dart said. "To the roof. Look up."

Gregor looked up. At first, all he saw was a mass of moving, black bats disturbed in their rest, pulsing and beginning to call and shriek. Then he spotted the opened square with its pull-down plywood ladder. It had been hard to find because the square was open on nothing but blackness, and because the ladder was swarming with bats.

"They must have gone up," Geraldine Dart said. "They must have gone out on the roof. She's going to push him off." Her voice sharpened with fear.

"Gregor, how did they get out of here?" Bennis asked. "How did they get past all those bats?"

"They didn't care if they got hurt," Gregor said.

"Are we going to follow them?" Kelly Pratt called out. "Do you want me to go out after them?"

Gregor rubbed his face with his hands. He did care if he got hurt. He especially cared if he got hurt by bats, which were often rabid in the United States. He had once seen a Bureau agent take the necessary series of injections for rabies. He hoped never to see anything like that again. He certainly didn't want to see it done on himself. I'm a desk man, Gregor told himself. If I have to be a great detective, I want to be a great detective like Nero Wolfe. I want to sit in an armchair all day and think great detective thoughts. Damn Hannah Graham and damn Cavender Marsh and damn Tasheba Kent and damn those bats.

"Mr. Demarkian? Are we going to get moving?"

"Gregor," Bennis said suddenly. "I know what to do. I know how to make it so that the bats can't get to us."

—— 3 ——

Bennis did not make it so that the bats could not get to them. That would have been impossible without specialized clothing. What she did do was to rearrange the clothing they did have to give the bats the least possible access to bare skin. She pulled Gregor's sleeves down over his hands and fastened the cuffs past his fingers. She took his sweater off and wound it around his head and the lower half of his face. Then she did the same for herself and called out to Kelly Pratt and Geraldine Dart to do the same for themselves. There was nothing she could do about the upper halves of their faces. They needed to see.

"Look at it this way," Bennis said. "We'd have had to have found some way through here no matter what we decided to do about Hannah Graham and Cavender Marsh. We have to get out to the roof to meet the helicopter."

"I thought we decided that the helicopter wasn't coming. I thought Geraldine Dart said it couldn't land."

"She did, but it doesn't have to land, Gregor. It just has to hover. That way it can drop some medical people off and pick some of us up."

Gregor thought of a helicopter hovering above this roof in this weather with a human being dangling from a rope, being hauled in or let out, and then he decided not to think of it. It made him sick to his stomach. He would think about it later.

"Come on," he called. "Are you two ready?"

"We're ready," Geraldine Dart said.

"Ready," Kelly echoed faintly.

Gregor started forward across the attic, very slowly, very carefully, trying not to disturb the bats. For a while, it worked. The bats were restless, but no more restless than they had been when Gregor first came to the attic door. They shrieked and shuddered and pulsed above his head. Some of them took off and flew in great swooping arcs among the rafters. None of them came close.

"Maybe we're going to get away with this," Bennis said.

"We've still got the ladder."

The ladder was a disadvantage Hannah Graham and Cavender Marsh would not have had. It would not have been pulled down when they arrived in the attic—or Gregor thought it wouldn't have. If it had not been pulled down, it would not have been covered with bats. Gregor approached the ladder and then stopped. Bennis stopped behind him. Kelly Pratt and Geraldine Dart stopped beside her. The ladder was carpeted in bats. Every rung had two or three. Some rungs seemed to have ten or twelve crammed in together. They were all moving incessantly. The noise they emitted made Gregor's skin crawl.

"Now what?" Geraldine Dart asked.

Gregor looked up through the open trapdoor. He expected to see black sky and feel the rain. Instead, he saw Hannah Graham smiling at him. She had the long iron instrument raised above her head. She was bracing herself on spread legs just beyond the lip of the trapdoor. It took a minute for all the elements to come together in Gregor's mind, and by then it was almost too late.

"Look out!" he shouted, as Hannah brought the instrument crashing down above their heads, just inside the trapdoor, on the top rung of the ladder.

The bats exploded into life. Shrieking and cawing, they wheeled into the air and made angry circles among the rafters. Gregor hit the floor with his hands over his head. A bat swooped down and tore at the sweater he had wrapped around his head. Another scratched at his thin cotton shirt.

"My God," Bennis said, on the floor next to him. "What are they doing?"

"They're protecting their home," Gregor said curtly. He looked up, hoping to catch sight of Hannah Graham again, hoping to find out what she was going to do next. What he saw instead was the ladder, almost empty. The bats on the ladder had been frightened off it by Hannah's blow. Their absence was only temporary. Gregor didn't have much time.

"Bennis," he said. "When I tell you to go, go. Run up the ladder. Get onto the roof."

"Just Bennis?" Kelly Pratt asked.

"All of you," Gregor said.

The bats were still cawing and angry. Gregor braced himself on his knees in a running crouch and got ready. They were going to have to be fast.

If I get out of this without needing a rabies shot, Gregor promised the universe, *I will stay home reading Perry Mason novels for the rest of my life. I will even go to church.*

Gregor launched himself forward.

"Go!" he shouted.

He hit the ladder running and scrambled ungracefully all the way to the roof, refusing to listen to the shriek and swoop of angry bats swirling around his head, refusing to look back to see how the others were doing. When he got to the lip of the trapdoor he grabbed it in both hands and pulled himself upward. A bat attacked the sweater on top of his head and he shook it off. A second later, he was out of the attic and onto the roof.

It was not a good roof to stand on. Parts of it were steeply pitched, as Geraldine Dart had said, but only parts of it. It was not a typical New England A-line. Instead, the patch of roof just beyond the trapdoor was flat, but inches away it fell off into a slope, and inches after that it began to climb again. All around the edge of it there was a cast-iron rail. There was a cast-iron rail along the widow's walk, too. The wind was strong enough to be a gale. The rain was like marble in heat.

Hannah Graham and Cavender Marsh were both well away from the trapdoor now. The two were standing on a narrow catwalk on the side of the roof that looked out to Hunter's Pier. They seemed to be at an impasse. Cavender Marsh had backed up as far as he could go. The old man was flat against the highest of the four square turrets that anchored the corners of the roof. His face was gray and his eyes were stiff with terror. One way or another, he was not going to get out of this alive.

Hannah Graham was at the very middle of the catwalk, standing still. The instrument was in her hands, but she was not swinging it. The wind and rain and hail were lashing against her body, but she didn't seem to feel them.

"What does she think she's doing?" Bennis asked Gregor.

"I think Cavender is going to die," Geraldine Dart said tremulously. "I think she's already killed him."

Hannah Graham turned suddenly and stared at Geraldine Dart. A smile spread across her face. She had never looked more like a mobile skull. Her hair was thick with water. Her bright green sweater was covered with beads of hail.

"I haven't killed him yet," she said. "But I'm going to kill him now. Just watch."

If there was anything Gregor Demarkian could have done about it, he would have, but there wasn't. They were both too far away from him over terrain that was much too treacherous. Hannah Graham had a catwalk to walk on, while Gregor would have had to climb up and down on the shingles of the roof.

Hannah Graham lifted the instrument high above her head. She swung it at the catwalk railing. The sound she made reminded Gregor of anvils. The railing shuddered but did not break, because it was made of cast iron too. Cavender Marsh shrunk farther back against the wall of the turret, but there was nowhere farther back that he could go. Hannah Graham walked toward him, still grinning.

"Gregor, for God's sake," Bennis said. "Can't you do something?"

"No," Gregor told her. "And neither can you."

The wind rose into a stiff hard gust and blew at their backs, making Bennis stumble forward. The rain began to fall more heavily, pelting against them with drops like needles. Hannah Graham didn't seem to notice any of it.

"Here I come," she said.

Cavender Marsh seemed about to cry out. He never got a chance. Hannah was close. She raised the instrument over her shoulder and swung out, like a batter hitting a baseball. Cavender Marsh did not retreat in time. Hannah hit the left side of her father's head with the full center of the round blob at the instrument's end. Cavender Marsh grabbed the wounded place on his face and staggered sideways. Hannah Graham hit him again, in the body this time, smashing into his gut.

"There he goes," Kelly Pratt said.

Cavender Marsh had been spinning slowly on the catwalk. Now Hannah gave him one more smash to the midsection and he pitched sideways, tumbling over the catwalk railing and onto the roof itself. His body slid down the shingles, dislodging two. It hit the gutter, hesitated for a moment, and then broke through. The next thing they knew, Cavender Marsh's body was in space, falling toward the sea.

"I told you I'd kill him," Hannah Graham said.

Gregor knew what was going to happen next. It was the only thing that could happen. He looked for a way to get onto the catwalk, but couldn't see one. Obviously, it had been meant for decoration, not for use. A widow's walk, some people called it. Hannah was walking back to the middle of it now, swinging the instrument in her hands. When she got to the place she had been when they first emerged onto the roof and saw her, she stopped.

"Here it goes," she said, drawing her arm back and pitching the instrument as far out to sea as she could. It went farther than Gregor would have imagined it could, making an arc like a rocket in flight, disappearing into the clouds and rain.

"Here I go next," Hannah Graham said.

"Gregor, for God's sake, what's she going to do? Can't you stop her?" Bennis clutched Gregor's arm.

Gregor could have pointed out that Bennis had asked

this question before, and that his answer now would have to be the same, but he didn't. With her back to them and her arms stretched out, she looked like a Druid celebrating ancient rites in a storm. Her wet hair could have been made of molten lead.

"Go *now*," Hannah shouted suddenly, at the top of her lungs.

She drew backward and then launched herself forward, pushing against the catwalk as if it were a diving board. She did not hit the shingles or the gutter as she went down. She went right out into the air and fell, screaming, straight into the sea.

"Jesus H. Christ," Kelly Pratt muttered.

Geraldine Dart turned her back to the rest of them and got violently and definitively ill.

—— 4 ——

Five minutes later, when they were all soaked to the skin and chilled to the bone and holding out on the roof only because they were more afraid of the bats than they were of the storm, they heard the sound of chopper blades in the distance, and looked up to see that the damn thing was right above their heads. The wind had been too high and blowing in the wrong direction for them to have heard it earlier. It was not an army helicopter, but a coast guard one—exactly the kind of detail, Gregor thought, that Bennis always did get wrong. It was, however, a serious vehicle, the kind with two propellers, one on each end. It had medical insignia as well as U.S. Coast Guard insignia painted on its sides.

"We've got to remind them to go down and get Lydia and Mathilda and Richard," Bennis said unnecessarily.

"What are we going to be able to tell them about Hannah and Cavender?" Geraldine asked.

Hannah and Cavender were the least of it. Gregor knew that. There were two corpses down in that house, and a third body that might be a corpse by now and might not. They were going to have to explain all of those before they got around to the denouement, and it wasn't going to be easy. Gregor knew what he would be thinking, if he were the law enforcement officer charged with the investigation of this case. He'd be thinking that the six people who were still alive and well in this house had a lot of talking to do.

A door in the side of the chopper opened. A man in rain gear and thick boots came swinging out, attached to a thick cord line. He blew around in the wind. The cord lowered him very slowly. Gregor and Bennis and Kelly and Geraldine stepped back to give him room to land.

The man was good at his work, and experienced. The wind was bad. Gregor expected him to fall at least once. Instead, he landed without difficulty, unhooked the cord, and looked around at the four people watching him.

"How do you do, sir," he said to Gregor, holding his hand out. Maybe, Gregor thought, I look like I have more authority here than I really do. "I'm Petty Officer Robert Moreby. We were advised of a medical emergency here."

"He's downstairs," Geraldine Dart said. "We couldn't move him."

"To get to him you have to go through bats," Kelly Pratt offered. "The attic is lousy with them."

Petty Officer Robert Moreby took all this in. Then he got his squawk box off his belt and spoke into it.

"Doctor will be down in a minute," he told them, when he'd finished. "You people can go on up if you want to."

"How are you going to get through the bats?" Bennis demanded.

"Rubber weather suits," Petty Officer Moreby said. "I was wearing one when I got hit with half a bucket of flying glass during Hurricane Andrew. If that didn't get through it, bats won't."

Gregor considered this. "Do you have any of these suits lying around that I could borrow?"

"Yes, sir," Moreby said. "But you don't have to do that. We can take care of everything from here on out. We'd just as soon you got into the chopper and let us take you to safety."

Gregor looked up. Another man was coming down at them out of the sky. The chopper and the man were bouncing around in the wind like hollow plastic balls in a blow tank.

"That's all right," Gregor told Petty Officer Moreby. "First you'd have to get me into the chopper, and if you ask me, I've had a bad enough day already."

EPILOGUE

LEAVING
IT UP TO
GERALDO

The headline in *The Philadelphia Inquirer* Monday morning was the worst Gregor Demarkian had ever seen. Standing in front of the stack of them in the rest stop in northern New Jersey, Gregor thought about buying all of them and shredding them in the parking lot. "TRAPPED BY A STORM," the enormous letters read, and then, underneath them: "Philadelphia's Own Armenian-American Hercule Poirot Captures a Killer on a Storm-Bound Island." Obviously, nothing serious had happened to the economy over the weekend. Saddam Hussein hadn't had a cold. Bill and Hillary had spent the last few days reading paperbacks and doing crossword puzzles. *The Philadelphia Inquirer* was usually a serious newspaper, and one Gregor liked. It was just when it came to Gregor Demarkian that the *Inquirer* seemed to go off its nut.

Out in the parking lot, Bennis was putting the top down on the tangerine orange Mercedes. Gregor could see her through the rest stop's plate-glass windows, walking around to the back of the car to make sure everything was secure. There was wind in her black hair and bright sunshine everywhere. It was one of those days in October that makes it possible to call fall "perfect." In the distance, the leaves on all the trees had turned from yellow to gold and brilliant red. Even the parking lot seemed to be full of color.

Gregor paid for one copy of the *Inquirer* (there was a large black-and-white picture on the front page of Gregor talking to two policemen; the caption said they were "consulting," but Gregor knew he was being read the riot act) and headed for the parking lot himself. It was colder than it looked. It was hard to understand how Bennis could walk around the way she did in nothing but a turtleneck and a J. Crew cotton sweater. Gregor walked over to the car and threw the copy of the *Inquirer* inside.

"It's getting worse all the time. The papers were much better about it yesterday."

"I don't want to talk about the papers." Bennis finished whatever she was doing with the canvas top and came around the side to get in behind the wheel. "I want to talk about Lydia Acken."

Gregor got in, too. He had to take the *Inquirer* off his seat to do it.

"I don't see why you want to talk about Lydia Acken. I have nothing to say about Lydia Acken."

"You didn't get her phone number," Bennis said.

"I know I didn't get her phone number."

"Well, does that make sense, Gregor? I mean, you find a woman you're attracted to, and she's attracted to you back, and you don't get her phone number."

"Believe it or not, Bennis, unlike you, the rest of us have other things on our minds more than occasionally."

"I wasn't saying you had to go to bed with her, Gregor. I was only saying you ought to call her."

"We weren't attracted to each other in that way."

"You were groping each other under the dining room table."

"Where did you get such an idea? Where could you possibly get such an idea? I don't grope."

"You ought to."

"If you go on driving the way you've been driving on the Garden State Parkway, Bennis, you'll get us both arrested."

Bennis bounced the tangerine orange two-seater Mercedes down the ramp, looked both ways to make sure the road was as clear of traffic as it had been all morning, and then stepped on the gas.

———— 2 ————

They were well out and away in the New Jersey sunlight before Bennis slowed down again, bored with the kind of attention she had to pay to her driving to keep up her speed. Gregor privately thought that Bennis only went really fast when either he or Father Tibor Kasparian was in the car. She wanted both of them to know how hazardous it was for them to assume she would drive them places just because neither one of them knew how to handle an automobile. Father Tibor didn't even have a license. Gregor had one that he kept current, but Bennis was always saying that it wasn't worth its little laminated shield. Gregor Demarkian behind the wheel of a car was not a pretty sight.

Bennis slipped a Joni Mitchell tape into the tape deck and turned the volume up so that she could hear the music over the roar of the wind.

"So tell me again," she said. "Cavender Marsh contacted Hannah Graham in California—"

"No, no," Gregor said. "It was the other way around. Hannah Graham had been writing and calling for years, trying to get her father to talk to her. And finally, a few months ago, Cavender decided to answer."

"And tell her that Tasheba Kent wasn't really Tasheba Kent."

"I don't know how the negotiations went, Bennis. I wasn't hiding in a closet when they went on. Eventually he told her that Tasheba Kent wasn't really Tasheba Kent. It was probably the only way he could get her mad enough."

"Mad enough to commit a murder."

"Mad enough to go along with his plans to commit a murder. Remember that there was only supposed to be one murder. Carlton Ji was Hannah going freelance. So was Richard Fenster."

"Richard Fenster didn't die."

"No, he didn't," Gregor said, "but that wasn't deliberate on Hannah's part. She was basically interested in getting rid of anybody who got in her way. I think she must have given her father quite a shock. Cavender had no way of knowing what she was like."

"Did she intend to kill herself, right from the beginning?" Bennis asked.

"I don't know," Gregor told her, "but I'll bet anything that she intended to kill her father. I almost sympathize. I mean, look at the two of them—the three of them, if you include Tasheba Kent—I mean Lilith Brayne. They never once thought of anybody but themselves. They never once cared what happened to other people as long as they got what they wanted. Lilith was perfectly willing to ditch her own infant child just to keep up the pretense that would allow her to spend her life with the man she was obsessed with. And Cavender Marsh—"

"What about Cavender Marsh?"

Gregor shrugged. "Hannah was his daughter, too. There was nothing to say that he couldn't have put his foot down and made his wife bring the child with them. Quite frankly, I think he was relieved to be rid of it. Squawling and diapers and interruptions. They weren't his style."

"You make them all sound like such lovely people."

"If there was one thing I learned pulling kidnapping detail in the Bureau, Bennis, it was that the last people on earth you want to deal with are actors and actresses. You ought to remember that the next time what's-his-name blows into town and wants you to run off for a weekend in the Bahamas."

"Never mind what's-his-name," Bennis said. "I still don't see how you worked it all out. I thought it had to be Geraldine Dart, myself, with all the sound effects and the lights going on and off and the things being moved around. I thought it had to be someone who was very familiar with the house."

"It *was* somebody who was very familiar with the house, Bennis. It was Cavender Marsh. But I agree with you. Geraldine was certainly a good guess. She was my first."

"So why didn't you stick with her?"

"Well, for one thing, I couldn't figure out why she would want to set up all the things that were being set up. I don't mean the ghost stories and the sound effects and all that. That might have been spur of the moment because Hannah Graham annoyed her. I mean all the distractions."

"*What* distractions?"

"Well," Gregor said, "there was all the makeup Tasheba Kent wore to dinner, and the strange clothes. Those things were deliberately engineered. I'm not a total recluse, Bennis. I read *People* every once in a while."

"Especially when you're in it."

Gregor ignored this. "I've seen the odd occasional photograph of Cavender Marsh and Tasheba Kent together—Cavender Marsh and Lilith Brayne, but I'm trying not to get confused. Anyway, they looked like any old couple photographed from a distance. No feather boas. No strange makeup. No bizarre clothes. No wigs. So why was it, when they had us in the house face-to-face, that the old lady suddenly turned herself into a bad joke from an even worse movie?"

"I don't know."

"Of course you do. Or at least you do now. She didn't want to take the chance that even after all this time, somebody might realize that she was not in fact Tasheba Kent. If you remember what Geraldine told us at the end, it was mostly Cavender who was worried about all this. Not that he told Geraldine specifically what he was worried about. He just said he wanted to make sure that nobody brought up all that business in 1938 during the weekend. That's how he justified the sound effects prank to Geraldine, too."

"Right," Bennis said. "So she set up the CD player, and then—what? Hannah went and changed it?"

"That's right. Cavender told Hannah where to go and what to do, and Hannah went and did it all."

"And in the meantime, she ran into Carlton."

"We think so, yes. This part is mainly conjecture, of course, because we don't have any of the principals here to tell us what really happened, but my guess is that Hannah saw Carlton Ji sneak off after dinner, and as soon as she had a chance, she sneaked off in the same direction."

"And found him in the attic."

"Looking through that trunk full of pictures the young man from the coast guard found," Gregor said. "Yes, I think that's it exactly."

"And being attacked by bats."

"I doubt if they stayed in the attic proper for very long, Bennis. My next guess is that Carlton Ji being Carlton Ji, he couldn't keep his mouth shut. He told Hannah Graham all about how he was sure that the Tasheba Kent who was living on an island off the coast of Maine wasn't really Tasheba Kent at all, but Lilith Brayne."

"Which he knew from all the research he'd done into the black feather boa."

"From that and from the pictures in the attic. You really should have taken a look at them, Bennis. They were a very interesting collection. Anyway, the warming iron or whatever it was was lying on the attic floor. There are half a dozen of them up there. She got one and bashed his head in and left his body where it lay."

"On the back stairs landing to the attic."

"That's right. There was a pint of blood soaked into the carpet up there."

Bennis tapped her fingers against the steering wheel. She pressed down on the accelerator and surged past a pale blue Toyota. Gregor could see the driver's face: a pale white blur as they raced by. "So then she came downstairs and fixed the CD player, and then she went to bed."

"She went to her bedroom and waited for the rest of us to go to bed."

"Then she went down to her mother's room? Carrying the warming iron?" Bennis was doubtful.

Gregor shook his head again. "Bennis, you're making this unnecessarily complicated. Try to remember that Hannah had been trying to contact her father for years. All she had to do was to go down to his room and to insist on talking to him. It would have seemed perfectly natural."

"While carrying the warming iron?" Bennis repeated.

"She could have carried anything she wanted," Gregor said. "Lilith Brayne was younger than her sister, but only by a year. Her sight was bad even with her glasses on. She slept on the far side of the bed from the door. My God, Bennis. Hannah Graham could have marched in there carrying a Sherman tank on her back, and the old lady wouldn't necessarily have noticed. And Cavender Marsh wouldn't have cared. He was *expecting* Hannah to show up with a murder weapon."

"So she went in there with the warming iron," Bennis said, changing lanes without checking for traffic, "and then what did she do?"

"Just what she was expected to do. She killed Lilith Brayne."

"Right there in the bed like that."

"That's right."

"With Cavender Marsh awake and watching."

"Right again."

"Yuck."

"I agree with you," Gregor said. "But there isn't anything pleasant about any of this. Anyway, Hannah did the job right this time and there wasn't too much blood. That was probably an accident, but it wasn't an accident that mattered. After that, Cavender Marsh took some sleeping pills that Hannah gave him. We think from something Mathilda Frazier said that she might have stolen them from Mathilda's room. Anyway, Cavender lay down and got ready to go to sleep. Hannah started to go back to her own room, but then the commotion started with the sound effects and she couldn't."

"But, Gregor, wait a minute. Tasheba Kent—Lilith Brayne—wasn't really dead."

"Sure she was. Or as good as. What she did, coming down in the wig and the negligee, isn't really all that unheard-of with head wounds. I could cite you a dozen different cases. That's not the same thing as saying that the woman wasn't really dead. She *was* dead. And try to remember, it's taking me longer to tell you all this than it actually took it all to happen."

"The sound effects were to distract us," Bennis said.

"Partially to distract us and partially to give Hannah a definite period of time when she could leave her mother's room without being spotted. And partially, of course, the whole incident was meant to ensure that the old woman's body was discovered, and that Cavender was discovered right next to it, sleeping peacefully away."

"Was that what all the birthday decorations were about later, too, the ones in Hannah's room and the ones downstairs in the dining room?"

Gregor nodded, keeping his eyes carefully off of the road. "Mostly. Hannah wanted us to find Carlton's body without going up to the attic to find it. There were lots of things in the attic that she didn't want us to see. Especially those pictures. She also wanted to say that she was being persecuted, so that it would look as if things were being done to her and not as if she were doing things. She also did not, in fact, want to discover the body herself. So she brought it downstairs—"

"Wasn't that dangerous, with all of us awake and wandering around?"

"Maybe she didn't wait until we were all awake and wandering around," Gregor said.

"I never thought of that."

"Just try to remember that with Carlton Ji and Richard Fenster, Hannah was on her own. Cavender Marsh had only bought into one murder, not two completed and one attempted."

Bennis was thoughtful. "Hannah Graham killed Carlton Ji because he figured out that the woman calling herself Tasheba Kent was really Lilith Brayne."

"That's right."

"Did she try to kill Richard Fenster for the same reason?"

"Of course. Richard Fenster had worked it all out from the shoes, you see. As soon as he saw the corpse of the woman calling herself Tasheba Kent, he knew she couldn't be Tasheba Kent, because of the size of her feet. It just took him a while to accept the fact that he was seeing what he was seeing."

"I guess I just don't understand that as a motive," Bennis said. "I mean, what difference could it possibly make if any of us knew that that woman was really Lilith Brayne? From Hannah's point of view, I'd think it would be preferable if we did know it. I'd think we would have been far less likely to believe that Hannah would have killed the old woman if we knew the old woman was her mother."

"Possibly," Gregor said, "but I think it was something really quite simple. I think Hannah was embarrassed."

"Embarrassed?"

"*Ashamed* might be a better word. I don't think she wanted anyone to know that her own mother had had no use for her even as a baby. I think the idea that anybody might know that tore Hannah up."

"Oh," Bennis said.

They were bouncing along to their exit now, not far from the turn that would put them on a straight shot into the state of Pennsylvania. Gregor thought about telling Bennis that it was too cold to keep the top down, but decided that it wouldn't do any good.

"People ought to be more careful about children," Gregor said instead. "Adults treat children as if they're still being formed in the womb in some ways, as if their emotions aren't complete. But their emotions *are* complete. They're subject to monsoons of feeling they can't understand and can't control and can't begin to come to terms with, and when they try to get help they're treated as if they've got nothing worse wrong with them than a cut finger. Adults think that what children don't understand, they don't feel."

"Wonderful," Bennis said. "A lecture on children from a man who basically thinks they're all right as long as they belong to someone else. Can I quote you, Gregor?"

"You can always quote me, Bennis. I don't see how I could stop you. I can't stop you from doing anything else."

Bennis seemed about ready to make an answer to this, but the road was widening out and there were signs she had to watch, and she reached for her pack of cigarettes instead. The Joni Mitchell tape had finished playing. Bennis popped it out and fished in the well for another one.

All the Joni Mitchell songs Gregor Demarkian had ever heard had been played for him in cars driven by Bennis Hannaford, and all of them had concerned the excruciating breakup of one love affair or another.

It was beyond Gregor's understanding why Bennis would want to listen to songs like that.

—— 2 ——

An hour and a half later, Bennis Hannaford pulled the tangerine orange Mercedes into the parking garage where she kept it while she was in town, raised the roof, took the keys, and made sure she had everything that had been scattered around on the seats safely in her shoulder bag. Then she walked the keys to the garage office and dropped them off. Several minutes before, she had dropped Gregor Demarkian off in front of the brownstone where they both had floor-through apartments. She had dropped the luggage off with him and told him to find a kid to haul it upstairs for him. There were always kids hanging around Cavanaugh Street, looking to make money doing errands. There hadn't been when Bennis first moved into her apartment, but in the meantime the Soviet Union had collapsed and Armenia had declared its independence and the refugees had come pouring in. Now Holy Trinity Armenian Christian Church was running a parish school of its own and most of the older women were placing displaced families in equally displaced housing and the neighborhood was expanding again, for the first time in decades. It was an immigrant neighborhood again for the first time in decades, too. Over the past several months, Bennis had been developing an ability to swear prodigiously in a language she hadn't even known existed until she was over thirty-five years old.

Bennis turned off Wessex onto Cavanaugh and checked out the windows of the Ararat restaurant, where Linda Melajian was sitting behind the cash register, reading a John Grisham novel and looking tired. Linda looked up and waved. Bennis waved back and kept going. The doors of Holy Trinity Church were open, but nobody was going in or out, and she couldn't see Father Tibor Kasparian anywhere. The windows of Lida Arkmanian's living room were open, and Bennis could see Lida. She was

moving back and forth in a flurry, tidying up for the arrival of the maid.

Lida Arkmanian's town house was directly across the
street from the brownstone where Bennis and Gregor had
their apartments. Bennis could see Gregor sitting on the
stoop there next to Old George Tekemanian and little
Tommy Moradanyan. Old George Tekemanian had the
ground-floor apartment in their brownstone. Tommy
Moradanyan and his mother, Donna, had the top-floor
apartment. Donna Moradanyan was Bennis's best woman
friend on the street. Bennis wondered where she was.

"So," Bennis said, coming up to the two men and the
small boy and sitting down herself. The luggage had disappeared, which she took as a good sign. Gregor hadn't just
sat down on the stoop and decided he was too exhausted
to cope.

"So," Bennis said again. "Where's Donna gone?"

"Donna is off at the art-supply store," Old George
said. "She will be back in a moment. Did you see this
wonderful thing my grandson Martin bought me?"

Bennis took the gadget Old George was holding out to
her. It was made of metal and cork and looked like nothing she had ever seen before.

"What is it?" she asked.

"It's a device for pitting pomegranates," Gregor said.
"Sterling silver."

Bennis handed it back to Old George.

The wind was rising and it was getting cold again, but
it was a good kind of cold, full of sunshine and the smell
of roasting chestnuts. In a few hours, they would have to
tell everyone they knew on the street everything that had
happened on that island in Maine, and they would do it,
because it was an obligation, like paying taxes and making
sure not to litter. Bennis was just glad that they did not
have to do it now. Bennis knew that Gregor thought she
was obsessed with what he called his "extracurricular
murders," but that wasn't quite true. Sometimes she was
and sometimes she wasn't. The weekend had taken a lot
out of her.

Now she got out her cigarettes and lit one. She blew a
stream of smoke in the air and suddenly found herself

attended by a furiously frowning Tommy Moradanyan, aged four.

"You're not supposed to be doing that anymore," he told her sternly, pointing to her cigarette.

"Well, I'm trying not to do it," Bennis told him.

"If you go on doing it, your lungs will rot," Tommy Moradanyan said. "They'll turn to black powder and fall out of your chest and then you won't be able to breathe anymore."

"Where does this kid get his vocabulary?" Bennis asked the air. "Where does he get his ideas?"

"From Tibor," Gregor Demarkian said.

"If your lungs don't fall out, they'll get full of junk instead," Tommy Moradanyan continued relentlessly. "They'll get so full of junk you won't be able to put any air in them. You'll turn blue."

"Tibor smokes like a chimney," Bennis said. "Israeli cigarettes. Without filters."

"When you die they won't even be able to bury you in the regular place," Tommy went on. "Your body will smell so bad, none of the other bodies will want to be around it."

Bennis Hannaford looked into Tommy Moradanyan's big black eyes and got the distinct impression that he was having a very good time saying these things to her.

Then she took one last drag on her Benson & Hedges menthol, dropped the cigarette to the pavement, and ground the lit tip cold under her heel.

Welcome home.

ABOUT THE AUTHOR

JANE HADDAM is the author of fourteen Gregor Demarkian holiday mysteries. *Not a Creature Was Stirring,* the first in the series, was nominated for both an Anthony and the Mystery Writers of America's Edgar Awards. Other titles in the bestselling series include *A Stillness in Bethlehem, Bleeding Hearts, Dear Old Dead,* and *Quoth the Raven.* She lives with her husband and two sons in Litchfield County, Connecticut, where she is at work on her next Gregor Demarkian mystery, *Deadly Beloved,* a wedding mystery.

If you enjoyed Jane Haddam's AND ONE TO
DIE ON, you won't want to miss the latest
entry in mystery's most celebratory series,
DEADLY BELOVED: *A Wedding Mystery*!

Look for Jane Hadam's DEADLY BELOVED
in hardcover at your favorite bookstore in
August 1997.

For a tantalizing preview of DEADLY
BELOVED,
please turn the page.

DEADLY
BELOVED
A Wedding Mystery
by
JANE
HADDAM

PROLOGUE

WALKING DOWN THE
AISLE TO THE
FUNERAL MARCH

There was a fog in Fox Run Hill that morning, a thick roll of grey and black floating just an inch above ground, like the mad scientist's dream mist in some ancient horror movie. Patsy MacLaren Willis moved through it much too quickly. There were stones on the driveway that she couldn't see. There were ruts in the gutters where she didn't expect them. It was just on the edge of dawn and still very cold, in spite of its being almost summer. Patsy felt foolish and uncomfortable in her short-sleeved, thin silk blouse. Foolish and uncomfortable, she thought, dumping a load of clothes on hangers into the rear of the dull black Volvo station wagon she had parked halfway down the drive.

That was the way Patsy had always felt in Fox Run Hill, all the time she had lived there, for more than twenty years. It was as if God had touched his finger to her forehead one morning and said, "No matter what you do with your life, you will always be out of step, out of touch, out of place."

The clothes on hangers were her own: navy blue linen dresses from Anne Taylor with round necklines and no collars; Liz Claiborne dress pants with pleats across the front panels under the waists; Donna Karan wrap skirts with matching cropped jackets. The clothes went with the Volvo in some odd way Patsy couldn't define. The clothes and the Volvo went with the house, too—a mock Tudor seven thousand square feet big, set on a lot of exactly one and three quarters acres. Fox Run Hill, Patsy thought irritably, looking up at all the other houses facing her winding street. An elegant Victorian reproduction. A massive French provincial with a curlicue roof and stone quoins. A red brick Federalist with too many windows. The only thing she couldn't see from here was the fence that surrounded it all, that made Fox Run Hill what it really was. The fence was made of wrought iron and topped with electrified barbed wire. It was supposed to keep them safe. It was also supposed to remain invisible.

Years ago—when the fence had just been put up, and the first foundations for the first houses had just been dug on the little circle of lots near the front gate—someone had planted a thick stand of evergreen trees along the line the fence made against the outside world. Now those trees were thick with needles and very tall, blocking out all concrete evidence of the existence of real life.

Patsy checked through the clothes again—dresses; slacks; blouses; skirts; underwear in pink satin lightly scented bags—and then walked back up the drive and felt fat wet strands against her neck. She shifted the waistband of her skirt against her skin and ended up feeling lumpy and grotesque. Three days ago, she had celebrated her forty-eighth birthday with a small dinner party at the Fox Run Hill Country Club. Her husband, Stephen Willis, had reserved the window corner for her. She had been able to look out over the waterfall while she cut her cake. She had been able to look out over the candles at the people she had been closest to in this place. It should have been the perfect moment, the culmination of something important and valuable, the recognition of an achievement and a promise. Instead, the night had been ugly and flat and full of tension, like every other night Patsy could remember—but it was a tension only she had recognized. If she had tried to tell the others about it, they wouldn't have known what she meant.

Nobody here has ever known what I meant, Patsy thought, as she came up out of the garage into the mud room. She kicked off her sandals and left them lying tumbled together, under the built-in bench along the south wall. She padded across the fieldstone floor in her bare feet and went up the wooden stairs into the kitchen. The house was cavernous. It should have had a dozen children in it, and a dozen servants, too. Instead, there was just Stephen and herself, having their dinner on trays in front of the masonry fireplace in the thirty-by-thirty foot family room, making love in a tangle of sheets in a master bedroom so outsized the bed in it had to be custom-made, and all the linens had to be special ordered from Bloomingdale's. Patsy stopped at one of the four kitchen sinks and got herself a glass of water. Her throat felt scratchy and hard, as if she had just eaten razor blades. I hate this house, she thought. Anybody would hate this house. It was not only too large. It was fake. Even the portraits of the ancestors that lined the paneled wall in the gallery were fake. Stephen had bought them at auction at Sotheby's, the leftover pieces of somebody else's unremembered life.

"I only paid a thousand for the lot," he'd told Patsy, when he'd brought them home from

New York. "They're just what we've always needed in this place."

Patsy put her used glass into the sink. That was the difference between them, of course. Stephen *did* like this house. He liked everything about it, just the way he liked everything about Fox Run Hill, and the country club, and his job at Delacord & Tweed in Philadelphia. Last month he had bought himself a bright red Ferrari Testarosa. This month he had been talking about taking a vacation in the Caribbean, of renting an entire villa on Montego Bay and keeping it for the three long months of the summer.

"The problem with us is that we've never really learned to enjoy our money," he'd said. "We've never understood that there was more that we could do with it than use it to invest in bonds."

Patsy had fished the lemon slice out of the bottom of the glass of Scotch on the rocks she'd just drunk and made an encouraging noise. The family room had a cathedral ceiling and thick useless beams that had been machine-cut to look as if they had been hand-hewn, then dyed a dark brown to make them look old. Stephen's voice bounced against all the wood and stone and empty space.

"Now that I won't be traveling any more, it'll be better," he had told her, "you'll see. I know that you've been terribly lonely, dumped in this house with nobody to talk to for weeks at a time. I know that you haven't been happy here."

Now the water-spotted glass sat in the sink, looking all wrong. Everything else in the kitchen was clean to the point of being antiseptic. The sinks were all stainless steel and highly polished, as if porcelain had too much of the roadside diner attached to it, too much of the socially marginal and the economically low rent.

"Damn," Patsy said out loud. She walked through the glass doors that separated the kitchen and the family room from the foyer and stared up the front stairs. The stairs made a circular sweep up a curved bulge in the wall that was lined with curved leaded windows looking out on the drive and the front walk. Outside the Volvo looked dowdy and frumpy and square— just like Patsy imagined she looked dowdy and dumpy and square everywhere in Fox Run Hill, next to all these women who worked so hard on treadmills and Nautilus machines, who came to parties and ate only crudités and Perrier water. The clock at the top of the stairs said that it was 6:26. Patsy stopped next to it, at the linen closet, and rummaged through the stacks of Porthault sheets until she found the gun.

Patsy turned the gun over in her hands. It

was a Smith and Wesson Model 657 41 Magnum with an 8³/₄ inch stainless steel barrel, muzzled by a professional silencer that looked like a blackened can of insect repellent. She had bought it quite openly at a gun shop in central Philadelphia, with no questions asked, in spite of the fact that it was a heavy gun that most women would not want to use.

Most women probably couldn't lift it, Patsy thought, walking down the carpeted hall. The only real sounds in the house were Stephen's snoring, and the whir of the central air conditioning, pumping away even in the cold edge of the morning, set so low that crystals of ice sometimes formed on the edges of the grates.

In the bedroom, Stephen was lying on his back under a pile of quilts and blankets, his mostly bald head lolling off the side of a thick goose down pillow, a single shoulder exposed to the air. When Patsy had first met him, he'd had thick hair all over his body. In the years of marriage, he seemed to have shed.

Patsy spread her legs apart and raised the gun in both hands. She had fired it only twice before, but she knew how difficult it was. When the bullet exploded in the chamber, the gun kicked back and made her shoulder hurt. She wished she'd thought to wear a set of ear protectors like the ones they'd given her when she went out to practice at the range. Then she remembered the silencer and felt immensely and irredeemably stupid. Could anyone as naive and ignorant as she really do something like this? Why didn't she just turn around and go downstairs and get into the car? Why didn't she just drive through the front gates and keep on going, driving and driving until she came to a place where she could smell the sea?

Stephen's body moved on the bed. He coughed in his sleep, his throat thick with mucus. He was nothing and nobody, Patsy thought, a cog in the machine, an instrument. He was the one who had wanted to live locked up like this, so that he could pretend they were safe. If I don't do something soon, he'll wake up, Patsy thought.

She tried to remember the color of his eyes and couldn't do it. She tried to remember the shape of his hands and couldn't do that, either. She had been married to this man for twenty-two years and he had made no impression on her at all.

"I know how unhappy you've been," he had told her—but of course he didn't know, he couldn't know, he would never have the faintest idea.

Stephen shifted in the bed again. A little more of him disappeared under the covers. Patsy aimed a little to the left of the shoulder she could see and took a deep breath and fired.

Stephen made a sound like wind and jerked against the quilts. Blankets fell away from him. Patsy changed her aim and fired again. He seemed to be dead, as dead as anyone could get, but she couldn't really tell. There were two black holes in the skin near his left nipple, but no blood. Then she saw the red, spreading in a thick wash on the sheet underneath the body. The longer she looked at it the more it seemed to darken, first into maroon, then into black. She let the gun drop and brought her legs together. She suddenly thought that it was so odd—even in this, even in the act of murdering her husband, the first thing a woman had to do was spread her legs.

Patsy walked over to the nighttable on Stephen's side of the bed and put the gun down on it. The air was full of the smell of cordite and something worse, something foul and rotted and hot. Patsy made herself kneel down at the side of the bed and look Stephen in the face. His eyes were open, deep brown with no intelligence left in them. She grabbed him by the hair and turned his head back and forth. It moved where she wanted it to, flaccid and heavy, unresisting. She let his head drop. His eyes were brown, she told herself, as if that really mattered. Then she walked out of the suite and into the hall, closing the single open bedroom door behind her.

The house was still too large, too empty, too hollow, too dead. Now it felt as if it no longer belonged to her. Patsy walked down the hall to the front stairs and down the front stairs to the foyer. She went through the foyer to the kitchen and through the kitchen to the mud room. She walked through the mud room door into the garage and then carefully locked the mud room door behind her. The Volvo was still packed and waiting on the gravel. The fog was still rolling in puffs just above the ground. No one would come looking for Stephen at all today. Anyone who came looking for her would assume that she had gone into the city to shop.

Patsy got into the Volvo and started the engine. Molly Bracken, who lived in the elegant Victorian, came out onto her front porch, looking for the morning paper. Patsy tooted her horn lightly and waved, making just enough fuss for Molly to look her way. Molly waved, too, and Patsy began to drive around the gravel and head for the road.

The sun was coming up now, forcing its way through the clouds, eating at the fog. It was going to be a a perfect, bright day, hot and liquid. There were going to be dozens of people down at the Fox Run Hill Country Club, hanging around the pool. The city was going to be full of teenagers in halter tops and shorts cut high up on their thighs.

I am going to disappear, Patsy told herself, smiling a little, humming the ragged melody of something by Bob Dylan under her breath. I am going to disappear into thin air, and it's going to be as if I'd never been.